THE HEALERS

by Gerald Green

Fiction

THE HEALERS
HOLOCAUST
GIRL
AN AMERICAN PROPHET
THE HOSTAGE HEART
TOURIST
BLOCKBUSTER
FAKING IT
THE LEGION OF NOBLE CHRISTIANS
TO BROOKLYN WITH LOVE
THE HEARTLESS LIGHT
THE LOTUS EATERS
THE LAST ANGRY MAN
THE SWORD AND THE SUN

Nonfiction

MY SON THE JOCK
THE ARTISTS OF TEREZIN
THE STONES OF ZION
THE PORTOFINO PTA
HIS MAJESTY O'KEEFE
(with Lawrence Klingman)

THE
HEALERS

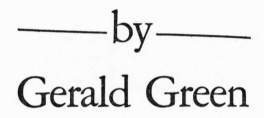—by—

Gerald Green

G. P. PUTNAM'S SONS
New York

Copyright © 1979 by Gerald Green

SBN: 399-12119-6

Library of Congress Cataloging in Publication Data

Green, Gerald.
   The healers.

   I. Title.
PZ3.G8227Hc   1979   [PS3513.R4493]   813'.5'4   78–24534

PRINTED IN THE UNITED STATES OF AMERICA

"THIS LAND IS YOUR LAND" Words and music by Woody Guthrie. Copyright TRO © 1956, 1958, 1970, Ludlow Music, Incorporated, New York, New York. Used by permission.

For
Melvin Hershkowitz, M.D.
and
Herbert Mark, M.D.

You do solemnly swear each man, by whatever he holds most sacred, that you will be loyal to the profession of medicine and just and generous to its members; that you will lead your lives and practice your art in uprightness and honor; that into whatsoever house you shall enter, it shall be for the good of the sick to the utmost of your power, you holding yourself far aloof from wrong, from corruption, from tempting others to vice. . . .

—Oath of Hippocrates

PART ONE
1950

1

It had been a quiet night in the emergency room except for the battle with the three-hundred-pound man.

The ambulance team—Matt Cross, the black driver, and Ed Riley, a young white orderly—had wheeled the sedated giant into the room. The man's left leg was splinted and extended. A city policeman had accompanied them, and had informed the resident and the medical student on duty that the injured citizen was one Johnny Farrell, address unknown.

"How'd he break his leg?" asked Dr. Abe Gold, chief resident of Mid-Island Hospital.

"Beats me, Doc. He was bombed. Stumbled out of a gin mill, fell off the curb. When you're that big and you hit the pavement, you gotta break something."

Dr. Gold laughed. Not a bad diagnosis. Abe had finished medical school after the war and pursued his medical career with the single-minded fervor of a poor boy from the Bronx. Farrell's huge gut rose and fell as he breathed.

"Fought us like a madman," Riley said. "I figured he was dead the way he was laid out in the gutter. Then he gets up like a Frankenstein and starts swinging."

Matt Cross, mahogany brown and dignified, nodded. "Got me right on the chops before we jabbed his big ass."

"Nice work, both of you," Dr. Gold said. "Nice splint."

Kevin Derry, a third-year medical student, studied the man's leg. It looked like a bandaged telephone pole. "Darn good job, Riley.

You too, Matt." Young Derry was always polite and cheerful to drivers, orderlies, kitchen help, lab technicians. A very junior member of the hospital, he was well known and well liked.

"Okay," Dr. Gold said. "Suppose we get him into radiology. Kevin, write up the admitting report and do a physical."

The policeman, seeing Farrell was in good hands, left. Riley and Cross rolled the doped giant to a cot. As they did, Kevin Derry noticed a spreading bloodstain on the sheet.

"Jesus," Riley said. "Where'd that come from?"

Matt Cross, the driver, nodded. "He wasn't bleeding none before. Least I didn't see no blood."

Kevin and Dr. Gold stood alongside Farrell. It took their combined strength to push him to one side. He snorted. Curses filtered through his bruised lips. He appeared to be in his thirties, a dark pork-faced man. The seat of his green work pants was reddish brown.

"If that's a hemorrhoid that's popped," Dr. Gold said, "it's the world's biggest."

"I swear he wasn't bleeding before," Riley insisted.

"Where'd you find him?" Dr. Gold asked.

"Outside Hanratty's. In the gutter, like a dead horse. The leg was like in three pieces. Some guy said he collapsed on it and it busted like a toothpick."

Kevin was snipping at Farrell's trousers with a scissor. He cut the work pants, the striped undershorts, and as Dr. Gold rolled the patient farther onto the bed, he ripped the clothing apart. Mr. Farrell's elephantine buttocks greeted them. One was a mass of blood. A ragged hole nested in the midst of the quivering flesh.

"Shot right in the cheek," Dr. Gold said. "Bullet wound."

"Get the cop back," Kevin said. "I bet he didn't know."

"No wonder he went down the way he did," Riley said. "Somebody plugged him in the ass."

The four men studied the marvel of Farrell's mammoth butt. Kevin applied gauze patches to the bleeding wound. When he had wiped it clean, and the bleeding had abated, he smeared the wounded area with Merthiolate.

"Call surgery," Dr. Gold said to Kevin. "They got a doubleheader here." He looked at the wall clock: five A.M. The trauma surgeons could go to work on Mr. Farrell—extract the bullet, put a

12

permanent splint on his fractured tibia, get him into traction.

"They can have a field day with this guy. Bullet wound *and* a compound fracture," Kevin said. He kept applying patches to Mr. Farrell's rear. Kevin knew that Abe Gold expected it of him. Junior medical clerks usually sat around, watched, wrote reports, and were regarded as several cuts below orderlies. Dr. Gold, dedicated and tolerant, let his third-year students do considerable clinical work.

"Can't figure how I missed it," Riley said miserably. He slumped into a chair and helped himself to coffee from the pot on the electric ring. "Maybe the fat kept the slug tucked in, and when we moved him, it started to bleed."

"Keep that up I'll get you into medical school," Dr. Gold said. He was listening to Farrell's chest with his stethoscope. "Healthy as a weightlifter. Bleeding, Kevin?"

"It's stopping. The bullet couldn't have gone far in that big Irish ass."

Everyone laughed. With the second application of disinfectant, the inert Farrell rose from the cot like Moby-Dick surfacing in the southern seas. He howled balefully and flailed about with ogre's arms. The back of his right hand caught Abe Gold in the mouth. The chief resident flew against an oxygen tank.

"Take it easy, buddy," Kevin Derry said. He ducked Farrell's left hand. Riley and Cross got up from their coffee and approached the patient carefully. They had been through this many times. But Farrell was the biggest fish they had ever landed.

"I said cut it out," Kevin said.

"Who the fuck are you?" Farrell mumbled. "Fuck are you?"

Like a dancing walrus, the wounded man was on his good leg now, hopping about the room, his splinted left leg extended in front of him. Pantless, blood streaming down his buttocks, he grabbed Kevin's slender figure and lifted him off the ground. Then he threw him against the instrument case.

"Riley!" Dr. Gold shouted. "Call for security! See if that cop is outside!"

The technician flew out the door. Farrell hurled a metal table after him. Glass shattered. "I'm goin' home," he bellowed. "Teach 'em to shoot Johnny Farrell in the ass. Mickey Mouse bastards. Kill the Mickey Mouse bastards."

He turned his rage on Matt Cross, the black driver, who was very

13

small. "You done it, you eight-ball. C'mere and fight."

Cross darted across the room and fled through the door to the garage. Farrell spit at him and spun around like Peter Stuyvesant doing a jig. "Gimme my pants, fuckin' Mickey Mouse doctors."

Abe Gold, wiping blood from his lips, cautiously circled the hopping giant. The bandages on the splint were coming apart. If it were not so dreadful, Gold felt, it would be laughable, a Laurel and Hardy scene.

"Let's be reasonable," Dr. Gold said. "Mr. Farrell, we want to help you. . . ."

"Break your chops, you little shit," Farrell shouted. "Out of my way, out of Johnny Farrell's way. . . ."

He headed for the door to the garage. With each hop, the room seemed to shiver. En route, Farrell swept the coffepot from the heater, rammed his fist against a wall cabinet, overturned a cot.

Kevin Derry beat him to the door. He had a metal stool in his hand.

"Kevin, please," Dr. Gold said. "Don't risk anything. . . . He isn't worth it. . . . The guards will be here. . . ."

"Out of my way," Mr. Farrell roared.

"Shut up," Kevin said.

The man wiped his muddy face. He stared at the young man in the doorway. Perhaps Kevin's pale gray eyes, choirboy face and curling orange hair looked to him like some vision of lost youth. Who in hell was this kid in a white coat? Doctor? Intern?

"I hear you say shut up?"

"That's right. Shut up and lie down."

"Kevin, please," Abe Gold cried.

"Mickey Mouse," the giant snarled, and lunged forward.

Kevin darted to one side, pushed the man's left arm, spun him around and shoved him sprawling over the examining table. He kicked the unwounded cheek of his buttocks.

Farrell tried to rise, gurgled, spat obscenities.

"For God's sake," Dr. Gold shouted. "Where's security?"

Cross came racing through the rear door with the policemen. They saw Kevin Derry bending over Farrell's lumpish back, talking to him. He had twisted the huge man's left arm behind his back.

"Mr. Farrell," Kevin was saying, "why not behave?"

"Fuck you; lemme up."

14

Mouth close to the patient's ear, Kevin whispered, "Know what you are? You're a *donkey*. A fat, drunk, stupid donkey, a harp. I know, because I'm Irish myself. Now shut up and let us take care of you."

"Bastard."

"Donkey. Harp. Mick."

Mr. Farrell turned his sodden face toward the young man pressing him against the table. The medical student was smiling even as he insulted him.

"Farrell, don't be a jerk all your life. Make your wife and kids proud of you."

"Mickey Mouse," the huge man wept.

The policeman had his billy in hand. He approached the table.

"Won't be necessary, officer," Kevin said. "He's ready to cooperate."

Dr. Gold and the EMT, who had returned with one of the hospital's aged security guards, wrestled Farrell back to the bed. "This time he goes *out*," Abe Gold said. He poised the hypodermic over Farrell's arm.

"Isn't it better to be a good guy?" Kevin asked him.

"Screw all of yez."

Gold jabbed the needle into the fat man's thigh. "Kevin, get me some more bandages." As he patched the bullet wound he asked, "How did you do it?"

Kevin Derry smiled. "Takes one to know one."

"But I've never seen you drunk in your life. Or carry on like that."

"You never met my relatives."

The resident shook his head. You couldn't tell with Kevin Derry. A good-natured, self-contained kid. From a poor family. Hard worker. But with a rare strength in him, something that made him able to reach people. Almost too much confidence for a third-year medical student. But Gold was grateful Kevin possessed it.

"Hail the conquering hero!" Potsy Luff shouted. There was a round of mocking applause from the people assembled in the attending physician's office as Kevin entered.

"Abe Gold's been talking again," Kevin said. He took a seat at the rear of the room.

15

"We weighed the guy later," Dr. Gold was saying. "Three hundred and two pounds, and he's dancing on one leg, breaking everything he can reach in the ER, and Derry whispers some Gaelic spell into his ear, and the guy starts to cry, and we get rid of him."

Potsy Luff—his real name was Walter and he was Kevin Derry's cousin—whistled. "Harp to harp, Abe. This hospital needs more Irish doctors to handle drunks. Jews are terrific on psychotics, but what do they know from alcoholics?"

Kevin shook his head, cautioning Potsy to go easy. Dr. Gold was sensitive. And he *was* chief resident. A scrawny, heavy-bearded, querulous man, Gold was reputed to be one of the most brilliant interns ever to come out of Mount Sinai.

"Kevin earned my gratitude," Gold said wearily. He had been up all night. Now he and his third-year students awaited morning report and rounds. "It was quite a performance."

Kevin studied his written report on the case. Dr. Alvin Rhodes, the chief of medicine, wouldn't care much about it. Trauma bored him. A chief of medicine didn't find much of interest in broken bones and bullet wounds.

"The crazy thing," Dr. Gold went on, "is that he isn't Irish. His name's Carmine Damelio. We found out when his relatives—seven of them—swarmed into the ward this morning."

"Carmine Damelio?" Kevin asked. He smiled.

"Johnny Farrell is a nickname, a *nom de guerre,* if you will."

"Sure," Potsy Luff chimed in. "Lots of guineas do it. Especially the wrongos. They take an Irish nickname. Status. There was a garment-industry hood named Doyle, real name Plumeri. And a fellow named Cassidy on the docks. He was Angelo Morelli."

"All this is beyond me," said Max Landeck, another third-year clerk. "Strange."

"So this guy is a Mafioso, right, Abe?" Potsy went on.

"Who knows?" Dr. Gold asked. "His brothers said they run a cartage company, and somebody was out to get the fat man."

"You're a hero, Kevin," Sally Hosmer said. She was also part of the five-member student group at Mid-Island. She was tall and slender, horse-faced but graceful, a native of Medford, Massachusetts, and a graduate of Wellesley.

Damelio, Kevin thought. And he had subdued the man by

16

insulting him as an Irish drunk. The giant had obviously been flattered. Status, an honorary degree.

They sat silently, studying their reports. Dr. Rhodes—"Dusty" to students and interns—was due any minute. Gold, chief resident, would be on the spot.

"Where is ole Dusty-butt?" Potsy Luff asked.

"Patience, Walter," Abe Gold said. Vaguely, he feared Luff—fat, loose-mouthed, glib. A different sort entirely from his cousin Kevin.

"You must learn to *wait* for authority," Max Landeck said.

Landeck was thirty-three. He had a blue number tattooed on his right forearm, souvenir of Auschwitz. He had come to New York in 1946 and immediately started medical school. He knew about authority. Dr. Rhodes' toughness was honey to him. Landeck had a wife and a child and lived in a tiny apartment at the edge of town. He was bald, bullet-headed, thick-bodied. He rarely spoke.

There was one other medical student from Danforth Medical College in Kevin Derry's group, a dark sweating man from Bombay named Rathman Lal. Lal had been on night duty on the third floor. He and Kevin would be expected to make their reports to Dr. Rhodes and then participate in rounds. Potsy Luff, aware that Wednesday was the day Rhodes took rounds personally, contrived to avoid Tuesday-night duties.

Dr. Alvin Rhodes came into the room with military snap, his starched white coat flapping, the watches, pens and rings sparkling on his sterile person. Rhodes was a former navy medical officer. His iron-gray hair was brush-cut, his face ruddy. Oddly, his eyes often seemed lost, wandering behind exaggerating lenses.

Gold was at Dr. Rhodes' side, showing him the reports, talking in a low voice. Rhodes nodded. He was just an average medical man (that was the word around Mid-Island General Hospital) but he made up for it with a dedication to detail.

When Gold told him about Kevin Derry's conquest, Rhodes smiled. "Sounds great, just great," he said. "See the kind of thing a medical career asks of us?" He proceeded to tell a long, dull story of his subduing of a violent marine aboard a ship off Tarawa.

In his notebook, Potsy scrawled, tilting it so Kevin could read it, OLD SEA DOG BORES THE SHIT OUT OF ME. MORE MEDICINE AND LESS NAVAL HISTORY.

"We'll skip the emergency room," Dr. Rhodes said. "Let the

surgeons take over. I take it Farrell has been operated on?"

Dr. Gold nodded.

"Very well. Proceed, Lal."

"Oh, yes, sir. Patient admitted at three A.M. with severe shortness of breath and chest pains. His name is Walker Mund, white male, aged sixty-eight. Patient had what appeared to be nonrelating pains in chest and upper abdomen. A marked shortness of breath. . . ." Rathman Lal's singsong voice induced yawns. "The patient has a history of congestive heart failure and is a known hypertensive since 1939. He says he is taking nitroglycerine, diuretics and other medications."

"*What* other medications?"

"I . . . I am not certain." Lal looked with sorrowing eyes at Dr. Gold.

Some administrative crisis sent Dr. Rhodes to the phone at the rear of the chief resident's office. With Rhodes' back turned, Potsy gave a Nazi salute, nodded his head at the chief of medicine and barked, "Und ve vill have *order!*"

Max Landeck shook his hairless head. "Dreadful accent, Potsy. Not German, not Hungarian, nothing."

"Let's get on," Rhodes said crisply. "Damned hospital is falling apart. Flak from the nurses. Doesn't concern any of you. House staff and students never give me any trouble."

Kevin smiled, thinking, Dusty Rhodes treats *us* like dirt. But the nurses were organized, tough, wise to him. There was a lesson there. Half the battle was moving with confidence.

"This patient, Mr. Mund, is a retired subway guard," Lal went on. "He thinks he may have had a myocardial infarct twelve years ago. . . ."

"*Thinks?*"

"Well, sir, as Dr. Gold said, he was a bit confused. I asked Records for his file, but as yet they have not located it."

Rhodes grimaced. Scarlet suffused his neck and ears. "No naval installation would be permitted to run down this way."

"The chest pains suffered by this man began at roughly two-fifteen this morning, when he learned of the death of his wife."

Dr. Rhodes rose vertically from his swivel chair. "Learned of the death of his wife? *The death of his wife?*"

Potsy drew a finger across his throat. Kevin tried to look away. He did not relish the imminent immolation of Rathman Lal.

Dr. Gold was on his feet, imploring Lal to talk. "Rathman, why didn't you tell *me* this?" the chief resident asked.

"I . . . I . . . did not think it medically important."

"But, Rathman," Dr. Gold pleaded, "you must start your report with this dramatic event. It's part of the medical picture as much as the patient's blood pressure."

Dr. Rhodes seemed to have found his voice. *"Learned* his wife had died? What the hell do you mean *'learned'?"*

"I, ah, perhaps did not phrase it felicitously," Lal blundered on. "His wife lived with him, suffering from terminal cancer. She expired this morning, and a few hours later, he—"

"And you spring this on us in the middle of your report!" Dr. Rhodes shouted. "Gold, these may be third-year medical students, but even that doesn't excuse such ineptitude!"

The Indian did a bit better now that the matter of the dead wife had been handled. Still, Kevin thought, it was the kind of dumb mistake that would do Lal no good. Rhodes was tough, and Mid-Island a rough place to take twelve weeks of medicine.

"His blood pressure was one-forty over ninety," Lal said hoarsely, "and the heartbeat was regular except for a possible gallop. There was no swelling in the abdomen, and no masses. Scrotum had a three-plus enlargement, and there was a four-plus edema of the legs. . . ."

Kevin Derry was thankful for the Lals of the world. They made it easier. *I'm no smarter than the rest,* Kevin thought, *but I'm luckier.*

"Let's look at the patient," Dr. Rhodes said.

"What about the giant?" Dr. Gold laughed. "Kevin's conquest."

Rhodes chuckled. "Oh, that's too good to use up in medical conference. Maybe he'll threaten to wreck the dump again and Kevin can go into his act."

"Once is enough, sir," Kevin said.

Rhodes led his party from the office to the ward.

Kevin watched Dr. Gold pull Lal away from Dr. Rhodes' earshot.

Mr. Mund was sitting up in bed. There was a look of surrender on his pasty face. Kevin saw it, and saw also his own father's tired eyes. Walker Mund, subway guard. Jack Derry, failed pharmacist.

"How're you doing?" Dr. Rhodes asked.

"Managing, sir," Mund murmured. "Didn't know I was worth all these doctors." His watering eyes took in the troupe of students. Dr. Milton DeBeers, the attending, joined them. He scowled a great deal, tried to anticipate Rhodes' temper. Dr. DeBeers also tried to avoid students.

Rhodes listened to Mund's chest, tapped his back, read the chart, asked a few questions. Then he threw back the covers to reveal Mr. Mund's swollen legs and the grotesque, pink-gray cantaloupe his scrotum had become.

"I've heard of a guy having big balls," Potsy whispered to Sally, "but this wins the brass monkey."

Dr. Rhodes' clipped head swiveled. "Luff, would you mind shutting up while I'm conducting rounds?"

Potsy was not fazed. Kevin smiled at his cousin, the nine-lived alley cat.

Dr. Rhodes asked, "Derry? What does this look like?"

"Hernia? Hydrocele?"

Rhodes studied the man's engorged legs and his turgid scrotum. Suddenly his head jerked up. "Was this man weighed?"

Gold looked at Lal.

Here it comes, Kevin thought.

"Weighed, *weighed!*" Dr. Rhodes cried. "How many times must I make the point to you people? Weight loss or gain is a key factor in medical management! Why, especially in this case? Miss Hosmer?"

Sally's New England tones seemed to calm him. "He's got a four-plus edema of the legs and a possible hydrocele. We'd want to reduce the water."

"And how will we ever know how much water he's losing unless we weigh him when he's admitted? And weigh him every day? Lal! *Get the scale!*"

Rathman Lal fled the ward. Kevin saw tears rimming his eyes.

As the rest of the party left, Lal blundered back, pushing a scale. Kevin turned and saw him floundering with the patient.

"Where's Derry's sparring partner?" Dr. Rhodes asked. He flashed his executive-officer grin at Gold.

"In the surgical ward. Took two bullets out of his butt, set the fracture, and put him in traction."

"Take a bow, Derry," Rhodes said.

Potsy applauded noiselessly, missing palms. Max Landeck managed a nod of his bald head.

"I like that kind of enterprise in students," Rhodes said. "You have to sock him?"

They walked into the orthopedic ward. Carmine Damelio's hulk rested under a canopy of pipes, pulleys and weights. A surgical resident was adjusting a counterweight.

Farrell-Damelio's glazed eyes roamed over the group. He was considerably subdued. "All a yez to see me? Jeez, I never had so much attention since communion." His black eyes found Kevin.

"There's the guy helped me out," he said. "I know a Mick when I see one. Give us a hand, kid."

"The name's Derry," Kevin said.

"Doctor?"

"Medical student."

The giant groaned as the resident adjusted pulleys. "Credit to the race, kid," he said. "You done right to belt me last night."

"What race?" Kevin asked. "Your real name is Carmine Damelio. You were shouting last night you were Johnny Farrell."

"That's what I mean, Doc. I got a great respect for the Irish. That's how come they call me Johnny Farrell."

"But I kept insulting you," Kevin said. He leaned down to Damelio's ear and whispered, "I called you a harp, a donkey and a Mick."

The whale looked as if he were about to weep. "Nicest things anyone ever said to me."

"What happened?" Kevin asked. "How'd you end up with a bullet in the ass?"

"That's my problem, Doc. When I catch those *sfaccimas* what done it I'll fucking break their chops. Johnny Farrell don't holler for cops. Anybody shoots a man in the back ain't fit to live."

Kevin smiled. The Damelios of the world were convinced they could be laid low only with a sneak punch. Kevin thought of aimless fist fights in the saloons and Legion halls of his hometown, Churchport. He had hated them. (But Potsy was never happier than when belting a drunk, swinging at a blear-eyed barfly.)

Dr. Rhodes glared at the X-ray on the viewing box. "We leave him to orthopedics and medical history. You handled it well, Derry."

The twelve-week medical "clerkship" at Mid-Island was known as

Little Buchenwald. Students at Danforth Medical College had seven training hospitals available to them for their clerkships in surgery, medicine, psychiatry, pediatrics and obstetrics. They were assigned by lottery, and Mid-Island—old, crowded and inadequate—was invariably chosen last, a place where, as Potsy Luff put it, "We specialize in alcoholics, malnutrition and clap."

The work was exhausting, with classroom sessions, advanced lectures, and clinical duties in the wards and the emergency room: cardiac resuscitation, hematology, pulmonary-function tests, infectious diseases. The program in Mid-Island's Department of Medicine, drawn up by Dusty Rhodes, was admired and hated in equal measure.

Most of the students survived. As chief resident, Dr. Abe Gold helped. Stooped, weary, Gold was an island of compassion and orderliness. He covered for latecomers, told white lies about inefficient reports, eased the path for miscreants who offended Rhodes.

Potsy read from the program outline. "Get this, fellow workers. 'One objective of medical training will be the mastery of problem-solving, which includes proper history-taking, adeptness at physical examination and ability to select appropriate biochemical and physiological laboratory procedures. . . .' "

Potsy, Kevin, Sally and Max Landeck were seated in the gray-green hospital cafeteria, drinking coffee. Lal had vanished. Not only had he performed badly that morning; he suspected he had done poorly on his second medical examination. Three hundred and sixty multiple-choice questions! Lal had come out of the examination with his coppery skin muddy brown.

"I'm worried about Rathman," Sally Hosmer said. She sipped black coffee.

"Dusty loves to ride his ass," Potsy said. "Lal's a wog to him."

Kevin shook his head. "He wants to make him a better doctor, Potsy. You don't give Rhodes enough credit. He likes Lal."

"*Likes*," Potsy sneered. "The only thing Dusty likes is a diagnosis of normochromic nomocytic anemia."

Max ignored them, his eyes locked on the New York *Times*. The students, interns and residents rarely read anything but medical texts. Dr. Gold mourned that he hadn't looked at a novel in five years. But Landeck, having passed through the furnace of history,

22

grateful for each day, felt an obligation to know something about a world that had left his family in ashes.

"What's the good word today, Max?" Kevin asked.

"Very little to give a man confidence."

Potsy nudged Sally Hosmer. "How'd you like to be Max's first patient? Cheerful Charlie. 'Mr. Cohen, you don't stand a chance with your subphrenic abscesses.' "

"Not funny, Walter," Max sighed.

Kevin laughed. "Ignore him, Max. Potsy's going into surgery so all he'll ever see of the patient'll be that little square surrounded by green drapes."

Max smiled. "I take no offense. But it's true. There is no good news anymore."

Landeck scanned the headlines of February 1, 1950.

President Truman had ordered a hydrogen bomb built for security: a subhead described it as a "triton bomb, the mightiest possible." France was protesting Russia's recognition of the Ho Chi Minh government in Indochina.

"And rain and cold today," Landeck said, in his careful voice. "Cloudy, continued cold tomorrow."

But never as cold as it was in Mauthausen.

Rathman Lal joined them. "I performed very poorly."

Kevin waved a hand. "Forget it, Rathman. It was your turn. Rhodes'll be on my butt tomorrow."

"I can't keep up. But why did he get so angry because I failed to mention the patient's wife died that morning?"

Potsy started to say something, but Kevin kicked him under the table.

"I think I flunked the last written," Rathman Lal said.

Max Landeck folded his *Times*. He wanted to shout at the Indian, *You fool, go back to India, and open a grocery store. A world full of hydrogen bombs will not need doctors.*

"Rathman, you always say that," Sally said gently.

"This time it's true. Three hundred and sixty questions. . . . I was lost . . . in a panic . . ." He held his head in his hands. His black hair gleamed under the fluorescent lighting.

Kevin and Potsy exchanged glances. Rathman had come to them pleading for coaching; they didn't believe it would help.

Landeck gulped his coffee and got up. Sally joined him. They had

23

night duty. Both were meticulous planners, careful with their time. If Kevin knew Max, he would sneak an hour of shut-eye in the residents' lounge. Sally would find an empty room and bone up on tissue diagnosis. Dusty Rhodes made that a specialty, and God help the student who couldn't differentiate between Hodgkin's disease and a sarcoid.

Lal's pleading eyes looked at Potsy and Kevin. He feared Potsy, but he respected Kevin.

"I was wondering, Kevin," Lal mumbled. "Perhaps if you would review some of the multiple choices with me . . . some evening . . . tonight perhaps . . ."

Kevin looked into the sorrowing eyes. "Rathman, what good will that do? You took the exam already."

"I know . . . I know . . . just perhaps . . . I might ask Dr. Rhodes . . . to let me take it over. . . ."

"You can try talking to Rhodes," Kevin said. "But you know what he's like."

"And may I come to you for help?"

Kevin nodded. Potsy scowled and got up. He had no time for losers. Nothing against brown-skinned brothers, mind you, he would say to Kevin. But they slowed down the action.

Abe Gold, harassed, unshaven, his white coat soiled, ambled in and reminded the students they were late for Dr. Hershkowitz's demonstration of peritoneoscopy. "Phone's been ringing for you, Kevin," Dr. Gold yawned. "Two calls in my office."

The students walked into the corridor—toxic-green walls, laminated with layers of disinfectant—and followed Gold.

Potsy whistled at a new nurse. *Ah, Miss Bezerska.* Straw-colored hair, thick-legged, ham-hipped, flat-nosed. Walter Luff, Jr., envisioned raising the crackling starched skirt, peeling down the encumbrances.

After Dr. Hershkowitz's slide show—he was a master teacher, unappreciated in Mid-Island, dedicated to his students—Kevin Derry hurried to Abe Gold's office. There were two pink chits for him: CALL YOUR MOTHER. CALL MISS MANSHIP.

Duty before passion, Kevin decided. Normally, students were not supposed to make calls—let alone long-distance ones—on hospital phones. But Dr. Gold was a tolerant man. Gold, scrawny, with

24

pitted skin and melting nose, seemed to find an alien strength in Kevin's good looks.

Once, after a few beers, Gold confessed, "It's the *Irish* in you, Kevin. When I was a kid in Long Beach they beat the hell out of me. But you're different. I don't think you hate anyone."

Embarrassed, Kevin blushed. "I try not to lose my temper. My mother always said, 'Think if it will help you, and ninety-nine percent of the time you'll see that it won't. So why waste time and energy getting sore at people?'"

"I like your mother without having met her," Dr. Gold said. "She sounds sagacious, temperate, tolerant and perceptive."

Old Adjectives at his best. Dr. Gold, besides being a medical hotshot, was a source of amusement because of his obsession with stringing adjectives together like verbal necklaces.

"Use my phone, Kevin," Dr. Gold said. "I've got missionary work with the fifth floor."

Kevin heard his mother's voice—soft, hesitant, as if minimizing a catastrophe.

"Ma?" he asked. "I can barely hear you. Maybe it's the switchboard."

"No, it's me, Kevin. I'm tired. Your father and I were taking inventory of the store. I get dizzy on the ladder."

Stacks of dusty bottles and boxes, he thought. A lifetime of Feen-a-Mint, Alka-Seltzer, Argyrol. His father's shelves were stocked with drugs that had long been rendered inutile—Anti-Phlogistine, Zonite. Jack Derry's problem was that he never could turn away a salesman, hurt a detail man's feelings. There was always a temptation to gab, to have a fast shot of rye in the back room amid the beakers and mortars. They'd talk while customers fretted at the counter, amid bowers of rubber baby pants, Venida Hairnets, Pepto-Bismol. The saleman would leave, unloading unsaleable items on Jack. The shelves became museums of ancient pharmaceuticals.

"You shouldn't have to do that work, Ma," Kevin said.

"Your father's legs are getting worse. Dr. Felder said he shouldn't be climbing the ladders. His varicose veins . . ."

She was not calling about his father's varicose veins. As much as she loved her children, Meg Derry communicated little with them. Kevin especially eluded her. She could not reconcile her penny-pinching existence, the downhill slide of the pharmacy, with Kevin's

25

cool ambition. She was ashamed that she and Jack had helped him so little.

"You didn't call about the inventory or Pop's varicose veins."

Silence again. She would go through life apologizing. A woman with no meanness in her, stranded in the lower-middle class. Several times a year Jack would start looking for "a new place," brag about the cut-rate pharmacy he'd open, the bank loan he could swing, and she would tolerate his boastful dreams, knowing they would be mired forever in the dusty store on Harding Street.

"Joseph is in some kind of trouble."

"Joe? Our Joe?" And he wanted to add, What else can we expect from that hardhead?

Joseph Derry, four years Kevin's junior, had dropped out of Whitman State College with no explanation, enlisted in the army, and was now with a base hospital in Germany. He went through life with a chip on his shoulder the size of a telephone pole. He did not pick fights, but he was always responding to some insult, some injustice. Strong, agile, a high-school linebacker, a kid with a squashed nose and a flat face, he and Kevin were physically unalike, except for the pale-gray Derry eyes and red hair. People were astonished to learn they were brothers.

"What kind of trouble?" Kevin asked. "How'd you find out?"

"There was this call from Germany. A friend of Joey's. He said Joe was in . . . what do they call it? The station house?"

"Guardhouse."

Kevin was not too disturbed. Joe's temper could have resulted in a sergeant's getting belted.

"What did he do?" Kevin asked.

"This man's name sounded like Budesa, sort of Italian or Polish, and he said Joe was arrested yesterday and . . . oh, Kevin, I can't believe it . . ."

"What?"

"He said Joe had done something bad to a German girl."

"Let me talk to Pop."

"I can't, Kevin. He's in a rage. He keeps cursing Joseph. He says it's that bad Cork blood in him. My family. Your father says he won't lift a finger to help him."

It figures, Kevin thought, *the burden would fall on me. Up to my ass in debt, struggling through my third year of medical school. Now I'll have to come to Joe's rescue.*

26

Something bad to a girl? Rape? Impossible. He knew Joe. He did not inflict pain. His violence was always a response.

He could remember a 240-pound kid who played offensive tackle for Clamtown spitting in Joe's face the first time they faced each other across the line of scrimmage. Joe, 165 pounds, cracked the side of the boy's helmet with the palm of his hand on the first play, cracked it again and again and had the fat bum walking in circles before the quarter ended.

"Pop can't desert Joe. Get him to call a lawyer, the Red Cross. Call Charley Felder. Joe's your son, dammit."

"Your father's at the store. He's finishing the inventory."

And cursing the air blue. All smiles and jokes with the customers, the salesmen, the cops and firemen, but fearful of facing a family crisis.

"I'll take the late train. Tell Bridie to call Charley Felder." His mother was crying softly. Bridie, his sister, was seventeen. Sometimes she appeared to have more sense and stability than their parents.

"I will, Kevin. God bless you."

He looked at the second pink chit in his hand: CALL MISS MANSHIP.

Damned near unbelievable. Cynthia never called him, except during the summer, when she was at her family's estate in Churchport Beach. A summer romance. Several of them.

He dialed the Manship apartment on Fifth Avenue. He'd been there a few times, doing heavy work for Mrs. Manship. And he remembered the fourteen-room duplex with its view of the Metropolitan Museum. Cynthia had been away at the time, skiing in Klosters. Buzzy Manship, her kid brother, had lounged about the place, talking on the phone to friends in Short Hills, New Jersey.

A maid answered. Miss Cynthia had just left. Where? To the airport to meet someone. Yes, she'd leave a message that Mr. Derry returned her call. Last I hear of her, Kevin thought.

"Keep notes for me, Potsy," Kevin said. "I hate to be yanked away like this. Maybe a phone call and Joey'll be all right. Dumb kid."

"A sucker," Potsy said. "Give you five to two he hit an officer for someone else. He doesn't even have the brains to fight for himself. It's always some Hebe or faggot he's defending."

Kevin buttoned up his reversible—purchased at the Churchport

27

Hospital Thrift Shop seven years ago—and walked to the door of their drafty third floor apartment. As he did, the buzzer sounded. He opened the door. Nurse Bezerska stood there, redolent of perfume.

"Ah, the gorgeous Madame Bezerska, Princess of Inhalation Therapy," Potsy said. "Welcome to the Ambulant Proctology Boarding House. Nobody in here except us poor medical students."

"Hi, Walter. Hi, Kevin."

"Hello and goodbye," Kevin said. Who could deny Potsy his conquests, most of which were bullshit? Kevin suspected they'd get bombed on beer, neck, pant a great deal, and then Miss Bezerska would straighten her blue skirt and return to the nurses' dorm.

He ran down the three flights of creaking stairs and, shivering in the February cold, walked to the bus stop.

2

Two hours later Kevin left the Long Island Railroad station and was walking again, hearing the distant Atlantic surf, smelling the sea wrack and beach scrub, feeling the tingling salt in the cold air. The sensations were wonderful—smells and sounds and textures he had known since his boyhood. But Harding Street had a way of dulling everything, reducing any enthusiasm he felt for his town.

In summers he had cleaned pools, mowed lawns, fixed gutters and leaders, done carpentry—not for the late arrivals in Churchport Beach, the advertising and television and garment-industry renters, but for the old families who had built mighty homes years ago, and who discreetly, invisibly, ruled the town, the beach, local politics.

Across the street from his gray home, weathered shingles and sloping roof, a malformed Cape Cod to which his father had added a wing after Bridie was born, stood the Derry Pharmacy. It seemed shabbier each year. The Venida Hairnet sign was crooked; the glass jars of colored water needed polishing.

The dwindling of business did not appear to depress Jack Derry—at least when he was behind the counter. He always had a joke, a crazy story for his customers. But rarely a smile at home.

Kevin shook his head in sorrow, recalling a typical scene. Ezra Munn, local fireman, asking Jack how much a new medication would cost. And Jack, in feigned seriousness, "Oh, this is going to run into money, as the monkey said when he peed into the cash register." In a curious way, his jokes and gabbiness did not encourage people to come to him. They had the sound of a man

29

whistling in a graveyard. *They're off, said the dog, as he backed into the lawnmower.*

Kevin crossed the street. The blinds were drawn. Dim light in the living room. Summer places in wintry months had a soothing aspect. He'd always enjoyed July and August—golden sun, visitors in garish clothes, girls in scant bathing suits, beach parties, an upsurge in his father's business. Yet he'd always felt somewhat an alien amid the crowds of visitors. After Labor Day he and Joe felt the town had been returned to them.

Kevin paused a moment on the canted porch of his house. The old man was letting the place fall into disrepair. With the boys no longer around to paint this, nail that, patch a leader, replace a floorboard, the building was beginning to sag with resignation.

Two ancient Flexible Flyers were stacked in one corner of the porch—his? Joey's? Was it possible Bridie ever used them? On the wintry grass, patched with dirty snow, the lawn furniture reminded Kevin of visits from relatives years ago. Crowds of kids shouting, climbing the crabapple and sourcherry trees that his father had once pruned. Now, the only relatives they ever saw were the Walter Luffs, Sr., Potsy's parents. The Luffs had stayed in Churchport with the Derrys. The difference was that Walter Luff, Sr., had made a fortune in real estate, buying up beach properties. Selling shrewdly, always a step ahead of the summer people. His yellow and blue sign, ANOTHER SALE BY WALTER LUFF REALTY, was plastered all around town.

Kevin's sister Bridie came to the door when she heard him fumbling with the key. She was not merely a pretty kid any longer, but a startlingly beautiful girl with perfect rosy skin, high cheekbones, elegant straight nose. Her eyes were a mutable gray and her auburn hair was thick, tied behind her neck with a blue ribbon.

"Kev, thank God you're here," Bridie said. "They're going crazy."

"Really bad?"

"Mama won't talk. Pop can't shut up, but nothing he says makes sense."

Kevin kissed her on the cheek. They showed little emotion in the Derry family. All of them were too concerned with survival. "Comes from being Irish Protestants," Jack Derry used to say. "We're neither here nor there, but we're independent."

Kevin was pleased to find Charley Felder in the living room. Charley was a young attorney, the son of Dr. Samuel Felder, for whom both Kevin and Joe had "office sat." (Doc Felder did not trust answering services, or possibly, Kevin guessed, could not afford one.)

Quickly shaking his father's hand, Kevin greeted Charley with pleasure. Charley looked chubby and rumpled. As a kid he had been the butt of jokes, anti-Semitic and otherwise. But he had survived, gone through Columbia College and Columbia Law School, and was now a leader in reform politics.

"So, how's the medical man?" Charley asked.

"Tired."

"You look okay, Kevin," Felder said. "Same baby-faced kid. Your father and I were remembering the day you and Joe beat Central Islip."

"I was a sub halfback and Joey played second-string linebacker, Charley."

"A good story anyway," Jack Derry said. "Kevin, want a bit of the disturbance?" He indicated a bottle of Imperial on the coffee table. Usually the old man did his boozing secretly.

"Jack, I wish you wouldn't," Mrs. Derry said.

"No harm," the pharmacist said. "Considering what he's got to hear. That goddamn Joseph, that rotten kid. Let him suffer."

"Pop!" Bridie cried. "You don't know what happened!"

"Whatever it was, it isn't for your ears, Bridget. Get out." But there was no conviction in Jack Derry's voice. Kevin winced at the spurious authority.

"It's family trouble," Bridie said. "I love Joey. I'm staying."

Kevin looked at his family and tried to throttle the pity that formed a chunk of ice in his chest. He longed to be like Potsy Luff, to mock everyone, to hide emotions with a leer.

"What did we find out, Pop?" Kevin asked.

"Ask Charley," Jack Derry said. "He talked to that fellow again."

"It sounds awful," Mrs. Derry said. "Kevin, why couldn't Joey be like you?" She buried her nose in a Kleenex. Bridie put an arm around her.

"This guy Henry Budesa," Charley Felder said. "I reached him while you were on your way out. He's a PFC. What is it? Hospital of some kind?"

31

"A base hospital," Bridie said. "The 325th, outside of Frankfurt."

"Budesa said Joe got caught in a black-market operation selling drugs."

Kevin shook his head. "No. Not Joe, Charley. You know him. Punch a guy in the mouth, but nothing like that."

"Don't be too sure," his father said.

"No, Jack, no," Meg cried.

"What did the guy say?" Kevin asked.

"Something about a racket in drugs. Not that Joe was *involved*, but that he had gotten into trouble because of it."

Kevin frowned. "But the business about a German girl . . . getting her in trouble . . ."

"Oh God, I can't listen to this." Mrs. Derry wept.

"Ma, you're not helping," Bridie said.

Kevin smiled at Bridie. A rock there, a reliable one. Joe might go through life getting his ass in a sling, but Bridie knew how to navigate. A fleeting joyful image passed through Kevin's mind— Bridie aged twelve, winning the hundred-meter freestyle at the Churchport Bath and Tennis Club, to the astonishment of the Manships and their Wall Street buddies. "Go, Bridie, go!" he and Joe had screamed.

"Budesa said Joe was charged with rape. A German woman. An officer's girl." Charley Felder looked at some notes on a pad.

"I don't get it," Kevin said. "How does this tie in with drugs?"

"I don't get it either," Felder said. "Budesa wasn't exactly articulate. Sounded like he was afraid to say much more."

"Damn that kid," Jack Derry said. He sipped his whiskey, slammed his pipe against a copper tray. Burning dottle settled on the threadbare rug. Meg knelt to pick it up. Kevin tried to hate his father and, as ever, found himself pitying him.

"Don't, Jack, please," Mrs. Derry whimpered. "Don't damn Joseph before we know what happened."

"And it's not true," Bridie said. "Joey never hurt people. He's got too much of a sense of justice."

"Joe was born to hurt himself and to hurt us," Mr. Derry said huskily.

Kevin waited, trying to find a way out. He had planned, organized, borrowed, labored, connived, to get to medical school. It had absorbed all his energies. A family crisis that now could upset

32

everything. He knew what the army did to rapists. Thirty years' hard labor was not uncommon. Joe Derry would die before he submitted. The kid would not survive a year in an army prison.

"Charley, you're the lawyer," Kevin said. "Tell us what we have to do."

Felder rubbed his nose the way he used to in algebra class when he knew the answer but was reluctant to respond because Potsy would taunt him about it later. "One of my classmates says there's a guy in Germany, a former officer, who takes on these cases."

"Probably charge an arm and a leg," Jack Derry said. Gloom made his pale face droop.

"I don't think so," Felder said. "Guy's name is Andrew Moss. He was a combat officer. Maybe you remember, Kev. There was this scandal after the war. Some colonel having guys beaten up. Moss got interested in the case and got the colonel transferred."

"How do we reach him?" asked Kevin.

His parents sat mute. The world was too much for them. *Hell of a thing,* Kevin thought. *My father is fifty-three and he can't ask a lawyer a question, and my mother is so frightened she'd let Joey rot in the guardhouse.*

"Can you call this lawyer?" Kevin asked Charley.

"I can. But one of you should go over. I can't leave the practice, or I'd go. Mr. Derry, it might be a good idea—"

Jack held his hand up. As he did, Kevin saw the hole in the elbow of the gray sweater. "Not me. Can't leave the store. I've got a deal cooking. Sell the old place and get a new location."

As naturally as if a vote had been taken, all of them—parents, sister, lawyer—were staring at Kevin.

"In the middle of medical rotation?" Kevin pleaded. "Have a heart, Charley. I'll miss a week."

"Kev, if it looks like a drawn-out deal, I'll go. But someone who knows Joe has to talk to him and see this lawyer."

Miss a week of medical work at Mid-Island! For a moment he was furious with Joe.

"I guess I'm elected," Kevin said.

Later, in the room he had shared with Joe, Kevin sat at the scarred desk and looked at the team photograph of Joe's last year at Churchport High. His eyes were rimmed with tears.

Joe and Vinnie Stabile, cocaptains, were holding the banner

between them: CHURCHPORT H.S. VARSITY FOOTBALL 1946. What the banner did not say was that their record was 0 and 8.

"Sucker," Kevin said. The odds had been hopeless, but Joe had refused to give up, continually barreling his small hard body into huge opponents. What had impelled him to go through that humiliating season? They'd lost ten seniors through graduation. Then there had been a sex scandal, involving two of the team's best runners. Coach Muranowski was left with three players with experience, one of them Joe Derry.

"Funny thing is, Kev," Joe told him one night, when Kevin had come in from Whitman State for a football weekend, "I don't even like the lousy game, and Muranowski's a rat."

"Why go through with it?"

"Someone's got to."

Kevin remembered the game. Churchport was being annihilated. In the last moments Joe decided that no matter what, he would hold the humiliating defeat to 64–6. They were on their own five yard line. Hamilton's all-state fullback, Ferrara, two hundred eighteen pounds, had run at Joe. Joe had met him head-on, driving his helmet into Ferrara's gut, saving Churchport from being the first league team to give up seventy points. And breaking his jaw in a gallant fight for a lost cause.

Bridie, without knocking, came into the room and sat on the bed opposite her brother. "Well?" she asked.

"I don't believe it," Kevin said. "Not Joey."

"I don't believe it either. But . . . maybe he went . . . you know Joe . . . that temper." Bridie leaned across the space between the beds and took her brother's hand. "I wish I could go also."

"Bridie, you're a high-school senior. I don't even know where I'll get the money for the flight. I can't take it out of my tuition money."

"I know where you'll get it."

"Everett E. Manship, the great benefactor. He might say no."

"It's not a gift. You're going to pay back every dollar."

"Sure," Kevin smiled. "Guys like E. E. Manship don't *lend*. They want the interest." He shook his head. "Just because he dated Ma a few times when they were kids he seems to feel responsible for this family."

34

"If he won't give you the money," Bridie said slyly, "borrow it from Cynthia."

"I don't see Cynthia out of season." He thought about the phone call.

Kevin looked at his sister's luminous face.

"The main thing is," Kevin said, "while I'm away, you have to watch that Ma and Pop don't go off the deep end. If it turns out Joey *did* do something bad, and Pop starts on the booze—"

"He won't. I'll see to it."

Kevin grinned at her. Not quite eighteen, she possessed a sturdiness and a fund of good sense that astounded him.

"Mr. Shapiro says I'm a cinch for a Regents' scholarship."

"Did he?"

"That's right. There are four kids in the class who have a chance, and I'm number one or two. He says he's going to try to get me an *extra* scholarship to Barnard."

"Good old Shapiro. I haven't forgiven him for that C-plus in English. Damned near kept me out of *my* scholarship."

"He said you didn't even deserve a C-plus, but he went easy, because you were the only jock who didn't give him a bad time."

He'd gone far on good looks, the ability to get people to like him, trust him. He'd always be an ordinary student and he knew it. People like Sally Hosmer and Max Landeck were a lot smarter.

"You dating anyone steady?" he asked Bridie.

"That jerk Frank Ferrara."

"The brother of the guy who broke Joe's jaw?"

"Yup. He's all-state in lacrosse. Lafayette offered him a scholarship."

"I have nothing against walyones, but I never liked the way his brother ran over Joey. Don't let him, you know, fool around. . . ."

"Run over *me?* No chance. They're all such *jerks,* these kids, with their duck's-ass haircuts and peg pants. Mr. Shapiro says I'm too smart for any of them except Alan Mermelstein. And he's got halitosis."

"Besides, he's Orthodox. What'd he want with an Irish Proddy?"

Bridie got up. "Kev, you have to get Joey out of this. It'll kill *them.*"

"And it might kill Joe. Go on. I'll worry about it."

35

As I always will have to, Kevin thought. She left him alone in the dingy room of trophies, old triumphs and defeats.

Kevin went to see Everett E. Manship in his office at 101 Park Avenue the following afternoon. At first Manship's secretary refused him. Impossible. Mr. Manship was in conference on new projects— shopping centers, high-rises, housing developments. But Kevin's polite voice won her over. She recognized the name. That nice Derry boy who used to work at the Manship house in Churchport Beach.

She checked with Mr. Manship. He would see Kevin at five-fifteen, after his squash game at the Yale Club.

Kevin stopped off at his apartment and found Rathman Lal seated in a sagging chair, hands locked between his knees, appealing to Potsy. Could Potsy and Kevin perhaps ask Dr. Rhodes to let Rathman take the exam over, on the grounds that he was ill that day? Kevin, unwilling to discuss his imminent flight, began to take out things he would need for the trip.

"What the hell?" Potsy asked. "You just got back from Churchport. Where you headed now?"

Kevin's eyes darted toward Rathman Lal, squatting on one of Mr. Parilli's Salvation Army chairs. Not in front of *him*, he seemed to say.

"I shall leave at once," Lal said. "You and Walter have something to discuss. Kevin . . . if you . . . you . . . can suggest . . ."

Kevin threw shirts and underwear into a valise. "Take it easy, Rathman," he said. "Maybe you didn't flunk the comprehensive."

"I am certain I did."

The cousins looked at him, Kevin with pity, Potsy with contempt. *Dumb bastard,* Potsy thought.

"Listen, Rathman," Luff said. "You're killing yourself with medical-student syndrome. Worries over nothing."

"My worries are genuine, Walter."

"You know the poem?" Potsy taunted. "Be like the guy in the poem." Luff recited:

" 'There once was a man from Bombay
'Who thought syphillis just went away
'And now he has tabes
'And saber-shin scabies
'And thinks he's the Queen of the May.' "

Lal's smile looked like a grimace of pain. "Kevin, what am I to do? I cannot return to India in disgrace."

Kevin shook his head. Ever since their first year in medical school, Lal, for reasons Kevin could not divine—their Irish toughness?—had tagged after them.

"Why don't you ask Max for help?" Kevin asked.

"Mr. Landeck has a wife and a child, and I cannot impose on him. Or Miss Hosmer. I am willing to pay."

Potsy walked into the leaky bathroom, urinated, came out zipping his fly.

"Hey, Rathman," Potsy said. "You want advice?"

"Yes, Walter. Very much so."

"Those exam papers haven't been marked yet. They're on Dusty Rhodes' desk."

Kevin was shaking his head. Potsy was a gambler, a con man. He had pulled a trick like this in their pre-med days.

"What does that mean?"

"Rhodes marks papers over the weekend. That gives you two days to get healthy."

"I don't comprehend, Walter."

"Your paper is on his desk. Walk into his office with a new exam paper with the *right* answers and substitute it."

Lal's round face went a shade darker. "Oh, but Walter, that is cheating."

Kevin turned from the dresser. "Don't do it, Rathman. The office is locked when Rhodes isn't there. His secretary guards the place as if it's a weapons room."

Potsy went back to his desk and took out a blue-covered examination booklet.

"Where did you get that?" Kevin asked.

"Ve haff vays," Potsy said. He shoved the booklet at Lal. "Don't say I ever did you a favor. If you say one word about this, I'll deny I gave it to you. Put in the right answers, write your name on it, and get it into Rhodes' office before he marks them. Beat it."

Lal clutched the leaflet to his white coat, mumbled his thanks and left.

"You'll get him in trouble," Kevin said.

"He's in trouble enough. I may save the gook's life. I hope he has enough brains to include some wrong answers."

Kevin tossed his toilet kit into the valise, tucked notebooks between his shirts.

"Weekend in Churchport?" Potsy asked. He opened *Pathology of the Heart*.

Kevin told him about the phone calls from Germany, the garbled conversation with Joey's friend.

"It's got to be a frame-up," Potsy said. His shrewd mind jumped ahead. "And if it's a frame-up, it can be unframed."

"Maybe I should have gone to law school instead of this grind."

"You mean you're hopping on a plane?"

"My passport's good from that hosteling trip I took in 'forty-eight. All I need is the dough for the plane ticket."

They shook hands. They had known each other a long time. Often, as kids and as teenagers, they had had bloody fistfights. Kevin usually won, unless Potsy fought dirty.

"So long, Kev."

"Keep notes for me. Don't let Lal screw himself up."

Everett E. Manship was in the bar of the Yale Club when Kevin walked in. The porter relieved Kevin of his valise and the envelope packed with case reports.

The high-ceilinged room should have made Kevin conscious of his bagging Robert Hall suit, his frazzled green tie. But it did not. He had learned in Churchport that there was something called "command presence" that helped enormously in confronting the very rich. Kevin knew he had it—the clear gaze of the gray eyes, the amiable smile, the erect bearing. Kevin was not a big man. But leanness and natural grace caused people to assume he was taller and stronger.

Everett E. Manship was seated alone; a scotch on the rocks was before him, a copy of the New York *World-Telegram* folded in his lap. The headline had to do with the coal strike. Manship put it aside and shook hands with Kevin.

"How's Churchport's young Dr. Kildare?" he asked.

"Weary, Mr. Manship."

"Let a non-medical man prescribe. A double J&B perhaps?" He held up his glass. Manship drank a great deal but never appeared drunk.

"A beer will be fine, sir."

38

Manship signaled a waiter and ordered a Budweiser for his guest. Kevin looked at the close-shaved, scented faces around him. Dark vested suits. Cordovan shoes. White shirts. He tried to find a common denominator, something that joined all these successful men, and decided it was *dullness*. An evening at the Churchport Bath and Tennis Club, where Kevin and Joe had worked as waiters, was about as stimulating as five hours of algebra.

But as the beer arrived, in a frosted crested glass—LUX ET VERITAS— Kevin decided he was being unfair to Manship. The King of Churchport Beach was a complex man. He was one of the few inheritors of wealth Kevin knew who could laugh at himself and his own kind.

"I've got to hand it to that little bastard Truman," Mr. Manship said. He slapped the *World-Telegram*. "Now he's threatening to throw the book at John L. Lewis. They deserve each other."

Kevin nodded. The beer was icy cold. It cleared his head.

"Oh, what the hell," Manship went on. "You and your folks voted for Truman. Frankly I was tempted to. Never liked Dewey."

"My grandfather used to say that as far as the working man was concerned, it's Tammany Hall or no hall at all."

Mr. Manship looked blank.

"I guess he meant the union hall," said Kevin. "That's how my mother explained it, anyway."

"How is Mother, Kevin?"

"With Joey and me away, she's lonely. You know she was never one for card games or church socials. When we're not around, she worries about my father losing the pharmacy or about his varicose veins."

Manship made a tent of his fingers. He was a fine-boned man, with a long, well-formed head. There was no fat on him—squash, tennis, long walks along the beach.

"The property's worth something," Mr. Manship said. "Why doesn't he get a good price and take a job in the chain drugstore? It could be arranged."

"Pop has his pride. It's his store."

"We'll work something out, Kevin. We can't let the Derrys of Churchport down."

No, you can't, Kevin thought. Twenty-five years ago his mother had dated Ev Manship. And surely slept with him. The town's richest kid and the beautiful daughter of Barney Lundigan, a Mick clammer. Kevin liked to think he had evened the score with Cynthia.

"I hate to bother you again," Kevin said. "Lending me all that money . . . the way you've given me and Joe work."

"You're Churchport. The town wouldn't be worth a damn without people like the Derrys."

Kevin smiled. The pale eyes fixed themselves on Manship. "We're donkey Irishmen, Potsy says."

"Your cousin is wrong. The town's lucky they have you. All right, what is it? I assume it isn't medical school. I know you're doing well."

"It's Joe."

"The troublesome brother."

Quickly Kevin told Manship about the phone calls. He did not use the word "rape," saying rather that there'd been some kind of "trouble" with a German girl.

"Military justice can be rough," Manship said. He had been an executive officer on an aircraft carrier. "What kind of help do you want? Shall I call someone in Washington?"

Kevin told him about Charley Felder's suggestion that he look up the lawyer who specialized in defending GIs.

"Why doesn't Charley Felder go over?" Manship asked.

"I can't ask Charley to do favors for me for nothing. He's just starting a practice."

"I can understand his problems. If he's got a tongue like his father, he's going to have a tough time. What about your studies?"

"I'm taking along notes. Some books. Actually they won't help much. I'm on medical rotation at Mid-Island Hospital. It's almost entirely clinical work."

"How can I help?"

"I need a round-trip plane ticket to Frankfurt and a few hundred dollars for expenses. I don't know what this lawyer will want, but I'll worry about it when I see him."

Manship laughed gently, a breathy noise. "Good God, Kevin, is that all you wanted?" He took a memorandum book from his jacket pocket. Kevin saw the label: J. PRESS. Manship made a notation.

"Call my secretary at noon tomorrow. She'll have the plane ticket and the money. We'll worry about legal fees later. Do you have your passport? Vaccination?"

"From that hosteling trip I took with Cynthia and her friends two summers ago." The mention of Manship's daughter evoked nothing from his narrow face. "Mr. Manship, I'm embarrassed to keep asking you for favors."

"That's all right. Joe may not be the world's most lovable man, but if he's in trouble, you should be there. I sometimes wish my children had some remote interest in one another."

"How is Buzzy?"

"He's in Paris. Trying to prove that he is this decade's answer to Picasso. We only hear from him when his funds run low."

Buzzy Manship, Kevin thought, *a prize jerk.* The blood ran thin in these people after three or four generations.

"I'm going to pay back every dollar you lend me. I've kept track."

They shook hands. "Let me know what happens."

Manship rose. His gaze went past Kevin to a young couple who were standing in the foyer. Turning, Kevin saw Cynthia Manship and a tall young man in an Oxford gray suit.

Cynthia's ash-blond hair was piled high over her forehead in tight curls, baring her ears and neck. She wore a double strand of pearls, a beige sweater set, a beige skirt.

"Come say hello to Cynthia before you leave," Manship said. "And the incumbent boyfriend."

What Dr. Gold would have called the "Seabiscuit Syndrome" (Abe was a horse-player) developed in Kevin's chest—a gallop rhythm. His first look at Cynthia after a long absence always affected him that way.

"Well, my goodness," Cynthia said. She had a low fluty voice. "It's Kevin. Hi, Dad."

She kissed her father and offered Kevin a gloved hand.

"Hi, Cynthia," Kevin said.

"Night off from the emergency room, or whatever it is interns do?"

"I'm not an intern yet."

The man in the gray suit stood immobile, out of the conversation, but not bothered by it. Clearly, he was not awed by the Yale Club or E. E. Manship. And certainly not by the ginger-haired young man in the cheap suit.

"Oh, I'm sorry," Cynthia said. "Daddy, you remember Wells Haslam? From North Carolina? Class of 'forty-five."

41

Wells Haslam shook hands with Manship. He had a chunky florid face and lank wheat-colored hair that fell over his left eye. "Privilege, sir. I read about the gift you gave to Yale."

"Wells is joining us for dinner, Daddy."

For a moment, a disapproving look colored Manship's serene face. "Splendid. I've reserved a table at San Marino for two, but I'm sure Mario can accommodate us."

Kevin stood his ground. Goddammit, he would wait until *he* was introduced. This was Cynthia at her bitchiest—the out-of-season Cynthia. In the summer, in jeans or tennis shorts, she mellowed.

"Oh, gosh, I'm sorry. Wells, Kevin Derry."

They shook hands—two dogs sniffing each other out.

"Mighty pleased, Mr. Derry."

"Nice to meet you, Mr. Haslam. Here on business?"

Wells Haslam of North Carolina looked with a wide smile at Cynthia, whose hand he had taken. "Might say so. Bit of vacation. Catch some theater, art shows."

Ridge-runner, Kevin thought. A high-class ridge-runner with an Ivy League education.

"I have a train to catch," Kevin said. "Mr. Manship, thanks for everything."

They said their goodbyes. Haslam managed to be looking the other way as Kevin spoke to Cynthia. *And screw you, too,* Kevin thought.

He turned once in the lobby and looked again at Cynthia. She had the power to fill him with a sense of inadequacy, clothed or unclothed. Her back was straight and hard. Almost a man's back. Breasts firm and spunky. What made men stare was the manner in which the narrow waist blossomed into hips and buttocks a shade too large and protruding for the upper body. It conjured up visions of stored treasure.

On the train ride back to Churchport Kevin tried to think of the five (precisely five) times he had made love to Cynthia Manship. Or rather, the times she had *let* him. She was a young woman who called the tune, named the game, set the stakes. Tossed out of Mount Holyoke, despite the fact that her mother and grandmother were graduates, Cynthia enrolled at Smith and graduated with the absolute minimum grades required.

She refused to be shipped to California, to "live down the shame," as Kevin had once overheard her mother say on the telephone. (He was raking leaves outside an open window. Mrs. Manship tended to be loud, a trait she found repellent in others.)

Kevin could remember each time, at what time of day, precisely where, what she wore, what articles of clothing they removed, what she said. She did not come easily or quickly. He had to work hard, restrain his bursting desire, to elicit one long sigh from her. The last time, at night atop an air mattress in the Manships' boathouse, she had practically dragged him to the rubbery bed, peeled off her slacks and underpants, caressed him to hardness in seconds.

But something held her back, would not permit release.

"This is the best it's ever been," Kevin had said.

"It's the best thing in the world."

As the train lurched out of the Jamaica station, he recalled how she always remained in control.

"Listen," Kevin had said, "I'm the happiest second-year med student in the world."

They kissed tongue to tongue. "It's very good," Cynthia said. "Oh, Kevin, I'm almost there. Can you wait?"

"Forever."

Moonlight poured through the windows of the boathouse. He raised his torso, better to see her hard body, marveling at the manner in which the narrow waist flowered into hips and butt.

This time she came with a slight crying noise. He could feel her heart flutter irregularly under his chest. He dug his fingers into the moons of her patrician behind, joined their mouths, let himself detonate. But she was past passion, retreating into a locked-in world, eyes shut, legs stiff and extended, her belly as hard as a middleweight boxer's.

"Did you mean it?" Kevin had asked. "Is it the best thing in the world?"

"Yes. When we're doing it."

"And afterwards?"

"Maybe."

"I don't understand you."

She ignored him. She had this capacity to hear only what she wanted to hear. "Got a handkerchief, Kev? I forgot to bring Kleenex."

He reached into his discarded shorts, found a handkerchief. With nurselike deliberateness, she cleaned herself. "God, what if you knock me up?"

"We'll get married."

"Maybe we will, and maybe we won't."

Kevin rested on one side. He embraced her, kissed her hair, her cheek. But she was unresponsive. "I always thought that was sort of understood."

"Why?"

"You let me lay you."

"Only five times. And please, Kevin, I don't want to hurt you, because you're sweet. But this is summer fucking, that's *all*. And you're the only one I've ever done it with."

"How do I qualify for winter fucking?"

She reached for her underpants. "There's no such thing. It's out of season. I mean it, Kev. You're the *only* one."

She pulled on her jeans. The blue denim stretched over her hips. He was hard again, hungry for another encounter. But she made the rules. She pushed his hands away.

"Kevin, drop the subject."

They kissed at the boathouse door. He began to tremble, ran his hands down her spine, caressed her buttocks.

"Don't. You can't get me started again."

"You'll marry me."

"Don't talk about it."

"Pharmacist's son. My dumb brother and my smart-ass sister, those parents of mine—the druggist who can't earn a living and the wife everyone feels sorry for. Pretty tough sneaking me into the Manship set. Is that it?"

"It is, and it isn't. I'm not ready to get married."

"But I make love to you. The best thing in the world, you said."

She was squinting into his eyes. "Funny. The light makes your eyes greenish. But they're *gray*. So gray I can hardly see them in the daytime. But I see them now. You have beautiful eyes, Kevin."

"To hell with my eyes. I said I love you."

She started up the gravel path to the looming stucco-and-timber mansion. Her parents were at the Cape for the weekend. Buzzy was

44

playing Wild Bill Davidson records in his room.

"Don't tell me that again, ever. Unless I tell you first, Kevin."

It was the last time they had made love. A year and a half ago. *Good luck to you, Mr. Wells Haslam*, Kevin thought bitterly.

3

Kevin sat in the kitchen with his mother and Bridie. How long would he be gone? He had no idea. What about his studies? Had he talked to the doctors at Mid-Island? Maybe Potsy could help, keep him up to date with work he missed, his mother suggested.

"Oh, that's a hot one, Ma," Bridie said. She had her chin nailed to a closed calculus textbook and was staring through glasses at the *Iliad*. "Potsy doing anything for Kev? When Kev dragged him through pre-med?"

"I don't need Potsy or anyone else," Kevin said. He picked at cold chicken on his plate, found he had no appetite. Food had never been of much consequence in his house, except for the fish and the clams he and Joe used to catch in the bay. Years ago, before the headache of the failing store rendered him indifferent, Jack Derry was one of the best fishermen in town, usually the first to come up with a big striper.

He told his mother about Manship's willingness to pay for his ticket. She did not react. The young red-headed Meg Lundigan. How many times? Kevin found that his feeling whenever these thoughts entered his mind was one of indifference. His mother, kind, vague, hardworking, was to him the most minimally attractive of women. Small-featured, small-boned, her red-gray hair in disarray, she seemed the ultimate denial of the Oedipal theory.

"It's not right you should owe him so much," Meg said.

"He'll get it back."

"Besides," Bridie said, "what will he do with his money anyway?

46

His rotten son, Buzzy, that freak. Never finished college, thinks he's an artist. Cynthia isn't much better." She looked insolently at Kevin. "They say she's a drunk."

"They're fine children," his mother said. "And we should be grateful to Mr. Manship for helping Kevin."

"Yeah," Bridie said. "He'd like to *own* Kev, the way he owns everything in Churchport."

"No way, sis. This is one harp who isn't for sale."

Before finishing his packing he called Charley Felder. The lawyer had a telephone number for Andrew Moss, the attorney. He also had sent a cable to Moss asking him to look into the case of PFC Joseph Derry, 325th Base Hospital, Frankfurt. He had advised Moss that the soldier's brother would be arriving in a few days.

"Thanks, Charley," Kevin said. "You're a good friend."

"For Joey? The man who refused to let Hamilton High score seventy points on us?"

Kevin laughed. Charley Felder had been in their "gang," their ball games, their weenie roasts. The only Jew. Because Kevin and Joe had insisted on it. Joe would knock anyone on his ass if he objected.

En route to pick up his ticket at Manship's office, Kevin stopped at the hospital to see Dr. Rhodes. A little soft-soaping was in order. He'd have to tell him the truth. Dr. Rhodes, an old navy type, would hardly appreciate a brother up for court-martial.

Hurrying across the hospital grounds, Kevin ran into Sally Hosmer, indifferent to the cold air in her white coat. Rugged New Englander.

"Oh, Kevin," she said. "Something awful's happened. Max Landeck phoned me. I was on night duty. . . ."

"What?"

"Rathman. Oh, my God. . . . Max said . . . he's . . . I can't believe it. . . ."

She began to sob and ran off the path leading to the entrance. Kevin caught her by the elbow.

"What? What happened, Sally?"

"He's dead."

Ahead of them were four police cars. The rotating red lights formed gaudy patterns on the dirty redbrick walls. There were a dozen policemen standing about. Kevin could see Dr. Rhodes, Dr. Gold, and Felix Vitti, the executive director of the hospital. There were a dozen other people gathered about, including Potsy and Max.

There was a cold sense of disaster in the air. Sally began to cry. "Killed himself, killed himself. . . . Why? . . ."

"Easy, Sal," Kevin said.

Policemen were shooing away kids. Two small boys retreated behind a hedge. "A guy hanged himself from that there window," Kevin heard one say.

Potsy saw Kevin and Sally and walked toward them. The smirk was gone from his face.

"Goddamn dumb Indian," he said breathily. "Look."

On the snowy ground lay an irregular mound covered by a green rubber sheet.

"Oh, dear God," Sally wept. "Rathman."

"What's left of him," Potsy said.

"I knew he was worried about his work," Kevin said. "But to kill himself . . ."

"Kill himself?" Potsy asked. "That isn't what happened."

Max Landeck walked over. He seemed the calmest person there, calmer even than Executive Director Vitti, who was shouting at an officer to clear the area.

"Look up there," Max said. "The fifth floor."

Kevin saw a heavy rope dangling from a window. It issued from a partly opened window and terminated several feet below the ledge of the room beneath.

"I don't get it," Kevin said. "Hell of a way to hang yourself. Lal even screwed that up."

"Kevin, don't," Sally sobbed.

Potsy turned to her. "It's true, Sal. The dumb gook didn't even mean to die."

Landeck said, "Rathman was trying to sneak an examination paper into Rhodes' office. He got into the men's room on the floor above. He tied one end of the rope to a toilet and tried to climb down and get in through the window. He was going to exchange his original exam for one with the right answers. They found the booklet under his body. He slipped off the rope."

Sally cried. "Oh, his wife and his child! Where did he get such an idea? And how did he get an extra examination?"

Kevin and Potsy looked at each other.

Dr. Rhodes detached himself from the crowd. An ambulance appeared, and Rathman Lal's body was removed. Rhodes had the booklet in his hand. A detective came over and asked for it.

"Evidence, Doc," he said.

"Just a second," Dr. Rhodes said. He faced his four students. "Any of you know anything about this?"

They were silent.

"All of you go to my office. I'll speak to each of you separately."

Kevin dragged Potsy into a conference room. The table was littered with coffee containers, ashtrays overflowing with butts.

"You son of a bitch," Kevin said. "You fed him that idea."

"I didn't tell him to try the Indian rope trick, for Chrissake."

"Potsy, one of these days I'm going to beat the shit out of you." He grabbed the lapels of his cousin's starched white coat. "Goddamn you."

"Can it, Kev," Potsy said. "You were in on it also."

"Like hell I was. You gave him the exam booklet. You told him to sneak it into Dusty's office."

"You didn't try to stop him."

Kevin shoved his cousin away and walked to the window. A metallic-gray sky lowered over Long Island. A hell of a day for Lal to die, far from his hot country, the palm trees and the burning sun. Who knew anything about him?

"Sometimes I wonder if it's worth it," Kevin said. He turned from the window. "I know, you were trying to help Lal."

Potsy swept containers and ashtrays from the table, kicked at a chair. "Fuck 'em all. He never had the balls for this anyway. So he sank sooner than later."

Kevin wanted to grab him by the throat again. But he walked past Potsy into the corridor. Sally Hosmer and Max Landeck were waiting. Both had overheard, but they were silent—the New Englander and the survivor.

Rhodes called Potsy into his office. When Potsy emerged, Kevin glared at him. "Well?"

"I didn't tell him anything. Just that Lal was scared stiff he was going to bomb out."

"Nothing about the booklet?"

Potsy shook his head. "Kev, don't go Boy Scout on me. You and me have pulled off our little scams. So this one went sour. Don't spill anything to Rhodes, huh?"

"I won't."

Potsy's lips formed the familiar smirk. "He got a shitty detail."

Gloomily Dr. Rhodes and Dr. Gold listened to Kevin's crisis. He was flying to Germany tomorrow, he told them. Some problems his brother was having.

Rhodes' brush-cut hair seemed to bristle. "That doesn't leave Dr. Gold with much help. How soon will you be back?"

"A few days. I'm sorry. This coming on top of Lal. I can't believe it."

Dr. Rhodes locked his fingers. "Maybe he's better off. Maybe he never should have been in medical school."

The chief resident's sallow face drooped; his unshaved cheeks went a shade darker. "He tried very hard, Dr. Rhodes. . . ."

"You sure Lal never said anything to you?" Rhodes asked Kevin. "No sir."

Rhodes dismissed him.

Gold walked into the corridor with Kevin. "Sorry about this, Kev. Everything happens at once."

"You'll manage, Abe. I'll be back in a few days."

It did no harm to be cheerful, to assure everyone that events turned out well.

In the corridor Kevin passed the ward in which Carmine Damelio lay in traction, his damaged hulk balanced by weights and pulleys.

Outside, four dark hefty men stood talking in low voices. They wore leather jackets, white turtlenecks, black silk suits. Rings sparkled on fingers. Kevin could see Damelio—ass wounded, leg fractured. An old Italian woman in black mopped his forehead.

"*Figlio, figlio mio,*" the old lady murmured.

"Ay, cut it out, Ma," Damelio said. Then he caught a glimpse of Kevin and Dr. Gold. "Ay, there's the guy, Vinnie," he shouted. "That's the guy saved me. Doc Derry. Doc, say hello to the family— Vinnie, Paulie, Dom, Tony. Come in and say hello to Mama."

Kevin waved to the old woman and nodded to the group.

One of them, an older man, silver flecking his perfumed coal-black hair, pumped Kevin's hand. "The Damelios don't forget,

50

Doc." He had a hoarse voice. "You need a favor, you wanna car wrecked, a guy roughed up, let us know." Kevin noted his diamond pinky ring.

Paulie, a squat junior member, added, "It ain't only cartage we do. Wait'll we catch the *scugnizz'* who shot Carmine."

"You're okay, Doc," Vinnie said. "You, too, Dr. Gold."

"I hope so," Abe said.

Kevin landed in Frankfurt in a heavy rain. Lights flashed around the airport tower in the wind-whipped night. The place had the look of a military base. He went through Passport and Health Control, a rare young face, not a tourist, not an army brat. It was a strange shadowy land, full of ghostly people. Even the loud American officers seemed of a different era.

He passed a display of American candies and realized he was starving, but he didn't stop. He had developed a talent for controlling his appetites.

A short young man in a khaki field jacket and overseas cap was staring at Kevin. He had a Slavic face, hair the color of buttercup blossoms.

"Derry?" he asked.

"Right."

"Mr. Felder called last night. He said it might be a good idea I met you. I'm Henry Budesa."

They shook hands. Budesa could not have been more than five feet three inches. The kind of lost soul Joe would adopt.

"How'd you know it was me?" Kevin asked.

"I cased the people on the flight. It's usually dependents, brass, business guys. You got Joe's eyes and hair."

"How is he?"

"They filed charges against him two days ago. It'll be his ass if he's guilty."

"You said something about trouble with a woman? Is it rape?"

"Rape and assault and a coupla other things. C'mon, I borrowed a Jeep from the motor pool. Me an' the motor sergeant, we're Cleveland Polacks."

Kevin followed Budesa into the cold rain.

"And that ain't the worst of it," Budesa said. "She's the colonel's private cunt."

Budesa said little else as they sloshed through the streets. They skirted the city, passed through military check points, came to a dingy suburb of cobbled streets, bomb-scarred buildings and run-down stores. At the end of the street loomed a tall institutional-looking building.

"The good old 325th Base Hospital," Budesa said. "Fuck-up City. Me and Joe work the same floor. Joe was up for corporal when he got in trouble."

"Is he there now?"

"Hospital's got no guardhouse. He's at the Military Police barracks. How you gonna see him?"

Kevin told Budesa about Moss. He would call him tomorrow. Budesa halted the Jeep in front of a three-story redbrick building with a sign that read GASTHAUS.

"The old lady, Frau Haft, she's expecting you," the GI said. "Look out for German hookers. They're all clapped up. Maybe I'll see you again. I got to watch out they don't know I'm trying to help Joey. He's been framed."

"Framed? Why?"

"That's what you got that lawyer for."

The Jeep farted off toward the hospital. Kevin picked up his suitcase and rang the bell. The door was opened by an elderly woman who spoke some English. She asked to see his passport, made him sign a register and took him to a narrow room redolent of disinfectant.

Kevin undressed, got into surgical greens—he and Potsy availed themselves of anything useable—and tried to sleep.

Rathman Lal, his father in the shabby store, Joe in the guardhouse. All kept him from sleeping. Winners and losers. And these three were losers. Not like the Everett Manships of the world. They were the big winners. It was clear that a man had to choose.

Kevin got up from the bed. He touched the envelope he had picked up at Manship's office—return ticket, five hundred dollars, and a note saying to call if he ran into trouble. Then he picked up a yellow pad and, under the dim light of the bed lamp, resting the pad on a copy of *Principles of Neurology*, wrote to Cynthia Manship.

Frankfurt, Germany
February 8, 1950

Dear Cynthia:

I don't quite know who Mr. Wells Haslam is. I hope he's a temporary.

The purpose of this letter is to tell you what my intentions are. I intend to marry you. I love you. I've loved you ever since the first time, that night in your room three years ago. The fact that we rarely see each other except during the summer means nothing. Up to now I've kept my mouth shut, played tennis with you, worked at your father's place, accepted his generosity. You're summer people. I'm one of the all-year-round serfs. But I realize now, on this dark, wet, cold, miserable night, in some god-forsaken house in Frankfurt, waiting to see my brother, who, as usual, is in trouble up to his eyeballs, that I love you, and I am going to marry you. Not only that, I intend to earn a lot of money in the practice of medicine. It isn't hard if you set your mind on it. Dr. Rhodes, the chief of medicine at Mid-Island, says that I should look to a specialty— cardiology maybe. He says I have the mind for it, and he's ready to help.

So all I ask of you is not to run off with someone or go for some big society wedding with Mr. Haslam.

I'll be back at med school in a few days and I'll call. I love you. You once told me it was "the best thing in the world." It is, and being together all the time will make it even better.

With deep love,
KEVIN

It was unlike any letter he had written. Kevin did not let his emotions surface. But there was something about the lonely room, the rain, the foreign city, that forced him to write the letter. It was as if the authority and status Cynthia possessed, by dint of birth and bank accounts, were signaling him to make a grand effort. Even if the letter proved nothing, even if she laughed at it. Even if rejected, the act of communicating his desire would sustain him in the days ahead.

53

Moss was a stocky man with a florid face and a mop of black curly hair. He had an impatient fast-talking manner, and he kept answering his own phone in his one-room office. Five years out of service, Moss wore a tan army shirt, brown Oxfords. An officers' trench coat, soaked by the morning rain, hung from a clothes tree. On the cracked walls of the office were photographs of Lincoln and a man Kevin did not recognize.

"Darrow," Moss said brusquely.

He told Kevin that while in service he had become convinced that for most enlisted men, military justice was a farce, a stacked deck. Following his discharge, he had tried to earn a living handling GI cases.

"Why didn't your parents come?" he asked Kevin bluntly.

"They're not up to it. My father can't leave his store."

"You work?"

"I'm a third-year medical student."

Moss swung his chair around, as if better to study the young man in the rumpled tan suit. "Felder didn't mention that."

"Charley and I are old friends. He thinks of me more as a guy he used to go clam digging with."

The clam digging seemed to mesh with Andrew Moss' preconception of the Derry family more than the fact that Kevin was a medical student. He nodded.

"Budesa tell you anything?" asked the lawyer.

"Not much. He said Joe was framed. The girl who claimed he raped her is a colonel's girlfriend."

"Budesa's not as dumb as he pretends to be. They may land on him next."

"They?"

"Colonel Curtis and his friends. Your brother got caught in the middle of a bad one."

Moss picked up a typewritten report from his desk. He fiddled with a pair of eyeglasses held together across the nosepiece with a Band-Aid. "Woman's name is Eva Baumann. Age twenty-eight. Your brother is alleged to have picked her up outside of an enlisted men's club, dragged her into a Jeep, beat her and raped her. They've got the torn panties. Bloodstains and a trace of feces. Don't look shocked. You're a medical student, aren't you?"

"I'm not shocked. I don't believe a word of it."

54

"They have a witness. Master Sergeant Bullard Hicks. Works at the hospital. He says he saw Joe Derry dragging Baumann into the Jeep."

"That sounds impossible. How can you drive a Jeep and force a woman to stay in it?"

"Hicks says he saw your brother beat the crap out of her. The police found bruises on her arms and back. Your brother turned up with a few black and blue marks also. He didn't like it when they came to arrest him at five the next morning. It took four MPs to convince him to go quietly."

"That's Joe."

"Anyway, the story is full of holes. Know why?"

Kevin shook his head.

"Eva Baumann is a whore. Before she became Colonel Miles Curtis's lay, she was working every American post from here to the Bremen Enclave. Fifty dollars a night. No deutschmarks, no marmalade."

"What do we do now, Mr. Moss?"

"We have a date with your brother. Look cheerful, Derry. The brass watches its step when I get into a case. I drink with the AP and UP reporters."

They waited in a bleak gray-walled room. There was no wire fencing. But there was a raised barrier between the two sides of the table that sat in the center of the room.

A black MP sergeant in a white helmet liner stood at the door, twirling his baton. He carried a .45 in a white leather holster and wore a white fourragère. A door opened and a second MP, a towering white boy, entered.

Then Kevin saw Joe, looking pale, the old anger flashing in the gray eyes. He was wearing a blue-denim fatigue suit, a size too big, with a large white *P* stenciled on the front. Incredibly, the next thing Kevin noticed was that Joe had the familiar scab from the football helmet above the bridge of his nose.

"Kevin."

"Hi, Joe."

Joe came toward the table. For a moment they looked at each other cautiously. Impulsively, Joe embraced Kevin, hugging him close, his powerful hands digging into Kevin's back.

"Hey. No contact." The MP sergeant moved toward them.

"Take it easy, Sergeant," Moss said.

They sat down facing each other. Moss introduced himself and told Joe about Budesa's conversation with Kevin.

"Keep it down," Joe said. "Last thing I want to do is get Budesa in trouble. They'll beat him once and he'll never get up again. I could show you some beauty marks on my ass."

Kevin smiled. Nothing about Joe had changed.

"How's Pop? How's Ma?"

"They're okay, Joe. Business picked up at the store." Kevin did not mind lying to a man who might find himself spending thirty years in prison. "Bridie's killing 'em at high school. Shapiro says he can get her a scholarship to Barnard."

"How about you? How come you can take time off to come here?"

"It's slow. I'm on medical rotation at Mid-Island Hospital."

They watched each other for a moment. It was not lost on Moss. He could see they had been rivals—dumb younger brother, smart older brother. They may not have been close through the years but they were united now.

"Talk," Moss said. "I'll take notes."

Kevin looked at the MPs. "Are they supposed to be here?"

"Yeah. I'm considered dangerous because I resisted arrest. But they're not supposed to listen."

Moss said, "Talk. I'll ask questions from time to time."

"I've been framed," Joe said. "That broad was never in a Jeep with me. I never laid a hand on her; I wouldn't screw her with someone else's dick. She's Colonel Curtis's whore."

"Why'd they frame you?" Moss asked.

"Curtis is running the biggest black-market operation in drugs in Germany," Joe said. "He and his staff officers and some enlisted men. Sergeant Hicks is the bagman."

"The guy who says he saw you drag Baumann into the Jeep?" Moss asked.

"He and some sergeants handle the shipping and selling. The officers make the contacts with the civilian black market in Berlin, Munich, Stuttgart. There's a story Curtis has three hundred thousand dollars in Swiss francs stashed away. The others aren't doing bad either. There's a shavetail drives a Mercedes. He's Curtis's accountant."

Kevin grimaced. "How do they let this happen?"

56

Moss laughed. "I know officers who've made fortunes cleaning up on Rosenthal china, automobile franchises, textiles. Anything goes. But drugs are a little hairy."

"Don't tell me," Joe said. "Five hundred percent mark-up on penicillin. Sulfa, morphine, insulin."

"How does all this lead to a phonied-up rape charge against you?" the lawyer asked.

Joe hunched forward. "I wouldn't be part of it," he said.

"And they framed you for this?" Kevin asked. "What did you do? Say you'd rat on them?"

"You know me better, Kev. When I got here last fall, I was assigned to Pharmacy. I went out for the hospital football team and played linebacker. We won the district championship. I was the colonel's pet. Couldn't kiss my butt enough after we beat the Twenty-eighth Division. I recovered a fumble in the end zone."

"That explains the helmet scab," Kevin said, and laughed.

"Around Christmas time Hicks takes me out for a drink. 'We've been watching you, Derry; want you to work with us.' I had an idea what he was talking about. Budesa and I had noticed something screwy about the inventories. If you get a typewriter and a mimeo machine, there isn't anything you can't fake in the army. Hicks said he and a few officers were doing business on the side. I was ticketed as a smart kid and they wanted me in."

"And you told him?" asked Moss.

"To shove it up his ass. I told him my old man worked his can off running a drugstore, that he'd never cheated anyone in his life, and besides, I didn't like the idea of making a living off stolen penicillin.

"They tried once again. Hicks and Curtis called me in. I could have a three-day pass to Berlin, all the drinking and screwing I wanted, if I'd carry medical supplies for them. I was to bring back five grand in Swiss francs, and they'd cut me in for ten percent."

"Did they approach Budesa?" Moss asked.

"No. They figured he was a dumb Polack."

Kevin studied his brother's homely face. Same Joey. Same trouble-bound kid.

"Why did they land on you?" Moss asked.

"I didn't want it. They transferred me out of Pharmacy. Budesa too. Made us bed-pan jockeys. About two weeks ago, a captain from the IG came down."

"Inspector General," Moss explained to Kevin.

"The guy was only here a day, but somebody must have dropped hints. Maybe the IG got suspicious about the bills of lading. I never talked to him. Not a word. Curtis issued new procedures for the dispensation of drugs. Last week they knock on my door at five in the morning and tell me I'm under arrest on a rape charge. Eva Baumann says I assaulted her."

Moss tapped his ballpoint pen on his pad. "You have witnesses to swear you weren't there when it was supposed to have happened?"

"Budesa and another guy. We were playing three-handed pinochle in the day room."

"It'll be their word against that master sergeant and Baumann," Moss said.

"Or maybe no word. The other guy was named Cohn. He was transferred two days ago to the Pacific. I like Henry, but he's afraid to open his mouth."

The black MP sergeant walked toward them. "Time's up," he said.

Joe got up. "Kev, you can't hang around here forever. Mr. Moss'll take care of me. Go back to school. Tell Pop and Ma I'm fine."

The brothers shook hands. Joe turned away. There was another *P* on his broad back. It enraged Kevin. He wanted to find Colonel Curtis and Master Sergeant Hicks and kill them. He would do it happily, explaining before he finished them off that they could not take thirty years of his brother's life and get away with it.

Outside in the misty rain Kevin asked, "What do you think?"

"I'm not happy. There's pressure from the German authorities to crack down on GIs. 'Ami Go Home' is replacing *'Deutschland Über Alles'* as the national anthem. Half the time I think we lost the war."

In the parking lot, looking more undersized than he had at the airport, Henry Budesa was waiting for them. He seemed to be wary. He said to Moss, "In the car."

The three got in. Budesa gave the lawyer a manila envelope. "I pulled these outa medical records. Don't tell no one. It'll be my ass."

"Medical records?" asked Kevin.

"From the civilian clinic," Budesa said. "We take care of civilians free. Goodwill, all that shit."

Moss began to open the envelope.

"Not here," Budesa said. "Make photostats and get 'em back to me." He got out of the Volkswagen. "It's how Curtis met that

58

broad. She was a patient here." He trudged off in the rain. *Henry Budesa,* he said to himself, *whether Joe gets off or not, we owe you a few.*

Moss took the papers out of the envelope. There were three sheets. Kevin joined him in the front seat. "You're the medical expert," the lawyer said.

Kevin looked at the top sheet. It read BAUMANN, EVA KLARA. She was twenty-eight, native of Frankfurt. An address was given, crossed out, another written above it. She had first come to the clinic two years ago. Then a few months later, then again in 1949.

"Well?" asked Moss. "Malnutrition? Diabetes?"

"She's had gonorrhea twice, and one infection of syphilis technica."

"Technica?"

"Syphilitic infection associated with profession or line of work."

Moss chuckled. "You'd think Curtis would have lifted the file or burned it."

Kevin found it hard to laugh. "I'm never surprised by the screw-ups in hospital records. He may have looked for the file and been unable to find it. Thank God for Budesa. What's this worth?"

"Maybe thirty years."

In two days' time, Moss located a warrant officer who was willing to swear out an affidavit that he had known Eva Baumann as a prostitute and had sexual relations with her. Chief Warrant Officer Vito Amalfi, of Queens, New York, also swore in front of a notary public that he had contracted gonorrhea a week later and had the medical records to prove it. He was furious with Fräulein Baumann because he was convinced she stole his watch.

"So his girlfriend's a whore and she's had venereal disease," Kevin said. "It doesn't prove Joe didn't rape her."

They were driving through the city to the hospital. Moss had—after several fruitless calls—succeeded in getting through to Colonel Miles Curtis.

"No, but it makes it less likely."

Kevin gasped as Moss sped around a prime-mover hauling a disabled Patton tank.

"You two are pretty close, aren't you?" Moss asked.

"On and off."

"Has he ever been in trouble before?"

Kevin's eyes widened. "Joe? That's his problem. He's so outraged by injustice he gets into trouble trying to do the *right* thing. I'm not sure I can explain it."

"You don't have to. I'm a little bit like that myself."

Moss flashed his ID card and they drove into the hospital parking lot. They walked past phalanxes of Jeeps, six-by-sixes, weapons carriers, ambulances.

"What about the black-market business?" Kevin asked. "We can't prove that."

"I'd like to have him think Joe didn't tell us, that we found out elsewhere. That'll make him sweat. Remember one thing. This guy is *not* an MD. He's a lieutenant colonel in the MAC. He's sort of an outsider."

"MAC?"

"Medical Administration Corps. They tend to be in awe of real doctors. He's also not the number one. There's a bird colonel over him, guy named Hawes. I may even introduce you as Dr. Derry, eminent young cardiologist from Long Island."

"Forget it. Everyone says I look too young to be a medical student."

Moss smiled at the young man. The kid had poise, manners. Better yet, he did not seem aware that he had these qualities.

A middle-aged WAC let them into the office of Lt. Col. Miles Curtis, MAC. There was a gold sign on the door under his name and rank: EXECUTIVE OFFICER.

It was a lavish office, a lot more impressive than Dusty Rhodes' flaking cubbyhole. Photographs adorned the wall. A group of officers standing around General Eisenhower. For a moment, Kevin felt outclassed.

Curtis was of good height, heavy-chested, paunchy. But he carried his uniform well—dark jacket, dusty pink slacks, gleaming shoes. He wore three rows of decorations. Kevin wondered how a hospital administrator could accumulate so many combat ribbons. There was a portable bar in one corner of the room, a massive Grundig radio, a carved bookcase.

They shook hands. Moss introduced Kevin. Curtis motioned them to two black leather chairs. He offered them cigars. The best the PX sold, he explained with a low laugh, then lit up himself when Kevin and Moss refused.

Kevin studied his face. Round, bland. Puffy cheeks, small mouth. He talked quickly, with the positive accents of a born salesman. Kevin noticed that when the colonel was not talking, his eyes darted to the walls or out the window that overlooked the hospital grounds.

"I'm puzzled why you came to see me," Curtis said. "It's a matter for the judge advocate's office. I didn't order Derry arrested. I'm just his CO."

Moss waited a moment. "There are cases where you turn the men over to civilian authorities, aren't there?" he asked.

"I know of none. But I'm no legal eagle."

"The charges were brought by a civilian woman. The military got into the act after the fact. Suppose the woman decided to drop the charges?"

Curtis' mouth formed a loose smile. "What makes you think she would do such a thing? There are witnesses who saw Derry beat her and drag her into the Jeep. She underwent a medical examination. Evidence of penetration. Her underpants were ripped. Traces of blood and feces, the examining officer said."

"Officer?" asked Moss.

"Well, the night technician. He's a sergeant."

Moss nodded. "I guess we can get his name and the report."

"No problem."

Moss said, "I'm very much interested in the woman's physical examination. I happen to know it wasn't her first visit to this hospital. She'd been here a few times."

"I don't see what bearing that has on Derry's attack on her."

Moss turned to Kevin. "Kevin, let me have those reports." He smiled at the officer. "I forgot to mention. Mr. Derry is a medical student. He was helpful in interpreting the medical data in Fräulein Baumann's dossier."

Curtis got up. "How did you get that? Hospital records are private. Moss, you and this man are in deeper trouble than you know. . . ."

"Settle down, Colonel. Kevin, you mind reading?"

Kevin stared at the officer. No, he was not afraid of him. But he hated him. He believed every word Joe had told him.

"What are you staring at?" Curtis asked. "I don't even know who the hell you are. But I know your brother. He's been asking for it since the day he came here."

61

Kevin's eyes did not flinch. "Asking for what, Colonel?"

"Never mind. Give me those papers."

"Curtis, relax," said Moss. "You've got a dime-store Clarence Darrow and a kid from medical school here. Two civilians. If you feel uneasy, you can ask Colonel Hawes to join us. He'd be interested."

Kevin read. "'Baumann, Eva Klara, admitted June twelfth, 1948, discharge and infection of genital tract, serosal surfaces also showing infection. Final diagnosis, uncomplicated gonorrhea, treated with procaine PCNG.'"

"This hasn't got a thing to do with a rape charge," Curtis said.

Kevin resumed. "'Patient returned January twenty-third, 1949, with similar complaints, discharge and cervical pain. Results of cultures were again positive, with same treatment prescribed—'"

The officer banged his fist on the desk. "That's enough. Who cares what this woman had? Your brother is accused of raping her. There are witnesses. He's going to go to trial."

"'December seventeenth, 1949, admitted for treatment of a hard chancre on the labia minora. Dark-field examination of fluid expressed from lesions, followed by serologic tests, revealed presence of syphilis, probably syphilis technica, since subject is an admitted prostitute. Procaine penicillin, eight million units, prescribed and administered—'"

"That's enough!" Curtis shouted. *That's goddamn enough!*"

Moss smiled at Kevin. "It helps to have a physician in the family."

"All right, Moss," the colonel said, "what do you want?"

Kevin looked at the photographs on Curtis' burnished desk. There was one of a plain-looking woman in a summer dress, with two fat children. Wife and kids.

"Eva Baumann is your girlfriend," Moss said.

"What if she is?"

"By the time I get this in front of a court-martial, you'll have a lot of explaining to do."

"Joe Derry is a bad apple. He's a misfit. One of those enlisted men who because he's been to some jerkwater college thinks he's as good as the officers."

Moss looked at Kevin. "I have a feeling the time has come to inform Colonel Curtis of his role in rebuilding the German postwar economy."

Kevin glared at Curtis. "Maybe he'd like to record this. Or bring in a stenographer."

"I don't know what you're talking about, Moss."

"You forget, Colonel, I'm one of *you*. I know the angles. Where shall I begin?"

"By getting out of here. I'm a busy man. The utilization committee is scheduled to meet in ten minutes."

"Colonel," Moss said softly, "you are running a dirty operation out of this hospital. You and some other officers are selling drugs to black-market operators."

The colonel got up and folded his arms. "So that's it. Nobody'll take your word against mine. Not with that son-of-a-bitch brother of yours in the dock."

"Colonel," Moss said, "let's open it up. My concern is saving Joseph Derry from thirty years of hard labor. I know what happens to men in federal pens. The boy's innocent."

"Then let him stand court-martial."

"Oh, no. Not the way you run those things. He's sworn to me and to his brother that he never told the IG a thing. He isn't that kind, as much as he hates your guts."

Curtis was standing at his window, his hands locked behind his back.

"He didn't talk?"

"Not a word," the lawyer said.

Curtis was rubbing his hands as if trying to restore circulation. "What do you want?" He walked to his door and locked it.

Moss scratched his unruly hair. "All charges against Derry dropped. Fräulein Baumann to make a statement exonerating him. Master Sergeant Hicks is to swear he was mistaken. You are to use your influence to see that Derry is released. There will be no punitive action. Nothing in his military record. He is to be transferred in grade to another command."

"What do I get?"

"Silence," Moss said.

"How can I count on it?"

"It's a chance you have to take. But from what I know of these young men, they'll keep their word."

Kevin shifted in his seat. "Don't count on me, Colonel. If I hear one word about you trying to get Joe, I'll open up." He waved the medical file.

"Mr. Derry intends to remain in Frankfurt until you arrange his brother's release and have him transferred," said Moss.

"And he's not to be beaten again," Kevin said. "Understand?"

Curtis, his cheeks scarlet, slumped in his chair. "Pretty shrewd pair, aren't you?"

Kevin could not resist it. "What are you kicking about? You can go on peddling penicillin and insulin to the Germans. Nobody's going to snitch. Unless you double-cross me."

Moss got up. "Colonel," he said, "I think we've had a constructive meeting."

The Derry brothers sat in the restaurant of the Frankfurt airport. Other soldiers looked trim and pressed in their uniforms. Joe's did not fit. They drank coffee and talked about the deal Moss had made for him.

"I'm sorry about one thing," Joe said.

"I know. We couldn't blow the whistle on those bastards."

Joe warmed his callused hands on the coffee mug. His fingers were gnarled. He had always gravitated toward positions of maximum punishment—catcher in baseball, linebacker in football, goalie in hockey.

They talked about Joe's future. He had six months to run on his enlistment. Curtis would transfer him to the Philippines. A base hospital near Clark Field. He had no bad time on his record. All the material on the arrest had been removed from his file. Moss had watched the destruction of the records, the wiping clean of the slate.

"Crazy, the way guys figure how to get rich," Kevin said. "I guess it's easy, so they fall into it."

Joe snorted. "The bastards clear over a million a year. There's a thousand percent mark-up on some of the stuff. No wonder they wanted me put away."

"Well, they learned about the Derrys."

The loudspeaker called Kevin's flight.

"It doesn't seem fair," Kevin said, grabbing Joe's hand.

"What doesn't?"

"Assholes like Curtis getting rich while Mom and Pop have to stand around that store all day."

Joe embraced him. "Nothing we can do about it. Hurry up and

64

get rich and famous. It'll give them something to brag about. They'll never get it from me."

Kevin picked up his valise. "Let me know what the Far East is like. We have Filipino nurses at the hospital, and they're like birds. They don't talk; they sing."

Two military policemen—white helmet liners, white scarves, armbands, clubs—came into the lounge. For a second the brothers looked at them. Joe got up slowly, his eyes following the MPs. But the shiny white globes vanished in a crowd of arriving army "dependents."

Joe and Kevin laughed and shook hands.

"Tell Bridie to go to college and finish, not like me," Joe said. "She's got more brains than both of us."

Kevin smiled. "And she's better-looking."

4

He decided against a trip to Churchport. It would take too much explaining. From his apartment Kevin called his parents and Charley Felder and told them that Joe was free and about to be transferred. Yes, he had been framed. (To his parents, he used the words "mistakenly arrested.") Moss was a hell of a man. Whatever he asked as a fee, the Derrys would pay. Charley laughed. He would write Moss a letter thanking him, explaining that the family had no money.

"No," Kevin said. "If he wants dough, we'll get it. Joe could be in prison now."

Jack Derry's reaction infuriated Kevin, but he said nothing. "I knew Joey was all right all the time," Jack bragged. "Had faith in him. The nerve of those guys, trying to railroad a Derry!" Kevin remembered his father's earlier condemnation of Joe, but he remained silent.

He asked for his mother and was gratified by her happiness. There seemed so little that made her joyful these days. Crazy, how a reprieve from jail—a negative circumstance, to be sure—could make her sound cheerful.

"And we have you to thank, Kevin," she said. "Always you."

The next morning he called Cynthia at her Fifth Avenue apartment. She sounded sleepy, but her voice had the exciting, fluty quality. It summoned up images of her fine-boned face, the golden hair.

"Kev, that was a dopey letter you wrote," she yawned. "You know, you can be a nut sometimes."

"Is that all I get? I meant every word of it."

"God, Kev. You know I like you. We can't talk about it on the phone. I didn't sleep."

"Over my letter?"

"That. Other things."

"Can I see you tonight? I . . . I . . . asked you to marry me. That's worth at least dinner or a drink."

There was a pause. More yawning. "You can't come here, Kevin. It's complicated."

"I'll meet you somewhere."

She agreed, after some persuading, to meet him after dinner at the bar of a West Side hotel. It was odd. The choice was hers. Kevin suspected why. She would not be recognized there.

Riding the train into New York, reading and taking notes from *Pathology of the Heart*, he smiled at a story that had been in the papers a few months ago. A young socialite—the kind of young man Cynthia dated—had been arrested in a raid on a whorehouse on West 68th Street. When he called his banker father for help, his father's response was, "What the hell were you doing on the *West* Side?"

After two beers, Kevin took her hand. "I took a room here," he said. "We're registered as Mr. and Mrs. George Haley."

"You've got to be kidding."

"I got here an hour ago. Valise, toilet articles. They made me pay in advance for one night. I said my wife was coming in from Detroit."

"No, Kevin."

He edged closer to her in the plastic-covered booth. The bar was empty except for two middle-aged men who were arguing about Truman's invoking the Taft-Hartley act to get the coal miners back to work.

Their thighs touched. He felt her hip. More of the great deception. The rich roundness below, the flesh of a Rembrandt nude.

"I'm not a summer lay anymore," he said. "You're going to be my wife. We'll make love tonight and I'll convince you."

"No." She began to get up. He grabbed her hand and pulled her to him.

"Then we'll announce our engagement. Cynthia, I mean it. I thought about it after that Indian got killed, after Joe got in trouble. The world's full of misery and brutality and dumb people doing dumb things. Let's do something that's good for both of us."

"Kevin, because I let you . . . a few times—"

"I remember every one. Two years ago, you came out of the Bath and Tennis Club in a striped bathing suit. Red and white peppermint stripes. You bent over to pick up a bathing cap and I went crazy. I've never recovered."

Cynthia put her fingers to his lips. "I know, I know. The demure, proper face, the serious green eyes, the straight back and suddenly— *wow!* It's all that muscle I put on from tennis and riding. You're crazy, Kevin."

"In five years I'll be a rich cardiologist with a Park Avenue address. Your father will like that. Most of the Manships get there on a pass. I'll pay my way."

"You know, Kev, you've developed a clever way of using your log-cabin origins."

"What does that mean?"

"Oh, that poor-boy, up-from-poverty routine."

"It's my Protestant-Irish charm. My father says I've got the best of both worlds—Irish blarney and WASP nerve."

"You aren't even aware of it. It's one of the reasons I've always liked you. And why I let you—"

He crushed her hand beneath his, began to stroke her arm. "The girl in the peppermint-stripe bathing suit. Thighs like a wild mare."

She laughed—large white teeth, broad mouth, the inner redness.

"God, what a compliment," she said.

"It's from *Darkness at Noon*. Bridie read the passage to me once. Two of these Bolsheviks are in prison, and one teases the other with a bunch of lies about the last woman he slept with. 'Thighs like a wild mare,' he tells the poor guy in the next cell."

She let her gaze travel from his curling ginger hair to the handsome features—the trusted face of the summer boy, mower of lawns, trimmer of hedges, trapper of raccoons. He had a right to brag about how far he had come and how far he intended to go. The story of his adventure in Germany had astounded her. She and her brother, Buzzy, confronted with such a crisis, would have fallen

68

apart, run to Papa for money, influence, the awesome power of the Manships. Kevin Derry, an impoverished medical student, had forced the army to back down.

"I have to leave," she said. "I told my parents I was meeting some girls from the office." Cynthia worked as a researcher for a television network. Her father's company were stockholders. Kevin never understood what she did.

"Does that mean they object to your having a beer with the servants?"

She shook her blonde curls. They were piled high, the hair drawn taut and glistening on her neck. Free-form gold earrings sparkled in her ears. "That's what I mean about your log-cabin routine. You can't make me feel guilty for being rich."

He took her arm. The fine golden hairs made him shiver. "We're going to love each other," he said. "Not in some boathouse, or a mattress in the attic, or behind the pro shop. In a locked room on a bed. Maybe I'll leave the bathroom light on so I can see all of you."

"No, Kevin."

He was helping her rise. She followed him—a woman too elegant for the shabby bar. The lobby of the hotel smelled of Lysol. Hardly the aroma of romance.

She looked at him with pleading eyes. Not like her, Kevin thought. She usually ran things. She made the rules in Churchport Beach. In the self-service elevator he seized her and kissed her, moved his hands down her sides, caressed her buttocks, drew the side of his palm down the cleft.

"Oh, what a romantic," she said, and sighed.

In the room she sat for a moment on the bed. "The boathouse was nicer than this," she said. "Who furnishes these places? Mauve carpet. Purple bedspread. Green drapes. Ugh."

There was a speaker with a selector on the wall. Kevin turned it on. Soupy music emanated—WPAT, Paterson. He began to undress. Naked, his hard body with its ginger patch of hair approached her. She had taken off her sweater, remained in slip and skirt.

He fell to his knees, dragged her skirt down, tugged at her underpants, stockings.

"I admire a subtle man," she said. She sounded mocking. "Are you trying to tell me something?"

69

But when she was naked and they had joined their bodies, the irony left her voice, and she gasped in rhythm with his thrusting. She locked her legs around him—gold, tan, perfectly formed.

It seemed to Kevin, as lightning sparked along his back, and he stared (disbelieving his good fortune) at her half-shut eyes and parted lips, that she was in *control*. Some part of her remained outside.

He was sure of it when she lowered her legs.

"Tired?" he asked.

"No. My earrings. I should have taken them off." She moved her arms from his back, unhinged the earrings, placed them on the night table. Then she took pins from her hair and let it fall.

"I'll love you all my life. It's never been better. I'll make love to you every day."

"Make me come, Kevin."

He plunged back into her, raised her thighs with his hands, dug his fingers into her nates. She moaned, but held back.

"I can't wait," he said. "I'm sorry."

Afterward he drew his head down her body, kissing throat, breasts, nipples, belly, the inside of her thighs. She was inert, sighing, stroking his head.

"Kevin . . . you must stop . . . please . . ."

Tongue and lips made her come, aroused against her will. She had never been like this before. She had been—in those uncomfortable sessions on dewy lawns and in splintery boathouses—pretty much the commander. They held each other for a half hour, dozing, saying nothing, and when he tried to pry her legs apart again, she resisted.

"What's wrong, baby?" he asked.

"Kevin . . ."

"I hurt you? Weren't you happy?"

"Yes, yes. You're marvelous."

He ran his lips down her spine. At forty, at fifty, she would maintain her figure and her grace. The good lines, the proper amalgam of musculature, glandular function, bone, and spirit, creating a conformation of flesh that did not wrinkle.

Cynthia got up from the bed and walked into the bathroom. He could hear her showering. He switched stations on the selector, found a newscast. Mike Quill was threatening another transit strike. Mayor O'Dwyer was trying to stop it. His father had phrased it

70

felicitously: "The English will forgive the Irish nothing, and the Americans will forgive them anything."

The shower trickled into silence. He heard her moving about the bathroom. Briefly he was ashamed of the depressing hotel room. She deserved better. But what mattered was what they had done with their bodies. And would do again. He wanted her immediately, under him, above him, the magical connections. His wife-to-be.

She came out of the bathroom with a white towel wrapped around her head like a turban and another around her waist so that her breasts and hips were covered.

"Cold?" he asked.

"A little."

"I'm hot. Body temperature and passion. Once more?"

She shook her head, sat in a mauve chair and pulled the bed cover around her shoulders.

"What's wrong, sweetheart?" he asked.

She shook her head and covered her eyes. He heard faint sounds of weeping.

"Jesus, I didn't want you to feel this way. Cynthia, stop."

"Kevin . . . oh, good God, Kevin . . ."

"What's wrong? What did I do?"

Her voice was firm and assertive, the voice of wealth and breeding. She'd screwed the groom in the hayloft and now she was ready to put on her jodhpurs and return to the mansion. "I have to tell you something."

"You're afraid I knocked you up. I'll arrange a rabbit test at the hospital."

"Kevin, listen to me. Wells and I are announcing our engagement next week."

"Wells?"

"You met him that day at the Yale Club."

"You're joking. *Wells,* for Chrissake. That isn't a name; it's a town or a disease."

"I never should have let you do this. But I like you so much . . . I like what we do together . . ."

He rose from the bed, knelt in front of her and reached for her arms. "Who the hell is Wells? What is this about, Cynthia?"

"Wells Haslam. I told you about him. From Raleigh. I've been

71

dating him for two years. He's a dear, kind man, and he loves me very much, and we're going to be married."

"Then why'd you let me? Why?"

"You insisted."

Kevin moved away from her. His nakedness made him feel foolish, a kid flashing his genitals. *"Engaged.* Why didn't you tell me that when we were in the bar?"

"I wanted to make love a last time," she said. "But not again. Wells and I are getting married in June."

Dressed, Kevin thought of the round-faced man he had met at the Yale Club. Southern accent, a loud authoritative voice, which in Jews or lesser breeds would be judged ill-mannered, but which in WASP overlords was considered charming.

"Where's the money?" Kevin asked cruelly. Cynthia was dressing.

"What money?"

"Wells's money. You people always seem to find each other. Charley Felder's full of crap when he says it's just as easy to marry a rich girl. For a rich guy, maybe."

She buttoned the beige sweater. Kevin stared at her. He would remember her forever in the beige sweater set—crew neck and cardigan, the double strand of pearls, the matching skirt.

"Knitting mills, that kind of thing," Cynthia said. "It's a bore."

"Lint-heads."

"They own a great deal. Pine-tree plantations, beaches. They make the Manships look like paupers."

"But not as poor as the Derrys."

They walked to the door. "Oh, Kev, you're so good, and sweet, and I could love you. But I don't know what love is. How do you find out? Who tells you?"

The elevator clanked dolorously. *Not quite the Haslam Estate in Turpentine County, North Carolina,* Kevin thought.

"Was he better than me?"

"Kevin, please. I can't see you anymore, ever."

"I'll look for the announcement in the *Times.* Thanks, anyway. It was a hell of an evening."

He hailed a cab for her on West 52nd Street. Before entering it, she kissed him dutifully on the cheek, and he did not respond. Indeed, the absence of passion gratified him. It told him he would manage his life, get on with his career without her. *Ah, there, Wells*

72

Haslam, in Raleigh, North Carolina, are you aware what your betrothed just did for me this evening?

Smelling of sweat and cigar smoke, Dr. Samuel Felder took Bridie's blood pressure. It was early June of 1950. She had been accepted at Barnard. A full scholarship. In a few weeks she would graduate. Mr. Shapiro hinted she was a good bet to be class salutatorian. Dr. Felder's daughter, Nan, would probably be valedictorian.

In the dim waiting room, Meg Derry waited for the doctor to finish the examining of her daughter. The college required it, and although Bridie was the healthiest of girls, Jack insisted they go through with a physical. It had been, Meg realized, his way of getting his wife to the doctor. Sam had been their family physician as long as they could remember.

It was appropriate, she supposed, her family's sticking with Sam Felder all these years. There were three younger physicians in town, men with modern offices. They drove big cars and dressed in tailored suits.

Doc Felder was like Jack—a man reduced to two-dollar office fees. But they trusted Felder, with his bad temper, and old jokes, and rumpled suits, and his trick of blowing on the stethoscope to warm it. She could remember him coming to their frame house on a sub-zero January day when Joe was choking with diphtheria. Or spending hours at Kevin's bedside when scarlet fever had almost killed him.

It was a shame he had made so many enemies. He had once threatened to punch a chief of psychiatry and had called him a scoundrel for overcharging. They barely tolerated him at the local hospital, and they laughed behind his back—at his bowlegged muscular figure, his foul cigars, his rattling old Nash.

"Never anything wrong with the Derry kids," Dr. Felder said, coming out of the examining room. "Good hearts, good lungs, good sense. Except maybe Joe gave me a hard time now and then."

"He gives everyone a hard time."

Dr. Felder made a lateral gesture with his left hand. "Ah, ancient history." He was a broad-chested man, with no suggestion of softness about him, no paunch. His face was angular, suggesting an American Indian—hooked nose, shock of graying black hair.

As he filled in the entries, Bridie looked at the photograph of Mrs. Felder on the wall. She had died five years ago. A timid woman who worked in the library. Her face was tilted upward in the photograph and she wore pince-nez. The sorrow she had lived with seemed to have been caught in the sepia-toned photograph.

"Looking at my wife?"

"I didn't mean to stare. I remember her real well. When she was a librarian, and—"

"Yeah. The concert."

He said no more. Bridie knew. She blushed, wishing she did not have to remember things like that. It was 1938 or 1939. A concert arranged for the library.

Mrs. Felder, possessor of a fine soprano voice, was to render several songs, including "The Last Rose of Summer" and "Just a Song at Twilight." It was a time when the German-American Bund had been active. There was a chapter of local hoodlums who strutted around town in stormtrooper uniforms, giving the Nazi salute.

Bridie, six or seven at the time, remembered sitting with her mother in the American Legion Hall as Mrs. Felder, smiling, bowing to the crowd, clasped her hands in front of her and began to sing.

"'Tis the la-hast ro-hose of summer . . .
Le-heft bloo-hoo-ming alone . . ."

Bridie stared again at the photograph of Mrs. Felder. And remembered the eggs thrown by the hoodlums. One hit Mrs. Felder on the breast; another splattered at her feet. She sang one more line.

"All her lo-hove-ly companions
Are fa-ha-ded and gone . . ."

Then she ran from the stage. The concert was over. Bridie could remember (her parents had talked about the incident for years) how no one except Dr. Felder and his son took out after the Nazis. They chased them a block or two, then lost them. Later, Charley swore he saw Potsy Luff running with them.

People saw little of Mrs. Felder after the aborted concert. She resigned her job at the library, even though everyone knew Doc Felder's practice was not that great and he had children to support. She stayed indoors, read, encouraged her children to get good grades, but was no longer part of the Churchport community. She died of cancer in 1945, still a young woman.

"She had great natural refinement, Bridie," the physician said. "Very much like your mother."

Bridie said nothing, thinking of Potsy. *Her own cousin!* Walter, Sr., caught up with him and beat the tar out of him. "I got no special use for Jews," Bridie's uncle bellowed at Potsy, whose ass turned to fire after a dozen whacks with a cane, "but you stay away from those Kraut bums. Dr. Felder and his family are part of the town."

The next day Walter Luff, Sr., and Jack Derry composed a letter to Dr. and Mrs. Felder and got about a dozen citizens of Churchport to sign it. What astonished Jack Derry was that so *few* people would sign. So what if the doctor's wife got hit with eggs? Nobody took the local stormtroopers seriously. A bunch of pretty-nice guys who drank beer at the Turn-Verein.

"Thanks, Jack," Doc Felder had said when he read the letter. "And thank your brother-in-law. But it won't make the pain go away. The wife thinks we should move. But I won't."

Felder had stayed and had seen his children become the best scholars to graduate from Churchport High. These days, Bridie heard her parents say, Dr. Felder was caught in the middle. The poor went to the free clinics, the wealthier residents to the smart young physicians.

"All set, Bridget," Dr. Felder said. "You're not only the prettiest Derry; you're the smartest also."

Bridie got up. She tucked her red-blond hair behind her ears. She was as fair as his own daughter was dark. Sometimes the world did not seem so painful. Doc Felder had lost a score of distant relatives in the gas chambers. He did not need rotten eggs to remind him of the nature of the world. But a pretty young girl, bright, mannerly, the daughter of his friend Jack, helped lighten the gloom.

Bridie left the humid room with its aromas of iodoform and cigar smoke. Her mother sat immobile, hands folded in her lap, with that faint, self-minimizing smile on her face.

"Mind if I don't wait for you?" asked Bridie. "Mr. Shapiro asked Nan and me to help with the decorations for the prom."

"Go ahead, dear."

Nan Felder, dark-eyed, bird-thin, shorter than Bridie, met her in the vestibule outside the waiting room. She and her widowed father lived upstairs. Charley had moved when he had opened his law office. The house had an unused quality about it. Not like the homes of other Jews Bridie knew, where there was usually a good deal of laughter, arguments, blaring music.

Dr. Felder got up, crushed the cigar, shook Meg's hand. "Nice to see you, Meg."

She had a history of a grade-two-plus systolic murmur, not severely abnormal, but a condition that warranted periodic check-ups. The old noise was there, the characteristic hissing. Meg sat primly, her blouse opened, the stethoscope against her breast.

"Is it still with me?"

"Oh, yes. But nonsignificant. You're anemic, Meg. I'm not sure you take the liver and iron pills regularly. Do you?"

"On and off. I don't like swallowing that stuff."

A bit of the martyr in the woman, Dr. Felder understood. Like his own wife. A woman of quality, deprived of education, doomed to a small frame house and a defeated husband. No wonder Kevin was the light of her life.

"It's the anemia that might be aggravating it," Dr. Felder explained. "Since your red blood count is low, the heart has to work harder, pump more blood so you can go about your work. That means a higher velocity of flow in the heart, and a reduction in the viscosity of your blood. It isn't serious, but you should take it easy."

He suggested an electrocardiogram. It was one of the few diagnostic machines he had installed.

Meg sighed and relaxed on the examining table. She took off her shoes and stared at the flaking ceiling. Like Jack's pharmacy. A place of the past.

A half hour later, Dr. Felder studied the rolls of film with the jagged white lines. He did not like what he saw. He compared it to an EKG he had taken a year and a half ago. His fault. Too long a wait. But he hated enforcing diagnostic work on people ill-equipped to pay for it.

Squinting through thick glasses, he said to himself, "Aortic stenosis. Maybe." It would explain the more insistent sound of the murmur. He would have to have her worked up by a cardiologist. As much as he scorned "professors," Felder knew when he was out of his depth. He considered dropping by the drugstore and telling Jack Derry. But he hesitated. Jack had enough worries.

Kevin, of course. The kid would understand. He had rarely seen Kevin upset. It might be a good idea to send his mother to Mid-Island.

"What does it mean?" Kevin asked when Felder had finished explaining his mother's symptoms on the phone a day later.

"I can't be sure. Not too much to be concerned about. But you know about pathologic murmurs. Did your mother ever have rheumatic fever?"

"I don't think so," Kevin said.

"It could be a possibility. I think we can rule out a congenital abnormality."

"That leaves . . . what?" Kevin asked. "Calcium deposits around the aortic valve?"

Doc Felder smiled. "I see you're doing your homework. Make an appointment for Mother, huh, kid?"

Back at the house, Kevin didn't look forward to his night off. He barely objected when Potsy begged him to take his duty.

"This is my night with Ruth Yanowski. I've been working on this one for three months. Anyway, they need you in the Emergency Room. And that Ferrara kid you admitted last week? He's going sour. Gold is climbing the walls."

Kevin smiled. Potsy and his endless girls. For a while Kevin and Potsy had dated two local sisters named Connetta—Angie and Jenny. They were student nurses, dark-eyed, willowy girls, full of gossip, willing to submit to an evening of necking and explorations.

Potsy had abandoned Angie, the older one, an aggressive type, who would surely be chief surgical nurse some day. He had not scored; she was not impressed with him.

Kevin still saw Jenny Connetta from time to time. They joked a great deal, went to the movies. She hinted that if he tried hard enough, he might succeed. He was so *cute*. And Irish. Italian girls considered it a step upward to date an Irish boy. They were more "American" than Italians.

77

Kevin found it difficult to sustain a conversation with her. She was full of ambition, forever asking him medical questions, discussing cases. They remained "friends." One problem, he realized, was that whenever he felt the urge to see Jenny Connetta, perhaps to take advantage of her hints, his mind became clogged with visions of Cynthia, whose wedding had been announced last month. Rather than muddle his emotional life, he preferred to hold fire. For a while at least.

On the fourth floor, Kevin found the new intern, Dr. Behari Ghosh. He looked upset.

"What's up, Behari?" Kevin asked.

"I'm so glad to see you. I have phoned for Dr. Gold, but I can't reach him. I'm trying to get one of the attendings or the boy's physician. Everyone seems away tonight."

Kevin wondered how much a third-year student could help. "Everyone's watching the UN. The Korea business."

"Bugger Korea; bugger all of them. Kevin, I am concerned about the Ferrara boy. He has gone sour."

Kevin thought, *Danny Ferrara.* The all-state fullback from Hamilton High. The kid who had flattened Joe Derry. Kevin had followed his career after high school. Busted out of two colleges, a brief time with the Manhasset Redbirds, a semipro team, then oblivion. He had been admitted for the first time last March. Weakness, asthma, shortness of breath, bronzing of the skin. He complained of double vision, drooping of the left eyelid. After two weeks of tests, Dr. Rhodes and Dr. Gold agreed that Danny Ferrara had a disease called myasthenia gravis.

"But he shouldn't be *that* sick," Dusty Rhodes argued. "Most myasthenia gravis patients get treated on an ambulatory basis and recover."

Since his first admission, Ferrara had been in and out of Mid-Island. Each time he seemed thinner, weaker, more dazed, less responsive. The physicians had hesitantly tried cortisone. It had just come into use. And it was controversial.

Kevin followed Ghosh into the ward. Danny Ferrara was sitting up in bed. His breathing was labored, his face drawn, his eyes dull. Months earlier, the powerful body had begun to turn flaccid. Kevin remembered the charging brute who had trampled over linemen and dragged tacklers into the end zone.

"Hi, Danny," Kevin said.

"Hi, Derry. Where's my doctor? Where's the other guy?"

"They're on their way," Kevin said. "Rest easy."

"Rest, shit. I can't catch my breath."

"I believe you." Kevin's eyes scanned the chart. Temperature 99.8. Pulse 72 with a regular sinus rhythm. Blood pressure 126 over 100. No indications of severe illness. But his right eyelid drooped badly.

Dr. Ghosh touched Ferrara's forehead and said, "Cool and dry."

"Shit," the patient said. "Can't breathe."

Kevin saw him straining for air, using every muscle in his chest. There was little expansion of the thoracic cage.

Dr. Gold entered the ward. "How's he doing?" he asked.

Kevin and Dr. Ghosh turned to the chief resident and said nothing. Abe Gold listened to Ferrara's chest. His narrow face was grave. Kevin knew what was troubling him. Two days earlier, Ferrara had been in the emergency room. It had been his fourth visit to the hospital in two months. This time, his tearful mother accompanying him, he had complained of asthma.

The intern on duty had been Dr. Dolan, a new man from upstate New York. Sally Hosmer had been assisting him, writing reports. There had been a nurse present. It had been a rough night. Three people admitted with severe burns.

Ferrara's "asthma" was dismissed as a recurrence of his spells of labored breathing. Ferrara was given something to help his breathing and sent home.

Two days later, Danny Ferrara was back, acutely ill. Dr. Gold had taken one look at the bronzing skin and ordered him readmitted. Weary to his bones, Gold had sought out Dr. Dolan and Sally and reamed them out unmercifully. Gold, in turn, weathered a bawling-out from Rhodes.

"Get him into an oxygen tent," Gold said. "Fast."

Kevin ran into the inhalation-therapy room and awakened the technician. He helped him wheel the tent to the ward.

Ferrara looked worse. He had to sit bolt upright to breathe.

"Get the mask on him," Dr. Gold said. "Give him an oxygen-helium mixture and give him intravenous epinephrine and aminophylline." Dr. Ghosh went out to get the floor nurse. "Move faster, for goodness' sake," Gold shouted. The failure to admit Ferrara was preying on him.

"Why'd we stop cortisone?" Kevin asked.

"He was showing signs of acute cardiac decompensation." Gold shook his head. He took these interrogations from few people. Kevin Derry was one of the few. "Cardiac enlargement," Abe explained.

Gold studied the patient. He seemed to be benefiting from the oxygen-helium mixture. "Prepare a point-five-percent solution of potassium chloride and have it ready. Somebody stay up here and see how he does."

Dr. Ghosh's head moved laterally. "I should be in Emergency, sir."

The chief resident was too tired to waste an angry look. If Ferrara died after the dust-up over admitting him, the shit would hit every fan in Mid-Island Hospital.

"Kevin, you're elected. I'm going to sleep in Dr. Rhodes' office. Keep an eye on him."

Kevin stood at Ferrara's bedside and forgave him everything, even the bloody fistfight he had once had with Joe during a hockey game in West Churchport.

He walked to the bedside and took Ferrara's hand. "You're going to be okay, Danny. The oxygen was all you needed."

Ferrara's glazed eyes did not believe a word. *He's played in losing games before,* Kevin thought.

Three hours later Ferrara went into convulsions.

Kevin shouted at the nurse to get Dr. Gold. Without waiting, he got another nurse to hold the thrashing body down and injected Dilantin into Ferrara's right arm.

Dr. Gold rushed in. "Well?"

"He's convulsing," Kevin said.

Ferrara labored for air, appealing for a last-minute reprieve. His skin was blue purple. His eyes were popping. Gold began to massage his chest. Kevin pulled the oxygen tent aside. The nurse moved curtains around the bed.

"Goddammit, hang in," Dr. Gold shouted.

"Come on, Ferrara," Kevin yelled in his ear. "You can make it."

The convulsions stopped. Dr. Gold watched the mouth cease moving. The limbs turned rigid in attitudes of surrender.

"Gone," Dr. Gold said. "Dammit to hell. Nothing worked."

"Kevin, you say you knew him?"

"Slightly."

"You mind calling the family?"

80

It wasn't a junior medical clerk's job. Abe Gold knew it, too. But Kevin had a vague connection with the dead athlete. *Mrs. Ferrara, I'm Kevin Derry; your son is dead, the one who played against my kid brother, Joe Derry. . . .*

Gold stopped him at the door. "Make sure you get the family's okay for a postmortem. This is one case Rhodes will want to rub our noses in."

Potsy stopped Kevin outside the auditorium next to the postmortem laboratory. "Rhodes is eating ass like it was steak. Dolan, the guy who sent Ferrara home? Came out of Dusty's office looking like he'd swallowed a turd."

"Myasthenia gravis isn't supposed to be fatal."

"That's what's breaking Rhodes' balls. A screwy case. Professor Howard's down from Danforth today. You know how full-time professors of medicine feel about chief attendings."

Kevin rolled his eyes to the ceiling. They walked into the auditorium with Max Landeck and Sally Hosmer and took seats in the rear.

Dr. Rhodes and Dr. Gold were standing behind the slate table. In its middle, in a basin, were the internal organs of the late Ferrara. Kevin had weathered anatomy courses, dissections, and handled more than his share of corpses. He thought he had developed a hardness where the dead were concerned. But for the first time he felt the need to gag. The connection of Ferrara with his past was damned near unbearable.

In the front row, apart from house staff and the attending physicians, was Professor Alan A. Howard, chairman of the Department of Medicine at Danforth Medical School. Black-clad, vested, gold chain winking across his paunch, he observed the proceedings with the hooded eyes of an old hawk.

"We won't get into the question of the patient's readmission," Dr. Rhodes said. "I'm sure that earlier treatment would not have saved him."

"He's all heart," Potsy whispered.

"This is a postmortem. I'd like the students to participate. We have here a twenty-four-year-old white male with a history of myasthenia gravis. Before we can examine the organs, I'll give clues and see if anyone can determine the cause of death."

Max Landeck raised his hand. "Sir? Don't myasthenia patients

81

have a low tolerance for shock, stress or injuries?"

"Right, Landeck. But what evidence is there that the patient sustained any? He was in bed a good deal of the time."

Sally raised her hand. "Don't they usually die of paralysis of the respiratory muscles? Or spasms of the larynx?"

"He had trouble breathing," Dr. Gold said. "Miss Hosmer has a point."

"But he responded to the oxygen and medication, didn't he?" Dr. Rhodes asked.

"Not enough," Gold said. "Derry was with me. How about it, Kevin?"

"He responded temporarily. When he went into convulsions he was finished."

Rhodes ticked off results of the postmortem. With each revelation, he lifted a section of one of Ferrara's organs. The lungs showed fibrous pleuritis. There was hemorrhaging in the lower lobes of both lungs. There was healed endocarditis of the heart. The adrenal glands were soft, brownish, friable. There was atrophy of the cortexes of both adrenal glands. The pituitary gland was reddish brown and had too many cells. . . .

Rhodes said, "Let's try again. House staff, hands down. Let the students give it a try."

"I'm confused," Potsy said. "Since when is myasthenia gravis tied in with the adrenal glands?"

"Wake up, Luff," Rhodes snapped. "There's a theory that it may have an endocrine cause."

"But are we sticking with myasthenia gravis?" Sally asked.

"Yes. Derry?" Rhodes asked.

Kevin leaned forward. He thought he'd caught a hint. The abnormalities in the adrenal glands were worth exploring. Dusty liked gamblers.

"What about Addison's disease?" Kevin asked.

"What about it?"

"As a cause of death. Adrenocortical insufficiency, isn't that Addison's disease?"

"A stickler for terminology, Derry?" Rhodes asked, with less than his usual acidity. "You're suggesting this patient *never* had myasthenia gravis? That he died of Addison's disease?"

"No, sir," Kevin said. "I'm suggesting Ferrara had *both*. He had

82

all the symptoms of myasthenia but he *also* had Addison's disease."

"And which one caused his death?"

"I don't know. It's just that people with Addison's disease have small toleration for shock and stress."

"What's usually given as the cause of death in Addison's disease?" Dr. Rhodes snapped.

"I . . . I'm not sure. Maybe fatal hypoglycemia."

Mouth behind hand, Potsy whispered to him, "Don't push your luck, kid."

Dr. Alan A. Howard had turned in his seat and was smiling at Kevin Derry, as if to say, *See what a fine grounding I have given these young people.*

"But there was no evidence of hypoglycemia," Dr. Gold said.

"I'm not saying it *was* the cause of death," Kevin said warily. "Just that this patient may have had *two* conditions, both potentially fatal, and that one acted on the other, each producing stress and shock."

"Not bad, Derry," Dr. Rhodes said. "The pathologist's conclusion is pretty much like yours. Two pathologic states. Unrelated. No single mechanism for death can be reasonably suggested. We'll settle for a fatal case of myasthenia gravis, complicated by Addison's disease. A unique case. Have we found anything in the literature like it, Dr. Gold?"

"Nothing, sir."

Professor Howard was pointing at Kevin. He had a soft voice. "Mr. Derry . . . I'm curious. What made you suggest the complication of Addison's disease?"

"An educated guess, sir. The pathology of the adrenal glands."

"Quite a good guess. And you're being modest."

Potsy dug an elbow into Kevin's side. "Friggin' genius. Your lucky Irish ass."

"You made the teaching staff look pretty good," Dusty Rhodes said sourly in his office. "Sit down." He locked the door.

Kevin was about to thank him, but Rhodes held up a hand. "Repeat after me, Derry: 'If the Ferrara boy had been admitted two days earlier, it would have made absolutely no difference. He was terminal.'"

Kevin edged forward. "Are we certain of that?"

83

"As certain as we have to be. Kid was bad, *very* bad. I've briefed Dr. Ghosh and Dr. Gold and the nurses and the admitting personnel. If we'd have admitted him two days earlier—so what?"

"I don't know . . . the medication he was on . . . maybe if he got it earlier. Oxygen . . ." He was disturbed by something sneaky, vaguely shady, in Rhodes' manner.

Rhodes was putting a finger to his mouth. His lips were locked. For the first time since he had known Dusty, that tough, honorable navy medic, he had doubts about him. Didn't Potsy say Dr. Rhodes had reamed out Dolan, the intern who'd turned Ferrara away?

"Nothing," Dr. Rhodes said. "Nothing would have helped Ferrara. If his family, or friends, or a lawyer, or a reporter asks, the answer is he got the best of care up to his last breath. Understood?"

"Yes, sir." He wanted to blurt out a half-dozen "buts" about the case, but Rhodes' abrupt demeanor deterred him.

"Third year will be over soon, Derry," Rhodes said, changing the subject. "What then?"

"I thought I'd catch my breath in August. Maybe get a job at a lab, something like that."

Rhodes laughed. "My God, if I lived in a place like Churchport, I'd spend August fishing, swimming and loafing on the beach."

"When you're brought up in a vacation town, you don't think of it that way. Besides, the best fishing is after the tourists have left. My kid brother and I were champion snapper fishermen. But that's in September when the baby blues are running."

"I tried it once. Bamboo pole, the bobber. Couldn't land a thing off the dock in Churchport Beach."

"You've got to troll from a rowboat and watch the birds. If you see the terns feeding, head for it. That means there's baitfish in the area."

Rhodes said, "Howard was impressed. So was I. What about your fourth-year elective?"

"I'm interested in cardiology. I thought maybe I'd apply to Hopkins or Mass General for a fellowship."

"I don't want to lose you, Kevin. I know this place looks like a dump, but we practice medicine here. I'm working on the feds for a grant for just what you're after—cardiology. I want the most modern cardiac-care unit in the area. I want to start a cardiac-surgery unit."

84

Kevin was silent a moment. He was flattered. But Mid-Island . . . forever? Dusty's dingy empire.

"You're a good medical man, Kevin, but you've got something else. What we called in the navy *presence*. People listen to you. It helps."

"I'm a druggist's son getting through school on money I borrowed."

"I know what Manship is doing for you. Professor Howard knows. He and Manship play golf at the same club. You'd make it without Manship's help."

Rhodes threw open the window that Rathman Lal had fallen from five months ago. Soft air drifted in. A hazy Long Island day.

"Stay with cardiology," Rhodes said. "But you'll be up to your armpits in it as a resident. I'd build up my background in related areas. Lung disease. Kidney and liver. You saw the way the Ferrara case involved the whole system. Don't become the kind of specialist who only understands his own field. I've known cardiologists who wouldn't recognize hepatitis." Rhodes complimented him again on his performance at the postmortem. "I won't blow my stack if you do go to Hopkins or Mass General. And remember—the Ferrara boy had no chance. None at all."

Kevin rested on the slanted bed that came with Mr. Parilli's apartment, head on his arms, and stared at the ceiling. He could not separate Danny Ferrara and his sobbing mother from the discolored pile of guts on the slate table. He felt a vague disgust with himself for making points with Rhodes, for his display of medical knowledge at Ferrara's expense.

He had never been so frighteningly aware of the frailness of life, the gossamer strands suspending the living over the edge. This artery clogged, that gland failing to function, a valve closed. And the miracle ended. The intricate machine ground to a halt, beyond repair.

He was lonely, gloomy. Potsy was on night duty, probably trying to drag one of the nurses into a broom closet. On entering the room that evening, Kevin had found a pair of blue-lace panties under Potsy's bed. Not the kind a nurse would favor. Probably the bovine waitress at the diner across the street.

He telephoned Jenny Connetta. "I'm alone and feeling sorry for myself, Jenny," Kevin said. "Potsy's on duty. Come over. We'll finish off a six-pack."

They did more than that. With no protest, she undressed quickly, joined him in bed, and they made love. She seemed to have a gratifying capacity for small orgasms. A lithe olive-skinned girl, with round black eyes and a fall of dark-brown hair, she participated joyously, without inhibitions.

"I didn't know Italian-Catholic girls could make love this way," he said, and was ashamed of himself as soon as he said it.

"I'm sort of an ex-Catholic," Jenny said. She rested her dark head on his chest.

She told him she had been married at eighteen to a local boy in her hometown. A disaster. She had been forced to live with her in-laws. Her husband's mother was a Sicilian virago who hated Jenny. Adored and dominated by his mother, he proved impotent and ended up in a mental institution.

"And after that fancy wedding," Jenny said, "all those bleeding hearts and crucifixes in the house, I got a divorce. I wasn't twenty years old."

"Brave girl," Kevin said.

They locked themselves together and he sensed mild guilt. He was using Jenny as a tonic, a dose of vitamins and iron. She was too good for that. She came, and clung to him—thin dark legs locked on his freckled back. Her eyes, rather than closing in passion (as most women's seemed to) would open wide, the shiny whites emphasizing the gleaming black pupils.

"Ox-eyed Hera," Kevin said. "That's from the *Iliad,* I think."

"Thanks a lot. Am I an ox?"

"No, Jenny. You're a marvelous girl." He meant it. She had come to him with no pretense, no deceit, no conditions.

Clothed, she sat on his lap later and stroked the bristling hairs on the back of his neck. "I don't go around sleeping with interns or students. But you're different."

"No I'm not."

She was staring at his glacial eyes. "You really are sweet. Dr. Rhodes has his eye on you. I mean, I'm not saying these things to try to lead you somewhere. Besides, what'd you want with an old divorced woman like me? An ex-Catholic, an Eye-talian."

They kissed gently and he did not know how to thank her for the warmth of her body, the goodness in her. He offered to accompany her back to the nurses' dormitory, but she refused. An independent soul, Jenny Connetta. But he did walk her to the street, and they kissed goodbye in the misty night.

"I wish you'd call me again," she said. "Maybe we could do a few things this summer. You think so, Kevin?"

"Sure, Jenny."

Like almost everything in his life, Jenny Connetta had come to him too easily. He was grateful. But he could not tell her how grateful he was. The words would clot in his mouth.

5

Some weeks later Meg Derry entered Mid-Island Hospital for a cardiological workup. Hearing that she was Kevin's mother, Dr. Rhodes agreed to supervise the work of the cardiologists. Then, learning that she was entering as Dr. Felder's patient, he disengaged.

"He called me a crap-artist once," Rhodes said. "I'm no anti-Semite, but Felder is impossible. Your mother will receive the best care, Kevin. But I don't want to cross swords with that lunatic again."

Silence was indicated. Kevin liked both men. No point in antagonizing either.

After four days of laboratory tests and examinations, Dr. Felder's suspicions were confirmed. Mrs. Derry had a systolic murmur caused by a narrowing of the aortic orifice.

"It's probably congenital," the cardiologist said, "though we can't be sure. These things are elusive."

"I never heard the murmur that loud before," Dr. Felder said irritably.

The specialist shrugged. "It isn't always audible. It probably became so after calcification."

"What do we do now?" asked Kevin.

"Not much," the cardiologist said. "Mild exercise, restricted diet. There's no way of knowing how advanced the stenosis is."

"Kevin's a big boy," Felder said. "Tell him the worst."

"It's something to be watched."

"Kevin, you tell me. What's the worst can happen?" Dr. Felder blew out a cloud of cigar smoke. One of the Derry Pharmacy's stale El Cheapos.

"I'm not sure. Left ventricular failure from coronary insufficiency?" He tried to be as composed. "And sudden death."

"Right, kid. Just so long as you know," said Felder.

The two older men looked for a reaction on the freckled face. Kevin showed them nothing. What was the point in wailing, wringing his hands, asking endless questions?

In medicine, you took the tests, went with the diagnosis, and trusted your peers and the specialists. *Your mother will receive the best care, Kevin,* Dusty had told him.

Doc Felder got up. He and the cardiologist walked into the hall. Kevin mused, *Like the "best care" Danny Ferrara had been given?* The refusal to admit him, when he was damned near ready to die and in fact *did* die a few days later?

It's how much we don't know, Kevin, Doc Felder used to say, *and how few of the bigshots will admit it. . . .*

He concluded there was no point in making comparisons between the mishandling of the Ferrara case and Meg's prognosis. Mid-Island Foul-Ups, the old MIFUs, as Jenny Connetta called them, were probably no worse here than at other hospitals.

In the screened tent, redolent of jungle rot and the chemical stink of the tarpaulin, Cpl. Joe Derry read the letter from his sister, Bridie. The letter had taken three weeks to reach him. With Korea going full blast, no one cared about dogfaces in the Philippines. Mail was rare.

Outside the tent, farmers from the village, Batati tribesmen, were trying to sell eggs to Johnson and Rashefski, two other members of Unit C of the 911th Medical Detachment. The corpsmen stared suspiciously at the small turbaned men and the beaded women, but did not buy the eggs.

The GIs were not cruel to the tribesmen, simply indifferent. They looked upon them as one would gaze at illustrations in a book. It frosted Joe Derry's ass. "They're human beings also," he had raged at Sgt. Maurice Johnson, the head of the medical detachment.

"Just barely, Derry," Johnson would respond. "Just barely."

"Ten cents. One eggy?" a shriveled woman in a flounced dress was asking. Wheels of beaded rings depended from her tiny ears. A dozen necklaces dangled from her neck, over her wrinkled bosom. The Batati were pagans, subsistence farmers planting upland rice.

Joe Derry tried to close out the chatter, the hum of insects, the draining heat. They were at three thousand feet, but it didn't seem to help. Clouds rolled over the rainforest late every morning. They could set their watches with the first clap of thunder—eleven-forty-five A.M.

He smiled at Bridie's neat handwriting, and for the first time since he had seen Kevin in Germany, he longed for his family.

July 2, 1950

Dear Joey:

First off, Mama and Pop and all of us wish you were able to tell us where you are. Yesterday there was news on the radio and in the papers that American soldiers had landed in Korea and were fighting. Oh, Joey, we hope you stay at the place in the Philippines or wherever it is you are. I notice your APO number is the same, so I've got my fingers crossed.

Mama is the worst. She keeps saying how you should have finished college and it's your own fault for wanting to join the army. And you know how Pop is. I think he's hitting the bottle again, but quietly at the store. So, please, *please*, Joey, write more often and assure them you're okay, and you're still at some hospital and nobody's shooting at you.

At the risk of being conceited, the big thing was my graduation. We missed you. Kevin came and so did Uncle Walter and Aunt Kate. I guess I did the Derry family proud (ahem) winning the English prize and the Best Journalist award. Nan Felder won just about everything else, including all the science medals—physics, chemistry, biology. She was class valedictorian also. And guess what! We both get scholarships to Barnard. Mama says I'll just about be able to afford it if I get a job.

Anyway, we miss you. Kevin's going to hang around Mid-Island for part of his last year at med school. They think he's the rising hot-shot.

Please write, and lots of love from your kid sister.

BRIDIE

Joe folded the letter and sipped halazone-laced water from his canteen. Home was light years away. He tried to raise Radio Manila for news, failed, walked out of the tent. It was an hour before sick call for the locals, but about twenty villagers had gathered. They squatted, leaned on sticks, lay on the ground.

Sgt. Johnson, a mulatto who claimed to have been light-heavyweight champion of the Second Division, was sitting on a folding camp chair behind a field table. Olive-drab boxes and crates surrounded him—aspirin, penicillin, antibiotics, laxatives, vitamin pills, iodine, bandages.

No one understood why Unit C of the 911th Medical Detachment was in Batati, one hundred sixty miles south, over mountains and forests, from the base hospital in Davao. They were in Mindanao, the end of the line.

"Fuck we doin' here, Sarge?" a young soldier named Flinders would ask Johnson every day. Flinders was not much more than one hundred twenty pounds, spare of body, barely literate, a product of Appalachian inbreeding.

"When I find out I let you know, Flinders," Sgt. Johnson would say. "By then you be one big chancre anyway." No one talked back to Johnson.

Joe knew why they were there. The older men like Johnson and Pepe Valdez also knew, but they would not talk about it. They were the fuck-up squad, troublemakers, screw-offs. Joe knew it the second day he arrived at Davao, a bomb-wrecked waterfront city, full of beggars and prostitutes.

Lt. Col. Kuyper, an M.D., had called Joe in for a briefing. He had Joe's 201 file open in front of him. Joe could read his name, in blue lettering, on the edge of the manila folder: DERRY, JOSEPH FRANCIS ASN No. 13456789.

"You have a lousy reputation, Derry," Kuyper said. Joe did not respond. How did the army know these things? How did they keep track of you, mark you lousy, stick you with it for the rest of your life? *That bastard Curtis!*

"There's a memorandum in here that says you were arrested and charged with the rape of a German woman," the colonel said.

"It's a lie."

"Sir."

"It's a lie, sir." Joe, stammering slightly, told him the story—the

91

frame-up, the deal Moss and Kevin had made with Curtis. Kuyper wasn't buying it. He glanced at the 201 file. Haltingly, Joe defended himself. There was never a court-martial. The woman withdrew all charges.

Three days later Joe was on a truck convoy for Batati. Unit C had been formed under the command of Tech Sgt. Maurice Johnson, who had beaten up a Filipino girl and broken her nose. But because he was the captain's pet—boxing, football—he had been spared a trial. The word was that Unit C would be attached to Batati Village to await and service a Ranger battalion. A convenient way, Joe realized, to rid the hospital of fuck-ups. The Rangers never arrived.

"It beats Korea," Johnson told them now, as Joe walked over to the medical table. "Them gooks there cut your balls off, they catch you. Stick your cock right in your mother-loving mouth."

Flinders scratched the pimples on his cheeks. "How long we gon' be here, Sarge?"

"Till your ass grow a beard, Flinders." Johnson—a strong man gone to fat, his belly bulging over his belt—turned to Joe. "Okay, Derry, handle sick call for the wogs. Me, I'm gonna get me sack time. Too much fuckin' last night."

Valdez, Flinders and the others laughed. Joe did not. He hated Johnson's guts. A thick-headed bully.

The *datu*, or chief of the Batati, was resting on an elaborately carved bolo jammed into a scabbard fashioned from a Coca-Cola box. He held up a hand. His name was Na Bong and he had learned English in a convent school. "Okay, boss? Okay begin sick call?" He had wide eyes, a small feathery beard.

"Yeah, Na Bong," Johnson said. "Bring the fuckers around."

Johnson lumbered into his tent. Joe could hear him opening and slamming the refrigerator.

That bastard Johnson, Derry thought. While the rest of them attended to the Batati he would be finishing off the last of the beer. Once a week a truck from Davao rumbled into Batati with provisions. The detachment had no airstrip and was considered too unimportant to merit air supply. They were always running short.

"Flinders, line 'em up," Joe said. He got out the bottles—aspirin, antibiotic unguents and pills, Atabrine, vitamins, a specific for ringworm, rolls of bandages and adhesive. Knife wounds, cuts from the long razor-sharp bolos, were frequent. The Batati would never say how they were inflicted. Datu Na Bong would shrug. "Accident, boss."

Joe and Valdez hurried through twenty patients with everything from arthritis to yaws. They'd been given no training in tropical medicine, just some old army publications. But as each person accepted his medication, he tried to kiss Joe's hand.

"Jesus Chris'," Valdez said. "They act like you a God."

"I wish I knew what I was doing," Joe grumbled.

"What do you care?" Valdez asked. "They're just fuckin' savages."

Joe detested his inadequacy. They needed a doctor if the unit were to mean anything. There were ten thousand people in Batati village, undernourished, crawling with parasites, victims of every tropical disease imaginable. The Japanese had left the area in ruins, destroyed crops, burned seed, killed livestock. Five years after the war nothing had been done to revive the place.

The last man on sick call was barely able to stand. His wife and son supported him. The man seemed half dead. But with that stoic indifference of the tribesman, his skeletal face told them nothing.

"Friend," Na Bong said. "Very sick, boss. Name Gantu."

"Malaria, maybe," Joe said.

"Don't think so, boss," the datu said. "Sicker."

"No help for him," Valdez said cheerfully. "Tell 'em to start digging the grave."

"Shut up," Joe said. He knelt next to the man. There was a peculiar rash on his chest and arms, hemorrhages below the skin. He touched the man's forehead. He was burning.

"Ask his wife how long he's been like this."

"Two days, boss. His food comes up from his mouth. Belly hurt."

Joe palpated the man's stomach. The liver was swollen. He took the man's pulse. It was fast and irregular.

"We gonna have us a dead gook here, Derry," Valdez said. "Stink up the whole village."

"That's how much you know, Valdez," Flinders said. "They leave the stiffs out in the jungle and animals eat 'em."

"Mouth," the datu said. "See mouth."

Joe peeled back the patient's lips. Blood gushed from the gums. At first he thought it was betel juice. But there was no mistaking the color or the odor. His gums were hemorrhaging. The man's eyes, sunken in the starved face, looked at Joe with the appeal of a wounded dog. *No,* Joe Derry thought, *wrong.* He had never seen more human eyes.

"Tell 'em sick call is over," Johnson shouted from his tent. "Can't spend all day giving out Band-Aids to gooks. You hear me, Derry?"

Joe ignored him and lifted the man's shirt.

Gantu's chest and arms were bruised—purple-black patches on the skin. "How long's he had these marks, Na?" he asked.

"Since he get fever."

"He's hemorrhaging," Joe said. He squinted at the other men of Unit C. They had drawn back. "He's got internal bleeding. Flinders, get me the tropical-disease handbook. It's under my bunk."

"What for? We got nothin' to help him."

"I said get it."

Flinders slumped off to the main tent and came back with the dog-eared book.

Joe found a passage. "I think he has Dengue Hemorrhagic fever. 'Philippine fever,' they call it. He may go into shock in a day or two." He stopped reading aloud. *Fatality rate is 10-50 percent.*

The disease, if his diagnosis was correct, produced abnormal blood clotting and reduced blood volume. According to the book it was virus-produced, probably transmitted by mosquitoes. *Areas of high Aedes Aegypti.* But the high forest was relatively free of mosquitoes.

"He lives in Batati?" Joe asked Na Bong.

"Yes, boss. But he farm by lake. Way down."

A place full of mosquitoes, Joe thought.

The book recommended oxygen therapy. Plasma loss, the usual cause of death, could be counteracted with fluids, electrolyte solution and plasma. *Plasma loss may continue for 24-48 hours.* Judging by the pallid face, he decided Gantu did not have long to go.

Johnson came slouching out of the tent. He had a half-empty bottle of San Miguel beer in one hand.

"I said sick call was over."

Joe got up and hooked his hands in his belt. "Listen, Maurice," he said. "This guy is going to die of internal hemorrhaging. He's got to get to the hospital in Davao before he bleeds to death."

"My piles bleed for *him,* Derry," Johnson said. "I ain't no fuckin' medical expert like you, but if you think I'm gonna get Kuyper on my ass by sending slopes to Davao, you're dumber than I thought."

Joe blinked in the scorching sunlight. "They got a helicopter at the hospital. They could land in the village and have him in Davao in an hour. At least let them send the truck for him. We might get him to Davao in time."

"That gook would bleed to death from the bumps. Give him what you got and send him home."

The other patients retreated. They were a timid tribe. Datu Na Bong had told him that since they were neither Christians nor Moslems, other local tribes stole their pigs and chickens, burned their houses, raped their women.

"Send everyone else home," Joe said. "Tell Gantu's family to stay here. Take him into the hospital shed, out of the sun."

Joe walked to the hospital shed with them—two tarpaulins suspended from a framework of bamboo. There were four cots in the shed. In one corner was a field telephone.

Joe cranked it a half-dozen times. He waited.

Johnson walked into the shed, drained his beer, and threw the bottle into the bush. "Fuck you think you're doin', Derry?"

"I'm calling Davao."

Joe cranked again. This time he heard the army radio operator. "Base Dodger, here."

"Unit Charlie, Batati," Joe said. "Patch me into the Nine-eleventh."

Johnson walked to the camp chair on which Joe was crouched. He ripped the headset off, grabbed the speaker from Joe's hands and turned off the switch.

"You forget who's in charge here, Derry. Git the fuck to your tent."

Joe got up. "Johnson, give the guy a break. What's a half-hour trip by chopper?"

"Ain't no chopper comin' in, and ain't no fuss gonna be made with the 911th or the colonel."

Joe turned his back on Johnson, threw the switch, and turned the crank.

Johnson grabbed Joe by the shoulders, spun him around and kicked the chair out from under him. Joe landed in the dust. As soon as he got up, Johnson belted him with a roundhouse right to the cheek and followed with a left hook below the belt. Joe gasped, fell against a tent pole, slid to the ground.

"Maybe now you understand who's in charge," Johnson said. He was breathing noisily. "You want more, Derry? Come out in the open. We'll invite the slants so they can see how us soldiers kick the shit outen one another."

Joe struggled to his feet. The blow to his gut was like an electric prod, radiating pain to his groin, his chest.

They stood in the checkered shade of the clearing. Joe was bent double, holding his abdomen. Johnson grinned, held his huge left arm out, boxer fashion, the right close to his chest. *He can hit,* Joe thought, *but I can block.*

Joe charged him, hitting him low and hard, slamming his head and iron shoulders into Johnson's soft belly. He had belted a hundred running backs this way.

The air whooshed from Johnson's lips with an affronted wheeze. He staggered backward, gasping for air, and hit the dusty ground like a rotting tree. In a second Joe was on him, pinning his thick arms.

"I gonna kill you, you Irish prick," Johnson screamed.

"You got to get up first. I don't wanna fight, Maurice. I just want to call Davao."

Johnson wrestled free and stumbled to his feet. Joe circled him, charged him again in a brutal blind-side tackle, and again the sergeant fell.

"If'n I don't kill you first," Johnson screamed, "you're gonna be in a goddamn GI jail all your fuckin' life."

"Let me call Davao," Joe said.

Johnson got to his feet. The sergeant raised his fists, but his hands were pawing the air. "Come on, Derry, fight like a fuckin' man. You're no better than these gooks."

Rare courage stirred in Flinders. "Hey, Sarge, you hit him from behind when he was sittin' down."

Valdez nodded. "That's right, Sarge. He's only tryin' to even things up."

Johnson hesitated a moment. Valdez nudged Flinders and whispered, "You know, I think Johnson's fulla shit. He was never no champeen. He's too fat."

Flinders and the others edged forward. "Yeah, Sarge," Flinders piped. "Call it a draw."

"Okay," Johnson said. "But next time, I'll break your neck, Derry."

Wiping dust and blood from his eyes, Joe returned to the telephone. In five minutes he had the dispatcher at the base hospital. Luckily Col. Kuyper was on a three-day pass in Manila. Maj. Kezerian, the second-in-command, an easygoing man, listened sympathetically as Joe described the case. Three hours later a helicopter landed at Unit C. The Batatis fled and hid under their thatched huts.

Two medics carried Gantu aboard. His family wailed. They were, Na Bong explained, less fearful of his illness than of the way the huge bird was devouring him.

The medics watched the chopper make a graceful ascent over the green forest. Soon it vanished, but its steady hum lingered long after it left their view.

Gantu came back a week later on the supply truck. He had made a good recovery. Maj. Kezerian had a special interest in tropical diseases.

When Gantu climbed down his wife and children ran forward and prostrated themselves in front of him. Then the women came to Joe and placed strands of beads around his neck. Joe fidgeted and tried to stop them. Gantu's wife kissed his hand.

Sgt. Johnson watched from his tent, spit into the clearing, said nothing. He'd fix that Mick bastard on his own time.

Na Bong slipped a bronze ring on Joe's finger. It was a brass metal band incised with a geometric design. "You are Batati," the datu said. "Kakai Joe."

"Kakai?"

"Friend."

Two weeks later, Unit C was recalled to Davao. Col. Kuyper called Joe in and advised him he was busted to private. Sgt. Johnson had accused him of stealing beer, and stirring up trouble with the tribesmen.

"He's a liar," Joe glared at the officer. "Ask the other men. Ask Major Kezerian."

"Always you against the world, eh, Derry?" Kuyper knew the type. Hardhead. Not content to ride with the system. He informed

97

Joe that the 911th was shipping out for Pusan, Korea. He would be assigned to permanent kitchen duty as punishment for insubordination.

Aboard the SS *Mexico Victory*, two days later, Joe, scrubbing pots and pans, made friends with a Filipino baker named Manuel. Manuel knew the angles. He recruited a squad of black soldiers to help them haul flour sacks, crates, cases of milk, in return for hot bread.

One day, crossing the South China Sea, Maurice Johnson saw Joe coming out of the bakery with a wooden tray stacked with hot bread—reward for the labor detail.

"Who authorize this?" Johnson asked.

"Volunteers," Joe said. The blacks swarmed around him, ripping off chunks of steaming bread.

Johnson kicked Joe in the groin, backed him against the bulkhead, punched him until his nose bled. Pvt. Joseph Derry spent the rest of the voyage under guard in the infirmary. Col. Kuyper decided Derry was more trouble than he was worth. He marked him for transfer to a combat-medic unit when they hit Korea.

In mid-September Joe was sent ashore at Wolmi Island with a tank unit. They fought their way across the island to the causeway linking it to Inchon.

It was the operation, MacArthur said, that would end the war. But for Joe the conflict ended much earlier in a burst of napalm from one of his own planes. Pvt. Joe Derry, rescued minutes later, was found to have severe burns of the back—eighteen percent of the surface area of his body scorched by jellied gasoline.

Insensate with pain, in shock, he was evacuated to a hospital ship, drugged with morphine and transferred by chopper to a dirt airstrip, where he was put aboard a hospital plane for Tokyo and special treatment. "War's over for you, kid," a fat medic said to him as the metal basket into which Joe was strapped was carried into the big-bellied airplane. "Broads and booze from now on so maybe them burns are worth it."

The medic read the tag tied to Joe's hospital pajamas. "Third degree, right, Derry? You get pain on the plane, holler. Some of them nurses are deaf. They say it comes from screwing officers too much."

But the pain eased. He dozed. He was glad he did not have to bother the nurses. The man on the litter next to him died of internal hemorrhaging and shock during the flight, and they were busy trying to save him. He was undersized and had yellow hair, and Joe, hazed with sedatives, thought he looked like his friend Budesa. But of course it was not. It was just some unlucky GI who'd caught too much shrapnel at Inchon.

A shitty detail. The world was full of them. Maybe you could do something about it. Joe wasn't sure what. Young men should not have to be blown apart; or black-market criminals be allowed to run hospitals; or poor farmers like the Batati forced to starve.

If ever he got healthy again (and he was certain that his tough elastic body would heal, the burns would leave him marked but undiminished in strength) he'd make a run at medicine, the way Kevin had. Maybe there was good to be done. There were surely people who needed help. The system, Joe felt, could stand a few changes.

Med school. Why not? Oh, his marks at Whitman State College had not been that great. He'd have a lot of science courses to make up. But the GI bill would pay for everything. He wouldn't need a dime from his father. Nor would he have to kiss Manship's ass to make it.

Kevin would needle him. The old busted-nose linebacker, the B-minus student laboring over qual and quant, trying to memorize the branches of the coronary arteries. *Needle him, but help him.* If he knew his older brother, Kevin would guide him, show him how to pass his MCATs, what courses to concentrate on, how to get into a medical school.

Joe Derry dozed, deep in morphine. He barely felt the plane bounce onto the Tarmac. His back ached now, wrenching spasms of pain, but he did not call for the nurses. They were strapped into their seats, sweating, weary, silent, and he did not have the heart to bother them.

A rush of optimism made him eager to be cured, get home, shape his future.

PART TWO
1954

Before entering the conference room for the overnight report, Kevin and Max Landeck stopped to discuss a puzzling new case.

Kevin, still the possessor of the boyish good looks that had been a standing joke at Mid-Island (*You a doctor? You look like the kid who delivers newspapers*), was now chief resident. He was on the firing line, a twenty-eight-year-old supervisor of thirty-two interns and twenty-one residents, most of them complainers. Mid-Island Hospital, despite Dusty Rhodes' politicking, remained undermanned, underfunded and neglected.

Landeck, close to forty, was a senior resident. Kevin made a point of keeping Max close at hand. Taciturn, brusque, his talent for putting diagnostic pieces together was superb. Another Abe Gold.

"You should have been chief resident," Kevin once said to him. "You're the best medical man on house staff."

Max shrugged. "No, Kevin. I'll defer to you when it comes to administration, hurt feelings and ER disasters. You were the right choice. Dr. Rhodes knew what kind of man he wanted."

A left-handed compliment? Kevin wondered. Not from Max. Max could never have dealt with chief nurses, inept junior medical clerks, pharmacy thefts.

The patient up for report was an attractive red-headed woman in her forties, Mrs. Randall. She had been admitted complaining of neck and back pains that radiated to both shoulders, incapacitating her. ("And me with four kids in school, and my husband on the night shift at Grumman," she'd told Max.)

A few days after being admitted, she complained of intractable pains in her back. X-rays revealed destruction of the anterior bodies of the third, fourth and fifth vertebrae.

"It's got the look of cervical osteomyelitis," Dr. Rhodes said.

Then Max recalled something the woman had told him on admission. She had had a urinary-tract infection two years ago. She had been hospitalized in Des Moines, Iowa.

"Do you recall what kind of infection?" Max had asked, as Kevin listened.

"I don't, Doctor. It burned and I had to urinate all the time."

Max ordered a urine culture. Kevin raised an eyebrow, unwilling to question his friend before a patient.

"There are cases on record of osteomyelitis secondary to urinary-tract infection," Max said.

"Why didn't anyone suggest it?" Kevin asked.

"Who knows? It's not a routine case."

Before the morning conference, Landeck had found an article describing pathology similar to Mrs. Randall's.

"It's rare, Kevin," Max said as they walked to the conference room. Dr. Gold greeted them. He would run the meeting. Dusty Rhodes was in Albany trying to raise money for Mid-Island for a new wing. Dr. Gold, associate director of medicine, increasingly ran the department.

Kevin took the seat next to Abe at the head of the table. The residents and interns gathered around. Those coming off night duty yawned and sipped coffee from cardboard cups.

Joe Derry entered the room late. He had carried out his decision to finish college on the GI bill. Kevin, impressed with his brother's determination, had got Dusty Rhodes to sponsor his application to Danforth. Now a third-year student, Joe was taking his junior clerkship on medical rotation at Mid-Island. The two brothers made a determined effort to stay away from each other.

"Slow night?" Dr. Gold asked. "Who was on duty?"

One of the residents began his report. A patient slowly dying in one of the wards—an old man with progressive anemia, transfusions not helping, the man's body a mass of bruises from internal hemorrhaging. Gold nodded. Not much hope there. Have the staff hematologist look at him again. "A typical case," Gold said. "Tragic, terminal, unresponsive."

After a few more cases were discussed Abe asked how Mrs. Randall was doing.

"Not too well," Max said. "Pain persists. She resists movement and has to be sedated." Dr. Landeck got up and put her X-rays on the viewer.

"There's destruction of the cervical vertebrae," Gold said. "What's the feeling?"

Max looked at Kevin. He seemed to be deferring to him. Kevin launched into Max's diagnosis. "Abe, the woman informed us that she had a urinary-tract infection two years ago."

Gold looked blank.

"Max and I consulted the literature," Kevin went on, realizing as he did that he was taking too much credit for Landeck's hunch, "and there are cases where a urinary infection, staph or proteus or E-coli, can cause osteomyelitis. Right, Max?"

Landeck nodded.

"Fascinating," Gold said. "A bacterial infection *two years* ago?"

Kevin said quickly, "Dr. DeBeers says the X-rays show nongranular sequestrums. She may have tumefactions in the upper-esophagal area. Swelling in the posterior pharyngeal."

Dr. Gold whistled. "Wow. You think the osteomyelitis is related to those swellings?"

Kevin nodded. "Max does, too."

Again, Landeck remained silent.

Joe Derry watched them. Something going on there. Joe suspected it was Max who had made the connection between the damaged vertebrae and the infection. It was a brilliant hunch. And it seemed to Joe that Kevin was taking the credit. Kevin was changing. Or perhaps had changed already.

In a few days the results of Mrs. Randall's cultures came in. The blood culture was sterile. But her urine revealed a strong concentration of E-coli bacteria. When penicillin and streptomycin failed to clear the condition, she was sent into surgery, where the orthopedic surgeon found concentrations of pus full of E-coli. Drains were inserted. The woman's spine was irrigated with penicillin. It was a long and painful procedure. But Mrs. Randall recovered.

"One for the literature," Dr. Rhodes said proudly to Kevin afterward. "Write it up. I'll get it published."

Kevin was about to say "Max Landeck had a great deal to do with it, Dr. Rhodes." But everyone seemed ready to give Kevin Derry the credit. So he said nothing.

Later he stopped Max in the cafeteria.

"Rhodes wants me to write up the Randall case," Kevin said. "I think you should do it with me."

Max's somber eyes looked at Kevin gently. "No, Kevin. You do it. You followed it through."

They paused on the serving line, awaiting their Salisbury steak.

"Max, we should do it together. It was your interest in urology that tipped us off."

"Not at all," Dr. Landeck said. "Your first published piece: 'Cervical Osteomyelitis Secondary to Urinary Tract Infection,' by Kevin Derry, M.D. I wish you luck." He did not sound injured.

Landeck ate in silence. His friend Kevin had taken the credit as naturally as putting on his white coat or reading a chart.

Joe Derry plugged away at his third-year clerkship. Many of the attendings refused to believe he and Kevin were brothers. They did not look alike, except for the gray eyes. They did not sound alike. They seemed miles apart in intelligence.

Joe was silent, shy, never ready to volunteer information. He was so deeply into his studies that he rarely slept, ate sporadically. And he was developing a marked stammer. From overwork, tension, Kevin said.

Hell of a thing, Joe thought while sitting through a pathology lecture, to end up in a teaching hospital where your older brother had been an all-star. Like the guy who followed DiMaggio in center field.

But he worked hard, harder than Kevin ever had. He had been prepared for it, making up his required science courses in a murderous year of pre-med after discharge. He had to isolate himself, sit glued to his desk, staring at the text, making notes in a meticulous hand. He rarely slept more than five hours.

Sometimes he wondered if he were too dumb to make it. Or if he ever got his M.D., whether it would mean a damn. One thing he knew: he would never use Kevin again or ask him for favors. Once was enough—the time Kevin had asked Dusty Rhodes to help with Joe's admission.

"It was the burn scars on my b-back," Joe said bitterly. "Rhodes loved them. I was a war hero."

Kevin shook his head. "Use it, kid. Use *everything.*"

Yet Joe was not entirely in Kevin's shadow. There were physicians at Mid-Island who liked Joe Derry and encouraged him. He could be the bane of an attending's existence, sitting moodily, rubbing his squashed nose, trying to get his words out. But when Joe's answers came, his instructors found them knowledgeable, thorough.

The nurses also liked Joe. He seemed a palpably frank and compassionate young man. They said he was shy because of the terrible scars on his back, his experiences in Korea.

Jenny Connetta, a floor nurse now, had shrewder instincts. Being Kevin's brother, she said, made him silent. She knew. She had slept with Kevin from time to time—whenever Chief Resident Derry felt the need. Their affair was a well-guarded secret. No one knew. She did not like the arrangement, and she had tried to prevent herself from falling in love with him. It would have been easy, too easy. But she knew about the Fifth Avenue princess who had left him for a millionaire. Once, when Kevin exploded in orgasm, he had uttered the name Cynthia. Jenny suffered the insult silently.

The next time he asked for a date, she accepted. Dinner in his apartment, a joining of their bodies, a kind of faked tenderness from him. "What Dr. Derry wanted he got" seemed to be the rule at Mid-Island. (Dr. Abe Gold, Joe noticed, was not so lucky. Abe had long nurtured a crush on Jenny's sister, Angie. Every time she swiveled down the hall he would sigh. *Attractive, intelligent, independent.* It did him no good.)

One night in May Jenny ran into trouble with a patient, when Joe was on duty on her floor.

A black woman, Mrs. Dakes, loud and incoherent, began to wander the halls. Jenny flew from the nurses' island the moment she saw Mrs. Dakes emerge from the ward, bathrobe open, shouting that she was going home and to hell with all them doctors and nurses.

"Joe," Jenny called. "Give me a hand."

Mrs. Dakes had been admitted with a compound fracture of the left wrist. It had been poorly set and the pain had been unbearable. Now, to the dismay of the Mid-Island staff, her fingers and lower forearm were manifesting a venomous orange inflammation. She was running a high fever.

Joe could remember Dr. Gold whistling under his breath when he and the orthopedic surgeon who had reset the wrist looked at the woman's arm. "If it's gas gangrene, we have a bad one," Abe had whispered. "Virulent, resistant, unique and potentially fatal."

Mrs. Dakes had been under sedation. Her injured hand was in a sling. The surgeon had been wary of covering the inflamed area. Now she removed her fractured wrist from the sling and waved her arms over her head.

"Mrs. Dakes," Jenny said. "Please go back to bed."

"I'm goin' home."

"You can't until your wrist heals. Please, Mrs. Dakes."

Jenny, a head shorter than the black woman, tried to guide her to the ward. Mrs. Dakes kept pulling away.

Joe could see Dr. Espinosa, the intern on duty, coming out of another ward, looking frightened.

Joe got on Mrs. Dakes' other side, and gently slipped her hand back into the sling.

"You'll be better inside, Mrs. Dakes," Joe said. "Won't she, nurse?"

"Of course. You want something to drink? Some orange juice?"

Joe could feel the patient's febrile skin against his bare arm. He had an uneasy feeling that the physicians didn't know what was wrong, what the orange blisters on her arm meant.

He and Jenny maneuvered Mrs. Dakes back to bed. Her wrist and arm gave off a rotting odor. Why wasn't more being done? Because she was black and poor? Or because no one knew what was wrong with her?

Jenny gave the woman a paper cup of orange juice while Joe placed a wet compress on her head.

Joe looked at her chart. "Doesn't anyone know what it is?"

Jenny shook her head. "Between the orthopedic surgeon and the director of medicine, they can't make their minds up. Dr. Gold said he's never seen this kind of inflammation before. They're waiting for lab tests."

They walked out, assuring a bemused Dr. Espinosa that Mrs. Dakes would probably not try another nocturnal stroll. "If she does, holler for me or Joe," Jenny said.

Joe sat down at the nurses' island with Jenny. She went behind the desk. Under the dim lights her skin glowed, a pale olive-brown.

It was three in the morning. Joe tried to remember a line from Fitzgerald about that time of terror in a man's life when it was always three o'clock in the morning. Fitzgerald had never been a medical student or an intern. The truth was, it was a pretty good time: you were on your own; you could help people, ease their pain, or, if they were about to die, make the last moments easier for them. There was a kind of satisfying power in medical work. Any doctor who denied it lied to himself.

"What are you staring at?" Jenny asked.

"You're very p-pretty," said Joe.

"Cut it out. You Derry brothers."

He watched her make entries in the night log. A red light flashed on the board behind her. A signal buzzed. Jenny dispatched one of the nurses to the room.

"Want me to go?" Joe asked.

"Only if there's a problem. It's the old lady with the irritable-colon syndrome. Wants someone to talk to."

"I wouldn't be m-much help." Joe opened his pathology textbook and began reading, making notes on a pad.

"You're a plugger," Jenny said.

"I have to be. I don't have Kevin's brains."

Jenny made a sniffing noise. "Kevin's smart, but he's no genius. He isn't in Dr. Gold's class."

"Or Landeck's?"

Jenny's eyes brightened. She was enjoying having fun at Kevin's expense.

"What are you laughing about, Miss Connetta?" Joe asked. He leaned forward.

"The Randall case. Dr. Howard got a full report on it and he complimented Dr. Rhodes on having such brilliant men on house staff, especially Chief Resident Derry."

"Say what you m-mean, Jen."

"Everyone knows. Dr. Landeck made the diagnosis. Kevin went along for the ride."

"I suspected it myself. But that isn't what Kevin's like, honest. He and M-Max both looked at Mrs. Randall, and . . ."

Jenny burst into laughter. "Joe, are *you* a square. Kevin's the golden boy around here. He always will be."

"He knows his medicine."

109

Jenny answered a phone. Someone was coming up from emergency. A ward bed had to be readied. A black male, internal injuries, hematomas.

"I didn't say Kevin isn't a good doctor," Jenny said. "But so are a lot of other residents and interns. It's been too easy for him."

Joe followed her to the elevator. The new patient looked at the hospital people with hostile eyes, tried to rise from the stretcher. Joe held him down.

"He's bleeding internally," the intern said. "Someone beat the hell out of him. Look at that hematoma on his thigh."

Mr. Pinkley's tan skin bulged with a purple-black lump.

A nurse came out of another elevator. "They want him X-rayed right away. Dr. Raff says it sounds like a fracture. He doesn't want anyone injecting anything into him."

Mr. Pinkley started to rise again.

Jenny pushed him back this time. "Take it easy, Mr. Pinkley." She turned to Joe. "Come on, Joe, keep me company."

Later, he asked her to go to the movies with him, some night when they were both off. She'd be glad to, she said. And he could even come to dinner at the apartment she and her sister Angie shared on medical row.

A resident emerged yawning from the lounge.

"Any action?" he asked.

"Nothing much," Joe said. "One ER. He's being X-rayed. Trauma surgery."

"Terrific. Didn't I hear you two waltzing someone off the floor?"

"Mrs. Dakes. The one with the infected h-hand."

"Great." He yawned again, scratched his back, leered as Jenny got up from her desk to check charts. "Lotsa good ass there." He winked at Joe.

Joe's face turned scarlet. He got up, folded the text, and advanced on the resident, who was a head taller.

"Listen," Joe said. "Keep your mouth shut about her, understand?"

Jenny walked down the hall. Someone on the other side of the floor was buzzing.

"Okay, okay," the resident said. "The terror of the army medical corps. Rhodes' favorite soldier boy. Son, I'm a Texan, and you New

York people don't mean doodly-squat to me."

Joe grabbed the white lapels and shoved him back a foot. "Don't ever say anything like that about Miss Connetta again or I'll beat the shit out of you."

The Texan decided sleep meant more to him than a fight. But as he walked back to the lounge, Joe was left startled by his unexpected feelings for Jenny. Some knight in armor he was, in a white coat, and not twenty dollars to his name.

The Derrys gathered for Bridie's graduation from Barnard. They sat with Sam Felder and his son, Charley. Nan and Bridie had gone through four years of Barnard together. Both girls were excellent students, but whereas Bridie was bright, Nan was a whiz. In her senior year she had been allowed to take courses in the graduate-science faculties of Columbia. Bridie, who had spent her first two years in liberal arts, and had written for the literary magazine, had switched to psychology in her last two years. She told Kevin and Joe she wanted to do graduate work in psychiatric nursing.

They sat in the warm June sunlight in Morningside Heights as the ceremonies proceeded.

"Proud, Ma?" Kevin asked his mother.

Meg smiled. "Oh, yes. I never thought a child of mine would graduate from such a swanky school."

Only Jack seemed depressed. He had lost the pharmacy a few months earlier. All the optimistic chatter about the new place, all the deals Walter Luff, Sr., promised, had come to nothing. Business dwindled. Debts accumulated. Now Jack worked in a chain pharmacy for seven thousand dollars a year. He stood behind the prescription counter and filled bottles with codeine, Pro-Banthine, Chlor-Trimeton. "I don't mind," Jack would say. "I hate television and I get to sleep late. It's an education seeing who comes in for what at night." But he was licked at age fifty-eight.

Kevin looked at Jack's pale face and wondered where the ambition and drive in the Derry children had originated. He could remember when his mother read a great deal—novels, biographies. She had also spent a good deal of time painting.

Kevin, studying the mass of graduates, the dark gowns and bright faces, felt a fathomless sorrow for his mother. In the musty attic he had once found some of his mother's watercolors—pastel shades, soft outlines, fruit and flowers and beach scenes as fragile and vulnerable as she was.

Handel's *Water Music* was piped over the public-address system. The graduates began the procession down the library steps and the ceremony was over. The families left their seats and gathered in groups near the sundial on 116th Street.

A heavyset man, wearing sunglasses, bumped into Joe, apologized, then hurriedly walked toward a young man in mortarboard and gown, evidently his son. Something about the man looked familiar. Joe started after him but lost him in the crowd.

Bridie came over. She was crying with happiness. Nan Felder, who had graduated Phi Beta Kappa and summa cum laude, seemed subdued. All of her graduate studies would be paid for with fellowship grants.

Joe watched Charley Felder kiss his sister, and he thought about Mrs. Felder and the day Potsy and those other bastards had thrown eggs at her. It seemed unthinkable that men should go out of their way to inflict pain and suffering on others. People had to die, and many of them died in agony, or lived in appalling pain. Why make it worse?

"Hi, Joe," Nan said. "Gosh, it's been years since I've seen the Derry family together."

Joe watched the bubbling life in the girls and thought of Mrs. Dakes, the black woman with the fractured wrist and the orange blistering. She had died a week after the infection began to crawl up her arm. Abe Gold had been right—gas gangrene.

Bridie suggested they have dinner at a Chinese restaurant on Broadway. Meg objected at first. She was tired. Too much excitement. Jack also needed some convincing.

"Great idea," Kevin said. "When do we ever get together anymore?"

"A terrific idea," Dr. Felder said. "As your physician, Meg—until Kevin hangs out the shingle—I prescribe spareribs and egg rolls."

Dr. Felder winked at Kevin. Kevin knew his mother's heart was not that strong and Doc was worried about her.

"In my day, chief residents didn't get a day off in the middle of the week. Even to go to their sister's graduation. You guys have a racket."

112

"Chief residents make their own schedules, Doc. We do all the work, so we treat ourselves well."

Joe walked behind Kevin with his father. Increasingly he felt the need to isolate himself from Kevin.

"Don't kid me, Kevin. Dusty Rhodes lets you run the dump."

"It's improving."

"Yeah, because they entice young hotshots like you in there. That old crowd, Rhodes and DeBeers, never paid attention to their floors."

Joe listened as Felder angrily described a case he'd recently sent to Mid-Island. Seated in the restaurant, Felder continued to record his grievances with rich specialists and professors, giving vent to the accumulated snubs of a lifetime of general practice.

"Okay, Pop," Charley Felder said, as his father threw in a few extra damnations. "Let's all have a beer."

They drank to the girls.

"F-future biologist and f-future psychiatric nurse," Joe added, holding his glass up.

Bridie squinted at him. Joe's stammer was always a surprise to her. It had been slight after his discharge from the army and had grown more pronounced during medical school.

Joe and Kevin teased the girls. Nan blushed. They remembered her as a shy skinny kid. Braces on her teeth, legs like a sandpiper's. *Sheeny. Mockey.* The local Bund kids yelling at her. And their cousin Potsy Luff sometimes joining in. Joe felt a sour shame inside himself. Kevin stared at Nan, a potential beauty—dark, small-featured, with deep hollows under her cheekbones.

The food arrived, and they began to eat.

Jack Derry leaned toward Bridie and kissed her cheek. "I had to do it, Bridget," he said hoarsely. "I'm proud. You, Kevin . . . Mother and I . . ." He stopped, flustered. The beer had loosened his tongue. "Great children."

"And Joe," Bridie said.

"Sure, Joseph also," Jack said, embarrassed that he had left Joe out.

"They're great kids, all of them," Doc Felder said.

A middle-aged couple and a young man entered the restaurant and sat down in a booth across from them. Joe saw it was the man in dark glasses who had bumped into him after the ceremonies. Joe

113

stared at the round face, the brush-cut gray hair.

Suddenly Joe made the connection. The man had put on weight. He was wearing a tan cashmere sport coat. And he kept averting his head, trying not to meet Joe's eyes.

Abruptly the man clapped the menu together, as if dissatisfied with it. He said to his wife and son, "Let's go. I don't like this place." He got up.

"Curtis," Joe said to Kevin.

"Who?"

"Curtis. The son-of-a-bitch officer who tried to railroad me."

"You sure?" Kevin asked.

"He recognized me and he's splitting." Joe got up. Kevin saw the anger rising in him, the uncontrollable temper.

"Joey," Bridie cried. "Will you sit down. Kevin, what's going on?"

"Joe," Jack Derry called. "What are you babbling about?"

Kevin whispered to Charley, "Joe says it's Curtis. Remember when Joe was in trouble in Germany? That colonel who framed him?"

Charley got up. Doc Felder turned from his sweet-and-sour pork and watched Joe run out of the restaurant.

"Stay here, Charley," Kevin said. "I'll handle it." Dodging a waiter laden with steaming dishes, he darted after Joe.

The tall man had started downtown, and was heading for a white Lincoln Continental. He began to open the door.

Joe and Kevin stopped short of the car.

"What do I do now?" Joe asked his brother. "I swore I'd kill him if I ever caught him."

"Get in, dear," the man said. "You, too, Lawton."

The woman, who in spite of the warm day wore a mink cape, entered the car. Looking at her drab face, Joe understood why Curtis had been obliged to seek the favors of Eva Baumann. The boy looked soft, overweight.

"Colonel," Joe said, walking toward him. "You are Colonel Curtis, aren't you? Remember me?"

Kevin saw Joe's face turn a shade redder. His fists were clenched. Kevin stayed a step behind him.

"I'm afraid not," Curtis said. He started to get behind the wheel. Joe yanked at his arm and pulled him into the street.

114

"Get your hands off me," Curtis said.

"Miles, who is that man?" his wife called. "Why is he bothering you?"

"Still don't remember me?"

"No."

"Joe Derry. Frankfurt. You had me framed with a whore because you were afraid I'd tell the IG about your black-market operation."

Miles Curtis looked at his wife and son. "I resent this. My boy just graduated. I don't want his day spoiled. I have no idea what you're talking about."

He followed Kevin and Joe a few steps from the car, out of earshot of the mink-clad woman, who was now rapping against the window with a diamond ring.

"I'm Dr. Kevin Derry, his brother. I sat in your office four years ago with a lawyer named Andrew Moss. You must recall that."

Curtis' cheeks flushed. He ran a hand over his brush-cut. "Yes, I sort of recall it. I happen to be president of my own pharmaceutical house now. If you want to talk to me, do so at my office." He handed Kevin a card.

CURTIS & LEMOYNE
PHARMACEUTICALS & MEDICAL SUPPLIES
MERIDIAN, NEW JERSEY

"Did pretty well on all that sulfa and penicillin you stole from the army," Joe said. "I should have r-ratted on you, you fuckhead."

"Now listen here . . . I don't have to—"

"You wanted to put me away for th-thirty years. You want your wife to know? Would that make graduation day complete?"

Curtis hesitated. "Dr. Derry, warn your brother he's asking for trouble. He was always a troublemaker, a liar and a brawler."

Joe started to swing, but Kevin caught his arm and deflected the blow aimed at Curtis' jaw.

The woman came charging out of the Lincoln, shrieking. "Police! *Police!* Help! Lawton, go help your father! Those men are beating him up!"

She was more terrifying than the ex-colonel.

"It's all right, darling," Curtis said. "These men are mistaken. They have me mixed up with someone else."

115

Bridie and Charley Felder appeared at the corner. Charley had a duck-sauce-stained napkin tucked into his shirt.

"What are they talking about, Miles? Who are these people?" Mrs. Curtis shouted.

"Crazy," Curtis gasped. "Mistook me. Get back in the car, darling. It's all right, son."

Kevin looked at the card. He knew the firm. Big advertisers, hundreds of detail men.

The Lincoln pulled away. Joe ran after it and kicked the side door. The Lincoln vanished down Broadway. Joe turned to Kevin. "You should have let me hit him. I hate bastards like that who get away with everything."

"You always did," Kevin said, "and you always will. Think up a story so the folks won't start to worry about you."

2

In December of 1954 Kevin finished his two years of residency at Mid-Island and moved on to Protestant General in Manhattan to work in cardiology with Dr. Melvin Mapes. Mapes was a chain-smoking eccentric, famous for his research with dogs and monkeys.

Dr. Rhodes had let Kevin go reluctantly. But the hospital's cardiology department was not in the same league with Protestant General's. With Joe serving his final year in Arizona on an Indian reservation, the only Derry at Mid-Island was Bridie, in her first year of nursing school.

Kevin rented a studio apartment a block from the hospital, on New York's Upper East Side, and settled into a routine of long lab hours. Coming home late at night, he would collapse with a beer and the *World-Telegram* and its two-inch headlines on McCarthy. Potsy's parents thought McCarthy a saint, even though the Senate censured him. But Kevin found it hard to care one way or the other. It was amazing what a sixteen-hour day with Mapes did to him. There was work in the cardiac clinic, the cardiac-care unit, and Mapes' lab with the yapping dogs forever eating, crapping, poor mutts with hearts from other mutts *transplanted* into their circulatory systems.

Mapes, who put in an eighteen-hour day, had at first been offhand, almost rude. His favorite ending to any order was the contraction "willya," pronounced with a rising inflection. "Hey, Derry, fetch me that clipboard on my desk, *willya?*" Kevin, in his quiet way, quickly proved that he was well trained and quick to get things done. The cardiologist's attitude changed.

117

"Cardiology, huh?" he asked one day, smoke ringing his thin face.

"It interests me," Kevin said. "Maybe internal medicine with a subspecialty in cardiology."

Mapes nodded indifferently.

Several nights before Christmas, when Kevin had fallen asleep on the couch, the phone rang at about eleven o'clock. Dr. Mapes, no doubt, complaining about misplaced data.

"Dr. Derry speaking."

"Hi, Dr. Derry."

"I give up. Who is it?"

But he knew at once. The musical voice had not changed.

"Someone you never expected to call."

"Cynthia."

"Did I interrupt something important?" She sounded wary, as if the act of calling him was improper.

"No, I was resting. Where are you?"

"At my folks' apartment. Here I am in New York on one of my rare trips, and I had the urge to call and see how my old Churchport flame is doing."

He sat up in bed. She had not called him in four years. Not since marrying the textile heir and going off to North Carolina. "The old flame is burning out, Cynthia."

She asked about his work. He answered curtly, minimizing his fellowship, saying little about his plans. No, he wasn't married, wasn't seeing anyone.

"Don't tell me I'm at fault," she said.

"I've thought about you. When I saw your father I learned you had a son. You know I paid your father back—every dollar."

"Who cares? He'd rather have you indebted to him. I have a *wonderful* little boy. Wells, Jr. He rides ponies and he has a Confederate uniform. Real plantation life."

It sounded like a parody of *Gone With the Wind*, but Kevin tried to sound enthusiastic. "I'm glad, Cynthia. It must be a good life."

"If you like magnolias."

She asked about his brother and sister. Her brother Buzzy was in Paris. He was going to have a show any day.

"And you're in New York with your family?"

118

"I left the Haslams, *père et fils,* in Lintville, USA, for a few days."

"And decided to call me?"

"I'm bored stiff. I've seen five shows, visited friends in Rye, Darien and Bucks County, and I've got the empty-apartment blahs. Mother and Daddy flew to Palm Beach yesterday, and I'm due to leave for Raleigh in two days."

"Is that an invitation?"

"The address is ten-thirty-five Fifth Avenue."

He showered, shaved, used the men's cologne Bridie had bought him for his last birthday and decided to walk from Second Avenue to Fifth. It was a damp chilly night.

The doorman halted him. Why were they all old Irishmen, with the look of country priests? Yes, Mrs. Haslam had left word that she was expecting Dr. Derry. But he would have to announce him.

Kevin surveyed the marble lobby. Burgundy drapes, gold paneling, oval mirrors, leather couches on which no one ever sat. He heard Cynthia's voice on the intercom.

In the elevator he began to sweat. What did she want? Why, after four years of silence, did she bother to call him?

She met him at the door. She was thinner, but her face, in the half light of the foyer, was as subtly passionate as ever. She wore a two-piece lounging suit, the blouse loose and belted, the trousers falling in soft folds. The outfit was honey-beige, her favorite color—neutral, yet suggesting something vital and lush.

"My goodness. The physician himself."

"You look marvelous, Cynthia. I'd forgotten how beautiful."

She bent forward, turned her cheek. "Kiss?"

He pecked at her cheek. A whiff of some musky perfume rose from her throat. As he put his hands on her waist, she turned her mouth on his. Lips apart, she kissed him, her tongue darting. He took his hands from her waist and stared at her. The glorious hips had maintained their athletic resilience after childbirth.

"Don't look so *worried,"* she said. "We're alone."

She took him not into the living room—an arena-sized place, done in greens and grays—but into her father's library.

"Even the fire in the grate," he said. "Where's the champagne in the bucket?"

She pushed the button on the stereo and Sinatra's voice infused the room with wispy memories.

119

"How did you guess?"

"Sinatra figures in these situations. High-school proms. Only you never went to one with me."

She poured two scotches for them, sat at the other end of the brown leather couch. He looked at the walls of books, rare editions, complete sets, fine bindings.

There was a Chippendale desk in one corner. He could remember standing on the oriental rug in front of that desk while Mrs. Manship wrote him a check for seven dollars for moving crates back after the summer.

"You look the same," Kevin said. "More beautiful. Maybe a little thinner. Tell me about your family, how you live down there in Tarheel country."

"You first. You haven't changed. My God, *Dr.* Derry. I bet you run everything at the hospital."

"I clean up after stray dogs." He told her about his work with Dr. Mapes, making it sound comical, minimizing his role. In a year he'd be ready for practice. Maybe after a year or two in internal medicine he'd take his boards in cardiology. He told her about Joe in his fourth year of med school, working with Indians. And about Bridie, studying psychiatric nursing at Mid-Island.

"I'm impressed, Kevin; really I am."

She was smoking, and he saw her through a blue-gray haze. "What about you? Tell me about your husband and your son."

"My husband is master of the Morganton Hunt," she said. "We ride to hounds. *You* don't look impressed. You should see us in our pink coats and white breeches and black booties."

"The pursuit of the uneatable by the unspeakable," Kevin said.

"Very, very good. Not yours, is it?"

"Oscar Wilde. Did you know his father was the leading eye doctor in Ireland? Did you know Chekhov was a doctor?"

Cynthia blew a jet of smoke at the ceiling. "Bridie probably told you that. Oh, you Derrys are so smart and ambitious. I'm jealous of all of you."

"Oh, sure. And we'd love to be as rich as you."

She gave Kevin his scotch, but before he could sip it, she leaned over and kissed him again—open-mouthed and clinging. Then she straightened up and walked to her father's desk. From it she picked

120

up a framed photograph of herself, her husband and their son.

"You look shocked, Kevin, if that's possible for an iceberg like you. Kissing in front of the happy family."

"I don't know what to say. I don't think you called me to check on my medical career."

"Behold the family Haslam. Mama is that snooty Easterner who can ride better than any of those Melanies and Scarletts, play better tennis and golf and drink them under the table. They hate my guts. And here's Husband Wells, heir to every knitting mill within a hundred miles. And my son, Wells III, my little boy. . . ."

Without warning, she slammed the photo down, and burst into tears.

Kevin got up and put his hand on her shoulder. "What is it? Cynthia, what is it?"

She sat up and dabbed at her eyes. "He's retarded."

"Your son?"

"They diagnosed it a few months after he was born. Look at him, Kevin. Can't you see the vacant stare in his eyes? His poor, empty head."

Kevin lifted the photo. The child was fair and very blond. Pale eyes. A hint of microcephaly. "Are they sure?" he asked.

"They're positive. He has PKU syndrome. You should know about it."

"Phenylketonuria. I'm sorry, Cynthia, I'm really sorry."

Her eyes were dry, almost angry. "The neurologists have explained it to me. Something about his metabolism being unable to transform harmful acids into beneficial acids. We noticed when he was a year old—he couldn't hold his head up, his arms and legs are flexed. . . ." She cried again.

"You don't have to talk about it. I know about PKU. Cynthia. They can do things for these kids today. I assume he's on a special diet. They train them; they work with them on coordination and motor skills. I'm not too up on it, but if I can help you, I will."

"Kevin, stop. It's hopeless. He's not much more than an idiot. He's been tested, and he has an IQ that's less than forty. Dear God, the sight of him, Wells Haslam III, struggling around the nursery babbling nonsense."

121

"Cynthia, you aren't the only person in the world to have a retarded child. PKU is common. If you want, I'll ask around and see what the best schools are."

"Too late, Kevin. It's ruined my marriage."

"Why?"

"Wells hasn't slept with me since the day the doctors diagnosed what was wrong with our baby."

"But why . . . why?"

"He blames it on me. He says I hid something from him, some genetic defect in our family. It's not true. I talked to some of the old servants. They swear there were these imbeciles in Wells' mother's family—relatives back in the hills."

Kevin sat on the couch and watched her come toward him. She knelt at his feet and rested her head in his lap. It was an uncharacteristic gesture of submission.

"Kevin . . . I like you. I like you a great deal."

He stroked her hair. "I always knew you did. Liked, but not loved."

"Maybe that, too."

"Like the line in *Death of a Salesman*."

She looked blank. Manships were not required to read.

"'It's important not only to be liked, but to be *well liked*.'"

"Wells hates me. When the doctors told us what was wrong with the baby, he stopped touching me. He sleeps in a different room. Not a problem in a twenty-eight-room house."

"Girlfriends?"

"Anything that walks. Kevin, I'm glad I have you to tell these awful things. He's laid every woman in the Hunt Club."

"With a wife as beautiful as you? I could give him references."

"Oh, shit, I deserve it. The way I treated you. I let you sleep with me that last time, and when it was over, I announced my engagement to Wells. How could I punish you like that?"

Kevin lifted her face. "It hurt. But it was good we made love that last time. I've relived it every day since."

She began to kiss his hands. "Strong hands. The hands of the healer. You're better-looking than ever. We wouldn't have had a retarded child." She began to weep. "A little idiot who barely knows his parents. . . ."

"Cynthia, let me tell you something. These things are easier to take when you're rich. You and Wells can put him in a special school. Have another child . . ."

"I told you. He won't come near me. We barely talk."

She unzipped his fly, reached in with a gentle hand and began to stroke him.

Kevin tried to remain indifferent. In spite of the passion rising in him he wanted to make her suffer—just a little. Let her realize what a mistake she had made.

"I do like you, Kevin darling. I like you so much."

She began to kiss him.

"Let me suggest we do this properly," Kevin said. "Here? Or in your room?"

"Here."

"Okay. Clothes off. If you're going to operate, prep the patient."

She laughed. "Oh, God, you haven't changed. Medicine on the mind all the time. Kevin, promise me that while we're making love you won't be thinking of someone in Intensive Care."

"Not with you. I've played some lousy tricks on a few fine women these last few years." He thought of Jenny—giving, uncomplaining.

"Really?" Her clothes had come off her in seconds—the loose blouse, the voluminous slacks, bra, pants. She was the golden girl again.

"Nurses. Technicians. I made love to them, and I thought about you every time."

Naked, they embraced. She put a towel from the bathroom over the couch. "Relax," she said, her voice again flat and assured.

"You're the one who sounds like the family physician now," Kevin said. "I could come back with 'wider, please,' only I'm not a dentist."

"There, that's better," she sighed.

Breathy, joined, they worked together. And yet, for all her surrender, she was withholding part of herself. Kevin prolonged his labors. It would be a long night. He could see himself stumbling into Dr. Mapes' lab early tomorrow.

"You do wonderfully. It's the best we've ever had it, isn't it, Kevin?"

Finally she moaned, locked her legs around him, and joined his ecstasy. They rested, arms around each other. He stroked her hip, marveling at her perfection.

"What are you going to do back in Turpentine County?" he asked.

"I don't know. We'll have to get a divorce. I haven't said a word to my parents. They think everything's peachy between me and Wells. Oh, that poor child."

"You've got to stop thinking about him or blaming yourself. People live with children like that. Or if they can't, they put them in institutions that provide special care. Try it. Maybe you can salvage the marriage."

She turned on one elbow, rested her mass of tawny hair on his chest. "I love you even more for being poor. You'll be rich and famous and you did it on your own. And you already paid Daddy back."

"And now I'm paying his daughter back."

"I deserved it. I treated you like shit."

They made love again and her involvement was deeper, as if the segment she had been withholding was now engaged.

Later, in the half light of the room, he stared at the white stretch marks of pregnancy on her abdomen.

"I know what you're looking at," she said.

"Perfectly natural. Must have been a difficult birth."

"It was. Those white scars. They say they go away. Mine didn't. Wells hated them. Said I'd grown old overnight."

"What a waste," Kevin said. "Maybe he's queer."

"I've had my suspicions. Not really a fag, but well, wanting to try everything."

Before morning they made love a third time.

"Oh, I love you, Kevin. Do you love me?"

"I suppose so. Anyway I love to lay you." He regretted his cruelty immediately.

"That's not the same."

"I know it isn't. You're the supreme woman. All the passion hidden. Don't touch. Special handling. But when you want it you're insatiable."

"Not true. It depends on the man. If Wells were doing this, I'd throw up. But I adore you. When we were kids at the beach . . . fishing for snappers, clamming . . . But don't talk. Love me."

He obeyed, commanded her into new positions, treating her a bit roughly as dawn illuminated the windows. They had moved to her parents' bedroom, and in the vast chamber of antiques, rich fabrics, and heavy leather, he had the sensation that he was less making love to her than trying to humiliate her.

He saw Cynthia every night that week. Twice he took her to dinner at obscure Italian restaurants on the West Side; she seemed reluctant to go to the elegant places on the East Side patronized by "her crowd." He could not afford them in any case, and he would not permit her to pay, although she offered to give him the money beforehand.

Once they went to a revival of a Marx Brothers movie, sat in the last row of the balcony, and kissed, and petted like two high-school kids. They could barely wait to get to the apartment.

That night, in the midst of their passion—it seemed to Kevin that each encounter roused her to a more intense response—the phone rang.

It was her husband.

Kevin, enjoying a satisfying moment of revenge, remained in her while she assured Haslam that everything was "super" in New York.

When she hung up, they laughed, enjoying the notion of Wells Haslam (drunk, according to Cynthia) blathering on about the new hunt season.

"That's what I call an understanding wife," Kevin said. But for some reason he felt a warped kinship with the man he had cuckolded.

Later that night, as he was dressing, he suddenly had a thought. "Something just occurred to me. Now that we're . . . well . . . ."

"Part of each other. Kevin, come back and hold me again."

He pulled on his trousers, tucked his shirt in. "Wells stopped making love with you *three* years ago? After the boy was born."

"It's true."

"Let me ask you frankly, Cynthia. In three years' time, if your husband wouldn't sleep with you, you must have—"

"Had lovers?"

"Yes."

She breathed deeply. "Only one. A man named Ed Crist. He's Wells' best friend. He was the best man at our wedding. We had a little affair until his wife found out."

"Wells' best friend? You people are beyond belief."

"I never loved Ed. He was a bastard, no better than Wells. And crazy. He calls me every day as soon as he thinks Wells is out of the house."

Kevin shook his head. "Excuse me if I'm lost. I'm the kid who clipped your father's hedges."

"And laid his daughter. You're strong. You mean something in the world. You're not just a rich parasite. That's why I love you."

Fully clothed, he sat in a wingback chair (where E. E. Manship rested after a bout with the icy Mrs. M?) and looked at her.

"So?" he asked. "What now?"

"Maybe it's up to you."

"It's happened too fast. How do you think you'd like my family as in-laws? A drugstore clerk. A dowdy Irish lady."

"I'd be married to you, not them. You'll have to adopt a—"

"Don't, Cynthia."

She cried almost inaudibly. "A vegetable. It's worse than I told you. He's showing autistic signs. They don't give us much hope."

I was not meant to be a savior, Kevin thought. He was sure he loved her. But in the five days in which they had slept together, he had the troubling feeling that it was the assault on her body, the *vengefulness* of the act, that had gratified him. Each time she submitted, he thought of her in a wedding gown, white satin and lace, surrounded by hundreds of rich and powerful friends at the Manship estate at Churchport Beach. Reducing her to a gasping, naked receptacle had its gratifications.

"Tell me more about Ed Crist. Was that his name?" he asked.

"Don't make fun of me."

"I'm not. If we ever get married, I . . . I—"

"Want to know what you're getting into? Isn't that the old dirty joke?"

"Not quite. Who else besides your husband's best friend?"

She closed her eyes. "His business partner. You don't have to know his name. Forty-five years old, Yale, squash, money. Don't ask me why. I wanted to punish Wells. I swear to you, Kevin, they were the only ones and I stopped. I hadn't slept with anyone this past year before you." She held her arms out. "Kiss me, lover. Please kiss me. I'll write to you, but you mustn't write to me. Wells has a vile temper. He's beaten me a few times."

He kissed her, breathing in the tang of her skin, her mouth.

"I'm late. Mapes wants me in on time."

"Goodbye, darling. I'll be back in a few months. I'll write every week."

Downstairs he weathered a disapproving stare from the doorman. A mild December day. He strode along the empty streets to the

126

hospital. He had not the faintest idea what would come of the week's encounter. But he was not concerned. Things broke well for him. They always had.

"You are now formally inducted into the Indian Health Service," said Dr. Hance, making no effort to mask the sarcasm in his flat midwestern voice. "Your first case of trachoma."

Joe Derry peered at the filmy eyes and deformed eyelids of the six-year-old Papago girl sitting on the examining table. The child screamed in long gulping waves, her mouth stretching her coppery face.

Through the ophthalmoscope Joe saw the inflamed cornea and the lymphoid follicles.

The girl reached out for her silent mother. They were gentle, uncommunicative people. Other tribes were starting new councils, agitating for better health services, better land. But the Papagos tended to be unprotesting.

A dozen more Indians waited at the other end of the small clinic. Officially Joe was attached to the Public Health Service in Tucson, but had been rotated to the Senita River Reservation clinic. He worked there six days a week, assisting Hance, a cynical man from Indiana.

"Do we . . . do you . . . make a lab d-diagnosis?" Joe asked, still peering into the girl's deformed eyes.

"Derry, you have to throw away those fancy New York ideas," Dr. Hance said.

The Indians sat in silence. The men wore battered Stetsons, blue jeans, Windbreakers. The women wore blankets and ragged coats. Joe had no idea Arizona could be so cold. It was a week before Christmas. An icy wind whipped across the dusty plains of the reservation, obscuring the hogans, the abandoned rusty automobiles, tin drums, starveling goats.

"I'm from Long Island," Joe said. "It's a little different from New York."

"Yeah," Dr. Hance said, "but neither of them is the Senita River Reservation. We don't take lab tests, because trachoma is goddamn near endemic here. Didn't you learn any of this in Danforth?"

"Not much."

Dr. Hance took the ophthalmoscope and looked into the child's frightened black eyes. "You leave this untreated and you know what you get, Derry?"

"I can g-guess." He was annoyed at the way Hance talked about the Indians as if they weren't present.

"Gross deformity, progressive disability and blindness. All caused by lack of sanitation, associated bacterial infections and the usual crap. *Chlamydia trachomatis,* the little bugger. Okay, what did I just say?"

"Bacterial infection."

"That gets you B-minus. It's an intracellular parasite, intermediate between a virus and a gram-negative bacteria. But we won't quibble. It flourishes in dusty places."

Dr. Hance prescribed antibiotics, lectured the mother on the need for soap and water, and cautioned her not to let other members of the family use the same toilet articles and towels that the child used.

"No external salves or anything?" asked Joe.

"It's an internal infection. Only antibiotics and sulfa drugs work. You'll be a trachoma expert by the time you finish your fourth year of med school."

Joe watched the mother take the howling child over to the dispensary window at the other end of the clinic. *Some clinic!* It was a repainted Nissen hut with two small stoves, an examining area, a minimum of medical equipment. Anything as complicated as a blood test, a urinalysis, an X-ray, meant a trip to Tucson.

"How about isolation?" Joe asked, as Dr. Hance listened to an old man's bronze chest.

"For trachoma? Not where there's so much of it. Or quarantine for that matter. They like to be together. Same goes for *otitis media*—middle-ear infection. National diseases of the American Indian. Gastroenteritis, strep throat, pneumonia."

Joe tried not to be a romantic. You didn't ride into the West and right wrongs, a penicillin-bearing phantom. Kevin had warned him before he left for Arizona that it would be frustrating work. Maybe he'd do a little good, but it would mean little when Joe went into his internship and residency. How many cases of trachoma would he find in the Bronx or Mineola?

He ushered another Indian woman with an infant toward the table and lifted the baby. The boy acted sluggish. A ribbon of snot decorated its upper lip.

Dr. Hance was opening the blanket, undoing the buttons on the infant's sweater, asking the mother to yank down its snow pants.

"He's skinny, Doctor," she said. "He don't eat right."

"Do you feed him?"

"Same as us, cornmeal, beans."

Dr. Hance scowled. For the first time Joe saw something that looked like compassion on his drawn face.

"Marasmus," Dr. Hance said.

Joe looked blank. "A new one on me."

"Sure. They aren't much concerned with it in a New York med school."

The infant's skin was wrinkled, inelastic to the touch when Dr. Hance pinched it. "No subcutaneous fat," he said. He raised the child's arm, rotated it in its socket, let it fall. "No muscle development, lethargy, slow growth. How old is he, Mrs. Kagami?"

"Four 'n' a half," the woman said.

Joe clucked. "He looks as if he's two."

"Chronic malnutrition. We had an eleven-percent incidence of malnutrition in pediatric cases last year. Chronic protein and calorie malnutrition. You know what a synergizing effect is?"

Joe looked at the lethargic child, doomed by bad diet, lack of sanitation, infection. It had burning eyes, like the Batati children. The brightness of illness. How did you turn these things around?

"I know what synergizing is. Combined action of t-two or more agents or causes, heightening the end result. I see what you're getting at. The malnutrition interacts with infection and the kids never recover. What do we d-do?"

"The best we can. I'll give her nutrient pills for the child, tell her to give it more milk, more meat, but what the hell. The national drink of the reservations is grape soda. The favorite food is white bread with all the vitamins bleached out."

"It's not their fault," Joe said.

Another woman, unhealthily fat, her face splotched with liver spots, approached the table. Outside, the wind kicked up dust devils. A pickup truck lurched noisily past the clinic.

"I guess not," Dr. Hance said. "They don't have much of a chance, and what's worse, they don't seem to care."

Joe, keeping the charts on each patient, asked the woman her name. Mabel Grounds, age thirty-eight (she looked fifty), complain-

129

ing of a skin rash, headaches, fever, dryness. . . .

Sometimes he wondered what Quixotic urge had prompted him to spend his last year of medical school in the desert. Maybe there was a desert in his mind, in his soul (Bridie would say), that propelled him into these backwaters.

A few days later a medical missionary driving a portable X-ray unit in a rattling white van arrived at the clinic.

Dr. Hance, jabbing a penicillin shot into the behind of a screaming three-year-old, said to Joe, "The Reverend Bates. Strange duck, but he's on our side."

A sparrowlike white-haired man entered the clinic and greeted some of the waiting women. Few Indian men came. They considered it a sign of weakness to take pills. The Reverend Bates shook hands with Dr. Hance, who introduced him to Joe.

"Our fourth-year medical student, Reverend. Joe Derry. He gets along fine with the Papagos. He keeps it up, we may move him up to Navajos."

The minister smiled. He was quite old, his face crosshatched by sun and wind. He wore a gray work shirt and pants, shoes no better than those worn by the Indians.

"Joe'll go out with you today, Reverend," Dr. Hance said. "He's enthusiastic about community medicine, so a day with the mobile X-ray should give him a good idea of the community."

"Splendid, splendid," Reverend Bates said. "I'll let you drive. I'm weary. Seventy-five years old, and the machine's running down. Both the car and the driver. The wife says it's from too much alkali dust."

"Try smoking and drinking, Reverend," Hance joked.

"Now, Doctor, that isn't fair." The old man winked at Joe. "I'm a Free Will Baptist, a small but distinguished group."

"Sounds like a contradiction in terms," Hance said. "Don't try to convert Derry. He's Irish."

Joe smiled, picked up his musette bag, and followed the minister out the door to the van. "I hope I won't be expected to help you convert Indians," he said.

Bates motioned to him to take the wheel. "Lord, no. The last thing I'm after is their souls. I just want to X-ray their chests."

"That doesn't sound much like a missionary."

"No, it doesn't." Bates laughed. "You might say I'm a relic of the social gospel. Give the poor heathen a better reason for living, and maybe he'll join the fold."

Joe started the engine and they drove off. Billowing clouds of dust kicked up behind them, a rooster tail of yellow powder, obscuring the hogans.

"When John Wesley preached at the pitheads of English coal mines," the minister went on, "he wasn't concerned with raising wages but with saving souls. I put it the other way around, with all due respect to the Great Man."

"So long as I don't have to d-distribute pamphlets or help you run a Mass, or whatever it is Free Will Baptists do."

"No chance, Joseph. The Papagos couldn't care less. Most of them are members of the Native American Church—peyote religion. You're a medical fellow; you must know something about it."

"A bit. Mescaline. Visions."

"Oh, it's a lot more complex than that. But our mission today is medical, so let's dispense with theology. Agreed?"

Bates explained to Joe that most Indian men were ashamed to have their X-rays taken on the reservation.

"Bunch of them working out in the onions today," he said. "We can take their chest pictures, and the womenfolk won't know they did a womanish sort of thing."

The desert sped by them—parched, barren, spotted with creosote and mesquite. They had left the reservation, land more barren than the surrounding area, and were now on a blacktop leading through cultivated fields.

"It's grand country," the old man said. "Not like back east, hey, Joseph?"

"We've got a fine ocean, and the best b-beaches in the world."

"I've never been east. Would you believe I have spent my entire life in Arizona, except for two trips to conventions in California? Didn't like the place."

He explained he was not an M.D., like some medical missionaries. But he had been given a training course in first aid, diagnostic techniques, emergency help, and lately in radiology. "Of course, I just take chest plates, looking out for TB and so on."

Some twenty miles to the north, where irrigation ditches ran parallel to the highway, and rotating sprinklers showered the budding plants, Bates told Joe to slow down.

"They use water as if Moses had struck the rock," the minister said. "You can't tell me it won't run short someday. Maybe not next year, or in ten years, but maybe in fifty. The Indians knew better. They conserved it."

Joe swung the van onto a dirt track. "You sound as if you're anticipating judgment d-day."

"I wish no man harm," Bates said. "I just want him to respect God's earth, and God's people. And that, Joseph, will be my last reference to the Divinity."

"I don't mind."

"You're a Catholic, aren't you?"

"I'm nothing. My mother was a lapsed Catholic, my father a nonpracticing Presbyterian."

Reverend Bates nodded. A moment later he told Joe to slow down. "There they are. In the onions. Backbreaking work."

"Whose place is this?"

"Mr. Travis. Never met him, but I hear he's one of the better ones."

Joe could see about forty men bending over the rows of bright-green onions, plucking them from the earth, shaking loose the dirt, laying them in cardboard boxes. They worked on their knees. The sun had become intensely hot. A hard wind whistled through the fields.

There was a cleared area under cottonwoods. The minister told Joe to park the vehicle beneath the trees next to some old buses and pickup trucks. Mangy dogs yapped at the white van. Indian kids played with empty soda cans under the trees.

Reverend Bates got out and gestured Joe to follow him. They walked into the field and approached a muscular man wearing jeans, a checked shirt and a Stetson.

"Howdy," Bates said. "Mind if I take a few X-rays when the workers are on break? I'm Reverend Bates of the Free Will Baptist Medical Mission. This is Mr. Derry from the Public Health Service. He's giving me a hand."

"Sorry. They're working." The man looked annoyed.

Bates smiled innocently. "On their lunch break? We could take an awful lot of X-rays on their lunch break."

132

"Papagos don't eat lunch. They work till they're tired of working and pack up."

"Suppose I ask them if they want to go into the van. It's piece work they're doing, so they can just work a little faster after they have had their X-rays. Okay, Mr. Travis?"

Travis laughed. His voice was loud enough for the Indians to hear. "Work *fast?* Hell, there isn't a Papago in the world understands that. We rate 'em lower than Tucson drunks, Nogales Mexicans and niggers." He turned to address the Indians. "Hey, any of you guys want to have your X-rays taken? See if you got TB, or the clap, or whatever it is you got?"

The Indians stopped working. They looked at the van, at the minister and Joe. Their dark faces were impassive, bland.

"Look, fellows," the minister said. "It doesn't hurt. Some of you must have had X-rays taken."

Travis chuckled. "Need a better pitch than that, Reverend."

Of the forty-odd Indians three young men got up, dusted their hands on their jeans and walked toward the truck.

Joe recognized one from the clinic, a chunky boy with a nose flattened almost as badly as his own. He was known as Rabbit.

"Hi, Rabbit," Joe said. "Think you can get some of the others to come in? Mr. Travis says it's okay."

The young Indian smiled. It was the same smile Joe had seen in the Philippines. It told you nothing. "Nope. They do what they want."

Bates was not discouraged. "Well, three is better than none. Joe, you can go in and set up."

Rabbit was about to enter the truck when a blue Ford pickup, raising a giant plume of powder, roared into the cleared area beneath the cottonwoods. From the cab, a red-faced man shouted at Travis, "What in hell is going on, sonny?"

"Just the X-ray truck, Papa."

"Like hell it is. Hey, you. Get the hell out."

"I'm Reverend Bates, sir. The medical missionary. Thought I'd take a few chest pictures while your men are on a break."

"Not on my land, mister. Start with X-rays, the next thing you got is free lunches."

Joe watched the man's face. He had not raised his voice, except to shout at his son. He seemed more amused than angry.

"There only appear to be three or four who want the X-rays," the minister said. "If they're healthy, they'll work better."

Travis senior shook his head. "Get off." He lifted a shotgun from the seat and leveled it at the truck. "You wouldn't want me to unload this on that van, would you?"

"Certainly not, Mr. Travis," Bates said. "We're going."

The old urge to strike, the outrage he could barely contain, bubbled inside of Joe. He felt like an idiot in his white coat.

He moved a step forward. "Pretty fucking brave, aren't you?" he said to the farmer. "Put that gun down and get out and we'll see how brave you are."

"Son, you better move," Mr. Travis said. "I don't know you, but I'll cripple you with a blast from this if you come around bothering my Indians."

The clergyman took Joe's arm. "It's their land, Joe. We'll try again. Matter of fact, we didn't get much of a turnout."

They rode back to the clinic in silence. The world, Joe decided, was divided between those who dished out the crap and those who took it. He was part of the latter. He always would be.

3

Bridie walked slowly across the lawn to the children's psychiatric ward. She was reading a letter from Joe which described his encounter with Travis. Realizing she was late, she folded the paper and hurried inside.

Helen McGrory, a former Ursuline sister who had gone "over the wall," supervised psychological testing. She was a plain, big-breasted woman who rarely smiled. But she knew a great deal, and was the pride of Mid-Island's psychiatric section.

The students, in white uniforms, took seats at the side of the room. A dozen children were present. An autistic girl of fifteen crouched in a corner. A small boy rocked back and forth in a chair.

"We're going to watch Jimmy take some tests today," Dr. McGrory said. "All of you make notes, but don't talk, or distract us while we're working. Come on, Jimmy."

A boy of eight turned from the window, where he had been methodically ripping off Christmas decorations, and walked toward Dr. McGrory. He was by outward appearances, a normal child, if a bit thin and pale. He wore a striped T-shirt, brown corduroy pants, white sneakers.

"Sit here, Jimmy," Dr. McGrory said.

The boy wandered toward the students. He leaned heavily on Bridie's lap, as if by digging his arm into her thigh he could establish some kind of attachment.

"Here, Jimmy," Dr. McGrory said. "In this chair."

He turned his back on Bridie, tried to stand on his head. Then he reached up to the wall thermostat and pushed it to its limit. "What's this?" he asked.

"It controls the heat," the psychologist said. "Miss Derry, please put it back to seventy-two degrees."

"How does it work? How does it get the heat here?" the boy said.

Bridie scrawled in her notes: UNABLE TO ORGANIZE CONCEPTS FROM STIMULI, FIXATION ON ONE OBJECT, SIGN OF BRAIN DAMAGE?

Finally the boy sat down and began to respond to Dr. McGrory's tests—copying drawings, matching wooden blocks, identifying the "wrong" picture in a group. At first he responded quickly and intelligently. Then he climbed onto the table and leaned over the work papers. When the psychiatrist ordered him off, he slumped into his seat, so that his head was below the tabletop. Again he was reprimanded, and this time he swung around, his behind on the chair, his head dangling over one side, his feet over the other.

"Don't you want to finish these tests, Jimmy?" Dr. McGrory asked.

"They're easy. What are these blocks for? I can copy all these easy. They're rotten."

Bridie wrote: IRRELEVANT QUESTIONS, FAILURE TO CONCEN-TRATE, ERRATIC, INABILITY TO INHIBIT ACTIONS AND SENSA-TIONS . . .

"All right, Jimmy, we'll continue tomorrow."

The boy climbed on the table, did a dance on the papers, climbed down. Then he ran to the window, where, with grave precision, he resumed plucking a paper Santa Claus from the pane. He used a repetitive pecking motion with his hand.

PERSEVERATION, Bridie wrote.

Dr. McGrory led her student nurses into a dingy classroom. Dr. Rhodes had yet to make his big score with the state for more funds, but he was trying. Miraculously the hospital attracted first-rate people.

"All right, Miss Soslovski," she said to one of the nurses, "what did we observe in Jimmy?"

"Lack of concentration, distractibility."

Dr. McGrory turned to Bridget. "Miss Derry, what else?"

Bridie was the only one of the three who had made notes. She had

136

learned their importance from Nan Felder.

"Strauss syndrome," Bridie said. "Hyperkinetic behavior. Perseveration."

"Which means?"

"Doing the same thing over and over. The way he kept ripping at the window decorations."

"Would you guess this boy has average intelligence?"

"Mmmm . . . I'm not sure."

Dr. McGrory consulted a card. "He tests at a hundred twenty-five IQ. Pretty high. He isn't stupid; he just can't control his perceptual handicaps or his distractibility."

"What can be done for him?" Bridie asked.

"A lot of special attention," the teacher said. "Classrooms all over the country are filled with children like Jimmy. Schoolteachers see them every day. They can be disruptive, antisocial or apathetic. And they're usually labeled hopeless even when they have superior intelligence."

"But what causes it?" asked Bridie.

Dr. McGrory cocked her head. "The new theory is brain damage. Possibly anoxia at birth. Not enough oxygen, concomitant damage to the brain. We're not certain. These are the kids who didn't cry right away or failed to nurse."

The girls looked at one another. *A lot of sad and injured people in the world,* Bridie thought. *And not too many ways to help them.*

Dr. McGrory adjusted her heavy-rimmed eyeglasses and read from a card. "As one of my colleagues put it, the brain-damaged child is the least loved, the most lonely, the most unwanted and often the most hated in the world."

Bridie wanted to object. She wanted to make some general appeal in behalf of all the Jimmys. "But . . . but . . . how do we help them?" she asked.

"We'll get into that tomorrow. It isn't easy."

Later that day, Bridie and her friend Sue Soslovski took a break for a smoke on the glassed-in walkway connecting the new and the old wings of Mid-Island. Exhausted from the long day, depressed by the children they had seen in the ward, they marveled at McGrory's patience and enthusiasm.

137

"Some nun she must have been," Sue said. "I mean, the Church lost a winner when she copped out."

"She must have had her reasons. Wonder if she's got a boyfriend." Bridie looked into the gloomy inner courtyard of Mid-Island below them. Hospital garbage brimmed over green bins. A truck backed in. Two burly men got out—one of them a giant who must have weighed three hundred pounds—and began hauling the cans with much clatter.

Bridie told Sue a story she had heard. How Dr. McGrory had been confronted one night in the psychiatric ward with a hysterical young man, a suspected schizophrenic whose parents often beat him and had thrown him out of the house.

"He was like a screaming baby," Bridie said. "So what does McGrory do? She takes off her blouse and her slip and her bra, and embraces, presses him, tight against her bosom, like she's going to *nurse* him—and he shuts up. You believe that story?"

"Wow. McGrory?"

In the snow-patched courtyard, Bridie saw Jenny Connetta, hugging herself against the cold, come out of a rear door and converse with the fat man loading garbage. They seemed to be arguing. Or rather the whalelike man was pleading with her. Jenny was shaking her head. At length he shrugged, signaled to his companion and they drove off. Bridie caught the name on the door of the garbage truck: *DAMELIO BROTHERS: CARTAGE.*

Later Jenny walked into the passageway. Bridie, always curious, asked Jenny about the garbage collector.

"Oh, that *jerk*," Jenny said. She rolled her brown eyes to the ceiling. "My cousin. Carmine Damelio. Calls himself Johnny Farrell."

"He looked like he wanted something," Bridie said, teasing. "More garbage?"

"The slob wants me to run bets and numbers for him in the hospital. He's got half the colored guys in the kitchen betting with him. Some cousin."

"You really are related?" Sue asked.

"Sure. The famous Damelio brothers. Seven of them. When they aren't hauling garbage, or taking bets, they have an orchestra. I played with them when I was sixteen. Piano. I was the only one could read music."

138

The younger girls giggled. They looked at Jenny Connetta with new admiration. Italians, Bridie realized, were resourceful and multifaceted. The Irish tended to underestimate them.

"Incidentally," Jenny said to Bridie, "Carmine always asks when your brother is coming back."

"Kevin or Joe?"

"Kevin, of course."

"Why? What's Kevin to him?" Bridie asked.

Jenny told her the story. It was part of hospital legend. How Carmine Damelio had been brought into the ER full of bullets, drunk and violent, and how the only one able to subdue him was Kevin Derry. Ever since then he'd had a special interest in "the Doc."

"And he isn't the only one who misses Kevin," Jenny said, sadly. "Kevin made this place easier to take. Boy, the chief resident we have now! Scared stiff of everyone above him and a rat to everyone under him."

"Well, the department has you and Angie to keep the residents in line," Sue said. "Dr. Gold says you're reliable, bright, energetic, well informed, goodnatured and—"

"Overworked. Listen, you two. Student nurses aren't supposed to smoke here."

She walked away.

"Wow," Sue said. "She misses Kevin for other reasons. Not just because he was such a hotshot chief resident."

Bridie felt sorry for Jenny. She was obviously in love with Kevin, incapable of hiding it. As Bridie walked to her next class she thought how sad it was that so many people were unable to love the people who loved them. Look at the way Abe Gold pursued her. A nice man, but the few times they went out she would abruptly end the evening at her doorstep; not even a kiss for sorrowing Dr. Gold.

Shrugging off gloom, she followed Sue into the hospital.

Kevin sprawled on the bed in his apartment on East 74th Street. Mapes appreciated him, knew a good mind when he saw one. *But am I that smart?* Kevin wondered. There was another doctor on fellowship working with them, a Midwesterner named Elliott, and Kevin knew that Elliott was the better man.

Kevin had known he was in fast company the first time they

139

helped Dr. Mapes in the heart clinic. He could recall Elliott's stooping over an elderly man, stethoscope to the ribbed chest, having no hesitation in announcing, "Mitral stenosis. First heart sound has an increased loudness."

Kevin dozed. He was hungry, but he was too exhausted to fry an egg. The phone rang. He looked at the clock: one-twenty in the morning, dreary December.

"Dr. Derry."

"Kevin, Angel. I had to call."

"For Chrissake, Cynthia. Are you back in New York?" She had been gone less than a week.

"No. I'm at home . . . well, at a friend's home." She sounded drunk.

"It's one-thirty," he grumbled. Why did he find it so hard to be civil? She was a woman who wanted sympathy. And he, having once pleaded with her, now resisted her. That damned middle-class miasma of propriety, fear, a denial of the flesh. *You hurt me once; I'll never forgive you.*

"Oh, you cruel bastard. Kevin, I need you."

For a moment Kevin heard another voice whispering. Good Christ, was she in the sack with someone—that friend of her husband's—and pulling the same trick she had on Wells Haslam? Making love, and soft-soaping another man at the end of a telephone line?

"Cynthia, is anyone there with you?"

"Well . . . yes. Jan is here."

"Who is Jan?"

"My best friend. Jan Crist. She knows all about us, Kevin. She's the only one I've ever told; cross my heart. I need Jan when I'm in trouble. You see, Ed—that's her husband—Ed and Wells went duck hunting somewhere."

He tried to absorb it all. Ed Crist, her husband's friend, was the man with whom she had her first affair. Her revenge on Wells, who would not come near her after the child was born. And her closest girlfriend, to whom she talked freely about her lovemaking with Kevin, was the wife of this same Crist!

"Jesus," said Kevin. "Does Jan know everything? I mean, besides what went on between us?"

"I've told her. She forgives me."

140

He looked at the phone as if it were a piece of laboratory equipment.

"Cynthia, what can I do for you at one-thirty in the morning? I'm exhausted. Mapes wants me to collaborate on a paper on fluid pressures. And here I am getting involved with you, and Wells, and Ed Crist and his wife."

"I want some hope from you, Kevin." She began to weep.

Another voice was on the phone. "Dr. Derry? Ah'm Janice Crist. Cynthia's told me a great deal about you. She is really in bad shape."

"Mrs. Crist, I'm far away and I don't see what help I can be."

"Y'all can be a mite kinder. I was listenin' on the other phone."

"Mrs. Crist, I have known Cynthia a long time but I can't solve her problems with her husband." Suddenly the whole situation disgusted him. He believed in hard work, ambition, an orderly and organized existence. There was something off balance in these people.

"Cynthia, are you on the other phone?" he asked. "Stop bawling. Take a phenobarbital and go to sleep."

"She loves you, Kevin," Jan said.

"Mrs. Crist, this is embarrassing. And it should be to Cynthia and to you. Cynthia, are you listening?"

"Oh yes, Kevin, yes. Remember when we used to go clamming in the bay? You were the best-looking boy in Churchport." Her speech was slurred.

"I'm going to hang up," said Kevin. "This whole conversation is senseless."

"I'm sorry, Kevin," Cynthia whispered. "Really I am. Please say you love me."

"Not on the phone and not with your friend listening. Cynthia, go to sleep. See about getting some help for your child. Don't come to New York for a few months."

"You are rejectin' her," Jan Crist said sharply. "That is cruel, Dr. Derry."

"I'm not cruel. I'm tired, and it sounds as if Cynthia is either drunk, or on drugs. If you're her friend, keep an eye on her. Good night." He slammed down the receiver.

He lay back on the bed, but couldn't sleep. The thought of her avenging herself on Haslam by screwing his best friend and then using the friend's wife as a crutch nauseated him.

141

Yet as he tossed and turned into the early dawn, the thought of marriage returned to plague him. He remembered his early passion, how exciting she was in bed. And always in the corner of his mind, the concept of her father's wealth. Marrying her would mean an ugly divorce, a burdensome child; but backed by Manship's millions, he wondered if it might not lead to a more rewarding life than he had ever anticipated.

During the week between Christmas and New Year's, the Walter Luffs, Sr., gave a dinner party. The Derrys were there—all but Joe, who could not leave his Indians—Potsy, fatter and now affecting a vested suit, and his fiancée, Rosemary Reardon. She was a rich, sharp-tongued girl from New York, pretty in a hard-edged way. But she was unable to hold her liquor, and she rebuffed Potsy's attempts to have her go easy on the Four Roses.

Bridie and Kevin, watching her stagger out of the living room for a fourth visit to the john, smiled at each other.

"Potsy doesn't take his eyes off her," Bridie said.

"How can he?" laughed Kevin. He was sitting on the window seat at one end of the enormous overdecorated room. Walter, Sr., was cleaning up on beach-front property.

"Kev, that isn't kind."

Kevin raised his ginger eyebrows. "Sis, that is a bombed lady if ever I saw one. Her old man may be a millionaire but she looks like a lush."

"She's beautiful," Bridie said. "The Irish ideal—black hair, pale-blue eyes, ivory skin."

Kevin frowned. "Yeah, but it's all slightly out of kilter. Get close, and you can see old acne marks on her cheeks."

"You were never that cruel when you were younger."

"It's approaching middle age. Watch it, here comes Potsy."

"All together," Potsy said. "The medical corps, courtesy of the Luffs, the Derrys and the Lundigan sisters. Wish Joey was with us. What does he want to spend his time on Indians for?"

Potsy settled into a wing chair, crossed his chunky thighs and began to reminisce about their student days at Mid-Island. What a hole that old place was! Compared to Upper County, where he was taking his surgical residency, Mid-Island was a place for losers.

"How about their chief residents?" Bridie asked angrily. Potsy got on her nerves.

"Kevin was too good for the dump," Potsy said. "And so are you. Nothing but jigs and spics for patients."

Potsy proceeded to brag about Upper County Hospital and his future as a surgeon there. He boasted, too, about his prospective in-laws, the Reardons. Rosemary hobbled back into the living room. Her white face had a bloodless look, as if she had just heaved her cookies.

"Here, sweetie," Potsy said. "Join the medical society."

Instead she lit a cigarette and leaned against the wall, swaying gently from side to side.

"You okay, Rosemary?" Bridie asked.

"Oh, she's fine," Potsy said, winking at Kevin and Bridie. "That's how Rosemary controls the disturbance. She ODs on nicotine and it counteracts the alcohol. The rocking motion helps, too. She'll be sober in a half hour."

"Rocking motion?" Bridie asked. But she said no more. A return to childhood? Back to the cradle? She had learned enough in her psychology courses to understand Rosemary Reardon's unorthodox method of sobering up. The rocking didn't last long. With a wave of her alabaster arm and another deep drag on the cigarette she returned to the bathroom.

"Aren't you worried about her?" Kevin asked.

"Rosie? Never."

"Potsy, she's throwing up every time she goes in there," Bridie said. "Let me go look after her."

"Leave her alone. She knows how to take care of herself. The rich always do. Her family makes the Manships look poor. They got a private plane, relatives in Houston in oil, three brothers all graduates of Holy Cross."

To change the subject, Kevin asked Potsy where he expected to practice.

"I'm not sure. Two more years of surgery. I like Upper County. Anyway, the Reardons have connections."

Rosemary returned and, as Potsy's parents watched sorrowfully, she walked to the wheeled bar and poured herself a half tumbler of whisky.

"Easy, Rosie," Potsy called to her.

Kevin had never heard such tenderness in his voice. Potsy had, as far as Kevin could recall, never shown respect for anyone.

"Maybe it's time we were leaving," Jack Derry said, his eyes on

Rosemary. "I should be getting down to work."

"Potsy's lucky," Katherine Luff said suddenly, as if answering some unspoken question. "Mr. Reardon says anything he wants he can have: he'll pay for the office and see to it that Potsy gets whatever appointment he wants."

"We're all lucky with our kids," Walter Luff said expansively. "By golly, three doctors and a nurse! Churchport'll know the Luffs and the Derrys better than ever. Don't think it won't help the realty business."

Jack was silent. He was hardly an asset to Walter's dreams of a dynasty. An old man at fifty-nine, working the night shift and weekends at Walgreen's, closing up, taking inventory. The owner, Harry Katz, treated him decently and it was work Jack knew. But what kind of life was that for a man with such bright kids?

He began moving toward the door.

"I'll walk you down to the pharmacy," Walter said. "The kids can take Meg home in a little while." Kevin and Bridie saw them out.

"Great bunch of kids," they heard Uncle Walter say again as he closed the door against the cold sea air.

Back in the living room Rosemary was swaying.

"Perseveration," Bridie said. "We see it in disturbed kids. I didn't know booze could do it."

"Whatcha say, Bridie?" Potsy asked.

"Just admiring Rosemary's pearls," Kevin said.

"Like hell. What was that about disturbed kids?"

"Dry up, Potsy," Bridie said. "And maybe you could dry her out also. I know her father owns private airplanes, but that's no excuse."

Potsy grinned, but it was not an amiable grin. "The same sharpie, hey, Bridie? Come from hanging around Nan Felder and those other smart Hebes at Barnard?"

"I haven't seen Nan in two years. And smart Hebes know how to behave in public."

Potsy's face flushed. He rarely was moved to anger. But Bridie, even as a kid, could upset him. "Kevin, work on her, willya?" he said, trying to keep his temper.

"Yes, forget it," Kevin said. "These family get-togethers run on too long."

He helped his mother and sister into their coats.

Outside, walking in the bitter salt air, he couldn't decide which depressed him more, his parents' poverty or the Luffs' overweening acquisitiveness. He managed to put any comparison between Potsy's gravitation toward the Reardons, and his own toward the Manships, out of mind.

Back in Manhattan, Kevin found accumulated mail—bills, medical magazines, and a letter. He recognized the slanting backhand script. Sitting in the sagging black armchair, he opened the envelope and began to read.

Dearest,

I've moved out of the house. I'm living with Jan and Ed, who have been kind enough to take me away from what has become hell on earth. . . .

You won't believe what happened. Wells came home drunk the other night, and after the usual ranting, blaming me for little Wells' retardation, he awakened the baby and *beat him,* and when little Wells wet himself and began to shriek, he began to punch the child, slap his face until I tried to drag him off, biting and scratching and screaming.

George, our houseman, came running upstairs and the two of us forced Wells to stop. It was the last straw. Phyllis, our cook, took the child to her room and let him sleep with her the rest of the night.

In the morning, Wells acted as if nothing had happened. No apologies, no remorse; in fact, he claimed he remembered nothing of the previous night. But he kept referring to our child—our *son,* Kevin—as that pinhead, the idiot.

I've left. I don't know what to do or where to turn. But I'll never go back to him, never. Darling, I think of you all the time. Help me, Kevin. Please call me in Morganton. I won't be at peace until I hear your voice. Oh, Kevin, I need you.

For all the emotional anguish, Kevin noticed the handwriting had remained perfectly spaced, the little circles crowning each *i.*

He put his feet up on the ottoman and tried to think. Cynthia would certainly marry him now. He remembered the first summer they had used her father's boathouse. The excitement of her perfect body, her thick fall of hair, the dim shadows. Her father would

145

probably be pleased that his investment in Kevin had paid off. Then, unbidden, the image of Rosemary Reardon came into his mind—the money, the private plane, the oil wells. Rosemary swaying drunkenly against the wall, self-absorbed. *Perseveration,* Bridie had said. *We see it in disturbed kids.*

Kevin shook his head. Why was Rosemary bothering him? He knew; there was something elusively unstable in Cynthia Manship Haslam also. One measured assets and liabilities, Kevin decided before falling asleep.

4

It was an hour before closing. It had been a slow evening for the pharmacy and Jack was pleased when two young blacks entered the store.

One wandered amid the shaving-cream section, hands thrust in his Windbreaker. The other, a short man with a bushy mop of hair, walked up to the counter.

"Help you?" asked Jack.

"Yeah." He pointed a snub-nosed revolver at Jack. "Gimme what's in the register or I blow you fuckin' head off."

The other man wandered to the front of the store and watched the street. Fat chance one of the town cops would pass by. Patrolman Al Kilduff, on night duty, spent most of his time drinking coffee in the Post Road Diner.

"Steady, kid," Jack said. "You might hurt someone. It's only money."

"Gimme the fuckin' money or I blow you head off."

Jack rang open the register. The black man raced to the opposite side of the counter and began scooping out bills. There wasn't much in it. Harry Katz always took the receipts to the bank before he left.

"There's another one here," the second man called. He pointed to the front checkout counter, where tobacco, candy, newspapers and film were sold. At night they locked the section and Jack handled the entire store.

"It's locked," Jack said.

"You open it."

"I don't have the key. The boss takes it with him."

He cracked Jack across the face with the revolver. "Jesus," Jack gasped, "it's the truth. I'd give you every buck in the store, but it's locked. Here, for Chrissake, take what I have in my pocket."

He reached in his trousers and took out seven dollars. The gunman grabbed it. From the register he gathered in twenty-two dollars. Risk his fuckin' neck on what somebody told him was a rich man's store, and he'd only come up with twenty-nine bucks!

Blood streamed down Jack's left cheek. He could not fathom the hatred, the need to inflict pain and humiliation.

"Gimme Dem'rol, codeine, phenobarb, all the shit you can put in here," the man said, holding out a paper bag. Jack began dumping capsules and tablets from the jars.

"Don't hit me again."

The man at the front shouted, "Someone's comin', someone's comin' . . ." He had seen Abner Welsh, the clammer, approaching from across the street.

"Take what you have and get out," Jack begged. "I won't say anything. Just get out. . . ."

Wrong thing to say, Jack realized, as the words came from his mouth. *I talk too much.*

"You ain't gonna have no chance," the holdup man said.

Maybe it's time, Jack thought. He slunk against the cabinets.

The gunman fired twice. Jack was hurled backward as if slammed by a giant hand. The bullets smashed into the pale freckled face, annihilating all the old gags and tired jokes.

Kevin got the call from his uncle Walter Luff just after midnight.

Dead immediately, no pain. No, they hadn't caught the killers. Abner Welsh had seen two blacks running out of the pharmacy and had found Jack dead. The local cops had called the county police for help. There'd been a series of attacks on late-night businesses— filling stations, drugstores, diners. Couple of addicts, the cops said. They'd got a few dollars and some drugs. Demerol and codeine tablets were scattered around poor Jack's body. Shot twice in the head. . . . Walter stopped. He'd give Kevin details later.

"How's Mother?" Kevin asked. *Be calm,* he told himself. *You're in charge now.*

"Bad, Kev. Felder gave her a shot. Katherine and Bridie are staying with her. Ah, poor Jack. Tried to get him out of the business years ago. Those animals, those black bastards. . . ."

"I'll call Joe. Uncle Walter . . ."

"Didn't give the man a fighting chance . . ."

Odd, Kevin thought, after Walter had hung up, he felt no desire to cry. That would come later. Shock could dull the nervous system.

He looked for Joe's phone number in Tucson. It had been weeks since they'd spoken. It would be ten o'clock in Arizona. If he knew Joe, he was at his apartment, studying.

Kevin's calm dissolved when Joe began to weep. Not so much for his father's death as for his life, Kevin sensed. The aching feet, the house that was falling apart, the once-beautiful wife with her drained face. At least his children would fare better.

Kevin told Joe he'd meet him at the airport, asked him to call their mother. And as he did, he had a dazzling vision of the first time his father had taken the two of them out in a rattling outboard to catch snappers.

Kevin saw the terns wheeling and dipping after baitfish, the wind kicking up whitecaps on the bay, the sun glittering behind the scudding horsehead clouds. He succumbed to a despair that made him wonder what all his efforts, all his ambition, meant. He saw his father, younger, freckled, smiling, and heard his kid brother's shrieks of joy as they hauled in the wriggling silvery catch.

"Joe?" he called on the phone. "Joe, stop bawling. Pop's dead; we can't bring him back."

But the choking noises continued. The same Joey who, alone in the attic, sobbed and could not be comforted after a Little League game lost in the last inning.

"He . . . he never had a break," Joe said. "Never."

"I know, kid. But there's nothing we can do now. Come on home."

He hung up and wiped his eyes. There were no more trains to the Island until early morning. He'd call Dr. Mapes and borrow his car.

As he dialed Mapes' number he came to a decision. Hard work for small rewards was not a life he wanted. He mourned his father but he had never respected him. Everett Manship had done more for him in many ways. And now Cynthia had appealed to him. He would respond. In turn, her wealth and her status would work for *him*. There would be no late shifts, no drudgery. Rewards would come quickly.

149

PART THREE
1958

1

The sight of Carmine (Johnny Farrell) Damelio playing saxophone at his brother's wedding was not the least source of amusement to Kevin, now an associate professor of cardiology at Danforth Medical College, and youngest member of the medical board at Mid-Island General. He and Cynthia, married three years, had come to watch Joe wed Jenny Connetta.

"It's Farrell's white-on-white shirt, *and* the white-on-white tie," Angie Connetta explained to a dazed Cynthia. "And the pinky ring on his right hand. Proves he's a wise-guy."

"Wise-guy?" Cynthia Derry asked.

"Mob."

Kevin's wife shook her golden mane. It gleamed like polished amber amid the coallike heads of the bride's family. The reception was being held in the trellised garden of Colucci's Manor in Cohammet Beach, Jenny's hometown.

"Mob?" Cynthia asked Angie. "You mean that fat man is a gangster? A *mafioso?*"

"He *thinks* he is," Angie said. She twirled spaghetti on her fork. "He's your husband's buddy."

"Kevin?" Cynthia asked. "You know the saxophone player?"

Kevin smiled. "This Love of Mine" drifted across the lawns. He recalled the times he and Jenny had made love when he was a resident at Mid-Island.

"Would you believe, Kev, I once played great piano?" she had asked.

"I believe anything about you, Jen." And he stroked her soft brown hair.

"My crazy cousins, the Damelios, the garbage kings, they got this band, and I was sixteen and the only one who could read music. They used to drive around playing dates weekends all over Long Island. . . . Carmine, and Vinnie, and Dom, and Leo and Chooch. . . ."

The Sweet Serenaders, thought Kevin, *could use Jenny right now to keep them in tune.* He looked up to see her dancing with Joe. Her veil was thrown back. Every time she kissed Joe he turned scarlet. Kevin hoped his brother did not know about their affair. He had treated Jenny like a piece of disposable medical equipment. A girl too kind for her own good. Now he had a feeling that events had come to a natural conclusion. Joe and Jenny would be compatible and fulfilled, Kevin decided, happier than most people. Jenny would make sure of that. For a moment Kevin felt a sense of loss. It passed quickly, painlessly. Marrying a Manship was not the same as marrying the daughter of a retired policeman.

Paulie Damelio was doing his accordion solo, giving it the Frank Sinatra touch with his vocal solo.

> *My life is hard . . .*
> *Now I'm alone . . .*

"You have a talented family, Angie," Cynthia said. She had sat patiently through the long nuptial mass and was struggling through the dinner. Kevin had noted the withdrawal on her face. But Cynthia was too much of a lady to comment critically. Besides, there *were* a few people there with whom she could communicate—Dr. Gold and his wife, Barbara, and Dr. Rhodes.

"That bunch?" Angie asked. *"Garbage* men, punk musicians. Jenny and I finished nursing school because we did it on our *own.* Italian families, Mrs. Derry, they believe the women should cook and wash floors and have kids."

"I wish you'd call me Cynthia."

Angie smiled. She was now chief surgical nurse at Mid-Island, a terror to residents and interns. The betting was she would never

154

marry. Surgery's gain would be some man's loss. Abe Gold's crush on her (like his crush on Bridie Derry) had come to nothing. No brilliant young Jewish physician, Abe's parents howled, would penalize his career by marrying an Italian nurse, even if she were intelligent. Why always *shiksas? Angie, Jenny, Bridie!* So Abe had married well and opened a thriving practice. But even now, as he approached Angie's table with his wife, his eyes looked on Angie with old, unused passions.

"Do you remember the night we subdued Johnny Farrell, Kevin?" Abe Gold asked. "Mind if we join you?"

"The first question is rhetorical, Abe," Cynthia said, "and the answer is yes, and the second question is interrogatory and the answer is again yes."

"Your wife has got to be a former English major," Abe said to Kevin.

"Just liberal arts," Cynthia said.

Kevin took her hand. "Cynthia's good with words. She worked at CBS for a couple of years. Public-affairs department."

"I figured," Abe said. "Anyway, that night was one of the first times I saw Kevin in action. He was just a kid, a student. And he handled that giant like a baby."

Barbara Gold wished Abe would not spend so much time praising Kevin. They both had offices in Cohammet, the largest of the North Shore communities. Though they were not exactly competitive— Abe was in internal medicine and Kevin practiced cardiology—Abe's constant lauding of a man who had been *junior* to him for years was not right.

Who was Kevin Derry anyway? Barbara Gold often thought. A lucky Irishman. Oh, there were stories. How he took the credit from Max Landeck on an important case. Played around. Borrowed a bundle from Manship. And, to cap it off, married one of the richest WASP princesses on the Island. There was a suspicion that Everett Manship had encouraged Kevin to wed his daughter. A high-priced keeper. Kevin was always the great pacifier and compromiser at the hospital. *Why not utilize these same talents to succor an elegant but unstable wife?* Mrs. Gold mused.

Dusty Rhodes came by and asked Angie to dance. He was a widower, overworked, struggling to keep Mid-Island Hospital from falling apart. His iron-gray crewcut had turned white but his back was navy-straight.

The Sweet Serenaders were into Italian airs now. They began with "Faccim' Amore," segued into "Sorrento." Carmine was standing, taking an endless solo on the tenor saxophone. Amazing, Kevin thought, how sweetly this ogre plays. There had been something in his immortal soul worth saving that night eight years ago.

The waiter came by to fill wineglasses. Cynthia put her hand over his and smiled.

"It's real Orvieto, lady," he said. "From the old country."

"I know. I've been there. One of the most beautiful cathedrals in the world."

"I never seen it. I'm a Napolitan'."

Cynthia put on her dark glasses. The long day was wearing her down. On the tennis court, on a horse, she was tireless. But too much communication with strange people exhausted her. She had tried, after her marriage to Kevin, working as a hospital volunteer. She had lasted two weeks. Afterward she told Kevin she would rather just stay home and run their household.

They had a fourteen-room house in East Cohammet, two in help, a busy social life, bridge, golf, tennis, horses. And two active, demanding children. (With governess naturally.) Karen, eleven months old, had been left at home, even though Jenny Connetta had begged Cynthia to let her come to the wedding.

Johnny Derry, born in November of 1955, two and a half years old, in robin's-egg blue suit and white shoes, a replica of Kevin with his ginger hair and gray eyes, was having a grand time. His governess, Miss Vessels, English and proper, was spending the afternoon separating him from a mass of Connetta and Damelio kids. These wild children raced in and out of the kitchen, crawling under the bandstand, throwing ravioli at one another. Miss Vessels dragged Johnny Derry from under a table. Howling and grass-stained, he was presented to his parents.

"I think he's overtired, Mrs. Derry," Miss Vessels said.

"Wanna play!" Johnny shouted. "Wanna play with Freddie! Daddy, see my friend Freddie?"

Freddie Damelio, the five-year-old son of one of the musical garbage men, was climbing a trellis. It swayed perilously, threatening to fall on Nick Connetta and his wife. No one paid any attention.

"Sit with your father awhile," Cynthia said. She smiled at Barbara Gold. At least some common ground there, even though Barbara was fat, overflowed her lavender gown, and had a Bronx accent. (But she was, Kevin made certain to tell Cynthia, an honor graduate of Cornell, with a degree in social work.)

"John leads a sheltered life," said Cynthia. "I suppose this is an education for him."

"Isn't he in nursery school?" Dr. Gold's wife asked. She recalled Cynthia's other son—retarded.

"Yes," Cynthia said. She looked away.

There was a loud roll from the drummer and Carmine announced their specialty—"a medley of old Glenn Miller favorites."

"Sunrise Serenade" sugared the air. They handled it rather well. Kevin and Cynthia went to the dance floor. She closed her eyes, and Kevin was thankful that the day had gone as well as it had. He suspected Cynthia knew of his old affair with the bride. But what did it matter to her? She'd won Kevin. He was almost thirty when they'd married. She would have expected him to have slept with a great many women. (The truth was, his affairs had been few.) Jenny was one of the rare people who had actually meant something to him.

"Holding up?" Kevin asked Cynthia.

"It's an education. I'm not the hothouse flower you think I am. I like Jenny's relatives a lot better than my former husband's. Really I do."

Potsy and Rosemary Luff danced by. How fortuitous, Kevin thought, that he and Potsy had landed wealthy girls. Almost as if they'd been big-game fishermen at Montauk, trolling the waters with their medical degrees until the big one struck. Joe, naturally, would fall in love with a policeman's daughter. And marry her.

It had burned Potsy when Kevin married Cynthia Manship, even though the Reardons were probably richer. "Kev, you scorched my Irish ass with that move," Potsy had said at the bachelor party they'd held at the Churchport Harbor Club.

"I love Cynthia," Kevin said. "I've loved her since I was a kid."

"Yeah, and her old man's connections won't hurt. They're worth even more than Rosemary's money. I thought I'd made the biggest score in the family. But Jesus, a *Manship*. . . ."

Kevin, holding his wife gently as they waltzed, caught a glimpse of little Johnny racing after a mob of small Calabrese and Sicilians. He saw Potsy and Rosemary join Joe and Jenny at the wedding table. Rosemary was pregnant again. This would be her fourth. In three years, she'd presented Potsy with twin girls—Fiona and Kathleen—and a son, Walter Luff III.

Pregnancy seemed to have reduced Rosemary's boozing. Her dress was a Balenciaga and her shoes were Gucci. Yet she seemed dislocated. Her disdain for the Italians was poorly hidden. Cynthia at least had a patrician's talent for appreciating people for what they were. She was sensible enough to realize that dull work existed in the real world, and there would always be a need for people willing to perform these chores.

"Let's sit with Joe and Jenny," Kevin said.

Cynthia smiled. She hardly knew her brother-in-law. Kevin talked about him a great deal—the man with the built-in sense of outrage. He had told her about Joe's trouble in Germany, his adventures in the Philippines, Korea, Arizona. The stories had the ring of romance. But Cynthia had difficulty envisioning Joe as a hero. He was shorter than Kevin, broad-shouldered, thick-chested, with a football-flattened nose with a white scar on its bridge.

Kevin and Cynthia sat opposite Joe and Jenny. Potsy and Rosemary were next to them. The tablecloth was littered with bits of ravioli, veal, chicken. Energetic Long Island flies feasted on scraps.

"I think it's wonderful the way your family has preserved so many old customs," Cynthia said to Jenny.

Joe nodded. "I'm learning every day. Get a load of this." He lifted a white silk bag, tied to Jenny's left sleeve. "Jen, tell them what this is."

"It's *a-boost*," Jenny said.

"A *what?*" Potsy asked. He fiddled with the gold chain on his vest.

"A *boost*," Joe said. "Just what it means. It's where we stash the checks, the money, gifts. Like a boost up for us. Right, Jen?" He kissed her neck.

"That's the way Italian Americans figure it," the bride said.

158

"Actually, it's from the word for envelope. *Busta.*"

"Kind of tough to stash a Magnavox color TV in there," Potsy said. "Or even an electric blender."

"We'll be eating Mid-Island's gourmet cuisine." Jenny laughed. "Kev, do you remember the day the chef made the rice pudding with bicarb instead of sugar?"

"Do I? Abe and I went crazy trying to figure out how everyone on our floor had alkalinuria."

"But it's a great place, right, Kev?"

Potsy disagreed. Mid-Island was a dump. He'd chosen Upper County, kissed the right behinds, used his father's leverage with the diocese, and got an appointment as a general surgeon. He was already removing appendices and gall bladders.

"One of these days," Potsy brayed, "Mid-Island may fall down. *Wham.* I can see those two old towers collapse in a heap. They'll be fishing alcoholics and psychos out of the rubble for weeks. Dusty and Abe and a few others try hard, and there isn't a better pathologist than Hershkowitz anywhere, but it's through."

"Joe's there because it's a good place to learn medicine!" Jenny said. Her brown eyes looked like hot chestnuts. She had never feared Potsy's tongue.

"Oh, yeah," Potsy said. "For a *resident* it's okay."

"Walter, I'm beat," Rosemary whined. "Let's split."

"Sure, Rosie."

"Hold it, Potsy," Jenny said. "Residents, nuts. Mid-Island's as good as Upper County any day. What have you got there? Bunch of phonies. Society dames with imaginary pains. At least Mid-Island takes care of anyone."

"She's right, Potsy," Joe said. "We run a pretty good out-patient service. And the f-free clinics may be overworked, but the p-people get attention."

"I know, kid. It's just that I don't think you draw the top line of M.D.'s anymore. Wogs, gooks, Ay-rabs, little brown people—"

"And my husband, you shit," Jenny said.

"T-take it easy, Jenny," Joe said. "Potsy's got a generalized contempt for anyone darker than he is. It d-doesn't mean anything. Comes as naturally as breathing, right, Potsy?"

Potsy was chastised. He could not figure Joe out. Kevin he

understood. But Joe—running off to Indians, worrying about welfare patients, fighting battles for people not worth it. Something boiled in Joe's guts. *Hell,* Potsy thought, *maybe getting laid regularly will end it.* Jenny looked like a terrific piece.

Jen nestled against Joe's chest. Kevin was sure his brother could not have made a better choice. She'd soften the hard edges, control his temper, love his homely face. Kevin smiled and realized Cynthia was also watching the newlyweds. She took his hand and when she smiled her eyes were misty.

"Everybody on their feet for the wedding cake!" Carmine bellowed from the bandstand. The Sweet Serenaders struck up (for reasons that eluded everyone) "Buckle Down Winsocki." Waiters wheeled in the four-tiered white cake.

There were cheers, a chorus of "The Bride Cuts the Cake" from Carmine, Vinnie, Dom and Paulie. Jenny was shoving a chunk of cake into Joe's mouth. He ducked, grabbed the knife, cut his own chunk, and returned the favor.

At the edge of the restaurant garden, Freddie Damelio handed a tumbler of Chianti to Johnny Derry. "G'wan, kid, it's good. Like soda."

"Gimme soda."

"Drink it, kid, it's good for ya," Freddie said. Street-smart at five, he knew what he was up to. His cousins watched the rich kid take the tumbler, spill half on his jacket, start to sip. In seconds, Johnny began to splutter, cough, and vomit on his Saks Fifth Avenue suit.

Miss Vessels came bounding over as Johnny regurgitated a torrent of wine, cake and spaghetti over her shoes.

"Which of you gave him that wine?" Miss Vessels asked.

"He ast for it himself," Freddie said.

Lean and tanned, Everett E. Manship sat up on the table as Kevin's nurse, Mrs. Cottrell, removed the electrodes from his chest and wiped the jelly off.

"Handy having a cardiologist in the family," E.E. said to her.

Kevin was looking at the tracery on the EKG. Not a sign of malfunction. "You don't need one, Dad," Kevin said. "I hope I have your heart when I'm your age. Not a thing wrong."

160

"Maybe Cynthia should have married a proctologist," Manship said dryly. "I seem to suffer from that indelicate condition more than anything else. God knows I exercise enough and try not to be chair-bound."

"If you want, I'll have them arrange a workup. Aren't you about due?"

"Kevin, I'm in splendid health. You were right last month, and you're right now. What I keep thinking is heart trouble, is that hiatus hernia. I'll chew a few Mylanta tablets and I'll be fine."

Mrs. Cottrell stuck her head in. Two patients were waiting. Referrals from Dr. Gold.

"I'll be a few minutes," Kevin said.

He sat behind his six-foot antique desk and settled into a Queen Anne chair. Cynthia had decorated the office. There were Piranesis on the wall, Japanese silks, an abstract by a local prodigy Cynthia had sponsored. Kevin disliked it—splotches of toxic green and fungoid yellow, streaked with purple. But he did not complain. Manship money had created the office, bought the equipment, furnished the rooms, furnished the home in East Cohammet.

"Practice going well?" Manship asked. His face had the high color of a hypertensive, the cheeks unevenly flushed, but the tests Kevin had taken indicated that the condition was not one for concern. Clothed, he looked thin and youthful.

"Getting there," Kevin said. He had opened the office three years ago after a second fellowship in cardiology.

"Cynthia and the children well?"

"Thriving, Dad." Kevin gulped slightly each time he called E.E. "Dad." His own father had always been "Pop." Manship had insisted on "Dad." Kevin had tried calling him "E.E.," but had been advised to say "Dad."

"No depression? Alcohol?"

"She's terrific. Busy, interested, attentive to the kids."

E.E. nodded. "You're the best thing ever happened to her. Cynthia gives the appearance of strength. I'm afraid her mother and I spoiled her shamelessly. And that business with Haslam almost destroyed her."

"I'm the one who benefited from the marriage, Dad. I've worshipped her ever since I mowed your lawns."

161

E.E., fortified by the good report on his daughter and grand-children, talked about his son, Buzzy, whose paintings were about to be introduced to the art world. Manship revealed that he had bought a controlling interest in a New York gallery. Of course, the owner would be *enchanté* to hold a *vernissage* for Buzzy's abstracts.

"I'm afraid I'll have to buy most of them myself," Manship said. "Of course, through third parties."

"Maybe Buzzy has talent."

"Maybe. The trouble is, Kevin, there's no way of knowing in modern art. That's why I don't feel badly about giving Buzzy's career a boost."

"You did the same for me."

Manship got up and buttoned his jacket. "Not the same thing at all. With or without me, you'd be on the way up. I've had talks with Mr. Vitti and Dr. Rhodes and they say they miss you."

"I send people there."

Manship cocked his head. "They wanted you for more than that. Rhodes says you have a way of getting things done. Of keeping people in line without raising your voice."

"The interns claimed I kept them surly but not mutinous."

"Vitti and Rhodes want you to be chairman of the medical board at Mid-Island."

Kevin walked to the door with his father-in-law. The Japanese prints bloomed around them. Cynthia was having a cabinetmaker install Philippine mahogany bookshelves with sliding glass doors. In an examining room, Kevin could see Mrs. Cottrell prepping one of Abe Gold's referrals, daubing electrode jelly on the man's chest, hooking up the cables. Kevin's practice covered a wide range—working-class people from Abe and other physicians he had known at Mid-Island; the upper middle class and the wealthy, who knew he was Manship's son-in-law.

"I'm pretty young to be a medical-board chairman," Kevin said. "I don't mind . . . but . . ."

In the waiting room, Manship said, "I don't think the deciding factor should be your age. You're more mature than most of my contemporaries. But Mid-Island isn't what you need. Upper County is your terrain, Kevin."

"I'd like to keep a foot in both."

162

"Of course." In the lobby, Manship said, "Don't be surprised if Upper County asks you to fill the next vacancy on the board."

Before Kevin could protest, the slim figure was gone.

Matt Cross, the black ambulance driver, was the first employee at Mid-Island hit by what was to become known as the "great mayonnaise epidemic."

Joe Derry was on night duty when Cross walked into the house staff office complaining that he was burning. His brown skin looked gray.

Joe took his pulse and listened to his heart. Both seemed normal. Suddenly, as Joe lowered him to the examining table in the emergency room and began to palpate his liver, Cross leapt from the table, raced to the sink and vomited.

"Man, I can't figure what hit me." He collapsed into a chair and complained of chills. "Pains in my leg muscles," Cross said. "Like I been beaten."

Joe decided Cross was too sick to go home. He was running a temperature of 103. He had the look of a man incubating something serious. Joe assigned him to a ward on the third floor.

Two days later, Ed Riley, Cross' partner on the ambulance, also fell ill. Both men began to pass dark urine. Riley started to jaundice and Cross' skin turned a sickly bronze.

"What the hell is it?" Dr. Milton DeBeers asked.

"We're taking blood and urine cultures, BUNs, the works," Joe said. "But it's crazy—two men on the night shift, both with identical symptoms."

Within four days, sixteen hospital employees were striken with the same ailments—fever, vomiting, jaundice, dark urine, muscle pains. And the gravest sign of all—enlarged livers.

When the lab tests came back, Dr. Rhodes scowled at them as Joe and Dr. DeBeers waited. "Hepatitis," Rhodes said angrily. "A goddamn epidemic. How many?"

"Nineteen," Joe said.

Rhodes studied the lab reports again. "How severe, Dr. De-Beers?"

He shrugged. "Moderate to moderately severe, you agree, Derry?"

"They seem pretty sick to me," Joe said. "Cross can hardly get out of bed, he's so weak. Riley can't eat. There are th-three nurses down with it, four people from the kitchen, and an orderly."

"A hepatitis epidemic?" asked Rhodes. "In a hospital? How?"

Joe hesitated before talking. He lacked Kevin's fluency. "One thing, Dr. Rhodes . . ."

"Yeah?"

"All of the people who are sick w-work nights."

Rhodes twirled his steel-rimmed glasses. "So?"

"Some common factor."

"What? Breathing the healthful June night air of Long Island?"

"In the food m-maybe."

DeBeers scowled and locked his hands behind his head. He was a loner, a man with little use for Rhodes' operation, Mid-Island, but too old to make a move to a better hospital. Golf interested him more than diagnosis. He looked at Joe's battered face. This one would never make it to the top like his shrewd brother.

"Food-borne hepatitis?" Dr. Rhodes asked. "Rare, Joe. I can't think of a documented case. Can you, Milton?"

DeBeers shook his head.

"Well," Rhodes said, "let's hope it runs a short course. We've tested for levels of bilirubin and transaminase, I see." He studied the lab reports again.

DeBeers yawned. "Yep. Elevated in all patients. No question, hepatic malfunction."

Rhodes shook his head. "I think we have a hepatitis epidemic. Joe, start collecting data on the infected people. And for Chrissake, let's not talk about it."

Two days later Jenny Derry was stricken while on duty. She had

165

been working the night shift on a different floor from Joe's. She was assailed by waves of nausea and cramps, ran from the nurses' island to the bathroom, vomited in spasms, then tried to brave out the rest of the night.

Stoic though she was, she soon had to leave. Joe came up from the second floor and found his wife stretched out on the bed in the lounge. She looked yellowish. Her bright brown eyes were clouded.

"I've got it too, Joey," Jenny said. "The Mid-Island crud. I think I have to heave again."

Joe and a nurse helped Jenny to the bathroom. This time, she was seized by dry retching. Joe felt her forehead. She was burning.

That night three more night workers came down with the virulent form of hepatitis.

Joe sat at Jenny's bedside until he was summoned to his floor. An old woman, recovering from gastrectomy complicated by a subphrenic abscess, was going "shocky and sour" in the same room. Jenny did not complain. She seemed more concerned that they'd be a nurse short on her floor.

"I'll be fine tomorrow after a few aspirins and Pepto-Bismol," she said.

"S-sure you will, kid." He knew she wouldn't. The staff people afflicted with what they were now calling "hospital hepatitis" were all terribly sick. They ran spiking temperatures, failed to respond to drugs. Headaches and vomiting persisted for days after the onset of fever.

Rhodes called in his house staff and the attendings. There were now twenty-six people, all hospital employees, all employed on the night shift, ill with the unexplained hepatitis.

"Anything in the papers?" Dr. Rhodes asked. "On the radio?"

It annoyed Joe. Dusty seemed more concerned with keeping word of the epidemic secret than in getting to the cause of the disease.

"Nobody pays any attention to Mid-Island," Dr. DeBeers said. "Mr. Vitti's Public Relations department is as silent as the grave."

"Not an apt metaphor," Dr. Max Landeck said. Max had a subspecialty in liver disease—he'd switched from urology when he realized he didn't have the money to set up a surgical unit—and had remained loyal to the hospital that had trained him.

"Hepatitis virus has no capability of replication outside living

166

cells," Max said. "It follows that the mode of contamination must be a *large* one, big enough to provide an infecting dose for many persons eating the food."

"Heavy *initial* contamination," Dr. Rhodes said.

Landeck's hairless dome gleamed. "It seems to me that a common food consumed by the affected people was the vehicle. There is a separate kitchen operation for the night staff. This kitchen staff and the food it prepares have no contact with patients or day staff."

"I'm not sure I buy it," DeBeers said. "How many outbreaks of food-borne infectious hepatitis have been recorded?"

"Less than a dozen," Max said.

"Problem is, Max," said Rhodes, "you know what the incubation of hepatitis is—onset of the disease a month after infection. How do we expect these people to remember what they ate a month ago?"

DeBeers said, "Examine everyone in the kitchen; give the place a scrub; check refrigeration; look for mouse turds; spray with disinfectants; whatever has to be done."

Dr. Landeck shook his head. "I am afraid that won't do. The severity of this outbreak leads me to believe that there is a *persistent* source of contamination."

"We can't fire the night kitchen staff," Rhodes said.

"No," said Max, "but we can check to see if there was a common food eaten regularly by the infected people."

"How?" Dr. Rhodes asked. "Stuff they ate a month ago?"

Dr. Landeck proceeded to describe a procedure he had read about—a "food-preference technique." Questionnaires would be prepared listing all the foods appearing on the night-shift menu. Then each patient—and an equal number of nonpatients—would be asked to respond as to whether he "always or sometimes" ate a certain food or "never" ate the food.

"It'll prove nothing," DeBeers said. "The differences won't mean a damn."

Landeck was not insulted. "It's worth a try. And the medical records of all night kitchen personnel must be reviewed."

"Get on it, Max," Dr. Rhodes said. "This thing almost sounds like a military operation." He looked at Joe. "As an old army medic there, what's your feeling?"

"All I remember is that company cooks hated to go on sick c-call,

167

so you never knew what they were incubating. They also had the highest VD r-rate. For whatever that's worth."

In two days' time—with a total of twenty-nine cases clogging the wards—Max had finished his charts, worked out computations, and had a good idea of what foods were under suspicion.

Joe himself interrogated Jenny, who was behaving like a caged raccoon.

"Joey, this damned thing," she moaned. "Why am I so weak?"

"It's the nature of the disease, Jen." He kissed her cheek. Her skin had turned an emetic yellow.

"They say I won't be able to work for a *month*," Jenny moaned.

"But you'll be able to make love s-sooner than that. Jesus, I miss you."

It hurt him just to look at her in the hospital bed. She never complained, never asked for special favors, did not nag.

He read over her questionnaire. Under "always or sometimes" she had listed tunafish sandwiches, egg-salad sandwiches, ice cream, coffee and milk.

Angie Connetta came into the ward with books and magazines for her sister. A reporter from *Newsday* had found out about the epidemic, Angie said. He was asking questions. Vitti and Rhodes and some of the attendings were making themselves scarce. The reporter, a young man named Sparling, had tried tracking down patients, but Rhodes had cleverly scattered them throughout the hospital.

Joe joined Dr. Landeck and his "search unit" in the basement room. In an hour Landeck had drawn up a table showing comparisons between patients and nonpatients. He showed the lists of figures to Joe and the others. Most of them were interns and junior medical clerks.

"Ice cream," said one of the medical students, a Filipino named Chuck Zavala.

"Why?" asked Dr. Landeck.

"One hundred percent of the patients answered 'always or sometimes.'"

Joe was shaking his head. *Wrong.* But he said nothing.

"Zavala, good try. But look at the nonpatients' responses. Ninety-eight percent responded the same way. Why aren't they sick also?"

Chuck Zavala shrugged. "Maybe they didn't like the taste and spit it out."

"Really, Zavala? Joe?"

"I vote for tunafish and egg-salad sandwiches. Tunafish gets one hundred percent on 'always or sometimes.' Egg salad rates ninety-nine percent with patients. But less than sixty-two percent of the nonpatients marked these foods 'sometimes.'"

"Mayonnaise?" Zavala asked.

"Possibly," Max said. "Remember we're talking about a strong concentration of virus that cannot replicate itself *outside living human cells*. Joe, let's look at the medical reports of night personnel."

Joe handed Dr. Landeck the folder. They were on touchy ground and he knew it.

"Let's talk to these," Landeck said. He had pulled three records. Two folders revealed recurrent alcoholism. The third, a man named Wales, had spent three months in Bronx Veterans Hospital for "erratic behavior." He was discharged, given a bill of health, and recommended to Mid-Island. He was in his late thirties, white, and had satisfied health requirements.

"I wonder what kind of erratic behavior," Landeck said. "Joe, would you and Zavala talk to these men?"

"See what being a junior medical clerk does for you, Zavala?" asked Joe, as they entered the kitchen. It looked immaculate. White tile walls sparkled; coffee urns and trays gleamed. The floor had been swept and mopped.

"Nobody will eat this crap anymore," a technician drinking black coffee said. "It's supposed to be a secret, but everyone knows. Them people got sick eatin' the poison they serve here."

A black man, Desmond, who'd worked for the hospital for ten years, came out and emptied coffee grounds, refilled the urn.

"Is Wales around?" Joe asked, deciding to start with him.

"In the back. Goldbrickin' as usual."

"Anyone else on duty?"

"Hooks."

Joe drew coffee for himself and Chuck Zavala. He asked Desmond to join them at a corner table, wondering what Zavala thought of his surroundings. It was rumored that Zavala's family owned half the Philippines—sugar plantations, steel mills, textile factories, newspapers.

169

"Desmond, who does what down here?" Joe asked. "I mean, how do you d-divide up the work?"

The black man explained. He was the boss, and he handled supply, inventories, purchasing, requisitions. He helped the other men on night duty, filling in where needed. Hooks was desserts and drinks. Wales was the sandwich man. A fourth man handled short orders—eggs, bacon, pancakes, hamburgers.

"Can I t-talk to Wales?"

"Yeah, send him out."

Joe's mind wrestled with the problem. Tunafish and egg salad. Mayo? He asked Desmond how he drew mayonnaise supplies.

"New jar of mayo opened every month," Joe said, when Desmond had told him. He looked at Zavala. "And people got sick about thirty days later."

"Gotcha. The accepted incubation period for infectious hepatitis."

Wales walked into the dining area, yawning. He was a pale man with slicked down dark hair.

"You finished with your work?" Desmond asked him.

"Don't amount to nothin'," Wales said. "We ain't drawin' flies these days."

Wales was a drifter, a bottom-of-the-barrel type. Joe had known them in the army—old-timers who had batted around for years, always with memories of "the islands" or "the zone." Wales was not stupid. He knew what Joe and Zavala were after. He told them to look at his monthly medical reports. All in order, no clap, no infections.

"Look, Ed," Joe said. "I was an army medic. I know lots of guys won't go on sick call. It's nothing to be ashamed of."

Desmond said, "Man, you had the GI shits, don't you remember? Damn near ten days you couldn't eat nothin' but oatmeal. Thought you'd disappear, you got so skinny."

"Everyone gets GI shits," Wales said.

"When was this?" Joe asked.

"Month ago," Wales said guardedly.

"You sure?"

"I'm sure. It don't mean nothin'. I had the runs, couldn't eat. But I didn't screw off. Did my job."

You sure did, Joe thought. Opened a jar of mayonnaise, slapped

170

sandwiches together and somehow knocked down thirty people with hepatitis.

"I'd like you to take some lab tests, Wales," Joe said. "Just draw a little blood."

On the way back to the lounge, Joe kept shaking his head. "What did he do? Wash his hands in the m-mayo? It almost comes together but not quite. You heard what Dr. Landeck said—an outbreak as serious as this means *unusually* heavy contamination."

"Beats me, Doc," Zavala said. "Where I come from, if his blood test was positive, we'd pull the bastard's cock off if he didn't tell us."

By six o'clock the lab confirmed that Wales' blood serum revealed anicteric hepatitis.

The next morning Joe telephoned the Bronx Veterans Hospital and asked for the psychiatric section. He got a resident and requested that someone locate the records on Edward Wales, admitted in 1957.

After a delay a psychiatric nurse got on the phone.

"What can you tell me about Ed Wales?" asked Joe.

"He wasn't violent, or alcoholic, or addicted, but his behavior was irrational. One of the doctors classified it as hebephrenia—disorganized behavior, adolescent traits."

"Any acts that reflected this irrational behavior?" asked Joe.

"He had one *really* bad habit. The men in the ward used to call him Pisser Wales."

"Pisser?"

"He had a disturbing habit of urinating wherever it struck his fancy. We caught him one day urinating into Dr. Bernstein's hat."

Joe looked at Zavala. "Chuck, we've found the source of that massive contamination. Go on, ma'am."

"He urinated into an umbrella stand, then into a nurse's tote. There must have been a half-dozen times we caught him. Once he urinated into my wastebasket, and another time on the night watchman's copy of the *Daily Racing Form*."

"Thanks, ma'am," Joe said. He told the story to Zavala, who laughed and slapped the desk.

"Oh, boy. He pissed into the mayo! Wait'll Dusty hears. I tell

171

you, Joe, that guy Wales should have his ass whipped."

Joe recounted his findings to Dr. Landeck, who lowered his head gloomily. "Subject had an attack of anicteric hepatitis. Subject, under strain of sustained illness, reverts to aberrant behavior. In some manner he infects food consumed by members of our night staff. Thank God he didn't relieve himself in the water supply. The whole hospital would come down with it. I'm afraid he's got to be fired."

Wales was discharged immediately. He denied that he had contaminated the food supply. He claimed no recollection of his past acts at the VA hospital and acted hurt when Joe and Dr. Landeck questioned him.

The papers were put through personnel and Wales was sent packing. Joe looked at his pale sick face and felt sympathy for the man. He seemed harmless. But how could he be trusted?

"What a case," Dr. Rhodes said. "A psycho pisses in the mayo, and I have an epidemic on my hands." He pointed his spectacles at the house staff. "Not a word of this to anyone. If that reporter comes around, dummy up."

A young man from *Newsday*, Eliot Sparling, did come around, looking for a story. Once, he cornered Joe Derry in a corridor and tried to pump him. "How about it? What happened? A hepatitis epidemic? Unsanitary conditions? Isn't that serious business in a hospital?"

"I guess so," Joe mumbled. He backed away. He was incapable of dissembling. He was disappointed in Rhodes for not putting out the truth. But the truth could hurt them. And how do you explain to the public that a kitchen employee had urinated in the mayonnaise?

"How'd it happen?" Sparling persisted.

Joe feigned ignorance. It was over. He wanted to get angry at someone, and found that there was no one. Finally Sparling gave up.

A few days later Kevin dropped by. He sent occasional patients to Mid-Island, consulted with Rhodes and Abe Gold and the staff cardiologist. Joe told him the story.

"Roll with the punch, Joe," Kevin said. "Medicine is full of screwball stuff like that."

"But why keep it a s-secret?"

"Because it's how we stay in business. A few cases of hepatitis?

172

Wait'll you get hit with a tough one. You'll learn to deny it ever happened."

Dr. Helen McGrory, the psychiatrist who had trained Bridie, had moved on to run a special hospital for retarded and disturbed children. Privately funded, it was located in an old North Shore mansion where the carefully tended lawns, gravel drives and stands of pine and hemlock belied the agony behind the limestone walls.

To Dr. Vitti's annoyance, McGrory had taken Bridie, Sue Soslovski and several other girls who showed promise. The ex-nun warned them that the work would be wearing and that unless they were willing to be abused, frustrated and exhausted, they should not accept her offer.

McGrory had a certain luminous power. Her compassion was never on the surface—a trait Bridie admired. Without any dramatics, she was able to combine empathy for the mentally afflicted with a shrewd talent for interpreting family histories and medical data.

Dr. Lowell Kampey, on the other hand, the director of the institute, was a pompous, didactic nitpicker. McGrory tolerated him for his fund-raising abilities, but they fought frequently over hospital policy.

A typical case began with the admission of Bernie Ulnik. Bernie was five years old. His mother had brought him to the Institute as a final hopeless gesture. There were four "normal" kids in the Ulnik house and Bernie was driving them crazy. His father, a night worker at an aircraft plant, had begun to beat the retarded boy and had given his wife an ultimatum: "It's me or him."

The first thing Bridie noticed when the boy was carried into Dr. McGrory's office by his mother was the flailing motions of his arms. Bernie Ulnik could barely walk. Even crawling was an effort. When his mother lifted him he tried to strike her with clawlike hands.

Bridie took the five-year-old boy from his mother's arms. As soon as she held him he spat in her face. She was tempted to slap him. It never did any harm to establish authority. Then she looked at his eyes. They were not angry or aggressive. He had spit on her and struck at his mother with little awareness of what he was doing.

"Bernie, be a good guy," Bridie said. "You'll get a nice toy."

He spat at Bridie again. She wiped her face and sat him into a padded chair.

"Oh, my God, I'm sorry," Mrs. Ulnik said.

She was a thin blonde woman with a worn face. Bridie's heart grieved for her. She said he had been in and out of institutions since he was three. But her husband could stand no more. Her other children were in rebellion against the monster.

Bridie looked closely at the boy's face as she tied the straps around his chest and arms. The lower, fleshy part of his nose was red, sore, forming a scab. It seemed blunted, as if severed with a knife, torn from the rest of the nose. The lower lip was a malformed scar.

Bridie pulled the straps taut. Bernie's arms and legs increased the frequency of their spasmodic gestures. His muscles did not seem weak, merely out of control. Now and then he jerked his knees or flexed his ankles. When he flailed his arms, she noticed a curious wormlike movement of his fingers.

"Wanna doggy," Bernie said.

"Get him a toy," Dr. McGrory said.

Bridie found a flop-eared toy dog and gave it to the child. With surprising strength he hurled it across the room.

For a moment the three women looked at the child in silence. Now he was trying to raise his bound arms and reach his face.

"How did his face get scarred?" Bridie asked.

"He done it himself," the mother said. "That's why he's got to be strapped up. He rips at his lips, his nose, his eyes, all the time. He don't even know he's doing it."

McGrory began to question the woman. The mother had had a normal pregnancy and delivery with Bernie. But by the time he was ten months old, it was evident he could not sit up, crawl or walk. His older brothers and sisters feared him. They called him "the nut." Soon, the flinging movements of the limbs began, the odd wriggling of fingers.

"Choreoathetosis," McGrory said to Bridie. "Involuntary, all of it."

"Was he ever given an intelligence test?" Bridie asked.

"Yes, miss. He ain't dumb. They said he had a mental age maybe only a year less than he is, five and a half. Bernie ain't dumb, he's just got this . . . this . . ." She began to weep.

Bernie's arms struggled against the bonds. He spat across the room. Saliva dripped from his tortured lip in a thin string. "Shit, fuck, shit, fuck," he shouted.

174

"He does that also," Mrs. Ulnik wailed. "The other kids teach him."

Dr. Lowell Kampey entered and stood, with arms folded, near the door.

Mrs. Ulnik went on. She'd noticed "sand" in Bernie's diapers since he was a baby. They'd had tests taken and there was something wrong with his urine.

"Hyperuricemia," Dr. McGrory said to Bridie.

"Fuck, shit, fuck," the boy shouted. A spasm brought his tiny legs into the scissor position.

To Bridie's astonishment the child smiled. She saw a transformation from hatred to a kind of lost beauty on the mutilated face. There was something querulously gentle in him. But some curse of biology had decreed a life of agony.

Oh dear God, Bridie said to herself. *He is one of us. He wants love. He wants to be happy.* She felt the urgent need to give Bernie Ulnik anything in the world, to let him leave the binding straps, to walk, play, learn, enjoy the happiness of childhood.

"Do you know of any other cases in your family?" Dr. Kampey asked.

"I heard of one, maybe, on the other side, in Europe."

"Are his brothers and sisters normal?" asked Dr. McGrory.

"Oh, yes."

"Does he have good moments?" Bridie asked. "When he's happy? Or laughs? Like he did just now?"

"Yes. He loves Rocky and Bullwinkel on television. But then he starts again—picking at his mouth and his nose, and cursing."

Bridie walked over to the boy. He was half smiling again, although his limbs had not stopped moving. She bent toward the scarred face and kissed his cheek.

"Give me a kiss, Bernie," Bridie said.

She offered him her cheek. The child kissed her. Bridie petted his coarse blond hair. "You're a good boy, Bernie."

She picked up the toy dog and gave it to him. They started to play. Bridie made the toy jump at him. She could hear Dr. Kampey and Dr. McGrory discussing the case.

"You want this doggy?" Bridie asked.

Bernie snatched it away.

"It's yours, pal."

McGrory and Kampey had finished talking. Nothing was resolved. Mrs. Ulnik would hear from them in a few days. Bridie helped the mother carry the screaming boy to the car, where a stout man sat, puffing a cigar. Inside the car was a seat with canvas belts. As they strapped Bernie in, he smiled again.

"Hopeless," Dr. Kampey said when the Ulniks had left.

"I'd like him here for a week of observation," Dr. McGrory said. "The mother will consent."

"Consent?" Kampey asked. "She'll *dump* him on us. Let's face it, Helen. You've got extreme neurological damage here. The child has an irreversible disorder."

"But he smiled," Bridie said.

Dr. Kampey ignored her. "Helen, there isn't a thing we can do for that child."

"It isn't my intention to keep him here forever," Dr. McGrory said. "I'm curious about the self-destructive behavior."

"Part of the neurological pathology."

"Are we so sure?" Dr. McGrory asked. "Couldn't he be reacting to his physical limitations? Hating himself, aware that he can't do what other children can?"

"Don't argue with *me*," Kampey said genially. "I'm a behaviorist from way back. I'm willing to accept the possibility that when he spits at Nurse Derry, or curses, it's environmentally induced. But we have no idea how deep the neurological insult is."

"I'd like him here for a week or two for observation," Dr. McGrory said stubbornly.

"Lost cause. I know our limitations. You may make the kid *worse*. We're a treatment center, not a home."

"It's only for two weeks, Dr. Kampey," Bridie said. "I'd volunteer to work with him."

"Look, I'll bring it up with the board," Dr. Kampey said finally. "But I'm telling you, that child has a metabolic deficiency that makes him behave the way he does. He isn't our kind of case."

"Bridget, would you mind leaving us?" Dr. McGrory asked coldly.

Bridie left. The door was no sooner closed than she heard the argument burgeoning.

Dr. Kampey agreed to accept Bernie for two weeks of testing and observation. Bridie called the house to ask Mrs. Ulnik to bring Bernie in. She was told that the child had died. Bernie threw a "fit," his oldest brother reported. His head arched back, his legs went back until they seemed ready to break off and his body was thrown forward. Then Bernie began to vomit, had another "fit," and died.

Bridie reported this to Dr. McGrory, whom she found with Dr. Kampey in the conference room.

Kampey twisted his mustache. "Opisthotonic spasm. They dislocate the vertebra, damage the spinal cord. That usually finishes them. Was I right or was I right?"

Neither woman responded. Kampey was not being cruel. Perhaps his neutrality was appropriate. Bridie thought she saw a misting over Helen McGrory's eyes. Or was it anger? Not so much at Kampey this time, but at their failings.

As Bridie went back to the day rooms, she wondered whether she had sufficient defenses for the work she had chosen. Both McGrory and Kampey, in very different ways, seemed to have found methods of handling the daily heartbreak. She still responded personally. Bernie's last brief smile haunted her dreams for weeks.

3

"Dad's broken up over it," Potsy said. "He knew the man personally. When Potsy said "Dad" these days, Kevin understood; he meant his father-in-law, Thomas P. Reardon.

"What man?" asked Cynthia.

"Pope Pius XII," Rosemary said. "He died yesterday."

"Oh. The pope." Cynthia tried to look concerned. She had never regarded Potsy as a devout Catholic. The unlikely concern in his voice was surely for Rosemary's benefit.

They were seated around Kevin's tennis court. It was October 9, 1958. Just a few more weeks remained in which they could play. Kevin and Potsy took Thursday afternoons off for a few sets. Cynthia did not relish the weekly get-togethers. She was a far better player than Rosemary. Potsy, fathering a paunch, was not as good as Kevin, and so they usually played one set as husbands and wives, then let the men play singles. Cynthia found the afternoons interminable. But she behaved graciously, except when the Luffs lapsed into what she called their professional Catholicism. They used it as a weapon, Cynthia said, an unassailable assertion of superiority.

"Kev, I'm afraid of them when they start on that," she said.

"Why? WASPs rule the world. You have nothing to fear. They want to be like *you*."

Cynthia frowned. "They're just so *sure* of themselves, so positive they have ultimate truths."

"Rosie's dad is going over for the election," Potsy was saying. He sipped his gin and tonic and surveyed Kevin's estate. Gatsby's, he

178

called it. Potsy was pissed off at his own father-in-law for not delivering the goods the way Manship had. Not that Dr. Walter Luff, Jr., was complaining—their ten-room ranch in East Cohammet was no shack, and the swimming pool would go in next year. But leave it to Kevin to land a better sponsor! E.E. Manship really appreciated a professional man in the family.

Potsy watched Kevin's children on the see-saw across the leaf-dotted green lawn. The Derry kids seemed to be fashioned of spun gold and marzipan, yellow-haired, white-skinned, unbearably beautiful children. His own three ran to lumpiness. Great kids, but sort of klutzy. Well, Potsy mused, let Kevin enjoy his fairylike children and his estate. Potsy had plans of his own. He didn't intend to restrict himself to appendectomies and gall bladders the rest of his life. *The heart.* That's where the action would be in a few years. Dr. Luff was going to get in on the ground floor.

"Election?" Cynthia asked. "Who's your father voting for?"

Potsy's eyes narrowed. "Rosie's dad doesn't get to vote. Cardinals vote. He's a Knight of Malta and a Knight of St. Gregory. You should see him in his uniform—plumed hat, sword, the works."

"Marching as to war," Cynthia said.

"That isn't as funny as it sounds," Rosemary said. "Daddy says that it *is* war we're in. He and his friends are going to make sure those radicals don't try to pull any funny stuff with the new pope."

"T.P. takes these matters seriously," Potsy said reverently.

Kevin winked at his cousin. The old smartass had changed.

"But your father has no actual vote?" Cynthia persisted wickedly.

"Oh, no," Rosemary said. "The *cardinals.* But you see, *we* call the tune. Daddy says it's American money that supports them, so we have a right to have a say. It's only fair."

Cynthia sipped quinine water and tried to mask her boredom. She'd been good about her drinking, was almost a teetotaler. Kevin watched her and usually was able to derail her when she seemed ready to head for the booze. He tried to keep her interested in her home, charities, and particularly the children. Yet some odd fear of them resided in her. She nurtured a draining terror of what had first issued from her straining womb. The memories of little Wells would never be exorcised. Institutionalized, isolated, he yet intruded on her memory. She loved the kids and fussed over them. But she was incapable of changing Karen's diaper on the maid's day off, shrank into an invisible iron cage when Johnny had a temper tantrum. In these moments, Kevin would come to the rescue, always calm, soft-voiced, competent.

"I'm jealous of you," she wept one night, when he took a screaming Johnny from his bed, hugged him, made him forget the nightmare. "I'm jealous of the way you handle people. Your own kids included."

Late afternoon sunlight sent shafts of ominous dark greens across the lawns and the tennis court. The pool had been closed for the year, covered with plywood. (Cynthia lived in mortal terror of one of the children drowning; she had horrid dreams about it.)

"When I was a student in Rome, my junior year, I guess," Cynthia said, "the Italians used to call Cardinal Spellman Shirley Temple."

Potsy laughed. Rosemary looked confused, then outraged. "Why? That isn't very respectful. Such a great man. I don't believe it, anyway."

"But it's *true*. He'd come tooling by in the biggest car in Italy. You could see him in the back, pink and smiling, and he was Shirley Temple to the Romans."

"Funny," Potsy said, lulled into carelessness. "Come to think of it, there is a resemblance." He noticed Rosemary's pout and stopped smiling. Something sour was happening between his wife and Cynthia. But hell, Kevin was a relative, a guy he'd grown up with. Besides, he needed Kevin. Youngest member of the medical board at Upper County, rumored to be the next chairman, Kevin was a power. Potsy didn't want any bad blood between wives screwing up their professional relationship. The Thursday afternoons would have to continue.

Cynthia did not accompany the Luffs to their car. Kevin wondered how long it would be before Rosemary would refuse to visit. Cynthia had gone out of her way to needle her; Rosie was no match for Cynthia's sarcasm.

When Kevin returned to the court he asked if she wanted to play a set of singles.

"No, darling," she said. "The leaves are covering the court. Sad, isn't it? Season of mists and mellow fruitfulness."

"Whatever you say, Cynthia."

"I behaved like a bitch to your cousins, didn't I?"

"You laid it on a little thick."

"Well, screw them. Your brother Joe's been wise to Potsy since you were children, and Joe knows him better than I do."

"Joe's sore about a lot of things."

"I know you and Potsy are cousins and medical buddies, but honestly, Kev, he's a fake. I feel sorry for that baby-machine he euchred into marrying him."

Cynthia watched the shadows cover the court, the lawn. Miss Vessels was escorting Johnny and Karen into the house for their bath and an hour of supervised television. Shivering, Cynthia gripped Kevin's arm. "I'm still afraid," she said.

"Of what, baby?"

"I don't know. Just afraid."

"We'll take a vacation. Barbados. St. Martin. That little place you liked, with the private beach and bungalows."

"I'm more afraid when I'm in strange places. I don't know what's wrong with me. I used to love to travel. Sometimes I'm afraid I'll die away from my children, and they'll never understand how much I love them."

He didn't answer. Leaving his hand in hers, he picked up the phone from the Florentine tile table and dialed his answering service. Kevin was meticulous about patients. If he and Cynthia went to the theater, or a restaurant, where pay phones were all that was available, he always carried a plastic cylinder filled with dimes. His patients knew he cared.

"Yes, Mrs. DeMott," he was saying. "Continue the nitroglycerin. Always under the tongue till it dissolves. If the drug's been sitting around the house a week or more, get a fresh supply. No, that's all right; I'll phone the druggist for you."

She watched him make his calls—confident, reassuring, calm. No wonder she needed him so desperately.

"The great healer," she said when he hung up. "A good word for everyone, isn't that it, Kev? I wish I had your power."

"It isn't power. It's based on training and experience. Why make people gloomy? Tell them the best. I lie a great deal in my work, Cynthia."

"It seems to come easily to you. Do you lie to me?"

181

"Never. You're not a patient. You're my wife."

He helped her gather up the tennis equipment and they walked across the lawn, past the hedges and fruit trees. Their monthly gardening bill was twice what Jack Derry had earned behind the prescription counter, Kevin thought.

Later, showered, perfumed, the children hypnotized in the nursery by Howdy Doody, Kevin made love to her. She sighed, came gently. She was too much like him in bed, he realized—not willing to give fully of herself. They could not consume each other in a great synergizing explosion. He tried to remember how Jenny had been. Much better, he concluded. And good luck to his brother Joe. She was the best thing that ever happened to the kid. Not just the joys of the bed, but what she would mean to his life.

"That was nice," Cynthia said.

She no longer forced him to remain locked to her. Passion spent, he rolled to one side and watched her walk to the bathroom. He still marveled at the controlled voluptuousness of her body. At cocktail parties it seemed she was the only woman in the room.

He was just dozing off when the phone rang. It was Dr. Rhodes. "Kev?"

"Yeah, Dusty."

"How's the backhand? Oh, for the life of a cardiologist. Us chiefs of services sit around and get hemorrhoids."

Kevin put on his terrycloth bathrobe.

"Trouble, Kevin. Hate to bother you."

"What kind of trouble?"

"Joe."

Kevin groaned. "Let's have it, Dusty."

"He socked Dr. DeBeers."

"*What?*"

"You should see the lump on Milt's jaw. He's threatening criminal action. I don't know what to do. The trustees don't know about it yet."

"*Socked a chief of services?* What got into him?"

Dr. Rhodes laughed. "The usual. An overactive sense of justice."

"What can I do?" Kevin had to walk on eggs. Joe was his brother. But Dr. DeBeers was a power in medical circles.

"Come down here right away. I don't want to discuss this over the phone."

182

"I'll be there in an hour." He paused. "Was it a right or a left?"

"I didn't ask. The whole mess began with your friend Sam Felder. Sometimes I think Joe wants to grow up to be just like him. What an ambition."

Cynthia came out of the bathroom. She sat at the vanity table and began combing her hair. She barely noticed that he was dressed—dark-blue suit, pale-blue shirt, maroon tie.

"Hospital calls? At five P.M. on your day off?"

"Minor emergency. Joe."

"Bailing him out again, I bet. Don't forget—we're due at the Flasts for dinner at seven."

"Who?"

"Harvey and June Flast—you *know*. Daddy's new partners in the beachfront deal. Kevin, I won't go without you. They're bores. I need you. Please don't get yourself involved in your brother's problems again. The last time, you wasted a weekend talking him out of telling a reporter about conditions in the hospital kitchen."

"This is worse, Cynthia. I'll be back in time. If I get hung up, I'll meet you at the Fleets."

"Flasts."

"Sorry. I must have enemas on the mind."

He kissed the top of her head and left.

The events leading up to Joe Derry's punching Dr. DeBeers were indeed triggered by Dr. Samuel Felder.

Contentious, outspoken, Felder had long been a thorn in the side of Mid-Island's administration. He was always spoiling for a fight, making crude remarks about "fancy professors in white coats." He had even referred to a distinguished visiting endocrinologist as a "scoundrel and ruffian," and had been threatened with a slander suit.

There was a bit of the paranoid in Felder. Patients left him because he was blunt and truthful. Colleagues resented him, because not only was he contumacious and sarcastic: he was usually *right*.

"I can't stand the old fart," the chief of obstetrics told Kevin one day, "but he's got one of the best medical minds in the county."

Joe Derry found himself one of Felder's few partisans. (Another was Max Landeck, whom Felder respected, and did not regard as a crap artist or whoremaster.) Oddly it was the gentle Landeck who was involved in the argument with DeBeers.

Ten days earlier, Doc Felder had brought a fifty-eight-year-old woman, Mrs. Kapustka, into Mid-Island for observation and treatment. The woman, a fat blonde, mother of four grown children, had complained of pain when urinating. It had got so bad she feared to relieve herself. Urine culture revealed a concentration of *proteus,* a bacteria common in urinary infections. It was decided by Dr. Landeck, and the floor chief, Dr. DeBeers, to put her on a course of pyridium and nitrofurantoin. The pyridium was to relieve the pain. The nitrofurantoin was a popular antibacterial agent.

Felder wanted to wait awhile before using the latter. "It's a punk drug," he said to DeBeers and Landeck. "I don't like it. With rest, she may get better without all that crap."

"Nitrofurantoin knocks the infection out in a day or two," Dr. DeBeers said impatiently.

Joe Derry, now in his second year of residency, said nothing, but he wondered what Felder was talking about.

Three days later Mrs. Kapustka's infection seemed improved, but she was afflicted with diarrhea. Doc Felder called Joe into the ward. "Stop the nitrofurantoin," he said. "She's getting better, and when they develop diarrhea, something rotten is going on. Okay, kid?"

"Dr. DeBeers says she n-needs it."

"To hell with him. She's *my* patient. Take her off it."

Two days later, Mrs. Kapustka was seriously ill. She could inhale and exhale only when standing or sitting up.

"Dyspnea, orthopnea," Felder said disgustedly. He took every illness, every symptom, personally. "Is she taking nourishment?" he asked Joe.

"Tried some light food, but she v-vomited twice today."

Mrs. Kapustka's stoic face looked at Dr. Felder in gentle appeal. Doc felt a personal responsibility to her. Damned few of the old-timers in Churchport still came to his Lysol-smelling office.

"You don't feel so hot, Mrs. K?" Felder asked. He took her pulse. It was rapid and irregular. He touched her jugular vein. The pressure seemed elevated.

"Not so good, Doctor. I'm better, you know, below. But I can't breathe."

What had happened? Joe wondered. He watched Felder carefully. Doc was like an old bloodhound, sniffing around for clues. Now he was examining her flaccid breasts, the ribcage. The muscles of

184

respiration were being strained. He listened to her chest. Then he handed Joe the stethoscope."

"What do you hear, kid?"

"Rales?"

"Yeah."

The examination was interrupted while Mrs. Kapustka threw up again. Joe held the basin and washed her face. It was a nurse's job, but he didn't mind.

Felder asked for an X-ray of her lungs. The woman was too weak to be sent to radiology. A portable unit was wheeled in. Max Landeck came by and expressed surprise at the unexpected lung involvement. The X-rays came back and Felder, Landeck and Joe looked at them.

"I can't believe this." Felder ran his hand over a shadowy area on the left lung. "Right-lower-lobe pneumonia. Pleural reaction."

"Has she had a history of this?" Dr. Landeck asked.

"No. Never had heart or lung problems, and I've known her thirty years."

Joe tried to put things in place. *Woman admitted for urethritis. A week later she's got pneumonia.* No wonder doctors hesitated to commit themselves.

Just then Dr. DeBeers breezed into the ward.

Felder described his physical examination of the patient and asked for corroboration from Joe. DeBeers listened, resting his head on one hand.

"I disqualify myself," Landeck said. "As Dr. Felder has told me, I'm out of my territory."

DeBeers ignored him. "She's got pneumonia and pulmonary edema," he said.

"You sure?" Felder asked.

"Look at that right lower lobe. Put her on positive-pressure breathing and penicillin. Digitalis."

"She's been off nitrofurantoin, the way I asked?" Dr. Felder asked.

"Yeah, yeah," DeBeers said.

Mrs. Kapustka was treated for pneumonia and pulmonary edema. Joe knew what was worrying Felder. Pulmonary edema was almost always the result of heart failure. No one had counted on that in a case of urethritis.

185

A few days later she began to show improvement. Felder, worried about Mrs. Kapustka's heart, ordered an EKG. It showed no troubling abnormalities, but the pulmonary-edema diagnosis didn't satisfy him. He had never liked DeBeers' offhand manner anyway. *One of those golf-and-bridge types,* Doc thought, *afraid to get his hands dirty.*

Then a new X-ray showed that the cloudiness in the left lung had virtually vanished. "Pulmonary edema?" Doc asked Joe. "Pneumonia, disappearing that fast?" He had his doubts, but continued to treat the woman as a potential cardiac case.

With her symptoms cleared up, Mrs. Kapustka was discharged. DeBeers bragged about the way he'd pulled one of Felder's patients through.

Irritably, Felder went back to Mrs. Kapustka's chart. He'd got careless in his old age, took the word of nurses and attendings for granted. He was standing at the nurses' island, reading the entries of the past few weeks, when his temper erupted.

"What the hell is this?" Doc yelled. "This patient was kept on nitrofurantoin *five days* after I ordered it stopped!"

The nurse shrugged. "It was given at night, Dr. Felder. Only the night shift would know."

"But goddammit, I gave orders to stop it! Joe! Where's Joe Derry?"

Joe came out of one of the wards. He also had failed to notice the night-shift entries. They were scrawled by a resident whose spelling left much to be desired. But there was no doubt that Olivia Kapustka had been receiving the antibacterial drug for five days past the time her doctor had demanded it be stopped. "For Chrissake!" Felder exploded. "There it is! In black and white! A hundred milligrams three times daily!"

"I don't get it, Doc," Joe said. "She got better, didn't she?"

"Better? What the hell do you think made her so sick? It was that drug! You ever hear of allergic pneumonitis?"

"Yes, but—"

"But, my behind. Where's DeBeers? I'm going to read him a chapter or two!"

Coattails flying, Felder barged into the medical conference in Dr. Rhodes' office.

"Sorry to interrupt, Dr. Rhodes, but I have something to say," Felder shouted.

"Please, Sam. Take a seat, and wait till I've finished."

"This won't wait."

Faces turned to stare at him. Joe could see Abe Gold making warning gestures at Felder: *hold it down; wait your turn; don't make things worse for yourself.*

"All right, Sam, I'll let you present your case out of turn," Rhodes said.

"You remember my patient, Olivia Kapustka?" Doc asked. "Woman with urinary-tract infection who developed pneumonia. I just discovered that woman had drug-induced allergenic pneumonitis. Nitrofurantoin produces symptoms imitating pulmonary edema, and anyone who doesn't know that should hand in his diploma and become a plumber."

"Are you saying," Rhodes asked, "that there was no pulmonary edema in this case?"

"Absolutely *none.* There was nothing wrong with that woman that the immediate stopping of nitrofurantoin wouldn't have terminated! Instead you started futzing around with digitalis, which could have killed her."

There was a strained silence in the conference room. Dr. Gold cleared his throat. "I must say, it's a new one on me," he said. "Toxic reaction is possible from any drug. But symptoms so close to edema of the lungs? How do you explain it, Sam?"

"I explain it because I ordered the woman taken off the drug after two days, as soon as her urinary symptoms began to clear up. Dr. DeBeers kept her on it five more days."

Bad tactics, Joe knew. Who knew what DeBeers had in mind? And maybe the resident or a stupid nurse had made the error.

"Dr. DeBeers decided that an *alte kocker* like me wouldn't know the difference. That woman was being made sick by the drug I wanted stopped. To cover it up, Dr. DeBeers insisted she had pulmonary edema and put her on a potentially toxic course of treatment."

DeBeers had turned a dull red.

"I'd like a comment from you, Dr. Rhodes," Felder said.

"Dr. Felder, I can't throw this case open to discussion now," Dusty said.

"Why not?" Felder asked.

DeBeers finally spoke. "Dr. Felder is making rash and pointless accusations. I insist the woman showed signs of pulmonary edema—"

"She had sensitivity reaction of the lungs, that's all."

They seemed in league against Felder, Joe felt. He'd broken the rules, made charges not only against a colleague, but one of Rhodes' friends.

"I-I'll back Dr. Felder up," Joe said. "And I-I'm partially at fault—"

"Stay out of this, kid," Felder said.

"N-no, Doc. I heard you tell Dr. DeBeers not to use nitrofurantoin. But it was being given on the n-night shift, and I missed it, because I was in ER most of the week."

"Dr. Derry, you aren't qualified to get into this," Rhodes said. He directed a cold smile at Felder. "Sam, calm down. The patient recovered, didn't she?"

"I don't like medication going on behind my back. Second, this patient got sicker than necessary. Third, if I hadn't caught it, she might have been put on a long-term treatment for cardiac failure. Totally unnecessary. Goddammit, digitalis can kill people!"

"Clear enough, Sam," Dr. Rhodes said. "But the discussion is over."

"I'd like to know what right an attending has to screw up another doctor's patient."

"That's enough, Sam," Rhodes said.

Felder bobbed his head, filled with the old conviction that *they* were after him. At the door he shook a fist at Dr. DeBeers. "I'll talk to you later. Maybe you should read up on iatrogenic diseases."

DeBeers reacted uncharacteristically. His face flamed. He rose from his seat and followed Felder and Joe out of the room.

"Milton," Dr. Rhodes called. "Forget it. We'll discuss this in my office." But DeBeers had left the room.

Rhodes shook his head, almost relieved to have the scene transferred to the hall.

"Felder," Dr. DeBeers said outside, "I demand an apology."

The old man waved him away with one hand. "Beat it, DeBeers. You're the one should apologize."

"I want a written apology and I am going to ask Dr. Rhodes to publish it in the hospital bulletin."

Joe Derry came between them. Two student nurses stopped to watch. One, behind Felder's back, made the "cuckoo" sign, twirling her index finger next to her temple.

"Look, Dr. DeBeers, and you, too, Doc," Joe said, "this is no way to h-handle it. Forget it."

"Derry, get out of my way," DeBeers said. "You're no better than he is. Listen to me, Felder—"

"*Dr.* Felder to you, you crap artist."

DeBeers swung, missed, swung again, trying to reach around Joe to hit Felder. Doc dodged Joe's intervening body, and went after DeBeers with both hands.

DeBeers swung wildly. One fist struck Joe, who was trying to keep the two men apart. Feeling the blow, Joe instinctively threw a short hard left at DeBeers' crimsoned face.

The physician, off balance, fell against the elevator doors. Unluckily, the doors opened at that instant, and DeBeers would have fallen onto a stretcher if Joe had not yanked him back.

"I'll get you for this, you dirty Irish bastard," DeBeers said. "You hoodlum, you have no right to be in a hospital."

"I was trying to s-separate you," Joe pleaded.

Raging, DeBeers stumbled back to the conference room. The noise of the altercation had brought Dr. Rhodes and the others to the corridor. They looked in horror at DeBeers rubbing his swollen jaw.

Dr. Rhodes locked the door of his office. Kevin sat in the maroon leather chair and faced the medical director. Dusty looked haggard. The navy snap had gone out of him.

"*Your* brother, Kevin," he sighed. "The kid I got into medical school."

"Joe swears he didn't mean to belt DeBeers."

"It sure didn't come out that way. At least if he'd socked Felder, nobody would be upset."

Kevin had to come to Doc's defense. "The old man was right medically, Dusty," he said.

"Nobody questions Felder's medical competence. It's the *way* Sam goes about it. The man has no idea what channels mean, how you submit something to medical conference. He comes storming in, makes wild charges."

"Not so wild. I asked Joe to talk to the night resident. DeBeers had countermanded Felder's orders."

"Felder had a legitimate complaint. But you don't go insulting a fellow physician in front of his peers. You'd better teach that to Joe,

Kevin. We'll have another Felder on our hands in a few years, and this hospital can't stand two of them. It may not even be able to tolerate *one.*"

"What do you mean?"

"DeBeers has got his lines out to every trustee. Nobody's going to stick up for Felder."

"I'm not following you, Dusty. Seems to me it's *Joe* who's in trouble. Not Felder."

"Kevin, the medical board held a meeting a few hours ago. There was a majority vote to kick both your brother and Felder out of the hospital. Terminate Joe's residency. Advise Felder he was no longer on staff."

"Who voted against them?"

"I'm not privileged to tell you, but Landeck and Gold were about the only votes to save your brother and Felder, and even Abe wanted disciplinary action."

There were seventeen physicians on the medical board, Kevin reflected. Not much support for Joe Derry and the old man.

"Didn't anyone bring up DeBeers' goof?"

"That's something for the medical conference. You can't hang DeBeers for what he thought was legitimate medication. We'd all be out of work if that were the case."

Kevin found it hard to agree, but he knew that Rhodes was arguing from strength. *Keep the mistakes in the family.*

Kevin said, "Felder says he won't quit. He's checked the woman again, found normal circulation time, which absolutely eliminates any heart or lung involvement. What's more, he's going to challenge the patient with small doses of nitrofurantoin, just to *prove* it was the direct cause of DeBeers' cockeyed diagnosis. Don't underestimate Sam."

"It won't help. He's out."

"And Joe?"

Rhodes nibbled at the earpiece of his eyeglasses. "With your help, Kev, we can work a deal."

"What do I have to do with it?"

"He's your brother. Felder was your family physician. He delivered you, I understand."

"And Joe, and Bridie. And looks after my mother."

"Fine medical man. But a pain in the ass." Rhodes shut his eyes.

190

"Landeck says he'll raise hell if we go ahead without giving the county medical society the whole story. He wants a report on everything that led to Joe's hitting DeBeers."

"Well?"

"I got Max to agree to a compromise. I had to give him a Chinese haircut to accept it, I admit. Joe stays, but he's under suspension for a month."

"Felder?"

"Out."

"So Felder's out on his can at age sixty-five. Where's he going to admit patients?"

Rhodes ran a hand over his brush cut. "That's his worry."

"What have I got to do with it?"

"They want your okay for the deal."

"Why me?"

"Come on, Kevin. It's no secret you're slated to be the next president of the medical board at Upper County. There isn't an M.D. on our staff here who doesn't want you in his corner. That's why this case was a sticky one. Both your own brother and your family doctor were involved. But if we can work out a deal that's okay with you, they'll go along."

Life, Kevin once heard a football coach mutter, is a shit sandwich and every day you take another bite. But right now, Dusty was asking him to swallow it whole. He did not savor the prospect.

"Say what you mean, Dusty. Nobody wants to be on E.E. Manship's son-in-law's blacklist?"

Rhodes smiled sheepishly but refused to comment further. One hell of a solution, thought Kevin. Throw Doc Felder to the wolves. Give Joe a slap on the wrist. And DeBeers would forget about the whole affair.

"What if I say no?" Kevin asked. "What if I think Felder is getting screwed?"

"DeBeers will be here with a lawyer tomorrow, and he'll drag Joe and Felder up before the medical society for breach of ethics."

Kevin mulled his options. The county medical society would back DeBeers. Joe was young, tough, and would survive. And Felder—maybe it would be for the best. He kept talking about retiring anyway. Kevin battled his conscience, remembering taking calls for Felder as a boy, delivering prescriptions from his father's drugstore for Doc's patients. And how Felder's son, Charley, had helped Joe beat a thirty-year jail term.

But sometimes you had to be cold. Almost anything could be rationalized, looked at from various angles.

"It's a deal," Kevin said finally. "Will Joe go along?"

"He's got no choice."

4

At his office, several days later, in the midst of reading EKGs, comforting a wealthy dowager friend of the Manships (assuring her that her "sighing respiration" was not heart failure), Kevin was interrupted by a phone call.

"I'm sorry," his secretary said, "it's a young woman, a Miss Felder. I told her you were too busy, but she won't be put off. She said she wasn't a patient, that it was a personal matter."

As Kevin took the call in his private office, a sense of shame gnawed at him.

"Dr. Derry," Nan said, "I'm calling about my father. He's been victimized by Dr. Rhodes and that crowd at Mid-Island." She knew a great deal, Kevin realized. How DeBeers had erred, tried to cover his mistake, and then rallied the board behind him because they considered Felder a wild man.

"I'm as sorry as you, Nan. I respect your father."

"Then get him reinstated. He's sixty-five. He needs a major hospital affiliation."

"But I don't make the decisions there," Kevin said. "The board voted on it."

Nan Felder paused. "I have to be frank, Kevin. Joe tells me Rhodes moved with your consent. Joe says you agreed to a deal. Joe stays and my father goes. Your brother is so furious he's thinking of resigning."

"It wasn't quite that way. The board made up its mind and we got them to suspend Joe rather than throw him out. I'm sorry for your father, Nan. I'll do all I can to get him an appointment." He damned Joe. Too outspoken, too honest.

"At Upper County, perhaps? Or would you worry about his sticking up for patients' rights there also?"

"You are your father's daughter."

"Yes, and Charley's his son. Charley is looking into the possibility of a lawsuit against Mid-Island."

"Take my advice, Nan. Forget it. You can't win. I'll be glad to write letters of reference for your father. Believe me, I tried to save his post at Mid-Island."

"Not very hard, Joe says. Kevin, I thought better of you."

All afternoon, he struggled with a sense of guilt, of an easy road taken, a failure of nerve. And rather than feeling annoyed with Nan, he admired her for calling. He wished he could see her and make her understand. She had obviously grown into a most unusual woman.

Joe remained furious with Kevin over the incident. He railed not only at Nan and Charley Felder but at Jenny and his mother.

"What right does he have to run my l-life," he shouted one night when they had stopped for dinner with Meg. "Felder's life is ruined, and I get another black m-mark on my record."

"I⌐ that all your suspension means?" asked Meg.

"Sure," said Joe. "And it's not the first. I sounded off a lot as an intern."

"Oh, Dr. Rhodes likes you," said Jenny.

"Only because I'm Kevin's brother." Joe couldn't help smiling at his wife. She was the best thing that had ever happened to him. She could work all night, come home exhausted, find the energy to joke with him and clean their plasterboard apartment on medical row.

"If I were you," said Meg, "I'd make my peace with Dr. Rhodes. Have you apologized to DeBeers?"

"No, and I won't."

"You will, you stubborn Irishman," Jenny said. "It never hurts to soft-soap people. Look at Kevin."

"I'm sick of looking at Kevin. Having him run interference for me. He does it to p-protect himself."

Jenny shook her head. "That has nothing to do with it. He has a loyalty to you."

There was some truth to what she was saying, Joe realized. Maybe if he didn't go banging his head against stone walls, he wouldn't need Kevin.

He smiled and changed the subject, but as he and Jenny were leaving, Meg said, "I can tell, Joe. You're angry with Kevin. Please don't be."

"I'm not angry, Ma. I know it could have been worse for me. I'm just sick of his running things."

"He wants to help you."

"If I'm not here, he won't be able to." He winked at Jenny. "Manship's son-in-law won't have any clout at the Papagos reservation, and that's where I'm thinking of going next year."

The mention of Manship's name made Meg flush. Her hands were twisting her handkerchief. "Joe, that isn't fair."

"What isn't?"

"The insinuation you just made. That Kevin's success is based on being Mr. Manship's son-in-law. Kevin would have been a success without him."

"Your mother's right, Joe. Don't say things like that."

"Who's fooling anyone? Every hospital board on the Island wants old Manship on its side. He gives me a stiff pain in the butt. So does my sister-in-law, with her g-goddamn horses."

"She's been kind to me," Meg said. "And Kevin loves Cynthia very much. You know, Kevin could have married dozens of girls. They were all after him."

Jenny took Joe's arm. "We know, Ma. Let's go, Joe. I'm tired."

Meg did not know what had impelled her to say it. She liked Jenny. But Joe's attack on Kevin irritated her. And she assumed that it was no secret. "Why, Jenny once had a crush on your brother, didn't you, Jenny? I mean, you and Kevin dated quite a bit."

"Ma, why bring it up?" said Jenny. "Kevin is great, but he was never really my type."

They drove home in silence. Jenny sensed her husband was about to explode. He didn't speak until they were in their rooms and ready for bed.

"What's wrong, Joe?"

"I never knew you d-dated Kevin regularly."

195

Jenny leaned on one elbow. "Look, this is no time for a third degree. I was twenty-seven when I married you. I'd been around a little. I was allowed to have boyfriends."

"So he was a boyfriend, huh? Not just an occasional d-date?"

"I don't like the way you're talking to me."

He seized her arms and held them tightly. "When? Tell me, goddammit! Why didn't anyone m-mention it?"

"Because I only saw him a few times. When he was working for Dr. Mapes. He was lonely, and he'd been hurt by Cynthia, and he wanted someone to . . . to . . . talk to."

"*Talk.* I bet." Joe got up and paced the carpet in front of the double bed.

"Joe, you have to stop this. You're developing an obsession about your brother. The world's big enough for both of you."

"So's something else."

"Oh, you bastard." She turned on her side, angrily pulled up the covers.

Joe yanked the blanket off. "Tell me. Goddammit, tell me. He s-screwed you."

"Go away."

"I said *tell* me. Kevin laid you. You went to that p-place he had on East Seventy-fourth Street. Why not? What Kevin wants, he gets."

"Joe, be quiet."

He tugged at her arm again, lifting her half out of bed. "How many times? Was he better than me? Did he make you come as much as I do?"

She began to cry. "You louse. You bad-tempered rat. Yes, I slept with Kevin. There was nothing between us. I didn't love him. He never wanted me. . . ."

"Except for a roll in the sack."

"That's right! I came to New York a few times; we never went out; we'd sit and talk. . . ."

"And *screw.*" He threw her back on the bed. "Dammit, I should have known. Kevin g-got there first."

"Joe, stop, stop," she sobbed.

"I should have guessed it. The way he l-looks at you." He sat heavily in the armchair and covered his face.

Jenny could not bear it. She got out of bed, knelt at his knees, rested her head in his lap. He did not move.

"Joe, I love you. I love you more than anyone in the world. I had an affair with Kevin. Don't hurt me by making me talk about it. I knew he never loved me, and all I had was a dumb crush on him. Every nurse at Mid-Island did."

"You should have told me."

"No. That's your trouble. Sometimes it's better to deceive yourself and be deceived. I don't want to say another thing about Kevin. I *know* you. When you get your mind set on something, you keep going until you're sorry."

Joe shook his head. "Goddammit, I'll see it all my life. The two of you in bed. At least if you'd l-loved each other, but that—"

"You want the world to be perfect, nobody dishonest, nobody sick, nobody selfish. It isn't that way."

"I could k-kill him."

"You won't and you *know* it. Put your arms around me."

But he would not, not until early morning, when shafts of light pierced the drawn blinds. Then he turned to her soft body and held her for a long time. When they dressed—she in her nurse's whites, he in slacks and a sweater (he was barred from the hospital for a few weeks)—he apologized.

"I'm sorry," Joe said, running his hand down the starched white back. "I'm a shithead. I love you, baby."

"I love you, dummy."

When she had gone, and he sat alone, his mind kept summoning the forbidden images, and he nourished them the way a man will scratch at an insect bite until it bleeds.

Joe picked a bad day to visit Kevin at Upper County.

Both Kevin and Potsy Luff were in trouble with a patient. Joe was told by the surgical nurse to wait in Dr. Derry's office. She knew, of course, he was the cardiologist's younger brother. But Dr. Derry was in the cardiac-care unit with Dr. Walter Luff and would probably be there another hour or so.

Joe wandered the color-coordinated corridors of the hospital. It was hard to conceive of people dying here, experiencing pain. The hospital was too wealthy for its own good. Manship and his

197

associates had lavished so much money on it that the medical board had to dream up new research projects and new lab facilities to justify the endowments.

In his office an hour later, Kevin told Joe about the case. A bad reaction to phentolamine in an elderly man who became hypotensive and finally died.

"Why didn't they measure the catacholamines in his urine first?" Joe asked.

"They did. Negative."

Joe asked, "Why didn't you try a half-milligram test dose first?"

"You've been studying, Joe."

"I'm suspended. I have lots of time for reading. Christ, a nurse's manual w-warns you about blocking agents."

"Easy, Joe. These things happen."

"Sure, though they don't always have to. But that isn't why I'm here."

Kevin looked at the blunt face.

"What can I do for you, kid? I was thinking I might ask Rhodes to cancel the suspension."

"I don't care about that. What the hell is a second-year residency, except p-picking up after attendings?"

"What's bugging you?"

Joe locked his hands in his lap. He was under stress, Kevin saw.

"You never told me you used to see Jenny."

"What about it? I saw her a few times. What has that got to do with anything? You barely knew her then, for Chrissake."

Joe kneaded his hands. Too much baseball, too many hard tackles, had thickened his fingers. *Always positions of maximum punishment*, Kevin thought.

"You should h-have told me. You and Jenny b-both. Kevin, admit it."

"Admit what?"

"You screwed her. She used to come to your apartment."

Kevin's pale skin reddened. He got up and sat on the windowsill. His voice was steady and comforting. "Joe, for God's sake, why make an issue of it?"

"Y-you both deceived me."

"You jerk, we didn't know the two of you would fall in love one

198

day and get married. What are you looking for—retroactive revenge?"

"I d-don't like being made a fool of."

"Joe, grow up. Jenny and I had an affair. It didn't mean anything. She was lonely. I was too."

"You laid my wife, and you thought about Cynthia Manship, w-wasn't that it?"

"She wasn't your wife then. I liked her. I respected her. I still do. You'd better do the same and stop this lunacy."

Joe swallowed and bent his head. He looked up and stared at the photographs on Kevin's desk. Cynthia in riding clothes astride one of her prizewinning hunters. Cynthia with Kevin's golden children, sitting on a lawn filled with sunlight and flowers and trees.

"Was she good?" Joe choked out. "Better than your wife? How many times, you bastard? What else did she d-do for you?"

Kevin leaped from the windowsill and grabbed Joe by the lapels. "Shut up, you idiot. Out of respect for Jenny, if no other reason. It's over, finished, in the past. You have this damned habit of never letting go of anything. If you want to hit me, go ahead, I never won a fight from you anyway. Go on, swing."

"No. It w-won't change anything."

"What's there to change? You're looking for some kind of abstract justice. You think less of your wife because I had an affair with her? Long before the two of you knew each other? Joe, I think you're crazy sometimes."

Joe shook loose from Kevin's grip. He had no desire to strike him. It would prove nothing. Yet he could not suppress that sense of betrayal, of deceit. The notion of Kevin—*as always*—getting there first.

"You have to learn how to handle your temper." Kevin offered him a cigarette. Joe shook his head. He noticed Kevin had become a heavy smoker. Hell of a note for a cardiac expert. The tension was hidden under the glacial exterior.

"I've made my mind up. I don't want to p-practice within a hundred miles of you. I'm sick of the big family star."

"Have I ever put you down? Have I ever tried to discourage you?"

"When I was in the VA hospital, recovering from the b-burns. You said I'd never make m-med school. Too tough for me."

199

"That's not the way I remember it. I went to Rhodes for you. I got you your internship. I—"

"And you b-broke in my wife for me."

"What a stubborn bastard you can be. If it'll make you happier, we can decide not to see each other again."

Joe stood silent. He knew confronting Kevin would only leave him more angry. There was nothing more to say. He started for the door just as Kevin's intercom sounded. It was Potsy's office. Kevin told the secretary he'd get back to him.

"Joe, you didn't hurt Jenny, did you?"

"Hurt her?"

"Did you hit her?"

"You think I'm some kind of animal? We argued, that's all. Maybe I shouldn't have been so t-tough on her." He looked into Kevin's imperturbable eyes. "Goddammit, it's always you. Always my brilliant big brother."

"I'm warning you, Joe. Forget it."

"It won't be easy. Every t-time I see her, wh-when we're in bed . . ."

"Joe, take my advice. Be good to her." He put his arm around the sturdy shoulders and the cheap tweed scratched his hand. Like Joe. Prickly, uncomfortable. "Listen to me, Joe. There isn't a finer person in the world than Jenny. She's better than either of us, better than Bridie, or any of our friends. She's just *good;* she can't be anything else." In an unguarded moment, Kevin looked at the photographs of his wife as if making the invidious comparison. "Some people seem to be born that way—generous and loving, without meanness or guile in them. I didn't let myself fall in love with her, because I had other ideas. You got a hell of a lot more than a wife when you married Jenny Connetta."

"You don't have to tell me."

"Maybe I do. You were always the kid who was shy with the girls in Churchport—the busted nose, the clothes that never fit. Don't let that leftover bitterness harm your relationship with Jenny."

Subdued, Joe punched Kevin softly in the arm. "Okay, okay. You'll need violins if you keep it up. I know what she is. That's why it hurt s-so much."

"Don't let it. Say it if you want. Dr. Kevin Derry is a selfish, ambitious SOB. Takes what he wants. But I'd never do it to you. I'm not quite the con man you seem to think."

"I never said you were. Potsy, but not you. Things just drop into your lap. Like—"

"Hold it. Not a word. Never mention this conversation to your wife. There are people in the world I don't mind hurting, but Jenny isn't one of them."

They shook hands. As they did, the intercom buzzed again. Joe, curious about the medical crisis that had just occurred, lingered. He could hear Potsy's fast-talking voice issuing from the speaker.

"Kev? I didn't guess wrong anyway. Postmortem revealed the guy had a huge pheochromocytoma in the left adrenal medulla. No wonder he was hypertensive. A shame I didn't get a chance to cut."

"A shame, Potsy."

When the intercom fell silent, Joe said, "Good old Potsy. He sounds sorrier he didn't get the ch-chance to operate than that he lost the guy."

As Joe left, Kevin invited him and Jenny for Sunday brunch. It was always an elegant, hard-drinking affair. Cynthia had picked up the custom at the hunt club back in Morganton. There was a French chef who specialized in omelets. Grilled meats, shrimp dishes, lots of booze. Board chairmen and executive vice-presidents turned red and sweaty, denounced Democrats and welfare recipients, complained about taxes.

Joe refused. Jenny and he had been to one such brunch. Jenny ended up calling the president of a plastics corporation "a lousy fascist." It was not their kind of gathering.

For some time Bridie Derry had been dating Eliot Sparling, the *Newsday* reporter who had covered Mid-Island's hepatitis outbreak. He had never learned the truth any more than he had learned about Sam Felder's sudden dismissal several months later, but he had become friendly with Joe.

A frustrated physician (Sparling's father had been a pharmacist, like Jack), the reporter liked pursuing medical stories. Joe had sent him to Bridie at the Brambier Institute to review new techniques used in handling the emotionally disturbed.

Sparling was stunned when he saw Bridget. She was a singular beauty. Fair-skinned, gray-eyed, with a pinned-up mane of thick red-gold hair. The reporter, an ungainly young man, with a long plain face and close-cropped brown hair, was single and lonely. Despite a glib tongue and a sharp mind, he tended to be awed by attractive women. And Joe Derry's sister was a vision.

They walked across the lawns of the Institute toward the narcotics clinic. Two small boys with Down's syndrome ran to Bridie, held her hands, refused to leave until she had kissed their coarse hair.

"Mongoloids?" Sparling asked.

"We don't use the word. Down's syndrome. They're affectionate kids. They can be trained to do a great deal. I've never seen one of them act mean or angry. We employ them as stock clerks in the shop."

It was late October, the sun brightening the green lawns and trees. A gardener was raking leaves into brown and gold heaps. Two soaring trees with purple-black leaves stood sentry at the gatekeeper's lodge, which housed the narcotics clinic.

"Copper beeches," Sparling said. "One of the man's great cases."

Bridie laughed. "Sherlock Holmes, wise-guy. Don't mess with *me*. I was an English major before I went into nursing."

"Never underestimate the Derrys. They say your older brother will be running Upper County Hospital in a few years. And that Joe. What a pistol."

"A loaded one sometimes."

Inside they joined a group at the conference table—Dr. Kampey, Dr. McGrory, two nurses, and a social worker in a tailored slack suit, pearls and expensive shoes. Dr. Kampey had approved Sparling's presence at the session.

Dr. McGrory read the admitting nurse's report. Kenneth Damelio, sixteen. Working-class family. White male. Unemployed. High IQ. High-school dropout. "He will take anything he can get his hands on," Helen McGrory said. "Methadone, Dilaudid, Tolenol, Valium, cocaine and heroin. He claims he averages fifteen Valiums a day and two bags of heroin. His father runs a private garbage business. The family threw Kenneth out two weeks ago."

Bridie made the connection at once. Her sister-in-law Jenny's cousins. Hard guys. Not quite mafiosi, on the edges.

"Dilaudid?" Dr. Kampey asked. He whistled. *"Doctors* have

trouble getting it. This kid must be a genius."

One of the nurses said, "He is. He's worked every clinic between here and Montauk. He knows every angle. What a line of chatter."

Dr. McGrory filled in Kenny's history. Undersized, thin, rejected in a family of tough characters. He dealt in drugs to support his habit, had been in and out of juvenile courts. Apparently his father had given up on him. The next time he was jugged, Carmine Damelio told the social worker, he'd let the little bastard rot.

Fascinated, Sparling made notes. By no means a hard-hearted man, the reporter was astonished that so much time and attention was given to one troublesome punk.

"Bring him in," Dr. Kampey said.

Kenneth Damelio was splintery thin, sallow, good-looking, with darting black eyes and (as the nurse had warned) a nonstop mouth.

"I'm an addict. The way you're a doctor, and you're a nurse, and you're a social worker. It's my life."

He rattled on. Hospitalized. Treated. Discharged. Mandatory detoxing. Hallucinating. Dealing, popping.

"What is your future, Kenneth?" Dr. McGrory asked.

"I got none. I got a bad self-image. My old man weighs two hundred and ninety-five pounds and can lift the back of a GMC truck himself. I'm a runt, a weakling."

"But you're not stupid," McGrory persisted. "You could finish school and find work. Do you have a girl?"

"I used to. I have sex problems. I masturbate a lot. I have premature ejaculation."

Sparling realized that Kenny was enjoying himself. But when he was dismissed and Dr. Kampey examined the medical data, the doctors were not optimistic about his future. They concluded there had been irreversible brain and neuromuscular damage.

"Keep him on tranquilizers another week and discharge him," Kampey said. He sounded bored.

No one had any other suggestions.

"Can't figure out what a sensational looker like you is doing in this place," Sparling said. Bridie had invited him to lunch in the Institute's cafeteria.

"I love the work."

"But that kid this morning. A dead loss. Don't you get discouraged?"

"I'm a Derry. We come up swinging."

"Like Joe. I wish I could get the story on why he belted some doctor at Mid-Island. I have the idea your older brother bailed him out. Ah well, the city editor didn't care."

"Did you get a story today?"

Sparling wasn't sure. He was appalled by the waste of time and energy on one self-destructive young man.

"They're not *all* like that," Bridie said. "Who knows? He may fool us and go straight."

Sparling preferred to talk about her. He stared at her clean features, radiant skin, and asked if she had ever thought of becoming an actress or a model.

"Too phony," Bridie said. "I like my work. You saw those kids who came up to kiss me? They make it worthwhile. I don't believe in trading on my looks. It isn't fair."

Sparling sensed she had some of Joe's sense of justice. He was convinced he had fallen in love with her, but for the moment he kept the feeling to himself. Instead he asked how all three Derrys had gone into medicine.

Bridie said she herself couldn't figure where the ambition had come from. She told him of Jack's failure, his pointless death. "I guess Kevin set the standard for the rest of us. People trust Kevin," she said, with evident pride. "They want to come to him. He's terrific." She told Sparling how her older brother was pioneering research in "invasive" techniques for cardiac diagnoses, directing a project to determine the relationship between heart disease and diabetes. And his practice was huge, his reputation growing.

They began dating. Sparling told her he was in love with her the first time they sat in Rothman's Inn. They laughed a great deal, found they had mutual friends at Columbia. He was funny, talkative, self-deprecatory. He complimented her endlessly, until, embarrassed, she had to make him stop. He hid his feelings behind a battery of amusing trivia—scenes from Marx Brothers movies, remarks by Dr. Johnson, old Broadway show tunes.

Bridie, after a half-dozen dates, decided she had never known a more engaging man. Yet she could not love him. His repeated requests that she go to bed with him were rejected.

"We have fun, don't we?" Sparling asked. "I mean, we're both terrific people."

"We have fun, Eliot."

"So I'm not Robert Taylor. I'm not even Elisha Cook, Jr. But I'll lose weight. I'll get a nose job. Get my suits at Brooks Brothers. Don't you know I have a great career beckoning?"

Bridie grabbed his hand, kissed his neck. "Oh, dear, you're such a good guy. But, please, *please,* Eliot, don't ask me again. The answer's just no."

Sparling continued to call her, to stop by the apartment she shared with Sue Soslovski, with beer and cold cuts, and take her out as often as she would permit. In return, Bridie rationed her affection. He was permitted a kiss, a hug, a touch of her hand. Sparling often had the sense she was physically stronger than he was, and if he attempted to force the issue, she would handle him the way she managed violent teenagers.

Moreover, Sue, a fat girl who rarely went out, was a convenient impediment to his advances. So long as she was present to make a third at Scrabble, or to watch Milton Berle with them, Eliot's lust was frustrated.

One night, when Sue was visiting her mother in upstate New York, Bridie, in a surge of pity for the adoring young man, let him make love to her.

His ecstasy and his wonderment were of such an overwhelming nature that he failed for about a half hour, muttering apologies.

"You're just trying too hard," Bridie said.

Her clinical attitude shocked him into success. He'd heard this about her older brother Kevin—cool, detached, always in command. And so she was in command of him now. Sex was like an assignment, she seemed to say. You did it properly or not at all. Sparling, rewarded and honored beyond his wildest dreams, believed he had reached the summit of human experience.

"I suppose I should light two cigarettes and give you one," he said afterward. He was fearful of touching her, stroking a firm thigh, the triangle of golden hair. She was a prize that he knew could never be his permanently.

"Only we don't smoke," she said. "You're also supposed to say, 'Was it good for you also?'"

"Well, was it?"

"Sensational." Bridie pulled the sheets up to her neck and smiled at him. "Satisfied?"

"No. I want to marry you. You're the greatest girl in the world." He touched her breasts with infinite gentleness, withdrew his hands. How did this happen? Did he deserve it? Was it possible that a serious clerical error was responsible for his good luck?

"Oh, Eliot, you are a nut, a first-class nut. But I like you."

"Marry me."

"No way. I'm not ready. You make me laugh and you make me feel good, and you're the world's Scrabble champ, but I'm not ready for the split-level house and the kids. It can wait."

"Why? On our two salaries we can live it up. I'm going to start free-lancing for the magazines. The world's ours, Bridie."

"Not yet."

He entered her again, this time more sure of himself. When he came, she patted his back as if consoling a child.

It was a strange Thanksgiving dinner, Meg thought. She did not understand her children at times. At the last minute Kevin had called saying Cynthia and the kids were away, and he wanted the rest of the Derrys to keep him company.

Meg, seated in the vast living room, sipping sherry, recalled Thanksgivings in the old house in Churchport. They were poor but they had happy moments. Kevin and Joe vying for the wishbone. Bridie teasing them, spilling cider, once throwing her cake at Kevin when he called her "pieface."

And Jack. Patient, quiet Jack. Once, the Felders had come. With guests, Jack opened up. All the old jokes from the drugstore were dusted off, paraded at the table.

"Well," Meg could hear her husband saying, "we sure made a monkey out of that turkey."

But this was a different Thanksgiving. They did not understand why Cynthia had chosen to go away. "She couldn't turn down an

207

invitation from the Crists," Kevin said without emotion. Maybe it was his fault, he told his mother, for being a stubborn Irishman. He had been included in the invitation, but he didn't like the North Carolina crowd, and he detested horses. In the last two years Cynthia had developed a passion for meets, jumping exhibitions, shows. She was forever off to rustic places in New Jersey, Westchester, Connecticut.

"They relax me," she had said.

He was a poor psychiatrist, but he wondered about the constant bobbing and thumping on the hard leather. They still made love. But he found, as he grew more passionate, she became increasingly detached.

Joe did not want to attend the Thanksgiving dinner. Jenny, furious with him, had Meg call him and insist that he accept Kevin's invitation. Joe could not hurt her feelings. But he was nurturing a dull anger at his brother.

"Don't say a word, *not one word,*" Jenny said, as they drove to the North Shore in their clanging Ford. "Remember our agreement."

"It's not just that. It's the way he rolls around on ball bearings. I'm spending my l-last rotation in the clinic with welfare cases, and he's curing guys with coronary occlusions. Did you know he's going to start one of the first cardiac-catheterization labs in the area at Upper County? And Manship's lending him the dough to put up a new professional building. Kevin'll be a landlord and collect rent from the other doctors."

Jenny looked at the evergreens, the gray lawns, the Tudor mansions and white rail fences of the North Shore. "Your turn will come, Joey. You'll be in practice next year."

"Yeah. Doing what? I'll never have his touch. Even when his patients die, the family wants to shake his hand. He's no smarter than any other heart man, but he sure gives them a line."

"It's no line. Kevin is sincere and smart."

"You'd know, wouldn't you?"

She punched his shoulder—not in play but in fury. "Dammit, Joe, I warned you."

"Sorry, kid. I'm a rat to you s-sometimes." He put his hand on her thigh. "You know I love you."

When they arrived at Kevin's house, the other guests—Meg,

Bridie, and Bridie's friend Eliot—were there, sipping drinks, sitting around the fireplace.

Kevin was talking to Cynthia on the phone in the study. *"Yes, dear. My best to everyone. Kiss Johnny and Karen. Oh, of course my regards to Jan and Ed. . . ."*

In her shrewd Neapolitan way Jenny knew there was something wrong. Wasn't Ed Crist involved in Cynthia's divorce? Kevin never talked about her North Carolina connections. They were people in a phase of her life he'd locked away.

Kevin hung up and took a drink. Chivas Regal, Joe noticed.

"Everything okay in Tarheel country?" Joe asked.

"Marvelous. The kids are having a ball."

And who is screwing your wife? Jenny wondered. She did not dislike Kevin. She knew him for what he was, and what he would always be—ambitious, lucky, respected, the man no one could refuse. When she smiled at him, he caught the faint derisive glint in her brown eyes. And sometimes he acknowledged it, as if to say, *You're wise to me, Jenny Connetta.*

Sparling, whom Bridie had invited out for the weekend, was telling a story about the last election in East Shinnaway, Jenny's parents' hometown. Sparling had complained to Mayor Parolo that he wasn't offering voters a "balanced ticket."

"He says to me, 'Kid, what could be more balanced? I got a Napolitan', a Sicilian', a Calabrese and a Barese!'"

They all roared. Even Kevin.

"That's like us," Jenny said. "Let us in the front door and we take over the house."

Cynthia's regal cook, Serena, called that dinner was ready. Kevin took his mother's arm and insisted she sit in Cynthia's place at the end of the table, facing him. She refused.

"Oh, I feel out of place in Cynthia's chair," Meg said. "She should be . . ." She broke off and quickly sat where Kevin had asked her to.

Looking around the lordly room, Jenny watched Kevin at the head of the table and thought, *A man in charge of everything but his family.*

As Serena passed the traditional meal, Meg asked if Cynthia would visit little Wells.

Jenny directed a knowing glance at Meg's sad eyes. Both women understood that the child was a convenient excuse for Cynthia's erratic behavior. Jenny was not intolerant, but she knew her sister-in-law. There was a fragile ego there. To Jenny, with her strong sense of family, the flight to North Carolina was an insult to all of them, further proof of Cynthia's instability.

"I'm afraid the medical knowledge about PKU came late for the child," Kevin said. "The restrictive diet, the nutritive regimen." He picked at his turkey. Serena forced him to take huge portions of everything—bird, yams, cranberry sauce, broccoli, sausage stuffing. He had never been much of an eater. Even now he got bored in expensive French restaurants, shoved the wine list away, let Cynthia make the selection.

"You should eat more," Meg said. "Kevin, please don't smoke again."

"It relaxes me."

Bridie had told Sparling about Kevin's fourteen-hour day—at the office, two hospitals, the cardiac clinic, the research projects. Not to mention several hours of teaching every week. He was even being talked of as a candidate for a city office! Health commissioner—a dollar-a-year job overseeing civil servants.

"How's the new batch of students at Mid-Island, Joe?" Kevin asked.

"Not too hot. The sh-sharpies all want to take rotation at P and S, or Mount Sinai. They're nice kids, b-but . . ."

"Dusty must be having fits," Kevin said.

Joe confirmed that he was. "The kids don't seem to care anymore. They just ask about the b-best place to practice. The clinic care is getting worse. The house staff hates working clinics."

Jenny agreed. "Maybe it's different at Upper County. You've got the funds, right?"

Kevin said, "Money helps." He looked at Jenny. "I'm recommending that we hire a full-time physician to do nothing but run clinics."

"Full-time?" Joe asked.

"A chief of ambulatory care. A first-class medical man. We'd pay him enough to make it worthwhile. I know what you mean about house staff detesting clinics. I hated them myself."

"Kevin, that's a sensational idea," Bridie said. "Why hasn't

210

anyone thought of it?" She held her right hand to her mouth, and in comic fashion, pointed with her left index finger at Joe. "Kev, keep it in the family. It's the one job which should satisfy Joe's lust for helping the oppressed."

"Knock it off, Bridie," Joe said. He did not want favors from Kevin.

"I think that's a marvelous idea," Meg said. "Joseph is so kind to people."

"Ma, l-lay off," Joe growled.

Sparling busied himself with his mince pie. Bit of a family strain here. He knew Joe far better than he knew Kevin, and he admired the tough-faced young physician. He was his own man, asked nothing, gave a great deal of himself.

"If Joe had experience in administrative work and a few years of practice under his belt," Kevin said warily, "he'd be considered. Maybe if he'd open an office on the Island he could work his way in."

Jenny took Joe's hand under the table.

"Joseph," Meg asked, "have you decided where you'll practice?"

"I haven't, Ma. Jenny's going to support me, right, Jen?"

"Joe might take a PG course in tropical medicine," Jenny said.

"You have to be kidding," Kevin said. "Why?"

"I don't know. It interests me. Most of those people in the tropics haven't got a chance. Parasites, infections, l-lousy diet."

"You want to be the Irish Schweitzer?" Kevin asked.

"No. But I get fed up with Mid-Island. People are ignored, kicked out of bed, a bunch of guinea pigs for rounds, d-doctors talking about them as if they weren't there."

"Ever see me do that?" Kevin asked.

"I don't mean you or Abe," Joe said. "But there are times when the attendings and the house staff act as if they were doing the patients a favor just looking at them."

After dinner Bridie, Jenny and Eliot played Scrabble. Meg watched a Bette Davis movie on television.

In the study Kevin and Joe faced each other. It seemed a good time for a cigar, Kevin said.

"Better than those butts you inhale," Joe said.

Kevin took two dark Havanas from a humidor. Manship's

personal selection from Dunhill. They nursed them for him in their Fifth Avenue store like incubator babies.

"Christ, it tastes like a ch-chocolate malted," Joe said.

"Good with brandy also. Want a belt?"

"Why not?"

The brothers sipped Remy Martin and let the room fill with blue-gray smoke. Joe's eyes absorbed the rewards of a rich father-in-law and a pleasing personality.

They talked of Joe's future, his interest in the Philippines, his experiences on the reservation. Kevin was concerned. Conditions in Arizona were worse. There was a job waiting for him there.

"If you're hipped on it, Joe, go. But it's a dead end."

"Is it?"

"I don't mean just the financial aspect. You'll get sick of it. Otitis, trachoma."

"Suppose I knocked some of that out? There's a g-guy working on ways of controlling those infections. Would that be a dead end?"

"But that sounds like a research project."

Joe dragged deeply on the cigar. He tried not to let himself envy Kevin. He'd never have a house like Kevin's or a reputation like his.

"And there's something else to think of," Kevin said. "Jenny."

"Tell me."

"She's got a career at Mid-Island. Jenny's odds-on to become chief nurse. If you held the election tomorrow the attendings would make it unanimous. She's a winner, Joe."

"We both know, d-don't we, Kev?"

"Lay off, kid." Kevin put his flannel-clad legs on the desk. Daks. Loafers from some place in New Haven. Argyle socks. Even on a holiday, he breathed power and success.

"I'm aware of it," Joe said glumly. "What the hell, Jenny'll do what I want. They could use her out th-there also."

"She'll do it because she loves you, Joe. But maybe she's got other priorities. She's got a career to think of. Why confuse the issue by dragging her to Arizona?"

"I don't know why."

Kevin leveled his cigar at his brother. "You're afraid of practice. What's scaring you? Me? You open an office in East Shinnaway or Cohammet, hell, in Churchport, and you'll be running a money

212

machine in a few years. Call yourself an internist and charge double. I'll see to it people get to know you."

Joe smiled. "Like DeBeers?"

"So what? We all make enemies. Take my advice. Stay here. Keep it a family affair. We might share an office someday."

Trying to be kind to the family loser, Joe thought. Or making amends for what he had done to Jenny. No, he would not be critical of Kevin. Kevin wanted him to succeed.

They talked medicine for a while. A patient of Joe's with acute tubular necrosis of the kidneys. The patient had been rushed into the intensive-care unit in septic shock. In minutes he might have suffered acute kidney failure.

Joe had acted quickly and saved the man's life. Knowing that he was dehydrated, he'd ordered saline intravenously, measured his central venous pressure. The patient was turning gray when they put him in the ICU. But loaded with saline solution, he'd come around.

"No attending around?" Kevin asked. He was impressed with Joe. In his stolid, self-effacing way, he was becoming a first-rate medical man. Max Landeck had said so, and Max knew.

"At three A.M.?"

Kevin swiveled his legs from the desk. "You know, I owe you an apology, Joe. I never thought you'd make it. I tip the O'Connor to you."

Joe hunched up his shoulders. "C-can it, Kevin."

Outside the wind swirled the last leaves across the lawn.

"Beautiful woman, isn't she?" Kevin asked suddenly, pointing to the photograph of Cynthia on his desk.

"Knockout."

Kevin got up. "E.E. says he couldn't handle her when she was a kid. I'm not doing much better."

Joe said nothing.

"She's fucking Ed Crist. This is her fifth trip down there in the last half year or so. The Morganton Hunt. Tally-ho, you son of a bitch."

"Get r-rid of her," Joe said.

"I can't. She comes back crying. She's sorry. She can't help it. She doesn't love him; she loves me."

Joe thought of the world in which Cynthia and her friends lived.

Screwing the husband of your dearest friend? In *their* house? The garbage-collecting Damelios behaved more decently.

"Get rid of her," Joe repeated. "She's going to screw up your life."

He shook his head and looked into his brother's eyes. "Nobody screws me up, Joe."

Joe raised his brandy snifter. "Good luck, buddy."

Bridie walked into the room to ask them to join the Scrabble game. "Kevin, come on. You're good at games."

Kevin put an arm around her. Following his brother and sister into the living room, Joe thought to himself, *You sure are.*

PART FOUR
1962

1

Joe Derry, his two-year-old son Nicky on his lap, was watching the seven o'clock news on television.

"Three times around the earth and a safe splashdown into the Atlantic at two-forty-three P.M., February twentieth, 1962."

Nicky was not impressed. He wanted cartoons. He should have been asleep. But his mother was working late. The baby spent the day with his grandmother, Carmela Connetta, but Jenny usually was able to get home for dinner. She sometimes thought of taking a year off, but they needed the money. Joe's practice was small, a GP in a sea of specialists. He was as he had always been—truthful, slow to make a decision, reluctant to force patients into expensive diagnostic procedures.

"Wan' Yogi Bear, Dad."

"He's not on now, Nicky."

"Change pitcha."

The boy—dark, chubby, a true Neapolitan—struggled from his father's lap. In bottom-heavy Doctor Dentons, he waddled to the TV set. *Christ,* Joe thought, *the kid knows more about television cartoons than he does about me, or his mother.* Joe pulled him back, kissed him to halt his whining.

An image of President Kennedy congratulating John Glenn flashed on the screen. Joe tried to explain the significance of the event to Nicky but was interrupted by the phone.

"Doc? Paulie Damelio. You gotta get here. Kenny's been stabbed. He's in the parking lot behind the supermarket."

"Carmine's son?"

"He was workin' on the truck. Some son of a bitch from Ravetta's gang done it. He's bleedin' like he's gonna die."

"Did you call for an ambulance?"

"Yeah. We're still waitin'. Carmine says he'll kill every cock-sucker in the Ravetta mob if Kenny dies."

Paulie gave Joe the address. It was the Fox Swamp Shopping Center, in back of a supermarket. Joe knew he could beat the ambulance there. Mid-Island's service had been declining. Dusty Rhodes had retired. DeBeers, his replacement as director of medicine, was a loser.

Joe wrapped a blanket around Nicky. He'd done this before in emergencies, trundling the good-natured kid next door where his neighbor, Mrs. Rackowski, and her daughter were only too glad to fuss over him.

"Do me a favor, Mrs. Rackowski," Joe called. "Phone my wife at Mid-Island Hospital so she'll know where Nicky is."

He drove through the development of identical Cape Cods, and sped onto the four-lane highway.

"Bleedin' like he's gonna die," Paulie had said. For some months, Jenny had heard that her cousins were feuding with a new family, the Ravettas, who were trying to muscle in on their routes. The Ravettas were "wise-guys" who had mob connections. They cleaned out their opposition through threats, and, if necessary, killing. The Damelios, tough as they were, did not kill.

There were four police cars, red lights flashing, in the lot where the stabbing had occurred. Mounds of dirty snow remained piled at the edges of the lot. As soon as Joe leaped from the car with his bag, he heard the Klaxon of Mid-Island's ambulance. A tie. Not bad for the old dump.

"Ay, Doc, over here," Paulie shouted. He grabbed Joe's arm and dragged him to the side of a green Damelio Cartage truck. They'd put a blanket under Kenny, another on top of him. The boy's small angular face—Joe knew about him through Bridie—was chalky pale. He appeared in shock.

Carmine was weeping. "The kid was just gettin' straight. We had him workin'; we had him innarested. If I catch the bastards done this to him, I'll tear their balls off!"

Joe lifted the blanket. The EMT, Ed Riley, hurried alongside.

218

Matt Cross and another orderly were unloading the stretcher. The police were questioning Paulie and Tony, who had been working the truck with Kenny.

A reporter and a photographer from *Newsday* appeared. Joe, studying Kenny's chest under the glow of a police flashlight, could hear the newsmen talking to the cops and the supermarket manager. *"Mob war . . . Mafia . . . I never had any trouble with Mr. Damelio . . . Terrible, it happened so fast. . . ."*

There was a crimson stain on Kenny's plaid shirt. But it seemed to be drying. Gingerly Joe lifted the shirt, then the bloodier undershirt.

He and Riley studied the boy's chest. How old was Kenny? Twenty? Joe remembered Bridie's stories of him—the runt of the family, the kid who ate sixteen valiums a day, washed them down with heroin.

Joe examined the knife wound below the breastbone. The cut was about an inch wide. How deep? He'd bet it had struck the wall of the heart. The dark fluid was issuing forth on each systolic contraction.

"He's bleedin' bad, Doc," Riley said.

"It looks like a transmural wound. That's why we're getting blood only on the systole. He can hang on for hours if he isn't agitated. I'll meet you in the emergency room."

A caravan of raging Damelios, led by two green garbage trucks, took after Joe's Ford. Paulie Damelio, one of the more articulate members of the brotherhood, rode with Joe and told him what had happened.

They were making their nightly pickup at the supermarket and the adjoining stores—Hi-Fashion, Von Ice-Cream Parlor, The Hobby Shoppy—when the Ravetta truck pulled up. The bastards were looking for trouble.

The Ravettas claimed they had bought rights to pickup in the shopping center. If the Damelios knew what was good for them, they'd clear out.

As Ravetta and his monster of a partner punched and shoved Paulie and Tony, Kenny had crept out of the cab and slid over to the competitor's orange truck.

On the seat of the cab Kenny saw Danny Ravetta's blue cashmere sweater. Even when he collected garbage, he dressed like a dude. While Ravetta and his goon kept threatening Tony and Paulie, Kenny nailed Ravetta's sweater to the Hi-Fashion Ladies Shop, then drove the last nails into the front tires of the Ravetta truck.

"Fuck's goin' on?" Ravetta cried. He had heard the pounding of nails, the hissing of escaping air.

Enraged, Danny and his partner descended on Kenny and began to beat him. Tony and Paulie ran to his rescue. They were giving as good as they were getting, when Ravetta's partner rammed the knife into Kenny's chest.

"This cocksucker rams the shiv into Kenny, pulls it out, and the two of them drive off in that fucking orange truck, the front wheels ridin' on the rims. Me and Tony was gonna go after them, but we figured Kenny was dyin'. Has he got a chance, Doc?"

"I think so, Paulie."

"Poor kid. For once't he was in a legitimate business and look what happens."

While a dozen Damelios waited outside in angry silence, the trauma surgeon, Dr. Gertz, worked on Kenny's heart. Joe scrubbed and went in to watch.

Gertz was precise, cool, undramatic.

"Lucky," he said finally. "Rip in the pericardium let the blood in the right ventricle escape into the thoracic cavity. He'll be walking around in a few days."

In the scrubbing room, Joe asked about postoperative maintenance. Gertz told him to keep an eye out for disrhythmias and bloodclots. The slow bleeding had saved him. "You know the kid?"

"My wife's cousin. And Angela Connetta's."

Dr. Gertz nodded, indifferent. Outside, the Damelios mobbed him, thanking him a thousand times. Carmine promised to pick up his garbage free, wreck an old car for him, rough up anyone who gave him a bad time.

Late that night Joe retrieved a sleeping Nicky. He and Jenny, too stimulated to go to bed, watched a late movie. Errol Flynn in *Charge of the Light Brigade*.

"Some family you married into," Jenny said.

"No complaints."

"I could tell. When they started suffocating Gertz, you wanted to die. Knife fights. Garbage wars."

Joe shook his head. "Not true. You read things into me sometimes."

"Then what is it? You've been too quiet," she said, sitting on his lap.

Through the purple flannel robe, he felt her soft body. A man had to be on good behavior with her, cheerful, upbeat. She did not demand this consciously. But one had no choice when confronted by her wide eyes, the happy face of a woman who found joy every day of her life.

"Watching Gertz, I guess. Smart, quick, knowing what he's doing."

"You never wanted to be a surgeon."

"I feel useless. Listening to old guys with shortness of breath, neurotic kids, housewives with pains in the womb, all the cases that specialists don't want. Had a guy in the other day who was convinced he was dying. The jerk was OD'ing on vitamins. I remembered Sam Felder had a case like it once. 'Stop eating all that crap and your fever will clear up,' I said."

"Did it?"

"Sure. From a high fever to normal temp in three days, as soon as the vitamins got out of his system."

"So? You did something good."

Joe ran a tender hand along her thigh. "It's not enough, Jen. Want to know the truth? I was happy in Arizona with those kids with ringworm. When I was a medic in Asia I felt worthwhile. I feel like a jerk now."

"You're saying it's my fault. I kept you here. In a split-level house, with a baby, my job. Right, Joey?"

He kissed her. They heard Nicky turning in his crib, sniffling. He always had a clogged nose, a cough, in the winter months. Maybe Arizona wasn't such a bad idea, Jenny thought.

"My practice doesn't just bore me," said Joe. "It isn't going anywhere."

"You marry a cop's daughter, you don't get the fancy office and the society practice. Joe, that doesn't sound like you. Since when were you so greedy for money?"

221

"I'm not. You don't understand, Jen. I feel useless. Some guys can be useless and haul in the money and that's enough for them. Others get a big charge out of what they do, and it doesn't matter if they get rich or not. Kevin's lucky. He's got it both ways."

"Nuts to Kevin. I'm sick of hearing about him. He's like a monkey on your back."

She turned off the television and they went to bed in silence. But the next day when she was putting together their Christmas-card list she took out the card they had received the previous year from Na Bong, the tribal chief. It showed a Batati family in a cart drawn by buffalo.

Jenny propped the card on the mantel and left it there.

Joe wasn't the only one restless in his practice. Kevin was finding that the excellence of the house staff at Upper County was robbing him of his most exciting cases.

"I enjoy teaching these bright kids," he told Abe Gold one day, "but sometimes I envy the time they get to put into a case."

"I know," said Abe. "That's why we try to treat as many patients as possible in the group. We put in all the diagnostic equipment. We even do minor surgery."

The "we" to which Abe referred was his year-old corporation, Cohammet Medical Group. He and five other physicians with different specialties had pioneered one of the first medical groups on the Island. With the ability to provide medical, surgical, obstetrical and pediatric care the group could service a whole community's needs without referring to an outside doctor. Now Abe was expanding to encompass more medical subspecialties.

The concept intrigued Kevin. To learn more about it he insisted that Cynthia invite the Golds to a dinner party. Barbara Gold, talkative and a bit flashy, was not Cynthia's cup of tea, but she could hold her own surprisingly well in any group. She went to the ballet and the opera, was a force in the League of Women Voters, and to Cynthia's astonishment revealed that she had ridden in jumping competitions when she was ten, but that horses now meant nothing to her.

The meal went smoothly. In addition to the Golds, Cynthia had invited one of her father's junior partners, a couple who seemed to do nothing but go on safari, and a third couple who collected art and artists. But when coffee was served, Kevin, bored by small talk, asked Abe to join him in the study.

After lighting a cigar, he began to pump Abe about his group. Abe smiled to himself, realizing Kevin's intentions, but not minding. He and his partners were doing too well to fear competition. Besides, Kevin was an old friend. He was describing the specialty breakdown when Cynthia walked in.

She was wearing a magnificent Indian silk gown, but Abe thought she looked thin and tense. "An insecure, sensual and secretive woman," Abe had told his wife.

"A snob," Barbara had replied. "And she doesn't like us either."

Abe greeted her gently. "That's a gorgeous gown. And no one can wear it the way you can, Cynthia. You really have—what do the kids call it?—pizazz."

Kevin could hear the guests discussing civil-rights demonstrations in the South. A man's loud voice was asking why no one had taken the trouble to "knock off" both Kennedys. Save the country a lot of trouble.

Abe fidgeted. He arched his eyebrows at Kevin. Noticing, Cynthia offered Dr. Gold her most disarming smile. "Ignore them, Abe. Barbara and I and DeeDee Dorsett are starting a bridge game. Do you want to make a fourth?"

Kevin did not play. Moreover, he found it increasingly difficult to be with Cynthia for long periods of time. The scent, the flesh, the beauty, had lost their attractions. She was like a picture, a cutout.

"Well . . . if you need me," Dr. Gold said.

"Oh, come on. It's no fun—four hens. Or having to listen to Dorsett expound on the need for another Hoover. He'll shut up if you're at the table." There was the unspoken suggestion that in her house people watched themselves in front of liberal Jews.

Abe looked to Kevin for guidance. He knew Kevin wanted to talk, but he was taken aback by the asperity in his voice. "I have things to discuss with Abe. Ask someone else to make a fourth."

Abe shrugged helplessly.

"Go on, Cynthia," Kevin said. "Play three-handed if you have to. Abe and I want to talk." He had all but said "Beat it."

"Try making your own guest list next time," she said.

She stalked out, but left the door open. Abe listened for Barbara's voice. Poor baby. Alone with that group of terrifying *goyim.*

As if divining Abe's mind, Kevin said, "Barbara'll do fine, Abe. Those people don't make anti-Semitic cracks anymore. At least not here."

"Kevin, old buddy, when I pulled into your driveway in my El Dorado, I heard one of the arriving guests comment that I was driving a 'kosher canoe.' His Imperial was longer than my Cadillac."

"Probably Dorsett. Inbreeding has shriveled his brain."

Kevin lit up again and turned the conversation back to Abe's group.

"Does the group have a head or senior physician?" Kevin leaned forward. He had always been a good listener . . . patient, involved, intense.

"You're looking at him." Abe was pleased to talk. It had been years since they'd had an old-fashioned session the way they used to when they were in training.

Abe's group was incorporated, paying a salary to each of the six members. Profits were divided evenly. Although officially its head, Abe insisted they all be paid the same.

"The fact is, Kev," Gold said, "I could make more on my own. But why kill myself? This is so much better, so much smarter. First, personal freedom. We get time off. There's a duty roster. So-and-so covers this weekend. I cover next weekend. Landeck has night duty Thursdays, Kaplan on Friday, and so on."

"You say you could make more on your own? That's hard for me to believe."

"Well, a real plugger, a man with a huge practice—"

"Like me?"

"I'm not in your class, Kevin. But even if an individual nets more, he can lay away a fortune in pension plans and benefits. I'd say that in twenty-five years every man in my group will have a retirement fund worth over a million dollars. Of course, that's no problem to you."

Abe went on to describe how he had put the group together, beginning with Max Landeck.

"I weeded out hustlers right off," Abe said. "Any guy who wanted to know how much he'd make in the first year was dismissed

224

out of hand. Most of them liked the area—good schools, good shopping, near New York. I found out a funny thing. I had to please the wives more than the men."

Everything Abe told him Kevin filed in his orderly mind. A group meant hiring a lawyer, an office manager, an accountant. All of these specialists charged more for the professional corporation than they billed individual physicians. The office staff had to be a large one—nurses, receptionists, technicians.

"Of course, Kev, you realize we're taxed *twice.* But it still comes out better for us in terms of benefits and free time. I'll have our accountant call if you wish."

"If you were to give a man starting a group some advice," said Kevin, "what's the most important thing you'd tell him?"

"Don't hire geniuses. Just noncomplainers."

"You've changed, Abe."

"Who hasn't?"

Cynthia, her hair glistening, stood in the doorway of Kevin's bedroom. She knew when she excited men. Dorsett had been giving her the knee all night, suggested they meet some weekend.

"Interested?" she asked Kevin.

He was sitting up in bed, rimless glasses on, reading a paper on open-heart surgery. Beside him was a yellow pad on which he made notes. *The surgery of the future.* Potsy Luff was going in for it with all his nerve, his charm, his street-smart aggressiveness. He had taken a year off to study in Cleveland. Potsy figured strongly in Kevin's view of the future.

"You look marvelous, Cynthia."

"If I found a red and white peppermint-striped bathing suit and bent over would it change things?" She sounded curious rather than plaintive.

She walked to the bed and sat beside him. The tensor lamp on the bed table sharpened the angles and planes of her long face. *She doesn't look like the woman I married.* Kevin thought.

"I've made my mind up to reform. Just the way I stopped drinking."

"I haven't asked you to."

"No, you never asked, never said a word, never harangued me

225

about those trips south. Just moved out of the bedroom and stopped making love to me. Not even a kiss, a pat, a caress. You knew everything, didn't you?"

Kevin found it hard to hate her. In fact, it was becoming more and more difficult to regard her with any kind of emotion.

She put a strong hand on the booklet he was reading, bent it away from him. "More machines? More techniques?"

"My work's never interested you. I like you better when you're honest."

"Then make love to me." She lowered her golden head on his chest. He let his right hand travel down her flank.

"Ed Crist called two days ago," she said. "I told him to go to hell. Kevin, I can't explain why I did it. He's a dreadful man."

"But he must offer you something I don't."

"No, no. I hate myself when I'm with him. But I have to . . . have to . . . to prove . . . ever since Wells stopped and then you stopped . . . as if I were a leper, a carrier of a disease. . . ."

"Get it right, Cynthia. If you were a junior medical clerk presenting a case, I'd bawl you out. 'Chronology, please,' as Abe would say. I stopped only after you started those trips south."

She raised her head. Her eyes were dry, flat. How easily she managed it all! Screwing left no scars on her. The beautiful, leggy woman survived on the surface at least. Whosoever entered was soon forgotten, dissolved, rendered as evanescent as a sigh.

"You don't look like a tortured woman," Kevin said. "Have you any idea what it did to me?"

"Kevin darling, you're *strong*. Nothing hurts you. You're smart. Good at what you do. And you love our children. I wish I loved them more than I do."

"Spend time with them. I'll spread the guilt around if you want. Sometimes I go a week without seeing Johnny. Maybe the kid would be better off in a boarding school than with us. And Karen—she thinks Miss Vessels is her mother and father."

"You have an excuse. You're busy all the time."

She put her hand under the blanket, moved it through his robe and into the fly of his silk pajamas. In seconds she had made him hard.

"Crazy, isn't it?" she asked, smiling at him.

"What is?"

226

"I got hot tonight looking at the way the Golds are with each other. He can't keep his hands off her. Barbara loves it. Those two ugly people. Why can't we be as affectionate as they are?"

He tried to remove her stroking hand but she would not let him. "You sure it wasn't Dorsett's knee that gave you these ideas?"

"No. Kevin, we should be more than two people who go to dinners together or spend a month at Churchport Beach. Why aren't we more of a family? Where's all that togetherness?"

"Largely in women's magazines." But this time when she touched his body, he moved closer to her. Sex could appease the hurt of unfaithfulness and undo (if temporarily) the coldness of selfishness, he decided.

"Please make love to me, Kevin. The way we did when we were kids. Before . . ."

She nestled close to him. There was a weakness, a vulnerability, in her that demanded sympathy. She was not unintelligent or insensitive. Maybe he had been to blame—a man devoured by a fourteen-hour work day.

"Oh, Kevin, love me. I promise I won't be rotten. I watched Abe and Barbara Gold and I was jealous. The way they adore each other."

"Abe knows when he's got a good thing. I like Barbara too. She's warm, and bright, and she's involved."

"And I'm not? Kevin, I can change. If you stop loving me, I'll drink, I'll starve myself. You don't know how strong you are, how you give people confidence. I see it with your patients. I saw the way Abe played up to you tonight—he told you everything in the world about group practice, and he won't even care when you start your group. People need your approval. I need it, darling."

Kevin solemnly opened her robe to reveal the burnished, healthy limbs. "You know me, Cynthia. Maybe better than I know you. Let's give it a try. We're healthy, rich; we have great kids. I want it to work."

They made love like trained athletes, coordinated, agile. She seemed more aroused than usual, and when they were done, she locked her arms around his back and would not let him leave.

She talked about a trip to Arizona her father was planning in a week—land deals, investments, horseback riding, tennis. They were invited.

Kevin disengaged her arms and sat naked at the edge of the bed.

"I can't, Cynthia. Too much on the schedule. You go."

"It's no fun without you."

"I know. I'm sorry."

She kissed his back, caressed his neck. "Do you like me again? Do you really want me? I promise I won't do dreadful things, ever again. I promise."

"I know, Cynthia. I believe you." He turned, kissed her, but he could not make love to her again. After she took two nembutals and fell into a drugged sleep, he went to his own room, read for several hours, slept fitfully.

2

"I'm a fly," the young man said.

"Swell," Bridie said. "Horse or dragon?"

The patient was a pale, thin man in his twenties named Drake. His golden hair was disheveled. He was on all fours, crawling about the narcotics clinic.

"Who told you you're a fly?" Bridie asked.

"I know I am." He crawled under a table. He rubbed his hands together in flickering movements.

"You see," Drake said, "I'm on the ceiling, and if I move too quickly, I'll fall off. Can't you understand? I'm upside down."

Drake's wife, Melinda, was seated against the wall in semitrance. Her legs were pulled against her chest. Her arms were locked around her bony knees.

"He *is* a fly," she whispered. "And I'm a bug on the wall."

"What's your husband's first name?" Bridie asked, with annoyance. At age thirty, single, with six years of psychiatric nursing behind her, she had found that a no-nonsense approach was best.

"Well, it was Jody," Melinda whispered. "But I think he's changed it. We've all changed." Her voice became a moan. "I'm part of the wall. Please help me. I'm in the wall. The two of you . . . please . . . *please.* . . .

Jody Drake settled against a filing cabinet and muttered, "There. That's enough. The spider can't catch me here."

Five minutes later Bridie terminated the interview. It was impossible to get through to these kids who had freaked out on LSD.

Helen McGrory came in to survey the new patients.

"How many does this make this month?"

"They're numbers eighteen and nineteen."

"Someone's spreading a great deal of that poison around," Dr. McGrory said. "Notice, Bridget, these are all educated people. It's an upper-middle-class phenomenon."

Drake curled into a fetal position alongside the cabinet. He was babbling about new insights into the world, the soul, the human condition. "I've found eternal peace. I know the meaning of life and I'm ready to impart it to everyone. Oh, if only they would listen."

"We hear you, buddy," Bridie said.

"He really knows. He knows. He *knows.*" Melinda rocked back and forth on the chair.

Incredible, Bridie thought. Son of a bank vice-president in Short Hills, New Jersey. Blair Academy. In the fourteen hundreds on his college boards. Yale. Public-relations firm. Enjoyed chess, skiing, cooking. They had started dropping acid at a party. A Harvard instructor had been present and had lectured on its virtues. He had promised that it would relieve anxiety, expand their consciousness.

"Who was this jerk?" Bridie asked.

"We don't have his name yet," McGrory said. "But he should be in jail."

"Please take me out of the wall," Melinda whimpered. "Please, I'm locked into these bricks."

"Try climbing," Bridie said under her breath.

Dr. McGrory looked at her with a mixture of disapproval and understanding. Sometimes she wondered if Bridget Derry was happy in her work. It was no secret that the girl had talked about quitting. The LSD outbreak was the latest in a series of depressing events that had left her feeling useless.

"Have we had *any* evidence that it helps people at all?" Bridie asked.

McGrory pursed her lips. "We've had five cases of prolonged psychosis after a single ingestion of LSD. As for multiple-ingestion cases, there's usually steady deterioration of personality. Instead of being able to function better, they suffer depersonalization. Symptoms recur. We aren't sure why."

"Oh, boy. And we have Harvard to thank for this. Is there anything we can do for them?"

230

"The usual," Dr. McGrory said. "Barbiturates to relieve anxiety and panic. And hope that the condition isn't prolonged."

"My body's disappearing," Melinda wailed. "I have no body anymore. Jody, where are you?"

McGrory nodded at Bridie. "Bridget, take them to the ward. Tell the orderlies to keep a sharp eye on them."

Bridie dragged the girl to her feet. "Come on, kid," she said. "How about a nice Fudgicle? You too, Jody baby. Up and at 'em."

"I'm all *mind*," Melinda said. "Help me."

"That's my intention."

Drake grabbed the leg of the desk. Bridie unclenched his fist. As if handling a toy, she yanked him up. She had Joe Derry's hidden strength. No wasted movements, no clumsiness.

With an LSD victim on each arm, Bridie left. "Now, aren't we a dandy group?" she asked.

The girl rested her head on Bridie's shoulder. "It's the oneness and suchness," she whimpered. But she did not resist. When Bridie asked patients to do something, they usually gave in.

Three days later Eliot Sparling arrived at the Institute with a camera crew from United Broadcasting. He had left *Newsday* ten months earlier to join the news staff of UBC in New York. The story on LSD, as related to him by Bridie, sounded interesting.

Sparling set up his cameras on the lawn of the Institute. It was a glorious October day. From an open window, the strains of a record player drifted out.

> *"This land is your land,*
> *This land is my land,*
> *From California, to the New York Island. . . ."*©

"That's what you think," Sparling said. "Bridie, can we have them either close the window or turn that thing off?"

He watched her, his heart (as always) beating desperately, as she walked to the dormitory window and called to a microcephalic boy. The boy issued guttural sounds, then closed the window. He waved, smiled through the glass.

231

They all love her, Sparling thought. As I do. But Bridie still rationed her time with Sparling, choosing the time and place for each of their encounters. Dazed by her beauty, he repeatedly asked her to marry him. Finally she warned him that one more proposal would terminate the affair.

And so Eliot remained grateful for favors, waiting for the day she might consent. And wondering if he could ever be man enough to satisfy her if they were married. She was getting bored with the Institute, the need to give continually to the maimed and limited, the outcasts. *I'm like one of them,* Sparling thought, as the camera was set up. *She knows I'm not strong enough for her.*

Sparling sat opposite the LSD-soaked couple. Bridie sat to his right, so the camera could move around and get her responses. She would later be filmed in close-up, giving the same answers or additional comments.

Dr. Kampey paced about, dropping suggestions. Why not in his office? Why not let him conduct a tour of the Institute?

"Yeah, later, Doc," Sparling said. "Okay, we're rolling."

Sparling addressed the young woman. "Mrs. D., tell us why you started taking LSD."

Brushing back a strand of hair, she said, "My husband said it would relax me sexually and expand my spiritual frontiers. A week ago I took two hundred micrograms and a half hour later I noticed the bricks coming out of the wall, forming a wall around me. The light was bothering me; it was around me, and in me, and everything I heard was very loud, almost like explosions. . . ."

Sparling thought, *Baby, it was the sound of the world coming apart. Yours and mine.*

Sparling was almost finished with the interview when a call came from the New York office. He put down the phone, subdued. "We're going to have to cut this short. Kennedy's thrown a blockade on Cuba. We may have a war tomorrow over those Russian missiles. LSD won't help."

He wrapped up quickly, stopped to give Bridie a kiss. "You were sensational, honey. Hope we can use this next week. But *war!* Maybe those creeps dropping acid have the right idea. Run away from everything."

* * *

232

Joe Derry heard the news bulletin in his office and wondered about reenlisting. He hated the army, but he had found a strange serenity there. Do your job, keep your nose clean, take your monthly paycheck. Then he dismissed the notion. Jenny would have a fit. There was Nicky to look after. The army would take one look at his record and laugh him out of the recruitment office.

The truth was, he was disappointed in his career, full of doubts about the profession. Financially, he was a bust. The better class of patients were flocking to the medical groups.

"You've got to learn, kid," Kevin told Joe. "They *want* to be coddled. You tell these people there's nothing wrong with them, and they go away sore. They'll keep trying doctors until they find one who'll put them on a medical-maintenance program and shove them under machines. Then they'll be happy."

"I can't do it, Kevin."

"Try. I do it every day."

"No you don't. There's something new in cardiology every month. I watched you run that cath lab. It's important work. You know your stuff."

Joe recalled the conversation as he assured Mrs. Minter for the sixth time that she had no heart problem.

"All tests are negative," he said wearily. The consulting room was small and plain. The office was attached to their split-level house—a converted garage, an extra wing.

"But the pain, Dr. Derry."

"I told you. It's a condition called a hiatus hernia and it has nothing to do with your heart."

After she left, he remembered the disappointment on her face. She'd wanted to be found ill, a woman truly suffering. But this blunt-faced young doctor wasn't any help. No wonder the waiting room was almost empty. Just a black woman with a snot-nosed kid on her lap.

Joe knew her, the wife of one of the workmen who'd converted the garage into an office. "Come in, Mrs. Hudson," he said.

Blacks were easier to take than the middle class. They had legitimate illnesses and they complained a lot less. Joe suspected little Eric had sickle-cell anemia—a widespread disease among blacks, maybe one case in every five hundred births. He could offer small cheer to Mrs. Hudson. The laboratory tests were in, confirming Joe's diagnosis.

Little was being done about it. A black disease. Let them look for help. No one really understood it.

Joe put Eric on his lap. The boy's skin had a bluish cast. Joe thought, *I should have caught this earlier.* Cardiac involvement. It was not uncommon in sickle-cell anemia. He stared at Eric's fingers and noticed the clubbing, the typical bulbous enlargement of the tips.

I'm a hell of a diagnostician, he thought.

"How does he look, Doctor?" Mrs. Hudson asked.

"Fine, fine."

He made a note. A full cardiac workup for Eric with Kevin. Congenital heart ailments and sickle-cell disease sometimes went together. He was disgusted with his own inadequacies, saddened by the limitations placed on the child's life. He asked Mrs. Hudson to undress the frightened child. Eric began to weep.

Not much hope, Joe knew. Kevin would look the boy over and in his suave way would have good news for her—maybe an operation, a course of treatment, new medication (all bullshit, Joe felt), and Eric would be healthy.

Joe charged Mrs. Hudson five dollars for the office visit. He felt guilty taking her money.

At the hospital, Jenny stopped him at the nurses' island. A haggard-looking man and woman in their fifties were standing to one side. The man looked familiar. Both looked stricken, terrified. The man was trying to get information from an intern who was playing the I-don't-know game. Joe could guess. There'd been a death. Nobody wanted to talk, not this soon anyway.

"It's a bad one," Jenny said. "One of our new wonder boys, Benton Graubart. You had him as a resident. One of his patients died two hours ago in the ICU."

"Family?" He indicated the couple. The woman was sniffling into a handkerchief.

"Parents. Woman named Olga Kelchak. Pernicious anemia."

Joe rubbed his nose. "Kelchak. I thought I recognized him. They were my patients. I made the diagnosis on the girl a year ago. Before Graubart grabbed the family away. How'd she die?"

"M-I-F-U."

"Mid-Island Fuck-Up," Joe said. "But how?"

"Graubart had her admitted for observation when her red blood count dropped. Single, twenty-five, pale as a ghost. The night resident, some genius from Uruguay, swears Graubart ordered transfusions. Graubart denies it. He's lying. One of my nurses heard him."

"Nothing wrong with that. You transfuse people with anemia."

Jenny's eyes turned to round brown discs. "Not before you draw off their own blood."

Joe frowned. "You mean to tell me they gave the girl blood without drawing off her own blood first?"

"The resident swears he got no instructions from Graubart. Graubart claims he didn't order the transfusions, that he merely discussed it."

At once Joe realized what had killed the woman. She had OD'd on blood. Her system had been overloaded with fluids which put a fatal strain on the circulatory system.

Mr. Kelchak, cap in hand, shuffled over to Joe. "Ain't you Dr. Derry? What happened? How'd Olga die?"

"It wasn't my case, Mr. Kelchak."

"Where's Dr. Graubart?"

Jenny said, "He's in conference, Mr. Kelchak. Why don't you and your wife wait in the family room?"

"It's been two hours almost. Not a word. Our daughter's dead and not a word."

The Kelchaks walked away—people in a trance.

Fifteen minutes later Dr. Graubart rounded the corner, talking agitatedly with Dr. DeBeers.

"What are they giving as the cause of death?" Joe asked Jenny.

"Cardiac arrhythmias."

"Beautiful. I'll give you seven to two nobody lays a glove on Graubart. Didn't he come over when she went into the ICU?"

"She was finished by then. The resident says it was irreversible."

Joe walked past the lounge. He got a glimpse of the parents talking to DeBeers, who was sitting, stiff in his white coat, hands covering his mouth. Dr. Graubart was leaning forward, slender and handsome in a vested Oxford-gray suit, pink shirt, charcoal-gray tie. His tanned face flashed a smile that was all confidence.

"Unquestionably heart failure, Mrs. Kelchak. Olga's heart could not work any harder than it did, given the lack of oxygen and red blood corpuscles. We tried. I came out immediately when I heard how sick she was. But sometimes it's better . . ."

And they were buying it. Not a word about the misapplied transfusions, the foul-up when Olga's body was filled with fluids it could not handle.

"Congestive heart failure," Graubart was saying. "Then the poor girl went into shock. . . ."

Shock, my ass, Joe thought angrily. Maybe he was in the wrong profession. Maybe it belonged to the Benton Graubarts and the Potsy Luffs.

Kevin's brother-in-law, Burton Maxwell (Buzzy) Manship, had returned from Paris for his first New York showing. His father had promised a leading art dealer that he would guarantee the purchase of every painting Buzzy displayed.

"How nice for all concerned!" Cynthia remarked caustically. She was not a great admirer of her brother. Kevin suspected it was because Buzzy had done precisely what he wanted to do—gone off to Paris, married a French girl, and pursued a "career" in the arts. Cynthia looked back wistfully at her brief tenure as a "public-relations gal" at CBS.

She looked dazzling for the showing—golden hair pulled back, face brilliantly made up. She wore a gray vicuna cape, a long black skirt, black crocodile boots. "A New Yorky crowd," she said to Kevin as they entered. "Very trendy."

The gallery was owned by a wealthy young Greek, Mr. Pirounakis. He was reed-thin and honey-skinned, with a child's hands and feet. He kissed Cynthia's hand and bowed to Kevin.

Potsy, followed by Rosemary, sneaked behind Kevin, gave Dr. Derry a discreet goose. Rosie looked reasonably sober but a bit out of sorts with the art lovers.

"Who's the bravest man in the world, Kev?" Potsy asked.

"Give up."

"Center on a Greek football team." He shook hands with Mr. Pirounakis.

Potsy waxed eloquent, cultured, manifesting an interest in ballet and sculpture. Rosemary remained mute. The six pregnancies had

236

dulled her. She turned out kids, Potsy confided, the way an A. B. Dick machine ran off mimeo sheets.

They wandered amid Buzzy's enormous paintings. He favored browns and yellows, fecal hues, excremental shapes.

Kevin said to Potsy, "They look like a pile of shit to me."

"But *good* shit, Doctor."

Several were marked SOLD—buyers anonymous.

Kevin shook hands with Buzzy. It was like picking up a dead whiting. The young man's gut bulged over his dark-brown sweater. He wore a ragged corduroy jacket and a tan muffler. His pants bagged properly—Montparnasse, Montmartre, memories of Modigliani and Soutine.

Buzzy's French wife was tiny, dark, with a hint of mustache. All afternoon she seemed angry, snapping. She had been a clerk in the local *papeterie* where Buzzy bought paper, pads, pencils. Her name was Celeste, and she spoke no more than three or four words of English. Frowning, stroking her hairy lip, she exuded the aroma of a once-a-week bather.

The crowd thickened. Women in outlandish costumes, clucking and nattering over the clever use of acrylics, Buzzy's mastery of the bone spatula, the emptinesses that characterized so many of his works, especially the series called *Digestive I, Digestive II, Digestive III.*

"I confess I'm confused," E.E. Manship said to Kevin, after kissing Cynthia. "But the dealers and the critics tell me my son has unique talent.

Just for this week, Kevin thought. *Next week it'll be someone else. Maybe a watercolorist who specializes in vaginas.*

"Oh, he's original all right," Potsy said. "Takes guts to try something new. Look at the first heart surgeon who stuck his thumb into a mitral valve."

Manship smiled. Behind him, staring balefully at the brown monstrosities her son had created, sailed Mrs. Manship. She wore a mink cape and a gray tweed suit. Cynthia said her mother always looked as if she were coming from a luncheon at the Fairmont Hotel in San Francisco.

"Joe not here? And his delightful *Italiana?*" Manship asked.

"He couldn't make it," Kevin lied. "Some crisis."

237

Joe and Jenny had not been invited. Bridie had been, but had chosen to stay away. She detested Buzzy Manship. Years ago he'd pinned her to the sand on the dunes, yanked up her skirt and tried to pull down her flowered panties. She was thirteen. She'd leveled him with a right to his throat.

Mr. Pirounakis, slithering between guests, giving orders to the waiters moving about with cocktails, sneaked up on Kevin's elbow. "There are a few paintings available, Doctor," the owner said. "Such an eminent physician as yourself, a member of the family . . . perhaps this one, Mr. Manship's *chef-d'oeuvre."* He pointed to a large canvas.

"I wouldn't know where to put it," Kevin said.

"I'd know," Potsy said. "But I'd have to roll it up tight. Maybe have to call in a proctologist to assist."

"Oh, you doctors," Pirounakis giggled.

Kevin surveyed the crowd with hard contempt. There were some of the beautiful people, a lot of Manship's austere friends, a few doctors from Upper County, and several people who fringed the "art world." Not quite dealers, not quite critics, not quite owners.

One was a ferret-faced young man in a loud houndstooth jacket who kept whispering in people's ears.

"Who's the dude in hound's teeth?" Kevin asked.

"Doberhauser," Potsy said to Kevin. "Land swindler. Lawyer. Art collector."

An hour later Manship suggested to Kevin that they "repair" to the Yale Club, then go to San Marino for dinner. He included only his children and their wives in the party, an intimate family affair. Buzzy, in his fat boy's whine, begged off. He wasn't dressed for it, he said, and Celeste was uncomfortable in fancy places.

In the bar of the Yale Club, where twelve years ago Kevin had asked E.E. for plane fare to Germany, the couples tried to relax, but people kept coming over. "Well, we finally got some action out of that idiot Kennedy," one man said, referring to the end of the Cuban missile crisis. "It can't hurt the market," another confided. "I'm told the Rockefellers had a hand in it," a third said.

When finally there was a lull, E.E. raised his glass. "I'd call this a banner day. Let's drink to it. Mother? Cynthia? Kevin?"

They responded. Mary Laura Manship's thinly powdered face betrayed no feeling. *Is she* that *stupid?* Kevin wondered. *A walking paradigm of the one truth about the rich that both Hemingway and Fitzgerald had missed, their inviolate dullness?*

"Kevin, you must tell Daddy about your new idea," Cynthia said. There was a hint of hysteria in her voice. Kevin worried about her. Each time he took a step upward, she seemed to get increasingly rattled.

"New idea?" E.E. asked.

"A group practice."

Cynthia's eyes widened. "A fabulous idea, fabulous. He picked Dr. Gold's brains."

Manship signed the chit for the drinks. *Amazing,* Kevin thought, *how he hears only what he wants to hear.*

"Love to hear about it, Kevin. It sounds fascinating."

E.E. helped his wife into her mink cape. Kevin let Cynthia manage her wrap by herself. He watched her walk into the street to the limousine and felt a sudden surge of pity and longing for the happy, arrogant girl in the peppermint-striped bathing suit.

At the restaurant Manship was given his usual table. When they finished ordering, Kevin tried to explain what he had in mind. What he envisioned was a "Multi-Specialty Group," with perhaps as many as twenty doctors. They would start with a nucleus of four or five crackerjack internists, aggressive young men with good connections, and continue to expand every year. Cynthia and her mother paid little attention. E.E. was intrigued.

His mind was racing ahead. The professional building he'd built for Kevin could be converted into a center for the group. Better yet, rent it, move Kevin's "Multi-Specialty Group" into a new complex. Part of a huge shopping and business center.

"We would need a cardiologist, gastroenterologist, a pediatrician, an OB man, a radiologist, a dermatologist, a urologist, an orthopedic man, a proctologist, a neurologist. . . ."

"Excuse a layman's ignorance," Manship said. "But aren't some of these doctors involved in surgery?"

"Of course. We'd have facilities for minor surgery, but we'd send complex cases to the hospital. But I think we'll do without general surgeons. They can be a headache."

"Your cousin, Walter Luff, Junior?"

"He's got other fish to fry, Dad. Now that he's back from

Cleveland and passed his boards in cardiovascular surgery, he has plans for pioneering open-heart surgery in the East."

Manship pursed his lips. Once, he glanced toward the rest rooms. Cynthia was gone too long. He worried about Cynthia, but he didn't like to mention his concern to Kevin. Instead he said, "Will you excuse a layman for offering a few notions?"

"Go ahead, Dad."

And why not? Kevin asked himself. Manship was no physician, but he was chairman of the board of trustees at Upper County and a member of the board at Mid-Island.

"I was talking to the senator the other day," Manship said. "He's convinced a federal program for hospitals is imminent. If not under Kennedy, then surely the next president."

"The AMA will fight them."

Manship laughed. "The AMA is a dinosaur, Kevin. The more they scream about socialism the faster the legislation will be passed."

Cynthia walked across the restaurant from the ladies' room. She'd put on outsized dark glasses.

"What I am getting at, Kevin," said Manship, "is that group practice may not only be a sensible plan, it may be the only answer. Doctors practicing alone will be the ones hurt."

Like Joe, Kevin thought. *Like Doc Felder.*

"All that sentimental nonsense about the old family physician," Manship went on, "the old gent getting up in the middle of the night—that's over."

"It wasn't a bad system."

"I quite agree," Mrs. Manship said.

Cynthia sat down. Her father and husband rose, both studying the pallid face.

"You all right, dear?" Kevin asked.

"Fine. May I have a *Perrier-citron?*"

Manship caught the captain's eye—*Damn,* Kevin thought, *I'll have to learn that trick someday*—and ordered mineral water.

"Then group practice is what medicine will be all about," Kevin said. "The old GP can't keep up. We'll have specialists to care for all the patients' needs with the most up-to-date methods. Why we'll eventually have our own hematologist, endocrinologist. . . ."

"How about the butcher, the baker and the candlestick maker?"

240

Cynthia asked. "Or a taxidermist, so you can stuff the patient after you've finished gutting him?"

Kevin leaned over to kiss her cheek. A sour odor emanated from her. She'd been throwing up in the bathroom. He had suspected this for some time. Secret trips to the john to regurgitate.

"I'm looking beyond your group, admirable as it sounds, Kevin," Manship said. "You see, we have to make certain that the enormous federal funds get into the right hands."

Mrs. Manship tilted her head. She looked rather like a bay mare hearing her groom's tread. "Everett is so full of surprises, Kevin. All his life he's been against government interference, those New Deal crackpots. Now I hear him talking in *favor* of federal money. Everett, are you joking?"

"I think I see what you're getting at, Dad," Kevin said.

"I may be wrong. But these millions, perhaps billions, of federal dollars will end up going to the largest and most prestigious institutions. Not to any twenty-physician multi-specialty group."

"We won't need it. We're a professional corporation supplying services. We'll benefit from more third-party payments. We'll do a bigger volume. . . ."

"Kevin, every man in your group should have a teaching position at a major medical center, like Danforth Medical College. Danforth will end up supplying physicians to every hospital in the region."

"Look out," said Cynthia. "Dad is building an empire again."

"I admit it," E.E. said. "But one in the public weal. Believe me, Kevin, I have an outsider's view of it."

"But you're not against a group practice?"

"By no means. Just lock it into a medical school. Get your men affiliated with Danforth, then put them into positions of authority in the local hospitals. That's where the money and power will be."

"Danforth isn't quite P and S, Dad," Kevin said. "Twelve years ago it even had trouble with its accreditation."

"We'll change that, Kevin. Demonstration programs. Research projects. Grants. Fellowships. And a lot of publicity. I tell you, we can make it the nucleus of—what did you call it, Cynthia—an empire?"

"Daddy, you really are too much. You've got them outfoxed and outclassed before the fight even starts."

Manship tried to ignore her. "There's no fight. It's a matter of who makes decisions."

Later, as Kevin and Cynthia drove across the Triboro Bridge, Kevin lapsed into silence. He had entertained some thoughts that Manship had, but had not seen the whole picture as clearly. Public funds were inevitable. Billions of dollars for research, complex technology, projects, staff. People who knew, people who would be in charge, had to be the ones who got the money and put it to proper use. And this would mean the medical-school connection.

But Manship was looking for something that went beyond that. What? Power for its own sake. He did not take his wealth lightly. "I'm no Rockefeller," he often told friends, "but I admire their public spirit." E.E. wanted something beyond the empire Cynthia derided.

And it can't hurt me, Kevin thought.

On the Northern State Parkway, Cynthia, who had appeared to be dozing, jerked upright, interrupting his thoughts. "I have to whoops."

He flashed his right signal, braked, moved the Mercedes gingerly into the right lane, weathering curses from a station wagon loaded with teenagers.

As soon as the car pulled to a stop on the soft shoulder, Kevin unstrapped his seat belt and undid Cynthia's. She appeared dazed. In seconds, she was leaning out of the open door, gagging and retching. A string of spittle depended from her mouth. He held her forehead.

"What is it?" he asked. "You hardly ate anything. You didn't drink."

She kept retching, bringing up spurts of liquid. Finally, she collapsed on the seat, weeping. Kevin wiped her mouth with his handkerchief. He located a box of Kleenex on the back seat and gave her a wad.

"You getting a virus?" he asked solicitously. "Do you feel warm?"

"No. It's nothing."

"Sounds to me like you're nursing a virus. You look pale. I'll give you penicillin when we get home."

"I don't need anything."

"You can't be pregnant."

242

He waited until the lane was clear, then drove off the grass.

"Don't be concerned about me," she said. "If I want sympathy, from you or anyone else, I'll let you know."

"I'm trying to be helpful."

She pulled away from him into her corner of the car. But for once he stifled his anger. Something was wrong. The tiny portions she ate. The vomiting. He was sure her father had noticed. In an odd way, he felt a kinship to E.E. If he had bought a son-in-law for a not-so-stable daughter, he had paid generously. Kevin knew he was in his debt; he would have to keep his part of the bargain with better grace. Reaching over, he patted Cynthia's shoulder.

"You'll be fine," he said. "I promise." But whether he was referring to her health or some deeper pact with the future he was not sure.

3

Some weeks after the missile crisis ended, Eliot Sparling asked his producer, a man named Christopher Ling, to screen the report he had prepared on LSD. The film had been shelved during the wild weeks of the crisis in Cuba. With a chance to get back to local reporting, the producer agreed to look at the footage.

Christopher Ling, despite his name, was no Oriental. The son of what he liked to call "Kansas dirt farmers," he was a descendant of Scandinavians, a self-made executive, arrogant, decisive, sharp-tongued, and by everyone's admission UBC's resident news genius.

Ling did not disagree. Lean, handsome, he had a craggy face, crooked smile, lush white-blond hair, and a fearsome social-register wife who was reputed to be smarter than he was.

If Ling had one disturbing quality, it was his almost inaudible voice, which forced everyone who worked for him to strain to catch his words. Sparling, to his everlasting regret, once produced an ear trumpet. His use of it amused the assembled staff, and Ling also laughed, but with an unpleasant edge.

"We are not the New York *Times*," Christopher Ling would whisper. "We are visual, kinetic." For a man who wrote for *Harper's* and advised corporations on their responsibility to the public, Ling had a remarkably vigorous anti-intellectual bias. He loved fires, riots, demonstrations, and fistfights. "Get me the blood on the sidewalk if you can't get the corpse" was his standing order to cameramen.

Sparling was relatively certain that his film of the LSD victims would not move the producer, but he felt he owed it to Bridie to have it screened.

They settled into the screening room—Sparling, Ling, a film editor, Ling's secretary.

Ling was silent as Melinda and Jody, the victims, recited. Then the camera turned to Bridie.

"She's the girl I told you about," Sparling said, with some pride. "Terrific dame. Medical family. She'd make a hell of an M.D. herself."

The film had done wonders for Bridie. Not that she wasn't naturally beautiful. But the reflector, bouncing October sunlight off her long face, highlighting her magnificent hair, made her as vivacious as any actress, prettier than most models. She was not hesitant in her denunciation of the new sensation-seekers, the peddlers of instant insights.

Ling watched her carefully.

"This is a crying disgrace," Bridie was saying. Her eyes were angry. "People who should know better—professors hustling the notion that LSD is good for you. At least the slum kids don't make any excuses. They pop anything they can lay their hands on and get high. But these hotshots who should know better; with their theories about expanding the mind, they're a menace."

"Amen," Ling said softly. He did not look at Eliot. "Interesting girl. How old?"

"Thirty."

"Looks younger. I like her."

The lights went on in the viewing room. There was silence for a while.

"Well, chief?" Sparling asked.

"Interesting. Cut it to three minutes. Hold for a slow night."

"That's all? I was thinking of making it part of a series on drug abuse."

"It lacks action. It doesn't move."

"I know. Three people sitting on a bench and talking."

"Let me explain what's wrong," Ling said comfortingly. "If you had actually *shown* these people in the throes of their LSD experiences, you might have had a story. The fellow crawling around thinking he's a fly. The girl moaning that she was part of the wall. Now, that would scare the pants off our viewers."

"I guess we weren't lucky. Maybe I could have slipped them each a bullet of LSD."

"I didn't mean that. But if you *know* that nurse, she could tip you off next time a patient is coming off the wall. I want to see them writhing, howling."

"It isn't what I'd call ethical."

"But people will watch."

Eliot raged inwardly but held his tongue. No one ever won an argument with Ling. He cut off director's heads, split writers down the middle with one whistling sentence.

He was about to leave when Ling told the screening room to run Sparling's piece again.

"Change your mind, chief?" Eliot asked.

"I want to look at the girl."

"Melinda? With the feet in the grass?"

"The nurse."

Again Bridie's glowing face appeared on the screen. They heard her voice—vibrant, firm, commanding attention. A viewer saw at once that she was pretty and worth listening to.

"Tell me about her," Ling said.

"Bridie? Department of Old Girlfriends. Thirty, psychiatric nurse, smart as paint."

"Full name?"

"Bridget Derry. She's got a brother who's a hotshot cardiologist on Long Island, and another one, a GP."

"Why isn't she married?" asked Ling.

"Ask her."

"Can you bring her in?" Ling said. "She's got quality. I don't know what it is, but it's real."

"What do you have in mind?"

"I never know until I talk to them. Maybe she's looking for a new career. How much can she earn peeling addicts off the walls?"

"Maybe she likes what she's doing," Eliot said.

"We'll find out. Everyone wants to be on television, don't they, Eliot?"

Sparling telephoned Bridie at the Institute. It had been a bad day. Two nurses had quit. A heroin addict, sixteen and violent, had escaped.

"Eliot, I've about had it here. I'm no saint—"

"Listen, maybe what I have to say will interest you," he said. "We ran the film of the LSD lovers. It wasn't a smash, but my boss wants to talk to you. The big producer. Guy named Christopher Ling."

"To me? Why?"

"He likes your looks. As Paul Stewart said to Kirk Douglas, 'You're pretty handy with your dukes, kid.'"

"What does he want?"

"Who knows? Maybe he wants to make you a distaff Cronkite."

"That's crazy. I'm no journalist. I can't act. My nose is too long."

"What can you lose?"

"I've lost it already, sport."

He laughed and told her to be at Louis and Armand's the following Thursday at twelve-thirty.

Joe Derry brought Eric Hudson, the five-year-old black boy, to Upper County Hospital for a cardiac workup. It would not be an easy day for the weakened child.

Eric cried a great deal. His feet hurt. He whined. His eyes burned. He was tired.

Kevin gave him a thorough examination.

"He's got *in vivo* sickling," Joe said, watching Kevin listen to Eric's chest and peer into his eyes. "I think it's associated with some kind of h-heart condition."

"You win the bet," Kevin said. He turned Eric's thin body, listened to his back with a stethoscope. "What odds on a tetralogy of Fallot?"

"I don't bet with specialists. I just said a cardiac involvement."

The boy was sent into the cardiac-catheterization laboratory under sedation.

Mrs. Hudson waited in the family room. She had told Joe she worked on an estate in Brookville. Her husband did odd jobs, sometimes drove a bakery truck. Eric was their youngest. He did poorly in school because of his weakness. Other kids teased him. But her older son, Jerome, was big and strong and a good student. Jerome tried to protect Eric, she said.

Joe listened and assured her Eric would be fine. Then he joined Kevin in a room next to the cath lab.

"Well?" Joe asked.

Kevin tapped the glass-topped desk. "Digital clubbing, atrophy of the optic nerve. He's got a grade-five pansystolic murmur. The heart condition may or may not be related to the sickling."

He knows his stuff, Joe thought. "So?"

"I don't know. The angiocardiograms'll be ready soon. Why don't you send them home and tell them we'll call?"

An hour later the brothers looked at the X-rays of Eric's heart pumping the injected dye from the catheter. Eric and his mother had been sent home.

"This stuff is new to me," Joe confessed. "You guys move so f-fast my head spins."

Kevin put on rimless glasses and studied the photographs.

"There's the venous-catheter tip," he said, pointing with his cigarette holder. "Apex of the right ventricle. See the defect in the ventricular septum?"

"If you say so." Joe felt thick-headed.

"Hypertrophy of the crista supraventricularis, severe pulmonary stenosis. See the stenotic area? It's much narrower than a normal pulmonary artery."

Joe asked what the prognosis was.

"It's a weird case. *In vivo* sickling combined with a tetralogy of Fallot? Maybe Potsy should see him. Potsy does beautiful work, you know."

Joe wrinkled his nose and Kevin smiled, seeing the white scar. All those blocks and tackles.

"Isn't there a risk operating on a k-kid like that?" Joe asked.

"There's risk in everything. It'll get worse if it's left alone. We'd pack him with red blood cells before surgery, try to keep him on bypass as short a time as possible."

"Who makes the decision on surgery?" Joe asked.

"The parents, I suppose. The boy is in no immediate danger, but he's weak, damned near nonfunctional. If we correct the cardiac defects, the kid may improve."

"I have to confess something, Kevin. I'm in over my head. I don't know what to t-tell them."

Kevin chewed on the stem of his eyeglasses. "I'd say operate." As usual, Kevin sounded very sure. After he left Joe continued to stare at the chart.

*   *   *

"How does six million dollars sound?" E.E. Manship asked.

"Excessive," the man from HEW said.

"I'm a little stunned myself," the senator said.

They were in the Senate dining room. Discreet colors, heavy furnishings, an air of quiet power—and the famous bean soup, which Manship insisted his son-in-law try.

The man from HEW, a former social worker from Brooklyn, watched Kevin narrowly. A fine-boned, cold-eyed Irishman. A little bit like the Kennedys. Talking only when he could add something to his father-in-law's appeal for a bequest to Danforth Medical College, he still seemed to attract attention.

E.E. Manship had arranged the meeting. The senator was not from New York, but he understood men like Manship.

"Dr. Derry has his presentation ready," E.E. said. "It'll be on your desks tomorrow. I think you'll find he writes clearly and to the point. He's no PR man, gentlemen, no fund-raiser. Even though he's my son-in-law, I'm not hesitant to say he's as fine a cardiologist as you'll find anywhere in the country."

The man from HEW finished his soup and stared at Kevin, trying to find something in the gray eyes. It was a face that took in a great deal yet did not offend. There'd been no bullshit about clubs or yacht races or important people. Just sound medical talk—the need for computers, new diagnostic machines, a new complex of buildings at Danforth. The man from HEW appreciated it. Somewhere in this doctor's background, the bureaucrat guessed, was a poor boy who had made it the hard way before marrying a Manship.

"Six million," he said.

"Not a large sum," said E.E. "New York City alone has been awarded in excess of twenty-one million dollars for hospital construction. Why not a bit for Long Island? We're taxpayers also."

"There's a medical need," Kevin said. "Danforth is the logical place to start."

"It's never been my idea of a first-rate medical school," the HEW man said bluntly.

"Good enough to turn out Dr. Derry," Manship said. "Kevin, do they know about your paper on—what was it?—the one you read at the American Cardiological Association?"

"Chronic constrictive pericarditis."

"That's really beside the point, Mr. Manship. Hill-Burton funds will run out next year. We have to be careful how we dispense the last of them."

"That's why Dr. Derry and I are here."

"You have some tough competition," the senator said. "Those characters in Houston and Cleveland are pushing for open-heart funding."

"We plan an extensive heart-surgery program at Upper County," Kevin said. "In fact we have two excellent surgeons: Dr. Luff and Dr. Mapes."

"I know about Mapes. Who's Luff?"

Manship let his eyes catch Kevin's. But Kevin was ahead of him. No point in underscoring the fact that Walter Luff, Jr., was his cousin.

"Walter Luff. Youngish fellow. Bypasses, aneurysms, valve replacements. He's a comer." Kevin lit another cigarette. "It's all in my presentation."

"*Two* heart surgeons?" asked the official.

Kevin coughed. A good question. "Dr. Mapes spends a great deal of time in research. We look to Dr. Luff to become our DeBakey."

"Sounds pretty good," said the senator. He knew nothing about medical schools or surgeons, but he trusted Manship.

"I can't make any promises," said the man from HEW. "But you'll get a hearing. I'm curious about one thing, Dr. Derry. You're just a clinical professor at Danforth. Why'd they pick you to make the presentation?"

All four knew the answer to that. Derry was Manship's kin. *Marry right, get it all,* thought the man from HEW. He resented Manship, but he found it hard to dislike the affable cardiologist seated opposite him.

"Look," HEW said, "Upper County is largely serving a white suburban community. Its residents get lots of medical care, don't they? The administration's got enough troubles with blacks without shoveling funds into areas like that."

"We've already done a great deal to improve clinical services," Kevin said. "I created one of the first fully staffed departments in the county to make sure poor people didn't have to wait six weeks for an appointment."

The senator smiled at Manship, who obligingly played his trump card. "I intend to raise a matching grant if the government gives us

250

six million for the Danforth complex."

The man from HEW laughed. "I must say your case looks better every minute." He pushed back his chair. "We'll be back to you after we have Dr. Derry's presentation. But I think you're on your way." He left then, torn between a genuine admiration for Kevin's charm and resentment for any young man whose father-in-law could buy him a whole medical complex.

"I'd like to see your hair fluffier, more bouffant," Christopher Ling whispered. "The color is marvelous, that sort of wheat gold. It'll show wonderfully on the tube, but you'll have to wear it loose."

"I don't like your tie, but it's none of my business," Bridie said coolly.

They were sitting in a corner booth at Louis and Armand's. Ling had ordered Sparling to cover a last-minute story. Sparling was thus effectively dispensed with.

"I liked the way you spoke on that film. The subject didn't grab me, but you did."

"I'm glad. But nobody tells me how to wear my hair."

Ling laughed—a discreet noise. The girl would be given a screen test. He was reasonably certain she'd be effective on TV. And the corporation was after him to hire more women.

"Sparling is in love with you," Ling said. This was part of his technique—the out-of-nowhere change of subject.

"Eliot is a good egg," she said. "I've known him since he worked on *Newsday*."

"You haven't responded."

"You didn't ask a question, Mr. Ling."

"Chris."

A waiter lit his cigarette. The food had been excellent. Bridie had ordered a crab, shrimp and avocado salad. The producer had eaten Dover sole sautéed in a lemon sauce. It had not been on the menu, but the chef had been happy to prepare it for Mr. Ling.

They lived well, these producers, Bridie saw. During lunch, Ling had told her about a reporter he'd sent to Paris, who had threatened to quit unless he was moved from the Hotel George V to the Plaza-Athenée. "Of course, we indulged him," Ling said. "The network is a money machine. News people don't contribute much but they're coddled."

251

She laughed. Ling had a certain cynical appeal.

"I'd like you to try your hand at a story," Ling said. "Stand you on a street corner with a microphone and talk a minute or so. Any suggestions?"

"Wait a minute. I like nursing. I have a career. I don't intend to chuck it overnight for a fancy lunch and some amusing stories."

"But that's what the business is, Bridget. Lunch and stories. And very good salaries. What do you earn now?"

"Twelve thousand a year."

"We'll start you at twenty-five. In six months you'll be earning thirty. It's a lot more fun than wiping up after incontinent children, or tying violent adults into straitjackets. Eliot tells me what you put up with—the worst cases. You're too pretty and talented for that. May I tell you my theory? You haven't married because you have guilt feelings that bind you to your patients. They are your symbolic children. I know someone must look after them, but why someone as beautiful as you?"

"I do more good in one day at the Institute than I could in a month of reporting murders for you."

This was the opening Ling had waited for. "I disagree. I think you might do more good working for us."

A well-known newscaster entered. Ling waved to him. The man stared at Bridie a moment and whispered something to a colleague.

"If it's what I think, forget it," she said. Bridie did not like the suggestion of sex in the whispered confidences.

"No, no. I don't dirty my own kitchen. I'm a farm boy, Bridget."

"You act more like the fellow at the county fair moving the pea under the shells—the one taking the farm boy's money."

"I like that. Now let me tell you what I have in mind."

"Go ahead."

"For some time I've felt we need specialists to report on specific areas, like the newspapers."

"How do I fit into this?"

"I want to try you as science and medicine reporter. I think there's a large audience for new treatments for migraine, developments in natural childbirth. You can even use the program to call attention to your addicts and handicapped children."

"How long do I have to think about it?"

Ling studied his watch. The Tokyo correspondent had bought it for him on the expense account. In addition to giving the time and date it showed phases of the moon and tidal conditions.

"You have ten minutes. Just the time it will take us to walk from here to the UBC building."

Outside it was cold and damp. Bridie thought of the work for which she had trained so arduously, of the children she loved, wandering in a twilight world, with so little done for them, so few who wanted to do it. But Bridie sensed she had come to a fork in the road. Even if it were selfish she felt she had to be free of the everlasting attachment to the abandoned and hopeless. Maybe Christopher Ling had put his finger on why she had not married.

They stood outside the granite and glass facade of the UBC building.

"You've got a deal, Mr. Ling. I'll give it a try."

"Close him up," Potsy Luff said briskly. His six-man surgical team took over.

All that could be seen of Eric Hudson was a small area of his chest. Potsy had excised the muscle of the outflow tract of the boy's right ventricle and closed the septal defect with a Teflon patch. The pulmonary artery was given a left-to-right shunt. Potsy had decided not to risk further surgical repair. The boy had been on bypass long enough.

"How does he look?" Kevin asked.

"Fair enough," Potsy said. "We want lab tests to see how the surgery affects the sickling. We'll give him multiple-packed red-cell transfusions for a couple of weeks. It'll reduce the sickling."

"I hope so," Joe said. "I'm lost with you guys. The idea is if the tetralogy of Fallot is corrected, it'll r-reduce the rate at which normal cells become defective?"

"That's the idea," Kevin said.

Joe shook his head. A new one on him.

The chief resident called softly, "Dr. Luff?"

Potsy walked back to the table. "Yeah?" he asked.

"Tricuspid insufficiency. The valve isn't working as well as it was."

Potsy frowned. "It'll correct itself. We couldn't keep him on bypass. Put him on digitalis when he's in the recovery room."

He walked back to his cousins.

"Look, how b-bad is that?" Joe asked. "I know I'm only a lousy GP, but if the tricuspid valve is regurgitating b-blood . . ."

"Take it easy, Joe," Kevin said. "Give it a chance."

Joe found Eric Hudson in an oxygen tent the next morning.

"He's holding on," the resident said.

"What about the blood t-tests?" Joe asked.

"He's anemic. Worse than before surgery. We're waiting for the results on the sickling and the oxygen-tension rates."

Joe walked up to the tent. The boy was sleeping, breathing shallowly.

"I might as well hang around. Maybe I can raise my b-brother and get an opinion."

Kevin had taken three days off. He was at the Manship house in Churchport, working on plans for Danforth. Joe woke him up.

"What about the blood picture?" Kevin asked.

"Worse than before."

Kevin whistled.

"Have Potsy look at him, will you?"

"If I can find him. Kevin, how about c-coming in?"

"Right now?"

"Right now. Look, he's my patient, and I don't want him left to the mercies of the house staff. Please."

Kevin arrived at the hospital at ten. Potsy came in from surgery. By then the boy seemed to be improving. The digitalis and oxygen had revived him. But the tricuspid valve was not producing a sufficient blood flow.

Worse, the tests revealed that the diseased cells were increasing at a rate *higher* than prior to surgery. Precisely the opposite of what Potsy and Kevin had predicted had happened.

The three physicians sat studying the laboratory results. Potsy shrugged. He was busy all day—a bypass, a valve replacement.

"Kevin," said Joe, "look at this. The boy's hemoglobin and his hematocrit are lower than before surgery. The lifespan of the normal cells is shorter. He didn't have *severe* sickling symptomatology before, but look at the k-kid now."

"We ran a legitimate risk," Kevin said. "The blood picture can change. The kid does look better."

"What do I t-tell his parents?" Joe asked.

"Tell them he's got a good chance of improving. Oxygen

254

saturation at venous points is higher. The left-to-right shunt is working."

Bullshit, Joe thought.

Kevin always made the worst sound okay. A doctor's privilege, he supposed. But he kept worrying about Eric, convinced that he was not really doing well.

A week before Christmas Eric Hudson died. Both Kevin and Potsy were out of town. Joe went in to see the parents alone.

"I'm sorry, Mr. Hudson. I'm sorry, Mrs. Hudson. We did all we could." *Useless, lying words,* he thought.

The woman wept quietly.

"Tell me, Dr. Derry," Hudson asked. "That surgery kill him?"

"No, of course not. Eric was a s-sick boy. There was something wrong with his heart and his blood."

"My baby. My little Eric." Mrs. Hudson dabbed at her eyes.

"Your brother around?" Mr. Hudson asked. "The heart doctor?"

"I'm afraid not. I spoke to him yesterday about Eric. Believe me, Mr. Hudson, we did everything we c-could. The nurses and doctors loved Eric."

Joe could think of nothing more to say. He sat with them for about fifteen minutes. Jerome Hudson, the older brother, continued to stare at him accusingly. Finally Joe asked permission to do an autopsy. It was a baffling case. Everyone would want to know why the boy's disease had worsened after the operation.

"All right," Mrs. Hudson said. "We are grateful, Doctor. You tell them other doctors also we are grateful."

In late afternoon Joe caught up with Abe Gold in the lunchroom and reviewed the case. Gold was always a good man to talk to. No crap from Abe.

Yes, he knew about Eric Hudson. One of the few Luff lost. He couldn't take it away from Potsy—he was one hell of a cardiac surgeon.

Joe showed Abe the blood reports.

Abe studied them. "What about his pH?"

"He had a m-mild alkalosis."

"Contributing factor, but that's all. . . . Wait a minute. The kid developed tricuspid insufficiency. So bad it led to heart failure. That tells me something." Steam from the coffee clouded Abe's eyeglasses.

"I don't understand it," Joe said. "His oxygenation went up. Why'd the disease get worse?"

"Circulation time. The kid had rapid circulation time before surgery. That's why the symptoms of the disease weren't pronounced. Rapid circulation *inhibits* sickling. If the red cells stay in the vascular bed, where there are low oxygen tensions, only a short time, then the process is less likely to occur. But the boy's circulation time *slowed* after surgery."

"Yeah. It didn't kill him, but it explains why he died."

"I know what you're thinking, Joe," Dr. Gold said. "You're furious at Kevin and Potsy. Don't blame them. If the surgery had been a success, and the boy's blood circulation unaffected, he'd be recovering."

"But it didn't w-work that way. I'm pissed."

"Don't be. Sickle-cell disease is a crazy thing. We should know a lot more about it."

"Maybe nobody cares because it's a disease that only hits Negroes, Abe?"

"Maybe." Abe saw the despair on Joe's battered face. "You and Jenny taking time off for the holidays?"

"No. I've g-got a couple of sour cases hanging fire. I'm in no mood for 'Jingle Bells' anyway."

"Joe, you've got to roll with the punch. It'll get easier as you get older."

"Not for m-me."

4

Bridie watched her image on the screen. They'd had a hairdresser wash and set her hair. It was red-gold, fluffy, blowing in the December wind. She wore a suit from Bonwit Teller, which Christopher Ling said she could keep even if she didn't get the job. The coat was of tan cavalry twill with an otter collar.

"Is that me?" she asked.

"Never looked better, Bridie," Sparling said. He'd sneaked into the screening room uninvited. Ling sat in the middle chair.

On the film the assistant cameraman clacked sticks together and shouted, *"Roll one, take one, test, Derry."*

There were a few false starts. She was nervous, fluffed her opening lines, and once, forgetting a word, shook her head and muttered, "Oh, shit."

As the final take began to roll, Bridie whispered to Sparling, "Know something? I'm excited. Even if I don't get the job."

Ling shushed them into silence and watched. He saw at once: natural presence, the undefinable ability to command attention, hold a viewer.

"This fortress, this prison," Bridie was saying, "is what the state of New York dares to call a mental hospital. Maybe the padded cells and straitjackets are missing, but the people who run this place have found a more efficient method of subduing patients. Drugs. And in some instances, a brutal attitude toward the patients. Where does the fault lie? . . ."

Sparling squeezed her hand. She was terrific. She'd be hired, and

257

have a great career. But he also knew it would be the end of their affair.

When it was over Ling waited for the room to empty. "Okay," he said. "You have yourself a deal."

"What do I do now? Dance? Sing?" She tried to be offhand. Her heart jumped deliciously.

"How soon can you start?"

"Mmmm—a month?" She thought of Dr. McGrory.

"Two weeks," Ling said. "I'd like you to come in on your days off to take a fast course in film writing. You can learn it in two days if you're bright enough. All you'll need is a stopwatch and a command of the language."

"I've been writing medical reports for years and no one's complained about my grammar."

He leaned toward her and put a fatherly hand on her knee. Sex or no sex? She couldn't be certain. Ling was married to a woman even more formidably intellectual than he was—a Ph.D. in botany—and he was reputed to live in mortal fear of her. "Just keep your scripts brisk and exciting. We have an obligation not to bore people."

"Do I need a trench coat? A press pass? Do I get to sit on the city editor's desk?"

"No. But I suggest an agent and a lawyer. UBC doesn't like to negotiate directly with talent."

Bridie shook her head. "This is crazy. But I like it. Where do I find an agent?"

"Sparling will know. Let's see. I think I said we'd start you at twenty-five thousand dollars, didn't I?"

She was not so flustered that she couldn't think. Hadn't he mentioned thirty thousand dollars at lunch? She could not remember.

"I think you said thirty thousand," Bridget said.

"I didn't make notes."

"Maybe you'd better make one now." Bridie was shocked at her own nerve.

Ling smiled and said, "I want to take you up to our publicity department. Good story for Friday's papers—local television's first science-and-medicine reporter. I like the sound."

"Ask him," Jenny Derry said.

258

She and Joe were decorating the Christmas tree in the den. Nicky, stumbling amid tinsel, angel hair, bulbs and lights, was making a prime pest of himself. It was long past his bedtime, but his parents were home at such irregular hours that he often awakened in the middle of the night. They had not the heart to force him back to his crib.

"Ask who?" Joe asked.

"Kevin."

"Screw him. Let him ask *me*."

Nicky tossed tinsel in the air. It landed on his dark round face, spangling him with flecks of silver. "Mommy. Look at me."

"You look great, sport. Aren't you tired?" She stood on tiptoe to place the plastic star on the upper point of the tree. Joe reached under her dress, pinched her behind.

"Not in front of the *bambino*," she said.

"Can't resist it, Jen. It's the best *cuolo* in the world."

"Really love me?" Jenny asked.

"Love you."

"Then ask Kevin about taking you into his group."

Joe released her. He picked up the box of bulbs and moved them out of Nicky's reach.

"Let him ask me," Joe said. "That's it."

"Oh, that damn pride of yours."

"He knows I'm a good m-medical man. If he wants me, he'll ask me."

Jenny put on the last bulb, picked up Nicky and carried him into bed with a warning to be quiet or he'd never get a rocket ship from Santa Claus.

"I shouldn't let you lug him around like that," Joe said. "But you move too fast."

"I don't mind. Comes from being in a family of garbage collectors."

They sat in the kitchen and drank red wine. Another gift from the Damelios. Carmine's father, eighty-two, made his own, drank a quart a day.

"Joey, Kevin's group is going to be the biggest thing that ever hit the Island. And you should—"

"Kevin can kiss my big Irish ass."

259

"Stubborn Mick. It isn't your ass that's big; it's your ego. You're worse than he is."

Joe rested his head on one hand. Not much of a day. Thirty bucks. Kevin got twice that for an hour's consultation. "I'm no internist. I never took the boards."

"The boards are minestrone. You can study for them while you're in Kevin's group."

"I said no."

"Joe, this is an opportunity. Kevin's probably afraid you'll think he's doing you a favor. It won't be, believe me. You're as good a doctor as any of that crowd, and for God's sake, you're interested in *people*."

Joe sipped the harsh wine. "That's just it. People think I go out at night because I need every buck I can get. They prefer the specialists even if they're never available."

The following evening Jenny telephoned Kevin at home from the hospital. Serena answered. Dr. Derry was having his dinner and could not be disturbed.

"This is his sister-in-law. He'll talk to me."

Cynthia picked up another extension. "Jenny, dear." The musical quality was there.

"Cynthia, I hate to bother you, but could I run over for a few minutes? I have to talk to Kevin."

"Of course, Jenny. Can we feed you?"

"No, thanks. I'll grab one of Mid-Island's gourmet bologna sandwiches and eat on the way."

Cynthia answered the door. Skinny, Jenny thought, looking at her lavender robe. Her cheeks were gaunt. But even in late December she was tanned.

"Something to eat, Jenny?" Cynthia said. "We've half a *blanquette de veau* left. Does chocolate mousse tempt you?"

"Nothing, thanks, Cynthia." And she thought, *No wonder there's half a dinner left. You look as if you don't eat at all; and Kevin eats cigarettes.*

The women stared at each other a moment: Cynthia, self-possessed; Jenny, ill at ease in her white uniform. *We both know*, Jenny thought.

Johnny and Karen were paraded in by Miss Vessels to greet their aunt. The brothers' families saw little of each other. The unspoken snobbery in Cynthia got the best of her at times. Jenny was a wonderful girl, everyone agreed, but she did not ride or play golf or bridge.

"Hiya," Johnny said.

"Kiss Aunt Jenny," Cynthia commanded.

The children did so and Jenny suddenly thought, *These kids aren't real. They are too handsome, golden and tan.* She was proud of Nicky, dirty, rugged, brawling, with his dark face and ebony eyes.

Cynthia excused herself. Too much to do around the house. *A lie,* Jenny thought. *She does nothing. Four in help, trips to Palm Beach, dinners for her friends.*

Kevin took her into his study. His desk was piled with stacks of medical reports.

"She's too thin," Jenny said, after she sat down.

"Who?"

"Oh, for God's sake, Kevin. Your wife. She looks half starved."

"She claims it gives her a better *seat.* The indoor jumping season is coming up."

"She still throwing up?"

"I haven't noticed," Kevin said, hiding behind cigarette smoke.

"Boy, you can be a heartless bastard. Has she gone for psychiatric help?"

"I've suggested it. She says she's fine, has two beautiful children, a successful husband, everything she wants."

Jenny cocked her head. "Tell me this, Kevin. When she vomits, is it spontaneous or deliberate?"

"I never asked. And she wouldn't tell the truth if I did."

Dr. Derry, she thought, *you have a problem. And like so many physicians, you are blind to your own family.*

"Noticed any cyanotic mottling? We've had a case or two like this at Mid-Island. Usually in teenagers, but it occurs in older women."

"I know what you're getting at, Jenny, but you're wrong. Please, let's get around to your problem."

"She's got anorexia."

"Jenny, you're a great nurse, but a punk diagnostician."

"She's got anorexia nervosa, Kevin. The two of you won't admit it."

"You didn't come here to lecture me. This isn't the nurses' training school at Mid-Island. Let's get off my wife's problems."

261

He changed the subject to Bridie. How wonderful her new career was. The network had great hopes for her.

"She have any regrets about leaving Dr. McGrory?" Jenny asked.

"Well, she'd go only so far in her field without an M.D. Anyway, why not be rich and famous?"

Yes, why not? Jenny reflected. Kevin looked weary but handsome, with his ginger hair and pale eyes.

"I came to see you about Joe," she said.

"Joe?"

"Your brother. Dr. Joseph Derry."

"What's wrong? I saw him just a few days ago. Is he angry about the Hudson boy? Is that why you're here?"

"You know why I'm here."

"I told him we can't save everyone. There are limits to our knowledge."

"Dr. Gold didn't think so."

"Dr. Gold should keep his nose out of other people's cases. Joe is angry because he feels every case is a personal challenge. It's an insult to him if a patient dies."

Jenny was silent for a moment. Then she said again, "You know why I'm here."

"You want me to take Joe into the group."

"Yes."

"Let him come and ask me."

"He's too proud. He's not jealous of you, Kevin. But he's proud and he's wary of you. He had to struggle so hard for everything. You always did it the easy way."

Kevin got up and put his hand on her shoulder. Beneath the white uniform he could see the outline of her bra.

"Don't touch me, Kevin. I don't want any reminders of the past."

"I'm sorry." He lowered his voice. "Tell Joe I envy him."

"Like hell you do."

Kevin walked away. "All right. It's done."

"What's done?"

"Joe's in the group. He'll have to do PG work. Get his certification as an internist. But he can take as long as he wants."

She grinned—a little girl opening a Christmas present. "You mean it? Oh, Kevin!"

"I have to clear it with the group, but that's no problem." He tapped a pile of papers on his desk. "Applicants. Three hundred at the last count. More M.D.'s than on the staff of Beth Moses. Know the ones I throw out? The ones who want to know how much they'll earn the first year."

"Joe would never ask that."

"I know."

He smiled. The old innocent smile.

Four days later Kevin hadn't called. Jenny caught up to him as he was finishing rounds.

"Kevin, is something wrong?"

He took Jenny's arm and guided her into the empty visitors' room.

"Did you speak to Joe yet?" he asked.

"No, you know I wouldn't do that. But something's wrong, isn't it?"

"Jenny, the others wouldn't let me do it. He doesn't have a subspecialty. Hell, he isn't even an internist. I couldn't fight them, Jen. He isn't qualified."

"Did you even try, Kevin? For your own brother?"

Kevin thought of the angry meeting. Benton Graubart, the doctor bringing in the biggest private practice, had trained at Mid-Island and had brought up Joe's past conflicts. His fight with DeBeers. His recent rows with other attendings. Graubart swung a lot of weight. He had threatened to pull out if Kevin insisted. The next day three other members of the group had called to say they would follow Graubart if Kevin overrode their veto.

"Jenny, there was nothing I could do," said Kevin. "The others threatened to quit."

"Maybe you should have let them. Maybe for once in your life you should have fought for what you believed."

"I tried, Jenny. I really tried."

Jenny surveyed him, her eyes hard and contemptuous.

"I wonder," she said. She walked out of the room. Shame hit him for a moment. He had a flickering vision of his brother valiantly playing out a losing season. Then he shrugged his shoulders and returned to his office. Joe would never know, and Jenny would get over it.

PART FIVE
1966

1

The rattling DC-3 barely seemed to be skimming the mist-shrouded emerald-green mountains of the southern Philippines.

Nicky slept in his mother's lap. He had been terrified at takeoff. The old two-engine plane wheezed and shuddered as if every rivet would blast loose. Then it roared down the runway at Manila airport, groaning as it gained altitude, just clearing the city, hovering over the mountains, and at last finding a comfortable channel in the dark sky.

It seemed to Jenny (as she quieted Nicky, normally a courageous six-year-old) that the aircraft would never make it. The vivid green mountains, enveloped in cottony clouds, rose menacingly about them. They never appeared to be flying much above the higher peaks, forever in danger of smashing into an extinct volcano.

"Can't he get this thing any higher?" Jenny asked Joe.

Joe was at a window seat, staring at the rain forest, the triple canopy of heavily leafed trees and the brighter green patches of cultivated land. The thatched huts looked like houses on a Monopoly board. Here and there, on some of the higher farms—they grew rice at incredible altitudes here—farmers would wave. Lakes and rivers abounded. Steely blue, inviting. But as Joe knew, they were packed with schistosomiasis, the endemic disease of much of the Orient. *Schistoma japonicum, you little bastard,* Joe thought, barely hearing Jenny's voice over the roar of the twin engines. One of them gave off sparks. It seemed charred, and deformed. *Christ, if we never make it to*

Batati, Jenny will never forgive me. But it won't matter by then. All three of us dead. And it was all my idea.

"Can't hear you, J-Jen," Joe said.

"I said can't he get this thing to fly any higher?" She had to shout. Nicky stirred, but was now deeply in slumber. It had been an exhausting two weeks for him—yanked out of school, the twenty-hour flight to Manila, and now a prisoner in this scary plane bound for a strange place. But the boy had the inner toughness of his mother. He'd manage. Jenny, wearing the khaki bush jacket and matching slacks Dr. Chuck Zavala had provided them, set him on the seat beside her. She fastened his seatbelt.

"Always trust a DC-Three," Joe said. "It may not look l-like much, but it g-gets you there."

"There's always a first," Jenny said.

She peered out the window. An awesome country—giant peaks, tiny farms, numberless lakes, unimaginable shades of green, almost like the gradations of red on a hemoglobin chart. No wonder Joe loved it. She had opposed the wild adventure, fought with Joe, and now she could not help but feel that she had done the right thing. Excitement inflamed her breast. If only the shivering plane would get them to their destination! And hurry up! With each revolution of the propellors it seemed to protest its overladen voyage, like a cranky old patient finding life too much of a burden. *Let me die,* the plane seemed to keep repeating. *Let me die, let me die, die, die.*

There were four other passengers on board, and a crew of two. The pilot, a friend of Zavala's named Manuel, favored a purple *barang tagalog* and lavender slacks, and chain smoked. Frequently—too frequently for Joe's comfort—Manuel left the controls to a fat Chinese named Chang, his copilot, who giggled incessantly, and, when not casually observing the instrument panel, turned pages in a two-year-old *Playboy.*

Two of the passengers were Filipino soldiers in mottled greens, peaked caps and combat boots. Each carried an Armalite, the standard rapid-fire rifle used in Vietnam. On the floor between them was a box of grenades.

"Why the soldiers?" Joe had asked Manuel when they boarded the plane—after passengers and crew had spent an hour hosing buffalo dung from the plane, a leftover of Manuel's previous cargo.

"Dr. Zavala's private army," the pilot said.

"But who are they?"

"Filipino constabulary. Bodyguards for you and the wife and the baby."

"Bodyguards?"

"Dr. Zavala feels he's responsible for you. Don't want the new doctor shot up before he gets there."

Joe swallowed. He did not convey the information to Jenny. As ever, she was in the spirit of things, vigorously hosing manure from the rear door of the DC-3. It was five A.M. and dark at the airport. They were on a remote runway used by charter planes. Beyond, the skyscrapers of Manila, the neon signs, winked in the indigo Pacific night. Manuel explained the early departure; he did not want to get caught over the mountains in the dark or in a late-afternoon storm.

But what was Dr. Carlos Zavala, whom Joe had known as a wild medical student, doing hiring Filipino constabulary? Manila was filled with armed guards. Joe tried to forget about the soldiers. After all, it was a booming business for World War II vets in the lawless country.

And who would want to shoot an American M.D., his wife and their six-year-old son? The rear of the plane was stacked with medical supplies Joe had brought from the states with Zavala's money—antibiotics, vitamins, fungicides, germicides, and basics such as alcohol, iodine, aspirin, cotton swabs, bandages, simple laboratory equipment.

The other two passengers were employes of Zavala's. One was a lawyer named Ramon Concepcion. The other was a man-of-all-work who had met the Derrys at the airport a week ago. He was named Danny Larrizabal.

Concepcion was quiet and mannerly, a tall dour man who was connected with the Zavala family's pervasive wealth—plantations, fisheries, knitting mills, food processing. He told Joe and Jenny he was a graduate of UCLA and its law school and considered himself an "old Bruin." He had Oriental eyes and lank black hair, but the pale skin of someone with an admixture of Spanish blood. Joe and Jenny liked him. He was articulate and thoughtful, and had brought a hand puppet for Nicky.

Larrizabal was potbelly fat, thuglike. He wore a gaudy flowered shirt. Under the tails, stuck in his belt, Joe could see the handle of a revolver. He was some kind of personal bodyguard for Dr. Zavala—gopher, stooge, answerer of phone calls, pimp.

The plane would land at Labat, a frontier town in a river valley.

Joe had asked Danny Larrizabal what it was like, and he had responded, "A snake's asshole, Doc. Carry a gun; keep the safety off and your hand on the trigger. They'll shoot you for your shoes."

Why hadn't Zavala mentioned this to him? Joe wondered. And this was where he was bringing his wife and child for a year or more? Dr. Zavala had hinted at minor troubles between the Batati and insurgents "from up north." But Joe had not bargained for Dodge City.

It was a five-hour flight from Manila to Mindanao. Nicky awakened and complained he was hungry. The Chinese copilot brought out paper trays with cold fried chicken, cold rice, fried bananas. Nicky ate greedily and gulped from a bottle of Pepsi.

"How much longer, Danny?" Joe asked.

"Hour anna half, Doc."

Joe walked to the rear, where the soldiers, looking efficient and tough, slept amid the medical supplies. The uniforms were U.S. Army issue, including the leather-and-canvas jungle boots with drain holes at the sides.

He walked into the malodorous john, relieved himself, felt an excitement growing in him. He discounted Danny's story. The guns and the soldiers were Chuck Zavala's game. A rich kid, an unimaginably rich one. This was his hobby when he wasn't practicing medicine in Manila.

As Joe zipped up his fly, he heard a metallic ping, then another one, then a series of short, loud, cracking noises.

He walked out of the bathroom. Larrizabal and Concepcion were peering out of the rear windows with binoculars.

"There's the prick," Larrizabal was saying. "Just ducked into the hut. He's got an automatic rifle."

Concepcion laughed. "Another one. He's still shooting, the jerk."

"Is that what I thought it w-was?" Joe asked.

"No sweat, Doc," Larrizabal said. "We always take a few pops when we're low over the plains."

The lawyer added, "I think they stitched us a few times, Doc. Usually they're not that accurate."

"Who?"

"*Ilagas.* Rats."

Joe could see villages scattered below them on the terraced slopes—bits and scraps of houses like bread crumbs on a green

270

tablecloth. People had vanished. Here and there a water buffalo grazed. Another swam in a muddy pond.

"Land grabbers, land stealers. Dumb bastards couldn't hit a dead horse if it was a yard in front of them." Larrizabal spoke with contempt. He took his snub-nosed revolver out of his belt, pointed it at the window. *"Pow.* Wouldn't I ever like this crate to have a few rocket launchers on it. Maybe a fifty-caliber machine gun."

Joe looked forward. Nicky was finishing his Pepsi. Jenny was reading. The shots must have struck the fuselage at the rear. Neither had noticed. The soldiers had not even awakened.

"But what do they want to shoot at *us* for?" Joe asked.

"They know the boss uses this plane for supplies, to ferry people in and out. They figure they might knock him off one of these days."

What have I sucked myself into? Joe wondered.

"No sweat, Doc," Larrizabal said. He tucked the thirty-eight back into his belt. "The village is secure. They don't come screwing around with Dr. Zavala's operation."

Concepcion patted Joe's shoulder. "And we need you there, Doc. Na Bong is calling a three-day holiday for your arrival."

"So long as it isn't a f-funeral mass."

The road that had led Dr. Joe Derry and his family from his office in East Shinnaway, Long Island, to the jungles of Mindanao had begun one hot August night of the previous year, 1965.

Joe had come home from an exhausting day. He rarely took a summer vacation, finding that he was able to earn extra money covering for physicians who took July and August off.

His own practice remained adequate, the fees modest, the work hard. People liked him. But competition from the specialists and the groups was hurting. The residents of the area were drawn to Dr. Gold's internal-medicine group, and now to Dr. Kevin Derry's Bay Medical Group, located in what amounted to a small proprietary hospital amid groves of lush trees, in North Cohammet. It was *the* place to go for medical care. Danforth College and Mid-Island and Upper County all worked closely with what had been termed in *Newsday* the "Derry Medical Empire."

Destined to marginal rewards, Joe found joy in his wife and son. Nicky was powerful and moved well and would be big-boned. He would be a better athlete than Joe because he had size. It probably came from his grandfather Nick, the retired cop.

Joe remembered the phone call from Chuck Zavala. Nicky had just belted one of his underhand pitches halfway down Eunice Drive. Jenny was summoning him to see the LA riots on the TV news.

"Good swing, kid," Joe said. "Always level, bat even with the ground, and snap your wrists at the end."

"Yeah, yeah, Dad. Once more."

Jenny called from the garage. "Joe. Don't you want to see Bridie? Los Angeles is burning; the whole city's going up in smoke. Twenty-one people are dead."

It was an evening ritual whenever they were home on time—to catch the UBC news to see Bridie. She had been promoted from the local news operation to the network. She was earning forty-five thousand dollars a year and had a lavish expense account, which, she admitted to a slightly shocked Jenny, she padded with "creative writing," adding an extra five thousand dollars, tax-free. Jenny could no longer see her as the Bridie Derry she had known— forthright, candid, honest. She sounded more like Kevin.

"Joe, you can't believe this," Jenny said. "The whole city is going bananas."

In the den the TV set showed a street in Los Angeles that looked like Hiroshima. Police in riot gear and National Guardsmen patrolled the area. There were blacks being hustled into Black Marias, laughing blacks laden with hair dryers and TV sets and cases of booze, racing defiantly out of smashed stores, a statement from Governor Brown denouncing the rioting, the fires, the deaths.

A reporter, looking nervously over his shoulder, as if awaiting a rock, was saying, "The death toll in the four days of violence has now reached twenty-one, with six hundred injured and damages close to one hundred million dollars. Of the twenty-one known deaths, nineteen are black, and two are white—a sheriff's deputy and a city fireman. More than twenty thousand National Guardsmen have been called up. . . ."

"Hate to be on emergency-ward d-duty there," Joe said. "Trauma surgeons are going to be up all night."

The image switched to Chicago. More rioting. Chicago's worst racial rioting in thirteen years. Then a local report—a near-riot in Brooklyn, when a black policeman killed a youth. He'd come upon six black kids beating and robbing a black man, tried to stop it, was attacked by the gang, shot back. Did anyone in public life, Joe wondered, understand how much these people hated, how much violence, how intense a craving for revenge, had been stored up in them?

"I always think of your father when I see these pictures," Jenny said. "Poor Jack."

"It didn't mean anything to those guys who k-killed him. A white face. They killed him so he couldn't identify them if they were caught. Somebody'd better start giving them work and get them homes."

They waited for Bridie to appear. She did at the end of the newscast. Although she was the program's specialist in medicine and science, she increasingly did general news or looked for some psychological angle on stories.

In her early thirties, she remained stunning, her hair lush auburn, her long face alert and compassionate. She was interviewing a black psychologist from NYU. He was commenting on the riots.

". . . hatred stored, compressed, boiling beneath the surface, will eventually blow the lid. I am afraid, Bridget, the lid has been blown, in LA, Chicago, New York, and eventually it will be blown in every urban ghetto. As the man said, the fire next time. . . ."

You nice, dumb professor, Joe wanted to yell at him, *you are only one ninth of the country. Look out they don't start building concentration camps and gas chambers and ovens for you.* Joe once voiced the opinion to Jenny. She raged at him. He was not in favor of these, he protested. He liked blacks, knew they had been given a lousy deal, that old crimes had produced the turbulent river of hate now flooding American streets. But he was a pessimist. He saw the worst coming.

Dirt-smeared, his Mets T-shirt sweaty, Nicky, with ball, bat and glove, entered, slurped iced tea from his father's glass. "Once more, Dad? Ten minutes? Mr. Plotkin can't pitch batting practice no more. His wife called him in."

"Pop's tired, Nick. Tomorrow's Sunday, all d-day. How about some fishing?"

"Yeah. And you promised me a new rod 'n' reel."

"Nicky, stop asking for things all the time," Jenny said. "And tuck your shirt in."

"Pop? An Arbogast reel? And a Rapala lure?"

"Sure, kid." He hugged him close. Ugly father, handsome kid.

273

Jenny wanted to cry. She could not imagine such unquestioning love. She adored Nicky, too. But not the same way Joe did. She had seen his tired eyes glow after coming home from a wearing day at the office and the hospital. Just looking at Nicky, kissing his round dark head, restored him.

The telephone in the kitchen rang. Joe got up, trudged upstairs from the patio and answered it. Jenny watched him—hunched, broad-backed, in droopy khaki shorts, a well-holed T-shirt from Mid-Island Hospital's discards.

"Dr. Derry speaking."

"Anyone pissed in your mayonnaise lately?"

"Who's this?"

"The guy who helped you solve the hepatitis epidemic, buddy-boy."

"Chuck, Chuck Zavala."

Eight years ago at Mid-Island. Zavala, the tiny medical student from Manila. He'd worshipped Joe. He was now Dr. Carlos Zavala. He had gone back to the Philippines. Joe had not heard from him in years. Zavala had gone to California for his internship and residencies. Like most wealthy men, he saw no need to correspond with old friends. Affluence made its own rules. Now and then a Filipino nurse or resident would come through Mid-Island with tales of the Zavala fortune, of the younger son who'd become a physician and ran his own hospital in Manila.

"Tell you why I called," Dr. Zavala said. "Couldn't think of the name of the guy who pissed in the mayo." He convulsed in giggles. "Wells? Weals?"

"Wales. Where are you, Chuck?"

He could hear a woman's laughter in the back. Party noises.

"The Plaza. Come on in, you and Jen. Still married to the world's best nurse?"

"Sure."

"Knockin' 'em dead, Joey?"

"I do all right. GP. Local practice. Kevin's the one b-burning up the track."

"Come on in and have dinner with me," Chuck said. "I'm bored as hell. Wanna see your ugly puss. And bring Jenny. Could we use her to train nurses."

Joe was drained. He looked forward to a quiet evening sipping beer, watching the Mets. Jenny usually read or worked in the garden patch where she'd planted eggplant, squash, tomatoes. It was mid-August and vegetables were ready for picking.

"I'll ask Jenny. Hold on, Chuck."

To Joe's surprise, Jenny agreed. She remembered Chuck well. It would take her an hour or so to fix her hair, get dressed. Joe returned to the kitchen (where Nicky complained he'd have to watch the Mets with Mr. Rackowski) and told Zavala they'd drive in.

"What room, Chuck?"

"The whole ninth floor."

The ninth floor of the Plaza. Joe had a jumbled recollection of furtive men carrying guns under their jackets. He and Jenny were met by a six-foot blonde and a somewhat smaller brunette, both bearing the trademarks of very-high-priced ass.

Chuck Zavala, pigeon-sized, in cowboy boots and a rancher's tailored suit, could not contain his joy at seeing Joe and Jenny. He chased the hookers and his flunkies (everyone but the lawyer Concepcion) out of his suite, and told Joe he had a business proposition. He wanted Joseph Derry to set up a clinic in Batati Village, in the forests of southern Mindanao.

Later at Twenty-One Zavala and the lawyer explained his mission to save the indigenous tribes.

"Old story," Chuck said. "Poorest people, not Christian, not Moslem. They are being forced to sell their land. When they won't they get shot, killed, tortured. But I got it under control now."

Concepcion nodded. "More than that, Doctor. The boss has a real program—save the land, save the people. New farming methods, self-government. Wait'll you see Batati. You won't recognize it. Stores, school, moviehouse. But the hospital stinks. We need you. Na Bong said you were the best doctor he ever knew."

"Kakai Joe," Chuck giggled. "Friend Joe."

"I w-was a GI medic and it was fifteen years ago."

"They never forgot," Zavala laughed. "Na says you beat the crap out of some coon sergeant to get a guy out in a chopper."

Joe remembered. The steamy forest, the people squatting outside the first-aid tent. A man with hemorrhagic fever.

It was Shangri-La, Concepcion said. Incredibly beautiful, high, clean air and pure water.

Joe protested—he had a practice and a home. Jenny had a career. They had a young son.

Zavala waved it away. He would talk to Dr. DeBeers, to Kevin, to Jenny's boss. Leave of absence. Nicky could go to the mission school. Father Kelly was a terrific guy.

For the rest of the week Jenny argued that Zavala was buying them the way he bought whores, gunmen, anything he wanted. But they were needed in Batati, Joe replied. The practice was boring him. He'd get into administrative work on his return.

She realized he needed the change, the challenge.

Concepcion called again in two days. The money wasn't much. Nine thousand for Joe, six thousand for Jenny. But they'd save every cent, bankable in U.S. dollars in the states.

By October she'd given in. Joe needed the boost to his ego. His own hospital, even if it had a thatched roof. He'd never be rich. Why not do some good?

2

Cynthia and Kevin were watching Bridie—"Bridget Derry" in her reporting—on the seven-o'clock news. It was a family occasion in more ways than one. The subject of Bridie's special report on medicine was Dr. Walter Luff.

Potsy had been on Bridie's back for a year to do a feature on him. Upper County had given him a new operating room, a new CCU, trained teams. Potsy was earning in excess of seven hundred thousand dollars a year, but was frustrated.

"I want recognition," he told Kevin petulantly. "I'm as good a surgeon as Cooley or Spencer. But nobody knows about me. Kev, that kid sister of yours has to help me."

Bridie eventually gave in to his endless phone calls reminding her of their blood ties. So now he was on national TV.

"Success has changed your cousin," Cynthia said. "He even speaks better. Did he take elocution lessons?"

Kevin said, "I doubt it. Potsy knows when to use the gutter and when to sound like he went to Princeton. One of the world's great fake-out artists."

The camera revealed Potsy and his team, bending over a sixty-year-old man who had been suffering acute chest pains—angina pectoris. His ailment was diagnosed as a severe stenosis, or narrowing of the main coronary artery. Bypass surgery was indicated.

The camera moved its lens under the bright lights. Viewers now saw Mr. Ramsgate's heart, ready to receive a section of vein from the patient's right leg. The vein would be sewn to the wider part of the coronary artery, then connected to the patient's aorta. Thus the word "bypass," Bridie said, speaking in reverential whispers. She had a sense of drama even if she disliked the assignment.

"What's happening now, Dr. Luff?" she asked.

"I'm attaching this piece of vein to the patient's aorta. Blood will flow freely into the heart. There'll be no shortage of blood, the factor that caused the pain."

Kevin watched, amused. Except for moments when he relaxed alone with Kevin, Potsy was a new man. His dignity was overwhelming.

"It's not the surgeon alone, Bridget," Potsy was saying, as he tied minute stitches, connecting vein to aorta. A nurse placed a sponge beneath the heart. "It's my *team.*"

Potsy identified the members of his cardiovascular unit, as the camera picked up each masked face in turn.

Cynthia stretched her legs, watched with concealed jealousy as Bridie, now outside the OR, her yellow sterile mask lowered, concluded her report. "And that, Fred, is a look at open-heart surgery as performed in a modern hospital. The bypass operation you witnessed is basically a simple one, but one that requires years of training—not just for gifted surgeons like Dr. Walter Luff, Jr., but for all the members of his team. Truly, they hold life in their hands. This is Bridget Derry, at Upper County Hospital, saying good night."

Kevin turned the set off. He had got used to seeing Bridget on the TV screen. She was prettier than ever, if a bit colder in manner. He could not explain it. Perhaps driving ambition was doing it. She had had her share of lovers and now, Kevin knew, lived with the vice-president for news, a terrifyingly intellectual man named Christopher Ling. Ling spent weekends with his wife and family in Chappaqua, New York. Weekdays he lived with Bridie in a high apartment on Sutton Place.

"The girl wonder of TV," Cynthia said. "She has your tenacity, Kevin, your ability to get what you want."

"Nothing wrong with that."

"Not at all. I was ruined by having so much early on. If I'd been a pharmacist's daughter, working my way through college, I might be doing interesting work."

"Nothing's stopping you. You've made threats for years about

278

getting back into PR. Your father could get you a job in a minute."

"I'm forty, wrinkled from too much riding and sailing, and I have no talent. Besides, I'm unstable. You told me so yourself. So did my father. So did the series of head shrinkers I ran through."

And the few who ran through you, he wanted to say.

The truth was, she was looking somewhat better. Bridie had been right four years ago. Cynthia Derry had been anorexic, a victim of *anorexia nervosa,* an aversion to food, a compulsion to stay thin. Kevin felt he was partly to blame.

It had come to a crisis a year and a half ago when after an extended vacation in St. Martin (he suspected Crist had joined her there) she came back, and for a month refused to eat, forced herself to vomit. A sour odor permeated the house. She was forever squirting lilac-scented deodorants.

Peaked, her eyes recessed in their sockets, she finally was persuaded to see Bridie's old teacher and idol, Dr. McGrory. *Anorexia nervosa,* Kevin knew, was usually a disease of young girls and teenagers. McGrory, with her wide experience with adolescents, might be able to help.

"The symptoms are classic, Dr. Derry," old McGrory told him privately. "She has a deep mental disorder that manifests itself in a refusal to eat. She's punishing herself for something. It's rare after thirty-five years of age, but by no means unknown. I'm surprised you didn't pick up the symptoms earlier."

Kevin remained silent. His ineffable charm, his fame, seemed to have no effect on the stolid ex-nun.

"Wasn't she overactive?" McGrory asked. "And didn't she rise feeling fresh and ready for another day?"

"That's what threw me off," Kevin said lamely. "No matter how thin she got, she was always ready to ride or travel."

"When did you last give her a physical?"

"About six months ago." He was stretching things. It was over a year ago. McGrory's blunt, honest face was shaming him.

"Your wife is hypotensive and has slight bradycardia. Excuse me for saying it, but it's always the physician's family that gets diagnosed last. I knew she was anorexic when she walked in here. Someone should have caught it earlier."

"She resists psychiatric help. She won't stay with it. It was an effort getting her to see you."

McGrory remained impervious to Kevin's charm. All she saw was a rather self-centered man, hiding his lack of emotions, his vaulting ambition, with a veneer of youthful agreeability.

"May I ask what your personal relations with Mrs. Derry have been?"

"You may. But I don't know that I'm required to respond. This isn't a divorce hearing."

"Dr. Derry, a man of your background knows that psychiatric therapy has to take into account family relationships."

"I'm aware, but not sympathetic. I like evidence, not theories."

"Then I shall give you some," Dr. McGrory said. She fiddled with her spectacles and read from the medical report. "'Because of malnutrition, patient was found to have diminished gonadal function. A marked decrease in urinary estrogens, an absence of cornified cells on vaginal smears and low urinary gonadotropins. There was also a decrease in urinary seventeen-ketosteroids.' That should tell you something."

"Thyroid function?" If she were going to play medical games, he was better at it than she was.

"Normal. All of which led us to a diagnosis of anorexia and not a pituitary malfunction."

"So we're back to square one. My wife is anorexic and she may be harming herself permanently."

"I am inclined to think so. Reduced sexual activity is a clear indication. Dr. Derry, you cannot underestimate the effects of serious psychosis in these cases. A psychiatric and social history is indicated. Your cooperation will be needed if we are to proceed."

"I'm not sure my wife needs that much help. It may do her more harm than good. It may open up windows she'd prefer left closed. Did she tell you about her first marriage and her first child?"

"No."

"There's your answer. She'll hide what she wants to hide. The marriage was a disaster. Her son is now sixteen and institutionalized. He is severely retarded, a PKU child, with extreme symptoms. She never recovered from the shock. Her husband blamed her for the defective child, the marriage fell apart and—"

"And how is your marriage holding together?"

"That isn't the purpose of this visit. If Mrs. Derry wants to see you again, I won't object. But I am not to be included in any couch sessions. I'm too busy. Besides, I don't know precisely what my involvement is."

She shook her head slowly. "You are a distinguished physician, Dr. Derry. But you're a shortsighted man. Your wife is on the edge of a total breakdown."

"I'm aware of it. I've lived with her for twelve years."

"Then help her."

"I'll try. But I don't intend to fill out MMPI forms or stare at inkblots."

"Then I guess we have little left to talk about. I warn you, though, if you permit her to neglect herself, there may be grave consequences."

Kevin asked about diet stimulants, ways of forcing her to eat. McGrory saw he was trying to divert her. "Try being more affectionate," she said. "Try making love to her."

Afterward Kevin had made some attempts to repair the relationship. Once, Cynthia asked him if he ever got laid. But his only answer was that if he did, he wouldn't talk about it.

Now as they turned off the television set, Cynthia, perhaps stimulated by Bridie's beautiful, provocative face, raised the topic again. "Maybe you're just not good anymore. Or maybe there has to be some real feeling. The connection alone isn't enough."

No, it wasn't. He was well aware of it. He'd made love to her for years with a kind of subdued vengeance, getting his innings for the way she'd run off to Haslam. Now he was preoccupied.

One night, drinking Glenfiddich with her father, the old man made him squirm with the frank revelation that he loved Kevin more than he did his own children. Suddenly Kevin had felt terribly sorry for Cynthia.

Worse, he was discovering that his sexual needs were limited. In recent years he had had two brief unsentimental affairs. He had dropped them as easily as he had begun them. One was with a publisher's wife, a blonde horse-lover, much like Cynthia, whose appetites far exceeded his. Her recriminations after he abandoned her disgusted him. Finally he had to threaten to tell her husband if she persisted in calling him.

Later he had pursued an affair with his receptionist's sister, a dark, sensual Greek girl named Rena Kostaris. She was brash, aggressive, shameless, accosted him in the parking lot at Upper County, and had gone to bed with him a few days later. They made love in motels. She had what Potsy called "cockroach eyes," ringlets of curling black hair. Yet he could not abide her brainless chatter for

281

five minutes. Passion was an interval between clumsy gaucheries. Yet he must have slept with her fifteen times before Potsy warned him. "Seems a well-known cardiologist was seen checking into the Highway Motor Inn with a dark-haired broad. Bad stuff, Kev. Not for a member of the medical board. You're a target. I know it's a problem with Cynthia sick all the time, but for Chrissake, *motels!*"

Perhaps it was guilt, perhaps loneliness, but he felt drawn again to Cynthia. He told himself he was concerned with Cynthia's well-being. McGrory was right; her health was at stake. That night, instead of answering her taunts, he took her in his arms, removed the robe and the nightgown, and with more effort than he realized would be necessary, made prolonged love to her.

"A surprise," she said. "A nice one."

"I want you to get better. We have a lot of years to work on."

"And I love you, Kev. Do you love me? Oh, I wish you did. The way you loved me in that letter you wrote from Germany."

"Sure, baby. You'll be fine. I loved what we just did. Easier than a cardiac catheterization and a lot more fun."

She cuddled against him, a terribly thin woman. "Please stay here all night, Kevin. I miss you."

"I will. It's a pleasure."

In the middle of the night she got out of bed, went to the bathroom and vomited.

"Are you all right?" he called.

Her gagging voice replied, "Yes, yes, I'm fine. Upset stomach. Too much to eat."

Anorexic, he thought. He would have to be more affectionate, more attentive.

"Lawton Curtis, Kevin Derry," Manship said, coming into Kevin's office.

Curtis was a beefy young man in his early thirties with extremely pale skin and limp brown hair that fell over his forehead. His eyes were widely spaced and unexpectedly shrewd. He was one of three men whom the Upper County Hospital search committee was considering for executive director. Kevin knew that Manship would make t'ie final judgment after consulting with him.

"I'm privileged to sit here," Curtis said. "I'm not an M.D. but I know about your paper on nutritional deficiencies and heart disease. Marvelous work."

Ass-kissing, Kevin realized.

"Kevin's working on a book now," E.E. said. "A primer for medical students on the pathology of the heart. How in the devil this son-in-law of mine finds time for all of it, I can't figure out."

Kevin studied Lawton Curtis' *curriculum vitae*. Blair Academy, Columbia College, a Ph.D. in hospital administration from Yale. He was currently assistant director of a volunteer hospital in Pennsylvania. His references were impeccable—the head of a large corporation, an eminent physician, a senator.

It was evident that Manship wanted Curtis for the job. Upper County was the biggest gem in the Danforth diadem, and it shone increasingly as Mid-Island faded.

"Upper County is the MGM of hospitals," E.E. told Curtis, who looked blank. "Before your time," E.E. elaborated, "I was involved in movie financing. Mr. Mayer, who ran MGM, so dominated the movie scene he let other studios exist on *sufferance*. Not a bad system. Why shouldn't the best run the show?" He went on to describe how Louis B. Mayer awarded studios to his daughter's husband, who promptly bankrupted them. The joke in Hollywood, Manship said, was that the fellow was "ruining the son-in-law business."

Kevin looked up. "I hope I haven't ruined yours, Dad."

"Hardly."

Curtis laughed nervously. "Dr. Derry, I'd consider it an honor to serve with you. Your reputation has reached Philadelphia."

"Not much of a trip," Kevin said dryly.

Curtis crossed his chunky thighs. "Of course, medicine runs in my family. My father is Miles Curtis. You know—Concordia Hospital Supply. It was formerly Curtis and Lemoyne."

"Oh. I see. *That* Curtis."

Manship rested his chin on his hand. "I was elected to their board a few months ago, Kevin," Manship said. "We've made a considerable investment in Concordia. It's the most impressive new firm in the field."

"I assume having Mr. Curtis as our chief operating officer will hardly put Concordia in an unfavorable position when it comes to contracts? I'm sorry if I'm blunt, but Mr. Manship will tell you that

I'm a working physician, not a financial man."

Curtis' face reddened, but he said calmly, "Absolutely not. I assure you, Dr. Derry, that would be the farthest thing from my mind. I insist on competitive bidding for everything from aspirin to a dialysis unit."

But it won't hurt, Kevin thought.

"Dr. Derry is a stickler on medical ethics," Manship said. "I have to watch my step with him. The fact that your father runs one of the country's largest hospital-supply corporations will not affect purchasing policies, correct?"

"Absolutely, Mr. Manship."

And you are both as full of shit as a lower bowel, Kevin thought. *My dear father-in-law, to whom I owe so much and whom I respect. And Mr. Lawton Curtis, son of the bastard who tried to stick my brother Joe in an army prison. . . .*

"You see," Manship was saying, as memories flooded Kevin's mind, "Lawton comes by his interest in hospital management rightfully. The elder Mr. Curtis was an army-hospital administrator."

"Dad was in World War II," young Curtis said. "A bird colonel."

I knew him, you asshole, Kevin thought.

"I'll be candid, Kevin." Manship said. "Of course we'll have competitive bidding. Miles and I wouldn't have it any other way. But we'll do each other favors. . . ."

Kevin thought of telling Lawton about his encounters with his father. Of the old man's criminal past. *Stealing U.S. Army penicillin and selling it at a one thousand percent markup in Germany.* But why muddy the waters? Lawton would know sooner or later. In fact, Kevin thought, if the new executive director ever steps out of line, I'll club him with it. But he was glad that Joe was in the Philippines, in some remote village.

As Curtis was about to leave, Kevin asked. "Have you mentioned me to your father? That you were seeing me?"

"I don't believe so. He knows who you are, of course. He's a great admirer of yours."

Kevin nodded. *Your father is a son of a bitch and he knows me, all right. Probably crapping his pants right now that I'll wreck the deal for him.*

When Curtis had left, Manship eyed Kevin with a cocked head. "You weren't your usual cordial self."

"I know his father."

"So do I. A little coarse but a superb businessman."

Kevin sighed and told E.E. the story. He was violating his part of the deal with Curtis, but he wanted E.E. to know. No, he would not vote against the ex-colonel's son, but he wanted his father-in-law to understand his lack of enthusiasm.

Manship did not seem upset. These things happened; they were best overlooked.

"Besides, Kevin," Manship said. "We only have Joe's side of the story."

For the first time since he had known Manship, he was faintly repelled by him. He said softly, "Joe doesn't lie, Dad. He's too thickheaded and honest to invent lies."

"You may be right," Manship said cautiously. "But that's old news. My goodness, things change in sixteen years. You wouldn't want to penalize Curtis over some old indiscretion."

Two months after Lawton Curtis took over as executive director of Upper County Hospital, its contracts with four major suppliers of drugs and other materials were canceled. Concordia Hospital Supply was appointed in their place. A week later Concordia's stock rose eight points. The corporation was mentioned prominently in a financial newsletter as one that was "virtually recession-proof."

Kevin was not even aware of what had happened. Nor was he aware, until after the trustees approved it, that Curtis had negotiated a $750,000 loan from a private bank to pay for refurnishing three floors of Upper County in "color-coordinated fashion." The interest charge was exorbitant, but Curtis made a persuasive case. These were the most expensive private rooms. Only weeks later was it discovered that both E.E. Manship and Miles Curtis were on the board of the bank afforded this favor.

After two similar loans were negotiated with the same bank, one for improvements in the OR, another for an expanded laboratory, it was decided to raise room costs five dollars a day.

Old Doc Felder, wandering around to medical-society meetings to raise hell about patients' being overcharged, ran into Kevin one night the following month.

"It's an outrage," Felder sputtered. "Those bastards are turning hospital care into a General Motors operation. Screw the patient; milk him dry; make the banks and the drug companies and the hospital suppliers rich."

"It can't be helped, Sam."

"Like hell it can't. Kevin, do something about it. You're chief of medicine."

"Sorry, Sam. I practice cardiology. I don't know what those birds are up to half the time."

"Well, I do. And they stink."

Kevin, seeing the rage in Doc's weary eyes, changed the subject. How was his daughter, Nan? And Charley? Terrific, Felder said. Nan was specializing in genetics in Boston. Her marriage had gone sour. Guy was jealous of her. But she was happy. Charley was the county public defender, giving legal aid to blacks, Hispanics and radicals.

Felder pulled out his wallet and showed Kevin a photo of Nan—a candid shot of her seated at a lab table, injecting a white mouse.

"Some girl," Felder said. "You remember her, don't you, Kevin?"

"I do, Sam."

He could see the beauty in the dark oval face. A beauty that went beyond flesh and hair and bone structure.

"You mean a child *died* of glue sniffing?" Bridie asked. Her eyes widened in shock. She had heard the case described before the camera began to roll, but she knew how to add a touch of drama. Each news report is a minidrama, Ling always said.

"That's what we suspect, Miss Derry," said Dr. Kaplan, chief of pediatric service at West Harlem Children's Hospital.

"The boy in question was thirteen. He admitted attending glue-sniffing parties for three years."

"Can you explain, Dr. Kaplan?"

The camera, beneath its padded "blimp," hummed softly. The technicians liked working with Bridie. Fast, smart, few retakes.

"Inhalation of fumes of hydrocarbons, usually what we call 'airplane glue,' or those extra-strong fix-it glues. The substance is a

286

benzene tuolene. It's become a fad among adolescents."

"But what does it do for them?"

"Do you mean what do they look for, or what damage does it do?"

"Both."

"Presumably it gives them a high. But we have documented ten cases of severe damage to blood and bone marrow. The boy who died had what we call an erythrocytic crisis—aplastic anemia, a shortage of blood cells due to failure of production by the bone marrow."

Dr. Kaplan turned to a group of youngsters seated against the wall. "These other youngsters are luckier. They all developed serious symptoms of anemia from sniffing glue, but we caught them in time."

"Can I talk to them?"

"Cothal, come here and talk to Miss Derry."

All the children were black. They had heavy-lidded eyes and moved sluggishly. Cothal approached the microphone.

Bridie heard a low-murmured "*sheeet*" in the background. She signaled the cameraman to cut and frowned at the children.

"You behave, all of you," she said firmly. "I used to be a children's nurse. If you don't shut up, I'll get Dr. Kaplan to ram a needle in your behinds. Would you like that?"

"Please, Miss Derry," the pediatrician said. "We try to be persuasive."

"I've got a job to do and a deadline. If I hear one more '*sheeet*' I'll throw them out."

The interview proceeded. In mumbled words, Cothal admitted her addiction to glue. It made her feel, "like, you know, real good." But then she began getting headaches and dizziness every morning, and got so weak her mama had to get her out of the bed, but then she wasn't strong enough to go to school. She kept "throwing up and all, so Mama brought me here, you know . . ."

3

Two hours later, wearing nothing but an apricot silk dressing gown, Bridie watched herself on the color TV in Ling's Sutton Place penthouse.

In a pearl-gray robe from Harrod's, Christopher Ling sipped champagne. This was a nightly ritual with them, Monday through Thursday. Fridays he took the train to Chappaqua.

Bridie said, "The lighting stinks. Those old newsreel hacks think they're filming waterskiing in Florida. When will they learn that when you film Negroes, you have to throw a double sun-gun on them."

"More wine, angel?" Ling asked.

He always referred to champagne as "wine." It seemed to give it an extra dimension. He was full of arcane knowledge. Presently he was writing an article on Byzantine icons in Yugoslavia for the *Journal of Religious Art.*

"Come fill the cup." Bridie stretched on the sofa, weary, unsettled. She worked hard. Setting stories up, researching them, doing interviews, standing over the film editor's shoulder. She had grown vain and demanding. A hairdresser and a secretary—all her own.

When the news program ended, Ling got up and went to the kitchen to look at the prosciutto, fresh asparagus and cheddar casserole he had in the oven. A gourmet cook, he was contemplating a book—the television-news cookbook, with recipes by his friends in the business. A perfectionist in all matters, he insisted on genuine

Indian mustard oil for his salads, made his own *mole* sauce from five chili powders and chocolate imported from Morelia.

In his absence Bridie gazed at the glittering skyline, the winking towers of affluence. She was part of it. And how easy it had been. What a warm, sweet, fulfilling sensation success gave. Damned near better than sex. And when combined with sex—*supreme.*

They dined near the glass wall overlooking the East River. Ling ate slowly, savoring his delicacies. There was *arugula* salad to accompany the casserole, more wine, hot bread from Zito's. Bridie was certain she loved him, but in an analytic, calculating way. She knew him for what he was—not a fake but a man who used every asset, every talent, every bit of knowledge, to make it all the way from a dusty Kansas town to head one of the greatest news empires in the country.

He stroked her hand, anticipating the programmed hours of sex that would follow. And typically, as flesh touched flesh, he began to talk trade. Ling was worried about doing too many stories on Negroes, like the piece Bridie had just completed.

"But you're a liberal, Chris."

That was just why he wanted fewer angry black faces on television. He feared a reaction from beer-drinking blue-collar workers in Queens. He did not want his power diminished by hordes of furious welders.

"We're walking on thin ice, Bridget," Ling said. "People are becoming terrified of their sons turning gay or their daughters being raped by Negroes."

"Sounds like you can't wait, Chris. It'll make a great three-minute spot for the evening news." She smiled at him. His face was a shade darker than his bleached eyebrows and pale hair. The coloration lent him a strange negative look that went well with his cynicism.

She lubricated herself while Ling put the dishes in the sink. In a few minutes he came in and turned off the lights. Often when he came, he was reduced to moans and soft appeals. She wanted to say "There, there," and pat his back. Yet he was a considerate and competent lover, and had long closed out such aspirants as poor Sparling.

"It gets more wondrous every time," Ling gasped.

She stroked his body—powerful chest, stringy muscles. "They

call me Ling's Thing, you know." He was kissing her breasts. "I don't like it, Chris."

"Tell me who. I'll fire them."

"It'll mean firing all the cameramen and soundmen. Anyway, I don't want to be Ling's Thing. I want to be his wife."

"Darling, you know my problem. Dolores will destroy me. She's a strong-willed woman. Give me a few more months to work things out."

"I love you more than she does."

"I know. I know, angel."

"Why are UBC wives different from ABC or NBC wives? They're all from Radcliffe and breed golden retrievers and work for Planned Parenthood. I hate them. I hate Dolores."

"She knows."

"Then for God's sake, why does she tolerate it?"

"Dolores is too intelligent to give me up."

"God, you people. Like my sister-in-law Cynthia. She was laying her husband's best friend—the husband before Kevin, I mean. I think she still sees him."

"Your esteemed brother is no different from Dolores. They are broad-minded, realists."

"And I'm an old-fashioned Irish girl from a small town." She kissed his open mouth. "Marry me, you conceited bastard. Divorce her and sell the house in Chappaqua, you hear me, Ling? I love you, goddammit."

He sighed, found her again, and they made leisurely love. She cried briefly. She really did want to marry him.

"Give me time, darling. I adore you, Bridie. But let me break it to Dolores slowly."

He was too much a cynic, a schemer. Maybe she loved him even more for that.

The DC-3 came in low, bounced noisily as it struck the dirt runway. Nicky screamed and held his ears.

"Keep your mouth open, wide open," Joe shouted.

"If he does, I'm afraid he'll whoops on me," Jenny said.

"Won't be the first time," Joe said.

At the rear of the plane, the stacked crates of medical supplies tumbled to the floor.

Ramon Concepcion and Danny Larrizabal were peering out the window.

"There's the boss," Larrizabal said. "When he says he'll meet us, he *meets* us. Hey, Ramon, see the boss?"

"Yeah. Got himself a new uniform."

Joe looked out the window. Labat Airport was a tin-roofed palm-thatched dump. The dirt strip ran alongside a filthy frontier town. Open drains, tiny stores, bicycles. Sweating under tropical vegetation, it might have been any impoverished town in Southeast Asia.

At the side of the strip Joe saw a military Jeep and two six-by-six trucks. Did he see right? Were machine guns mounted on them?

Dr. Carlos Zavala, in tailored khaki uniform and combat boots, was waving. He wore an old-fashioned army campaign hat with wide brim. Around his waist, Patton-style, was a bullet-studded belt, with two pearl-handled revolvers. Behind him were six more armed constabulary.

Joe scowled at Concepcion. "I thought you said this p-place was secure."

Concepcion waved at his boss, but did not look at Joe. "The boss likes to put on a show."

Jenny looked angrily at Joe. But she could say nothing. They were committed. And if Nicky didn't stop screaming, she'd scream herself. At last the steps were lowered and they could leave the old plane.

Joe stared at a group of ragged men who glared at them with sullen eyes. All wore peculiar glass amulets around their necks. They seemed far more undernourished than the Filipino constabulary who were supervising the unloading.

Jenny and Joe were greeted with warm hugs, kisses, laughter by Dr. Zavala. Joe nodded at the ragged men.

"Who're those guys?" he asked.

"The enemy," said Zavala.

"They don't look like much."

Ramon Concepcion winked at Dr. Zavala. *"Ilagas.* Rats from Ilo-Ilo. Christian land grabbers. They got pushed off *their* land by the loggers so they come down here and try to drive the Batati off. Burn their houses, rape the women."

Joe gulped. He was glad Jenny had taken Nicky to the toilet to clean him up. He felt the sweat form pools in his neck, under his arms. "You fed me a pile of crap, Chuck. You said this place was secure. You got a w-war going on. We were shot at on the plane. Now I learn you have to keep an army around you because of those hoods."

"Relax, buddy boy," Zavala said. "You think those creeps would start something in broad daylight? And against Dr. Carlos Zavala's friends? Right, Ramon?"

"Right, boss."

Jenny came out of the baking terminal building with Nicky. Poor kid, he looked gray, Joe thought.

A fat man in a gray suit, white shirt, black tie, appeared on the fringes of the crowd. He was whispering to some of the amulet-wearing men.

"Who's the dude?" Jenny asked Zavala.

"Perpetua. Local political boss. He's wanted on two murder charges in Luzon. Nobody's got the guts to grab him. He's behind the land stealing. Gets a cut on every acre his goons rob from the Batati." Chuck waved to the stout man. "Hi, Perpetua! *Mabuhay,* you son of a bitch!"

Perpetua waved back. He did not smile.

"This planeload's got them scared stiff," Chuck said joyfully. He helped Jenny and Nicky into the back of the Jeep. Nicky was fascinated with the machine gun mounted over the cab. It was the biggest toy he had ever seen.

"Why?" Joe asked.

"I had my spies spread the word," Zavala laughed. "You're special forces. That's why I got you and Jen the bush jackets. You're here to train the Batati with weapons. See that load of medical supplies?" He pointed a finger at the truck. "Those Ilaga jerks are convinced they're loaded with machine guns, grenades, ammo."

"Oh, Jesus," Jenny moaned, "they'll be after us."

"No way," Zavala said. "They don't mess with the compound."

"*Bam! Bam! Bam!*" Nicky cried. He made a rifle out of his brown husky arms, pointed them at the airstrip. "*Dut-dut-dut-dut-dut-dut!*" Pop, c'n I shoot the machine gun?"

"No. It doesn't work anyway. Right, Dr. Zavala?"

"Only when I want it to." He fell over the wheel laughing. "Christ, *special forces!*"

"It's nothing but antibiotics, antiseptics, bandages, vitamins and ringworm k-killers," Joe said.

"That's what *you* think, buddy boy," Zavala shouted.

The Jeep turned, following the lead vehicle past rice paddies and groves of palms. Little stands selling soft drinks and cookies were posted every hundred yards. A naked child squatted in the street. Nicky watched, fascinated. "He's makin' doody in the street, Pop."

"You mean you packed guns inside the crates m-marked 'medical supplies'?" Joe asked. He was furious.

"Couldn't pass up a chance like that."

"But what about Customs?" Jenny asked. "That long manifest Joe and I made out? I listed everything, down to the last syringe."

"Customs, *wow!*" Zavala hooted. He swerved to avoid a scrawny sow and its troop of piglets. "This is the Philippines. What Zavala wants, he gets."

As he opened the doors for sick call, Joe had to admit Dr. Zavala had done miracles with the village. Neat dirt streets, bamboo-and-nipa houses, a cooperative store, a school, a workshop where the women made beads, batiks and carvings for tourist shops in Manila. There was also a two-story concrete lodge with a bamboo veranda, where Zavala had his headquarters, and where the Derrys were housed. The doctor had also financed agricultural experiments with upland rice, the staple of the Batati diet.

The first patient came in and stood before Joe. He was an older man and his symptoms were disturbing—an enlarged liver, signs of hypertension. Joe sent him into the shed to leave stool and urine samples.

Joe had no laboratory to speak of. The specimens would have to be flown to Davao for analysis. Then, via telephone and shortwave hookup, the results would be read back.

The village was at three thousand feet, cold at night, foggy in the morning. Usually there were several hours of bright sunlight, and then one could set one's watch with the rainstorms, which arrived a bit before noon. In late afternoon, it cleared again for an hour or so. At night, more dampness.

Yet it was shiveringly beautiful. Concepcion had not exaggerated when he called it Shangri-La. The sloping terraced hills formed a

293

natural basin around the rows of cheerful huts. Beyond, the rainforest rose, giant mahogany and narra trees climbing the slopes. Above the forest were fearsome stone peaks and secret caves.

As the next patient came in Joe suddenly wished Jenny had not gone out to one of the perimeter villages.

"Someone go with my wife?" he asked Na.

"Danny sent a soldier. They don't mess with the boss's Jeeps. Ilagas attack only when our people got their backs turned, no guns, can't fight back."

The patient, squatting in pain, got up and told Joe, through Na Bong, that his belly hurt. Joe palpated the liver—swollen, tender. He sent the man into the shed for specimens.

"What do those guys do?" Joe asked Na Bong.

"Buffalo drivers, Kakai. Breed buffalos, sell."

"They spend a lot of time in the water?"

"Sure, boss. Wash buffalos, make them drink, swim."

Joe chewed on a pencil, frowned. His face was creased and freckled from the sun.

"Most of the Batati don't use the buffalo lake, do they?" he asked Na. A woman brought a baby to him. Otitis media, middle-ear infection. Like the Indians. The child had what looked like a strep throat and seemed to be generating a peritonsillar abscess. He told the Batati nurse to give the child a shot of penicillin. Again he wished he had his own lab facilities.

He detained the two men who had come to him with swollen livers. He turned to Na. "Ask them do they see snails in the buffalo pond."

"What's that, Kakai? New word for me."

Joe drew a picture on his prescription pad—coiled shell, the body with the antennas emerging. Both nodded vigorously and laughed. Yes, the pond was full of them. No good for anything. They had bad stink.

Schistoma japonicum, Joe thought. Zavala had sworn that the lakes and ponds around Batati were free of schistosomiasis, the dreaded *bilharzia* that infected whole villages.

Joe reread from his handbook on communicable diseases.

A trematode or blood-fluke infection, with adult male and female worms living in the veins of the host . . . symptomatol-

ogy related to the location of the parasite in the human host
. . . most important pathologic effects are the complications
that arise from chronic infection . . . liver involvement.

S. Japonicum, the blood fluke, led a wild life. Water buffalo, dogs,
wild rats, were often the hosts. But the persistence of the disease
depended upon snails, which were *intermediate* hosts. The fluke's
larval form developed in the snail; after the eggs left the mammalian
body through feces, the eggs hatched in water and the larva entered
the snail. Then mature free-swimming larva left the snail, and found
their way into another host—penetrating human skin through small
wounds.

An awful lot of trouble to make a man ill, Joe thought. He would
have to do something about the buffalo pond. He'd seen naked
Batati boys swimming in it, women taking water from it, even
though there were wells nearby. If it were infected with *S.
Japonicum,* he'd have to enforce rules. He'd read there were poisons
that got rid of the snails. He made a note to take it up with Zavala.

Sick call ended and Joe turned on the radio. There was usually an
English-language broadcast from Manila. Most of it was about
Vietnam. *All bullshit,* Joe thought, *a lost cause.*

One of the nurses, layered in colored cloths, tinkling with brass
hoops, brought him his lunch. She set it on a wooden table. She left
bowing, a habit neither he nor Jenny could break them of.

Not bad chow, Joe thought. On a banana leaf were pieces of spicy
fried chicken, fried bananas, shaved coconut. He ate better here than
when he was a resident at Mid-Island.

"Coke, Kakai?" Na asked, winking. He stole them from Zavala's
private hoard.

"Sure, Na."

The datu walked across the village green, where two swaybacked
stallions were flailing at each other. He returned with two Cokes.

"Radio was on," he said. "Some guy trying to reach us. Says he
got shot at this morning. Ilagas in the hills."

"Where?" Joe asked.

"We lost him. Breakup on the shortwave. Radio operator is
trying to raise him again."

Joe jumped up. "Where? Jenny's out there. If she's in trouble,
we're g-going after her."

295

"No trouble, Kakai. Ilagas won't go near a village in daylight."

"My wife may be dead by then."

Joe got up and ran across the field to the radio shack. The operator was on the pipe. "Bedroom One, Bedroom One, do you read me?" he was asking.

There was no response.

"Where the hell is Bedroom One?" Joe asked. Na was a step behind him.

"Perimeter station."

"Where?"

"North farms. Little Batati, Tamok, Suraga. Not to worry. The operator's probably out screwing a Batati girl."

"My wife is in one of those villages. I heard her say she was stopping at Suraga. Try to r-raise him."

"Bedroom One, Bedroom One, do you read me?"

There was humming and crackling at the other end. But no one responded.

Jenny had been curious to see one of the underdeveloped villages. Compared to Batati, Suraga was in the Stone Age. A treeless patch in the forest, it consisted of no more than a score of disintegrating huts and a few barely cultivated fields.

"They're Batati also," said Danny Larrizabal, who was driving. "Same language, same religion. But they're backward. The boss is trying to fly a generator in so they can have power. Maybe start a school."

Seated on the tailgate was one of the constabulary, a wiry soldier named Santiago who had flown from Manila with the Derrys.

When Larrizabal stopped the Jeep, Jenny was utterly unprepared for the welcome. Hordes of minature people came running out of the houses and fields to embrace her. Larrizabal they knew—Kakai Din—a friend of the greatest Kakai of all, Kakai Chok. But Jenny was new, a friend from far away who would fix the babies' eyes and ears.

"What a welcome," Jenny gasped. "Do they always do this?"

Larrizabal shrugged. "They haven't seen a doctor in a year."

"Danny, don't tell them I'm only a nurse. I like it."

Larrizabal walked with Santiago to a bamboo lookout tower and surveyed the countryside.

Jenny was borne, feet off the ground, by the murmuring crowd, to their chief. He wore an old U.S. Army shirt and a blue breechclout. He carried two bolos on his shrunken hips, and he kissed Jenny's hand.

A crude table had been set up. Jenny began shooing people away. They obeyed, retreating with tinkling of brass, rustling of long skirts. Then she opened her medical kit—aspirin, antibiotics, disinfectants, stomach pills, specifics against ringworm and other parasites.

"Danny," she called. He was descending the switchback ladder from the watchtower. "Can you help me with the language?"

"Sorry, Jen. I'm no good at Batati. Should have brought Na Bong or one of his sons."

"Oh boy," Jenny said. "This will be fun. Blind medicine. Well, Italians can talk with their hands, too."

She summoned two girls who had had a little schooling, and were supposed to function as "nurse's aides." The parade of patients began.

There were people with cuts, suppurating sores, and one man with a left foot twice its normal size. He'd been bitten by leeches, tried to cut them away, and developed a serious abscess in his instep. It was suppurating pus and stank terribly. Jenny gave him a shot of penicillin while the women clapped and shrieked.

"I'm a hit in Suraga," Jenny said. She was enjoying herself. An hour and a half later she washed her hands with Phiso-Hex, and taught the girls to do the same. With patient gestures she made it clear they were not to hand out medicine indiscriminately. Once a month either she or her husband, Kakai Dokka, would ride out to visit them. They were to enforce cleanliness, the use of disinfectant soap, and get the chief to build a latrine for men, another for women, and to pour lime over it. This dirty place, she explained, was to be built far away from the river from which they got their drinking water.

A meal had been prepared for the visitors. In one of the larger houses, Jenny squatted on the floor with Danny. They were served banana leaves heaped with rice, chicken, strange green vegetables. Inevitably Cokes appeared.

"Where do they get these?" Jenny asked.

"Peddlers. Couple times a year peddlers come around, sell them

297

thread, needles, cloth, nails, jewelry. They have no money, so they trade rice. The boss wants them to grow cash crops. They don't understand. Sometimes they get screwed out of their land."

"What happens then?"

"The boss takes 'em in. Settles them on other farms or in Batati. There's less land stealing since the boss moved in. Perpetua has a price on the boss's head, but no one would dare shoot a Zavala. The guy I worry about is Na Bong. Perpetua says he'll give three pigs to anyone who kills Na."

She thought of Na's clear-eyed, honest face. Joe said he was one of the most truly noble people he had ever met.

"We'd better move out," Larrizabal said. "Want to get to Batati in daylight."

The chief looked hurt. He wanted Kakai Jen to stay. Maybe for the night. Big dance, roast a pig.

"Thanks," said Jenny, "but we have to—"

The screaming stopped her. A long, shivering sound. And more screams.

"Stay here," Danny said. He yanked the gun from his belt and ran toward the sound. Outside men were racing about, brandishing bolos and ancient rifles. On the watchtower Santiago was waving to Danny. Above the treeline Jenny saw plumes of smoke.

Santiago, braced against the bamboo walls of the watchtower, ripped off a series of shots.

"See anyone?" Larrizabal shouted.

"No. Gone."

"What happened?"

"I don't know. Burning."

"You're a big help. There's a buffalo path to the farms. We'll take the Jeep."

Santiago flew down the steps. He and Danny ran for the Jeep. Jenny grabbed her medical kit and ran after them. Two Batati, long-haired boys carrying rifles, climbed in and helped Jenny over the back.

"You stay here," Danny said. "Doc warned me to look after you."

"What makes you think it's safer here?"

"Your choice, Jenny. But if you get hurt, I don't want the boss landing on me."

The Jeep bounced onto a dirt track. It was nothing more than a cowpath.

"See anything?" Larrizabal asked. He was driving with one hand, his .38 in the other.

"More smoke." Santiago leveled his rapid-fire rifle once, shook his head. The growth was too thick.

They burst abruptly out of the forest on to a field of high grass.

Three houses were cones of roaring flames. Great coils of black-gray smoke rose, stained the tropical sky. A group of women and children huddled beneath the raised platform of one of the houses that had not been put to the torch.

A tall man with a ring in his nose came running toward them. He was bleeding from a bolo slash on his thigh. He chattered hysterically with the Batati boys.

"Son of a bitch," Larrizabal said. He leaped from the Jeep and ordered the soldier to follow him.

The man began to weep, pointing toward the burning huts.

"He says his family was inside," said Santiago.

"Oh God," gasped Jenny. The huts began collapsing as they watched. A roar of flame, a crackling and a rush of air, and they were levelled.

Danny began zigzagging, first toward the burning huts, then to the woods beyond.

"Shit," he shouted. "I don't see them. Santiago, give 'em a blast."

The soldier fired into the woods beyond the clearing. There was no sign of movement.

"They gone, boss," the soldier said. "They burn and run."

"I hope they didn't do anything else." He pointed at the bawling man. "He says there were people in the huts. He's afraid to look." He noticed Jenny waiting behind him.

"Get back to the Jeep. There's nothing you can do."

"There may be people wounded."

"Go back and fix this guy's leg." Larrizabal was breathing hard.

"Ready, Santiago? Tell the boys to wait. We'll check the huts."

Larrizabal ran to the nearest mass of burned bamboo. "Jesus." He turned. Seeing Jenny waiting, he violently motioned her back.

A Batati woman's corpse lay on the scorched grass. Her skirts had been pulled up over her head and she had been disemboweled. The bright wet internal organs were covered with angry flies. Jenny gagged.

"I told you to stay away!" shouted Danny.

The man in black fell to his knees and pounded his turbaned head against the earth. Behind them, a dozen villagers stood in silence.

Larrizabal picked up a stick and pushed the woman's skirt over her mutilated abdomen. As he did, they saw that her upper torso was bare. Her breasts had been cut off.

"Oh God, oh God," Jenny moaned. "Maybe some of them are alive. . . ."

"No way. The bastards always hit the houses at the edge of the village. Catch the women in the fields."

One of the Batati boys shouted at Larrizabal from the burned house nearest the forest.

"Kakai Din," the boy called. "Here."

A second woman, much older, had been murdered and mutilated.

Jenny tried to comfort the villagers. But it was no use. Two men, the husband and a brother of the young woman, pounded their heads on the ground beside her.

Santiago and the Batati boys came out of the forest.

Santiago was dragging a man's body by the heels. One of the soldiers was carrying a baby.

"They cut this guy up in the forest," Santiago said to Danny. "Tell Kakai Jen not to look."

Jenny could hear him. "Cut off his, you know, stuck it in his mouth. They took their time with him."

"You think you winged any of the bastards?"

"Maybe. They run off as soon as they heard the Jeep."

The baby in the Batati boy's hands was shrieking. He looked to be two or three years old.

Jenny looked the child over. He seemed unmarked, but thoroughly coated in red dirt. And his screams were potent.

"They buried the kid alive," Santiago said. "Head down in the earth. We saw his feet kicking and dug him out."

"Give him to me," Jenny said. She took the screaming child. He had skin like brown satin. She dusted the dirt from his eyes and nose, listened to his tiny heart. *Buried alive.* She would offer her own life if she could murder the people who had done this.

"You get used to it," Larrizabal said. "Jen, we catch a couple of those Ilagas, you'll see some fun. Poor little guy. Is he okay?"

"He looks all right. Whose is he?"

There was some chattering between the Batati boys and the villagers. The man in black said he was nobody's child now. He was the grandson of the old lady who had been killed. He had no parents and he lived with her.

"He's mine," Jenny said. At the Jeep she washed him with canteen water and wrapped him in her bush jacket. He stopped crying when she gave him a lollipop.

Then she dressed the wounded man's thigh and applied antiseptics and antibiotics. He told her the baby's name was Pipil. At Batati Village Na Bong would decide what to do with Pipil.

When they returned to Suraga there was more wailing. The word had spread quickly. The chief had more dreadful news. He had sent a party up the mountain to the wireless station. The operator had been ambushed and his throat slit. The radio shack had been burned and his shortwave transmitter smashed.

"Let's go," Larrizabal said. He looked at Jenny. "You taking the kid?"

"He has no family. Someone in Batati will look after him." Jenny knew who it would be.

4

"Do you really think, Kevin," Cynthia asked, "that if we lose Vietnam, the whole Pacific Coast of the United States will be exposed?"

They had just watched the eleven-o'clock evening news. Bridie had not appeared, but there was talk of the network's sending her to the Far East.

"Who said that?" Kevin asked. "That the Pacific Coast will be exposed?"

"Senator Dirksen. Daddy had lunch with him last week."

Kevin shook his head. The Vietnam war was of no concern to him. His son was too young to be threatened by the draft, or to protest. A few physicians in the group, notably Horace Gottlieb, the dermatologist, and Alma Carey, the radiologist, were outraged, but Kevin refused to sign their petitions.

"You swing a lot of weight, Kev," Dr. Gottlieb had said.

Kevin had just shaken his head. "Have to watch my step. Too many committees. Have to be neutral."

Kevin sat on the edge of Cynthia's bed. It was May—balmy, lovely. Soon Johnny and Karen would be off to sailing camp on the Cape. Kevin had bought a weatherbeaten, twelve-room home in Orleans. "The right kind of people go there," E.E. assured him. He sneered at Hyannis—Kennedys and tourists. Wellfleet and Truro were interesting, but there were too many lawyers and psychiatrists. . . .

Psychiatrists. . . .

Kevin studied Cynthia's skeletal face. She had shown progress a few months ago, putting on weight, looking healthier. But now he could not deny Dr. McGrory's diagnosis; he knew his wife was severely ill again. She had come back from a cruise to the Caribbean looking frightful. He was certain she had had an affair aboard ship. Even undernourished, she seemed to attract men.

Her skin was fine and dry, and he had noticed the faintest growth of babylike down on her arms—*lanugo hair.* She did not menstruate and she seemed forever constipated. All the signs.

At meals she made a great play of cutting her food into pieces, moving it about the plate, complaining that she was terribly hungry but didn't quite care for the dish. Serena would angrily take away the fried chicken, the salad, the potatoes au gratin. She was insulted enough to quit.

Yet in the irrational way in which the disease manifested itself, Cynthia remained full of energy, riding every morning, shopping for hours on Manhasset's Miracle Mile, rearranging the house.

"You need help, Cynthia," he said. He touched her thigh.

"Do I?"

"It isn't your fault. It's a sickness as much as a weak aortic valve is. You must be helped."

"I like being thin. Maybe because you used to make such a fuss over my behind years ago. A little bit of revenge."

"I doubt it. You must not destroy your body," he said. He recalled a chilling statistic. The mortality rate in anorexia was twenty-two percent.

"I'd like you to see Dr. McGrory again."

Eventually she agreed. She asked him to kiss her. He did. He made love to her. Afterward he held her a long time and she cried, and he assured her she could be cured.

They met once more with Dr. McGrory, who explained that the Brambier Institute was primarily a children's hospital. She recommended a private sanitarium in Connecticut that specialized in alcoholics, addicts and anorexic patients.

When Cynthia was in the bathroom, McGrory told Kevin that recent work in anorexia nervosa established that people afflicted by it were undergoing deep personal struggles—searches for self-respect, identity, effectiveness.

"We do not see too many cases in women of your wife's age," she added. "But the later the symptoms begin, as in Mrs. Derry's case, the greater the likelihood that another illness, perhaps schizophrenia, is primary. Her MMPI test revealed a great deal of masked depression."

"She has no reason to be depressed."

"I'm afraid husbands are not always the best judges."

The Indian Ridge Center—they casually avoided the word "institute" or "sanitarium"—was run for people of means. No charitable organization, it depended on huge fees. It was located in a grove of maples on a secluded road north of the Merritt Parkway. The circular driveway, where the patients left their Jaguars, Rolls-Royces and Lincolns, surrounded a lawn as smooth as a putting green.

Kevin looked at the three-story stone mansion. It had once belonged to a chewing-gum heiress. He sometimes felt the way Joe did—disgusted at the way no-talent people accumulated so much. But he did not begrudge Dr. Alonzo Train and his associates their success. They had good reputations.

Dr. Train took Kevin and Cynthia to his office and explained that his program for people suffering from anorexia nervosa fell into four parts. First, separation from home. This was to remove the patient from pressure by other family members to eat.

Kevin tried to make light of it. "Eat, eat," he said. "I assure you, Dr. Train, no one acts like a Jewish mother with my wife."

Cynthia smiled and took his hand. "Maybe I needed one."

Dr. Train nodded. A loving couple. Intelligent people. He knew of Dr. Kevin Derry's reputation. The man no one turned down. Surely he has been a good husband. Anorexia in older patients could have deep roots.

The psychiatrist went on. Treatment of malnutrition, the second phase of therapy, was vital. Then psychotherapy, free and open discussion of anger, frustration and dependence. This would often be continued after the patient was discharged. Finally a program of active work involving the whole family.

"How old are your children?" Dr. Train asked.

"Our son is eleven and our daughter is nine," Kevin said.

"Good ages. Perhaps when the treatment is concluded, the four of you could take a trip together. Camping, fishing, that sort of thing."

Kevin explained that the children were off to a sailing camp on the Cape. Cynthia would be nearby in Orleans—assuming she was discharged from the Indian Ridge Center early enough. How long did the therapy take? Kevin asked. It varied, the psychiatrist replied. They had success in as little as a month. It could take as long as five months.

A nurse entered to take Cynthia to her room.

"Miss DeVaux will be Mrs. Derry's personal consultant," Dr. Train said. "One of our best."

Miss DeVaux was round-faced and gray-haired, with a prominent nose. She looked motherly and firm.

"Good luck, darling," Kevin said. "I have a feeling you'll set a record for a quick cure."

"I'm sure I will. Give my love to Johnny and Karen. Make sure they practice the piano. Don't let Serena go hog-wild buying food."

Later Dr. Train studied Mrs. Derry's record. A troubled woman. Deep, hidden depression. She had disguised it cleverly for years. Now it had surfaced as anorexia. Train had checked with her parents and learned that she had twice been committed for psychiatric care as a child. The family had kept it a secret. Even her husband had never been told.

A week after admittance Cynthia showed improvement. At first she had been fed in a private dining room. "Time to feed the animals," she would joke, as Miss DeVaux entered with the tray. They started with modest amounts—a cup of soup, a veal cutlet, minuscule portions of vegetables, a dab of Jell-O.

Miss DeVaux would eat with her. She was compassionate, but tolerated no nonsense. If Cynthia began to cut her meat into tiny portions, move the broccoli around the plate, she would stop her with a joke, a diversion. She watched her carefully for forced vomitings and was full of praise when Cynthia seemed to stop. The patient's luggage, purse and clothing were searched for laxatives and emetics.

Later, in the cheerful dining room, they dined together. Cynthia found she liked the plain, outspoken woman. She reminded her a bit of her mother-in-law: frustrated by life, but doing well with what was given her.

One day Cynthia began to chop her steak into pieces, stare out the window at the pink and white dogwoods.

"No games, Mrs. Derry," the nurse said. "Those trees didn't get that beautiful without nourishment. Eat your steak. Stop playing Scrabble with the pieces."

"I feel idiotic. A woman my age being treated this way."

"Don't be ashamed. I had a charming Jewish lady here some years ago. Very witty. She said when she was a child her mother used to read her funny stories with a Jewish accent by a man named Gross. Can't think of his first name. The book was called *Nice Baby*."

Cynthia looked blank.

"With an accent it's '*Nize* Baby.' Anyway, the mother was always ramming food down Nize Baby's mouth, and each story began, 'Nize Baby, eat up all the Brussels sprouts and Momma's gonna tell you about the Battle from Bunker Hill.' And she'd tell this story in a funny accent, and at the end she'd say, 'Nize Baby ate up all the Brussels sprouts.'"

Cynthia drank her milk in slow sips. "I'm afraid, Miss DeVaux, I was never a very nice baby. I'm a selfish and spoiled woman. That's why I starve myself. It's punishment."

"Let's take a walk on the grounds. Tell me about your brother in Paris. It must be wonderful to be artistic."

She made progress. Each day, the dietitian increased her caloric intake. Dr. Train himself met with her for several hours a day. They decided on a target weight. No hurry. They'd get there. She would proceed slowly, until she enjoyed eating, found no shame in it. In another week she would be allowed to dine alone if she wished, or with other patients. It astonished Cynthia that the staff was so little interested in her problems, her unhappy life with Kevin, the distances she kept between herself and the children.

"You don't probe very deeply," Cynthia complained one day to Dr. Train. They had just finished discussing the image she had of her body, what she expected of it, why she had chosen to punish it. Train shrugged her criticism off. Indian Ridge saw many women

306

like her. She was there to be taught to eat again. That was all. Other psychiatrists would get at root causes.

"But the root causes may start me starving myself again," Cynthia said.

"Our job is to break you of a bad habit. We want a better body image. In your case that shouldn't be hard. You are an eminently attractive woman. Being attractive to men has never been a problem with you."

"But I have other problems."

"Don't be disappointed in us. When you're on a normal regimen of food, we can explore your relationship with your husband and children. I can tell you'll be ready for it soon. You're showing signs of spontaneity, self-interest and a sense of humor."

"I was always accused of not having one. Especially by my husband."

Her husband again, Train thought. Maybe Dr. Kevin Derry needs therapy. Break down that appealing exterior. But he was functional, a workhorse, a *doer.* The Danforth medical establishment was becoming the envy of the state. It was no wonder she felt left out. Father and husband teaming up to create wonders. And she was left to her horses, her clothes, her vacations at Hobe Sound or Orleans.

"Why do you say I'm showing a sense of humor?" she asked.

"Miss DeVaux said you laughed at her *Nize Baby* stories."

By early June the air around the Indian Ridge Center was fragrant and warm and the heated pool had been opened. Cynthia had regained half of her lost weight. She had usually weighed about 130, being tall and big-boned. Now she weighed almost 120. At her worst she had been a starved 104, frantically buying new clothing, ordering her dressmaker to refit old riding habits, suits, coats.

She sat on the lawn, finishing a lunch of cream of broccoli soup, lamb chops, mixed vegetables and rice pudding. Miss DeVaux walked by and from the side of her mouth whispered, "Nize Baby."

One of the good people, Cynthia sensed. She had always been so wrapped up in herself, her needs, that she had failed to notice gradations in other people's characters. Yes, there were decent and kind and generous people, and there were mean, selfish and self-centered people. Where was she? God, she had tried to be helpful and giving. But she wanted to scream at Dr. Train, *I am an adultress.*

I have slept with more men than I can keep track of. She wanted to tell them that she got no soaring reward out of sex. Her strayings were an intricate form of vengeance, a way of reassuring herself that she was wanted, needed, functional.

Ed Crist. And Ed Crist's friend Ray, the golf pro, and Warren the tennis pro, and this member of that hunt, or golf, or bridge club. A piano-playing playboy of Back Bay lineage. A governor's aide. A man she knew only as Mac—crude, fat—whom she met on a cruise. *They enter me and I feel I have done something worthwhile, Doctor. My own orgasms are elusive. Please hear me out, and forget about that chicken pot pie. . . .*

She finally told Train of her first marriage, of the retarded boy, of Haslam's rejection, his refusal to touch her. Train nodded. Yes, a deep understandable cause for depression.

Casually Dr. Train asked one day, "And how is your sexual life with Dr. Derry?"

"On and off."

"We needn't look further into it. We're living in the present, and we will treat current symptoms. If you lick this illness, you may find he is more attracted to you. You'll look healthier, prettier. A healthy sex life is important."

"I see," she said. "From pork chops to orgasms in two easy lessons."

It remained for Kevin to accept her, forgive her and understand her. The first two parts would be easy. If she admitted past entanglements, he would be loving. Perhaps once more their bodies could be locked in passion. She admitted to herself that she had never enjoyed sex more than with him. His lean, freckled body was hard and trim at forty-two. What lunacy had impelled her to climb into strange beds?

Kevin came to pick her up in early July. Dr. Train spent more time talking about Kevin's new Mercedes than Cynthia's recovery. What was there to discuss? She was fine. She was eating again. She had sworn off forced vomitings and laxatives.

"You look marvelous, Cynthia," Kevin said.

"I feel pretty good. How are the kids?"

"Seem to love camp. I had Leo Damelio drive them up in the station wagon. He imitated Donald Duck and Porky Pig all the way to Brewster."

Jenny's cousins always seemed to be available to Kevin for chores, favors, odd jobs. "Need a patio cemented, Doc? Roof leaking? Engine tune-up? Wanna wreck a car for the insurance?" Cynthia never quite understood them. They appeared to be ruled by a hideous fat man who called himself Johnny Farrell. She remembered him from Joe and Jenny's wedding.

"Which one is Leo?" Cynthia asked. She was not sure she liked entrusting her children to a trash man.

"I can't be sure." Kevin laughed. "He's either the drummer or the bass player. It can't be Paulie. He's the one who was murdered. Anyway, he's delivered them safely and returned the wagon with a full tank of gas and six live lobsters."

"The Cape sounds like a splendid idea," Dr. Train said. "Fishing, clambakes, tennis, sailing. Your children are nearby and you can see them. By the way, the National Park Service runs nature walks with the rangers. I spent a whole week doing nothing but trekking up and down dunes. Why not take them together?"

"I'd love to," Cynthia said.

They got up to leave. Cynthia walked ahead.

"Dr. Derry, I must emphasize to you," Train said, "home-life follow-up is essential. It would be good if you could take a month off and be with her. She is a woman in need of love."

"A month? Impossible. We're putting up a new wing at Danforth. I have to be there."

"Two weeks?"

"Perhaps. Thank you for everything. The billings can go to my office. The Bay Medical Group."

"That won't be necessary. Mr. Manship's paid all the costs. Mrs. Derry requested that he do so. We got his check yesterday."

Kevin turned his head and looked at her straight-backed figure. Cynthia's idea. A bit of revenge. Showing him he was still the boy who trimmed hedges and raked leaves.

"Thank you, Dr. Train," Kevin said. "You've done wonders."

"You may have to perform a few minor ones yourself, Doctor. But I think she's on the road back."

Their luggage was in the Mercedes—summer clothes, fishing gear, tennis and golf equipment. Kevin yanked off his tie and jacket, rolled up his sleeves. Cynthia appeared relaxed. She wanted the windows open for a while, no air-conditioning.

They sped on to the Merritt Parkway and headed for Massachusetts.

"Why did you ask your father to pay the clinic's bills?" he asked.

"I wanted to. You are my wife."

"An impulse. Daddy had guilt feelings about me. I doubt that you have."

She stroked his thigh as they rode, and he responded, put his hand between her legs, withdrew when she began to moan.

"Tonight, please," she said. "We can listen to the waves, and see the stars, and it'll be the way it was in Churchport."

Kevin's mind drifted back to work. They were having a battle with Beth Moses Hospital. Some of the hotshots there, led by Abe Gold, were resentful of the way Danforth was expanding. Danforth Medical College was the new power. It had the prestigious appointments, the professorships, the money. Beth Moses, although affiliated, felt neglected. They wanted more important research facilities, more students. Abe had suggested that Danforth sever its affiliation with Mid-Island. The old place remained a dump. Moreover, it was now located in the midst of a slum. It functioned almost entirely on government subsidies.

"And I thought you were a liberal, Abe," Kevin had taunted. "You and Barbara were always for the Negroes, for improved medical care. Why cut Mid-Island off?"

"That's exactly why. The place is nothing more than an excuse for medical students and house staff to experiment on people. The clinics are a disgrace. You tried to improve them, but it didn't work. Your brother was right years ago. Why not redirect funds into local medical care for the people?"

"And Beth Moses would take up the teaching slack? You'd expand house staff?"

Abe nodded. He earned $150,000 a year, yet he looked as sad as he did in medical school. "Why not? We should be a major part of the Danforth complex. Don't think we can't match you and Manship dollar for dollar at raising funds. Jews are terrific at collecting money."

"You're silent," Cynthia said, interrupting his thoughts.

"Hospital problems. I wish Danforth ran as smoothly as my group."

310

"That's because you give the group your personal touch, darling."

Kevin noticed cars on the parkway had their lights on. "What's that all about?"

"It means you favor the Vietnam war. Patriotic Americans answering the protestors. Rosemary Luff told me. She and Potsy and her friends drive with the lights on all the time. It means bomb Hanoi, kill the gooks."

The radio newscast began as they passed Stratford and continued east through Connecticut. President Johnson had denounced "the knee-jerk liberals" who were betraying their country and "their own fighting men."

"Boy, is he up the wrong tree," Kevin said. "He'd better stick to the Great Society."

In Orleans they first visited the children's camp. There was a lot of whistle blowing and lining up. It was a strict camp run by a couple who owned a boarding school in Massachusetts. Kevin felt ill at ease watching kids in sparkling whites march to activities and wait at attention. He thought of the way he and Joe had grown up in Churchport—the freedom, the laziness, the exciting summers.

"Johnny looks wonderful," Cynthia said. "Maybe camp will bring him out of his shell."

"I think he's coming out already. Told me a joke this morning. Something about two boys named Trouble and Get-Out. I couldn't follow it, but I laughed."

"I guess he's inherited my lack of humor."

Kevin squeezed her hand. He had to encourage her, be supportive. It was parents' visiting day. Cynthia chose to stay away from the other mothers and fathers. On the pond, the children wrestled with the sails, tied ropes, maneuvered the boats.

Sunlight, sparkling water, green lawns, healthy children. Kevin mused, *Are we really part of this world?* Maybe he would be able to overcome his feelings about her past acts and make love to her tonight. She looked stunning, tanned, her hair plangent with light.

He would try to spend more time with her. His group practice was supposed to have liberated him from long hours. Dr. Gottlieb and Dr. Trask and Dr. Graubart always seemed to be taking long weekends, doing all kinds of family things with their wives and kids. He remained up to his neck in work. Boards, committees, fund-raising.

A sailing race was on. Johnny's boat trailed. It swerved and the sail settled gently into the water and two boats passed it.

"Oh, dear, he didn't do very well," Cynthia said.

Johnny was swimming to shore, disgusted. He had no stomach for helping his partner right the boat. A counselor with a bullhorn chased him back. "You capsized it, John Derry. Get back and help Courtney get it up again."

Johnny stomped back to deeper water and began to swim. *Not like me or Joe,* Kevin thought. We'd damn well get the boat up and finish the race.

That night Kevin steamed clams and boiled lobsters with an expert knowledge he had not put to the test in years. The lobsters were cooked for precisely fourteen minutes after the water returned to a rolling boil. Cynthia could not look when he dropped the two green-black "bugs" into the iron pot.

"Don't get nervous," he said. "It doesn't hurt and they have no awareness of death."

"But they make that dreadful hissing noise. I remember it when I was a kid. I used to say to our cook, 'Maybe they're begging for mercy.'"

"And what did she say?"

Cynthia embraced him from behind. "She said, 'Honey, lobsters can't talk.' And I said, 'Maybe they can, but we don't understand them. Just like people.'"

He turned and kissed her on the mouth.

"You taste of melted butter, husband."

They ate on the screened weather-grayed porch facing the Atlantic. They had a magnificent view of Nauset marsh and the distant ocean.

"Maybe we have no right to be so lucky," she said.

"Someone's got to be. It might as well be us."

They finished the clams, half the lobster. Kevin said he'd make lobster salad tomorrow. Cynthia promised to look for a housekeeper and gardener. The house was enormous. It seemed something of a waste. The children would rarely use it and they had few friends in Orleans. Kevin wondered why in hell they'd bought it for

312

$175,000. Churchport would have made more sense. But Cynthia had insisted. She had fallen in love with the weathered gray shingles, the widow's walk, the dunes, the view.

After they cleared the table and washed the dishes, they sat on the porch again. It had turned chilly. Kevin put a sweater over her shoulders. She seized his hands. "Kevin, we'll be happy here. Just the two of us, and the kids when camp is over. It's what Dr. Train was talking about. Stay for a month."

"Impossible. The funds committee—"

"Please stay. We'll make friends. That professor from Amherst and his wife. And there's a TV producer here. We can meet interesting people, get away from medical talk, aneurysms and aortic insufficiencies. I'll hide your calipers so you can't go around measuring P-waves."

"By God, you've picked up the jargon. In a year's time, I could make a cardiac nurse out of you."

"A bit late for a career, Kevin."

"It's never too late."

"For me? If I'm good? Eat up all my spinach? Stop doing the things I used to do?"

"Why not?"

He leaned over the beach chair and held her. Lights glinted in the house around Nauset marsh. They had consumed a bottle of Chablis with their dinner and felt warm and relaxed.

Frogs croaked belligerently, like children demanding attention before going to bed."

"*Brek-ke-ke-koax, koax, koax,*" Cynthia said.

"What the devil is that?"

"From *The Frogs,* by Aristophanes. I don't remember anything about the play, except someone calls them 'uncommon musical frogs.' Yalies use it as a cheer. Haslam taught it to me."

"I'd rather not hear about it."

Kevin dragged deeply on his cigarette. He was a three-pack-a-day man now. Potsy's warnings, his colleagues' disapproval, had no effect on his addiction. When he occasionally got out on a tennis court (and he had once been runner-up in the Churchport sixteen-and-under) he gasped after a set.

"Please think about taking time off," she pleaded.

"Maybe I can come up later," he said. "We could spend a week with the kids when camp is over."

"It would be good for them," said Cynthia. "And me."

"Someone should work on Johnny's tennis. Sailing and riding are fine, but I'd like the kid to get into competition. When Joe and I were kids, we went out for everything. Name the game, we tried to play it."

"But you quit football and Joe didn't."

"I wanted a whole pair of knees. That hardhead didn't care. He's got tendonitis for all his heroics. And that senior year. Zip and eight. Maybe that's why . . . why . . ." He struggled for words.

"Why what?"

"I love Joe more than I ever admit. More than he knows. Being a loser doesn't stop him. Show him a stone wall and he'll ram his head against it. Good thing he's got Jenny."

"Am I to feel guilty over that remark?"

"Not at all. I know people who call me a money machine. We do what we do, and so long as it isn't criminal, what's the difference? Joe and Jenny aren't saints. They're getting paid and they like what they're doing."

They got mildly drunk on brandy then went to the bedroom. It was a huge low-ceilinged room furnished with Boston rockers, heavy dressers, a four-poster.

She clutched at him. He was tender and loving, but the cigarettes and the long hours had taken their toll. After fifteen minutes of encouragements from her hands, her tongue, her legs, he shriveled and gave up, apologizing. Toward morning, he tried again. This time he was successful but reserved.

After four days Kevin left. Cynthia implored him to stay the full week. She could not face it alone in the huge house. But other women did it all the time, Kevin said. She should invite people up. Buzzy and Celeste would be over from Paris in a week. But she hated her brother, she responded. Then she should invite her parents. Or some of the women she rode with. Cynthia realized it was hopeless. She dropped the subject.

Two days after he left, Cynthia invited a twenty-one-year-old counselor from the children's camp to the house for a drink. He was tall, bronzed, a surfer from Laguna Beach. She let him seduce her.

He stole a bottle of scotch and four pairs of Kevin's Allen Solly sweat sox before leaving. But she invited him back, got rid of him a week later for a television producer who knew Bridie. If less talented in bed, he was not a thief.

5

Returning to work, Kevin plunged into the problem of Mid-Island Hospital. Dr. Gold lost no time in broaching the matter. Except for Max Landeck, leading physicians in the area were sick of Mid-Island. Activist groups were raising hell. Hospital supplies, drugs—anything moveable was fair game for addicts and hoodlums. It was getting impossible to interest medical students in the place. Virtually all of the house staff came from foreign schools.

The Danforth medical board, by overwhelming vote, decided to elevate Beth Moses at the expense of Mid-Island. Eventually the old place would be phased out altogether as a teaching hospital. "Won't hurt anyone," Gold said after the vote. "The minorities complain we use them as guinea pigs. So we won't use them anymore."

"But it also means less funding," Landeck said. "Those people need care."

Ever the conciliator, Kevin said, "We won't shortchange Mid-Island. We'll make it more responsive to the needs of the community."

"By closing its psychiatric center, as this plan envisions?" Max asked. "By cutting back clinical services? By lowering the quality of house staff?"

"We can't do everything," Dr. Graubart said. "Max, there are empty beds all over Mid-Island."

"Because the middle- and upper-class whites won't go there, and the Negroes and Puerto Ricans don't trust the place. Gentlemen, we are abandoning a whole area to inferior medical care." He wished Joe were present to support him.

"I don't agree," Kevin said.

Landeck smiled ruefully. "Ah, Kevin. Upper County and Beth Moses will end up with the new wings and the expensive equipment. Mid-Island will wither away."

"Maybe it should," Graubart said.

After the vote was taken, Landeck took Kevin aside. "I am sorry Joe was not here to back me, Kevin. He'll be angry when he gets back. He would understand my feelings. So would his wife."

Kevin lit a cigarette. "Come off it, Max. I'll see to it Mid-Island stays afloat. We'll get you what you need. And it's just as well Joe wasn't here. He'd have belted someone. Maybe me."

A few hours later Kevin took a call from Dr. Felder. Kevin's mother was in his office. She had suffered a seizure of angina. Typically she had not called Dr. Felder, but had walked to his office.

"That stenosis of the aorta, Kevin," Felder said softly, "what we suspected years ago. It may have gotten worse. You should come out and look her over."

"I'll be right there. Take me an hour. Sam, don't send her home or put her in Mid-Island. Can you take an EKG while I'm on my way?"

"Sure. You think I have to be a fancy specialist to read QRS complexes?"

As soon as Meg saw Kevin she began apologizing for bothering him. It was nothing, some chest pain. She'd had a few of these attacks before and they went away with aspirin. This was just a bit worse. Kevin did not have to come running out to Churchport, with all he had on his mind.

Meg was sitting in the ancient Morris chair, resting her head against the maroon leather. God, how Kevin remembered that chair! He used to sit there, feet on the ottoman, "minding the office," doing his trig and physics homework when the Felders went to the movies.

"She had another seizure a half hour ago," Felder said. "My guess is she's having coronary-artery spasms. Nothing really serious."

Kevin sat down alongside his mother and kissed her cheek. "How's it now, Mom?"

"Better, Kevin. Dr. Felder has been very kind."

"Your old lady," Felder fumed, "had to *shlep* here. I'd have been there in five minutes if she called."

Kevin felt tears forming in his eyes.

"Much pain, Ma?" Kevin asked. He took her wrist, felt her pulse. Normal.

"A bit. Kevin, I'm sure I can go home now."

Felder showed Kevin his second EKG. There was a depression of S-T segments and an inversion of T waves during the second attack of angina. But the first EKG, taken when the pain had subsided after the medication, did not show abnormalities.

"Doesn't tell us much," Felder said. "It's the underlying cardiac state we have to know."

Kevin smiled. "Know your stuff, don't you?"

"I've seen a lot."

"The aortic stenosis?" Kevin asked. "It could . . ."

"It could be. It could be a lot of things."

They said no more. Both understood. The attacks could have worsened and affected the blood supply to the heart. Angina often antedated a myocardial infarction, the death of part of the heart.

"She was in a lot pain when she got here," Felder said gently.

They sat in the examining room and discussed the possibilities. The pain, Meg said, was not localized, but it had been oppressive, heavy. The nitroglycerin had relieved the agony in five minutes—a pretty-certain sign that the pain was anginal, or that she had experienced a period of coronary insufficiency when the attack hit her.

"Sam, you're still a hell of a diagnostician. You did all the right things."

"Yeah, yeah, save the compliments." His weary eyes said, *And you let them throw me out of the hospital.* But he remembered all of the Derry kids with affection.

"I'm going to take her to Upper County and give her a cardiac workup. I'll have Dr. Luff look her over."

"She's your patient, Kevin. Your mother."

Kevin arched his brows. "I know you don't think much of my cousin."

"Terrific surgeon. He'll have you on the heart-lung machine before he's taken your temperature. The great cutter."

318

"Not fair, Sam. Potsy's one of the best. She's well enough to ride in my car, don't you think?"

"Sure. She'll be reassured just having you next to her. You're her hero, Kevin. The best child, she always says."

Meg resisted going to the hospital. Sam and Kevin had a hard time persuading her. Finally she agreed. Sam promised to have her sister Katherine bring over whatever she would need.

Meg rested her pale head against the cushioned black leather of the Mercedes. Kevin turned on the all-news station. They were plugging Bridget Derry's exposé of drug companies for charging ten times what medications sold for under their generic names.

"Be sure to hear this report on the UBC network news tonight," the plummy-voiced announcer said. "Another exclusive by Bridget Derry."

"My goodness, my famous children," Meg said.

Kevin nodded. Bridie was a source of pride to him also. Even bigger jobs were in the offing for her, he'd heard. But he said nothing about her affair with Christopher Ling. Meg did not know.

And he didn't want Bridget hurt, even if she was getting to be a bother to his associates. One of the drug companies she was drawing a bead on was Concordia. Lawton Curtis, Upper County's executive director, had heard of Bridget Derry's crusade. He had asked Kevin to get her to go easy. But there was nothing he could do, Kevin thought. Bridie had worshipped him when she was a kid, but as she got older and more attractive and more famous, she had also become more stubborn.

"Great girl," was all Kevin said to his mother.

"She amazes me."

Me too, he thought. If only she'd find a target outside of medicine.

Three days later, after an arteriograph, a cardiac catheterization, and other painful diagnostic tests, Kevin and Potsy looked at the results. The cusps of Meg's aortic valve were thickened. The old diagnosis by Doc Felder had been an accurate one, but it had remained a stable condition for years. Now, with advancing age, natural progression had afflicted the valve. It explained the seizures of angina pectoris.

319

"Coronary-artery spasm," Potsy said. "The valve is stenosed."

"So?" Kevin asked.

"Operate."

"Is my mother healthy enough?"

"Sure. She's got low blood pressure, general good health."

"She's sixty-seven."

"So what? I've done valve replacements on older people."

"We've had this discussion a hundred times," Kevin said. "You always seem to win. But when it's my own mother—"

"The angina is going to get worse. It could be the precursor of an MI. Give her a new aortic valve and she'll be a new woman."

"For how long?"

Potsy opened his chubby hands. "No guarantees. But the pain'll come back if we don't operate. You can't have Felder maintaining her on nitroglycerine forever."

Dr. Felder did not approve of the swift decision. He reached Kevin at a utilization-committee meeting.

"Just like that?" Felder asked. "Operate?"

Kevin reviewed the diagnostic findings. His mother was resting comfortably after the prolonged tests. But there was no question that she had aortic stenosis. The valve was in bad shape, failing to deliver blood to the left ventricle.

"What's the hurry?" Felder asked. "Wait a few weeks. The pain can be controlled with drugs. Maybe all she needs is the nitroglycerine. Kevin, forty percent of all deformities of the heart valves are aortic. In your mother's case, given her age and her health, she can be maintained medically."

"Potsy feels she'll get worse. He thinks there are calcified masses on both surfaces of the cusps."

"Okay, you're the professor. I'm just a dumb old GP. Can I visit her?"

"Of course, Sam. If you get any lip from the head nurse, mention my name."

"Yeah, yeah. I was a founder of the lousy dump."

Kevin's eyes sought the ceiling. Felder was off and running. Yet he could not dismiss his adversary view.

"One last thought, Kevin. Aortic stenosis is better tolerated than

320

almost any other kind of valvular deformity. People manage with it."

"I know, Sam. I'm a cardiologist."

"Me and my big mouth. Give my love to your mother. Don't let them keep her on the pump too long."

Kevin's other phone was ringing. Cynthia was calling from Orleans. She was bored. Buzzy and Celeste were coming for a week. Couldn't he *please* find time to fly up to Provincetown? She could not face her brother and his aromatic French wife alone.

He told her of his mother's impending surgery. A few more tests and Potsy would replace the malfunctioning valve with a plastic one. Cynthia—genuinely, it seemed to Kevin—expressed her sympathies.

Bridie, whom he called a few minutes later, wept a little. She'd come out and visit.

"Will Mom be okay?" Bridie asked. "Level with me."

"Of course. It's a simple mechanical procedure and I can't think of a better man to do it than Potsy."

Christopher Ling telephoned the newsroom as soon as Bridie finished taping her first five-minute report on the outrageous pricing of drugs.

"How did it go, love?" the vice-president asked.

"I don't know. It's rough. The producer's phone has been ringing all day. PR men from the drug houses want equal time."

"Good," Ling said. "Did you include the scene with the pharmacist throwing you bodily out of the cut-rate pharmacy?"

"Opened with it. There's Mr. Cohen shoving me, and me shoving back, and the soundman getting jostled. Sorry, no head-clubbing. Listen, Chris, I can't see you tonight. My mother's in the hospital."

She told him of the impending surgery. Ling expressed his sorrow. Was there anything he could do? He knew DeBakey fairly well.

"I'll miss you, love," Ling whispered. "Miss you terribly."

"Tomorrow," she said. "Chris, I love you." She kept her voice low during these office talks. Not that the affair was a secret. Everyone from the copyboys to the network president knew that they were living together.

Later Ling watched the news. A good, punchy report, made forceful by her indignant manner. A beautiful girl with her heart in the right place. And she was sincere, outraged. It was no act.

When the program ended Ling had trouble envisioning her family. He had met the older brother once—a handsome, likeable man. The younger brother was a do-gooder off in Asia. He suddenly realized he was falling in love with Bridie Derry. The four-nights-a-week routine was no longer enough.

His malaise took a quantum leap when his wife unexpectedly phoned. Up to now she had tolerated Ling's affair. But, she informed him, she had been attending group-therapy sessions, along with her yoga and meditation exercises. It would be his choice—Dolores Ling, or that Irish bitch. And she wanted him. If he insisted on Bridget Derry, she would nail him with the fattest divorce settlement since Bobo Rockefeller. Moreover, news executives were not supposed to have scandals.

"Easy, dear, you're being irrational," Ling said. She cursed him, using language he had never heard from her refined Mount Holyoke lips. Ling thought of his sprawling 1789 home in Chappaqua, his three daughters. In winter his estate looked like the Paramount set for *Christmas in Connecticut*.

"I am seeing a lawyer," Dolores said. "I suggest you do the same."

6

Six weeks after the attack in which three people were hacked to death by the raiders, Dr. Charles Zavala returned to Batati. Gloomily, he listened to Na Bong's account. Zavala swore vengeance.

Two days later Santiago walked into Batati with an Ilaga raider he had flushed out of a rice field. He brought him to the main village. The man was kept in a bamboo cage. A bullet had shredded the prisoner's right arm. Joe insisted on dressing it.

"I'd let the bastard suffer," Larrizabal said. "He's one who hacked up the women. Let him die slowly."

"Did he admit it?" Joe asked. He was crouched on the floor of the cage, winding gauze around the man's wound.

"They won't admit they're alive," Concepcion said.

"What are you going to d-do with him?" Joe asked.

Na Bong grinned. A gold tooth winked. "Make him talk."

Joe anchored the bandage with elastic and walked out of the cage. He didn't want to be around.

Amazing, he thought; the starved captive in the long black shirt, dirty white pants and sandals, could easily have passed as a Batati. He swore to Na Bong that he was a farmer, thrown off his land in Ilo-Ilo by a logging company. The loggers had killed his son, tied him up in a sack, and then raped his wife. Many Ilo-Ilo people had wandered south to Mindanao looking for land. They were told by powerful men from Labat that there was farmland there owned by cannibals who tortured strangers and did not believe in Jesus Christ.

Larrizabal pointed to a glass bottle depending from a leather thong around the prisoner's scrawny neck. In it was a live frog.

"I wondered about th-that," Joe said.

"These guys have a crazy religious sect," Larrizabal explained. "So long as they have the frog, they're convinced they can't be killed."

Concepcion explained that if interrogation failed, a prisoner would sometimes be made to eat the frog. This was the direst punishment.

Joe shuddered. Concepcion and Larrizabal swore they were telling him the truth; they'd torture the bastard if they had to. But what about the logging companies with their hired guns who had kicked this poor peasant off *his* patch of ground? It didn't concern them.

Joe trudged back to the hospital. He could not solve the social problems of Mindanao. His sympathies were with the Batati. He had seen too many mutilated farmers to have much pity for the raiders.

Meanwhile he and Jenny performed wonders. They'd stopped the schistosomiasis outbreak in its tracks. Zavala had flown in a shipment of a toxic agent that killed the snails. (The same flight brought in a new mistress from Beverly Hills for Zavala.) The antidote for the infected men was simple tartar emetic, administered intravenously. It made the buffalo breeders sick, but it cured them.

He and Jenny were happy in the village, happier than they had ever been. Joe confessed he enjoyed the power. In practice, he had always sensed he was being nibbled to death. Odds and ends, unpaid bills, patients lost to the groups, arguments with attendings. Here, Kakai Dokka was boss.

"You like running the show," Jenny teased him. "Admit it."

"Guilty." His battered face would twist into a smile, and he would kiss her.

A major change had occurred in their personal life. They had adopted the orphaned Pipil. Jenny had bathed him, fed him, tried to determine his age. Weeks after his ordeal, he cringed and cried a great deal. He always seemed to be hungry.

"I want him," she finally told Joe. "He's ours."

"Don't ask me. Ask Nicky."

"But do *you* want him?" She pointed to the tiny boy, playing in the dust with an empty bandage can, filling and refilling it with red dirt.

324

"Sure, Jen. Souvenir of our w-wild adventure."

"But I love him, Joe. Poor little squirt. We'll make a Derry out of him."

"I hope we're doing him a f-favor."

They were dining on the veranda of the main house. Unidentifiable vegetables, mounds of rice heaped on banana leaves. Pipil cried that he was hungry, even though he'd just had his own dinner.

A Batati girl carried the boy up to the veranda. It was dusk. The sky was charged with lavender and orange streaks after the afternoon rain. Joe and Jenny could not envision any place on earth more enchanting.

As soon as Pipil saw Jenny, he struggled free, toddled across the bamboo flooring, and clutched at her leg. "Kakai Jen," he shouted. "Kakai Jen."

She fed him bits of rice. He laughed and buried his head in her lap. He was an exquisite child—his eyes wide and gleaming black, his features small and regular. If undersized—they guessed he was about two and a half—he seemed sturdy. Joe had examined him for parasites, infections and sores and found none.

"I guess we have a new s-son," Joe said.

"I guess so, Joey."

Nicky, browner than his new brother, came out of their bedroom. He was a muscular seven-year-old now, well adjusted to the Catholic mission school, learning to play soccer barefoot with Batati kids.

"I don't want him," Nicky said. "Send him away."

"Nick," Joe said. "He's got no mommy and daddy. He needs us. You'll like your little brother."

"I hate him. Gonna call him Knucklehead."

Jenny rolled her eyes. Sibling rivalry so soon?

"Knucklehead," Nicky said. "He can't talk."

"Give him time, Nick," Joe said.

"He can't talk. Give him back."

Joe grabbed Nicky's head and pressed it against his chest. Nicky had become an older brother overnight. He remembered the way he himself had tagged after Kevin, imitated his moves. Pipil would, Joe hoped, look up to Nicky the same way.

"Knucklehead," Nicky insisted. "He doesn't even know how to catch a baseball."

"You'll t-teach him, pal." Joe said.

325

Concepcion cut through the red tape for formal adoption. Joe and Jenny flew to Manila one day with Pipil—now Peter Francis Derry, thanks to Father Kelly's obliging baptism—and had the documents registered at the American Embassy.

He was theirs now. A second son. Jenny, in a burst of nationalism, and as a tribute to her father, Nick, who always led his precinct in the Columbus Day parade, selected October 12, 1964, as his birthday.

The night the Derrys returned to Batati with their adopted son the Ilagas struck again.

It was an arrogant raid. Zavala, whom they feared and hated, was in the main village. He had flown in a few days earlier with the payroll for his bodyguards, and the six-foot "starlet."

The girl, Alicia Wells, looked like a blonde giraffe, ten inches taller than the Filipino physician, towering over the Batati people. She'd lounged about in a Balenciaga jump suit, ooh'd and ah'd over the "adorable little people" and insisted on telling the Derrys her life story.

"I'm an artist at heart," Alicia said. Dr. Zavala stroked her neck.

"Well, acting is an art," Jenny said.

"I don't mean that. I paint. I sculpt. My photography has won several prizes. It's much more satisfying than mumbling someone else's lines in front of a camera."

Jenny and Joe said little to her. When Zavala told her that Dr. Derry was the brother of the network correspondent Bridget Derry, the "starlet" came alive. "Oh, I adore her. It's funny, Joe—may I call you Joe?—you and she look nothing alike."

"Yes, they do," Jenny said. "They have the same shape ass. Joe, let's beat it."

"What did I say wrong?" Alicia asked.

Zavala was doubled over laughing.

The Derrys walked to the edge of the veranda. Joe was smiling. He understood Jenny's rage at the woman's implication—Joe was ugly, Bridie beautiful.

"Simmer down, J-Jen."

"That bitch. I hate having to make conversation because she's Chuck's whore. I sometimes feel we're no better. On his payroll."

326

"Not the same th-thing, Jen, and you know it."

"I wonder. We're part of the rich boy's show. *Time* is sending a reporter here next week. We'll be part of the act."

She put her arms around him. They rested against the bamboo railing, necking like teenagers with no place to shack up. Jenny gave a little cry.

"Oh, Joey, look."

She was pointing toward the outermost reaches of the Batati farmlands. In the blackness a glowing orange ball had appeared. Seconds later another fiery mass blazed in the darkness. Then a third exploded, shooting orange-gold flashes in the night.

Zavala leaped to his feet and ran to the railing.

"Son of bitch," Chuck said. "They're at it again. Danny! Ramon! Raise Ferdie on the shortwave."

Larrizabal flew upstairs to the radio shack and roused the operator. They could hear the crackling on the shortwave and then someone shouting, "Lizard, Lizard, this is Eagle. Do you read me?"

Zavala was bending over the rail with a pair of binoculars and peering into the hills. There were five bright burning orange splotches in thé distance.

"Oh, my God," Jenny said, weeping. "The people . . ."

Zavala remained crouched, trying to discern movement. It was impossible. The burnings were taking place three or four miles away. The flames against the inky darkness gave an illusion of closeness.

Larrizabal raced down the steps. "Ferdie says there was a mob of them. He popped at them with his rifle, but they're gone. Never seen so many on a raid."

"What about our people?" Zavala asked.

"He doesn't know. He won't leave the radio shack."

The actress wandered over and draped herself around a column. She studied the burning houses far away. "Oh, how beautiful. If I could paint it. That *gold* and *yellow* and *orange* in the purple black. I'd do it in acrylics."

Jenny turned, ready to insult her.

"Easy, Jen," said Joe. "I d-don't think she understands what's happening."

Larrizabal, Concepcion and Santiago, the latter pulling an ammo

327

belt over his head, were talking with Zavala in a corner of the veranda.

"I want to go after them now," Larrizabal was saying. "Let's get in the Jeeps and see can we catch the fuckers. I'll get some of the Batati trackers."

An ashen-faced Na Bong came running up. "The people are running in. A dozen of them. Wounded, shot. They won't stay out there. They're afraid."

"Goddammit." Zavala seethed. "Get on the pipe and tell that prick Ferdie to get down from the tower and *make* them stay. Let them sleep in the ditches."

"Na, where are the wounded?" Joe asked.

"Clinic, Kakai Dokka. One guy has a bullet wound in his back. Woman looks like she won't make it—blood all over her chest. Two guys with bolo wounds. A dead kid."

"L-let's go, Jen," Joe said.

Na was strapping on a sidearm. Tifak, a Batati tracker, was jabbering to Na Bong, pointing to the mountain range.

"He says they're easy to find." Na translated for Zavala. "A wild pig is hard to track but a man is a fool in the forests. He says he can catch them."

As Joe and Jenny left for the clinic, they heard Zavala saying they could not chase the raiders at night. But by God, they'd go after them the next day.

"We got that guy in the cage?" Zavala asked.

"What's left of him," said Larrizabal.

"Oh," the starlet cried. "The man in the cage. I want to watch."

"You go to your room, sweetie," said Chuck. "Wait for me. Nobody watches."

Joe was glad Jenny had not heard. They hurried to the clinic. The Batati nurses had turned on the kerosene lamps and put the wounded on cots.

A four-year-old girl was dead. She had been sliced down the middle with a bolo.

Jenny clapped a hand on her mouth. She told the nurses to wash the corpse, wrap it in cloth.

"Kakai Chok want photograph," the girl said. "Always take photo when bad thing."

"Kakai Jen says no. Talk to Na and see that she's buried."

The woman also appeared doomed. She had been repeatedly slashed in the abdomen. The men, stoic and uncomplaining, seemed better off. They had made a run for it. Their wounds were deep but not lethal. The man with the bullet wound looked as if he would survive. Joe went to work with scalpel and forceps, dug out the misshapen slug and showed it to him.

"You're lucky, Kakai," Joe said.

"You good, Kakai Dokka."

He and Jenny worked for several hours, patching, cleaning wounds, trying to stop the woman's bleeding.

"She isn't going to make it, Joey," Jen said. The woman's pulse was gone. She was exsanguinating rapidly. Minutes later she died, silent, accepting. Her weeping family gathered around the bed.

Father Kelly walked in. To Joe, he suggested a graduate student in physics, his mind on abstract symbols. He was in his thirties, soft-spoken, good-natured, always willing to help out despite Zavala's edict—no conversions.

"Can I assist?" the priest asked. He wore ragged suntans and sandals.

"You can help the girls clean up," Jenny said. "Grab a mop."

"Glad to." Father Kelly began to swab the blood-covered floor.

The family of the dead woman wrapped the body in leaves and carried her out. They had some secret, unrevealed ceremonies with their dead. Father Kelly shoved his loose eyeglasses up his snub nose and shook his head.

Outside they heard howling. Not a dog, not any animal.

"They're working over that prisoner," Joe said. "G-gonna make him talk. Chuck wants to lead a raiding party."

The priest frowned. "Disgusting. I'm going to stop him."

"It's Asia, Father," Joe said.

Jenny, maneuvering an IV pole and tube, called to them. "You two stop arguing, huh? Come here and give me a hand."

Joe and the priest walked over and helped the wounded man to a prone position on the narrow cot. Jenny jabbed the needle into a vein.

As she worked, she chattered, not looking at the priest. "You know, Father Tom, if I'd known priests like you when I was a kid in

East Shinnaway, I might never have left the Church."

"Oh?"

"They were all Irish, and they made us Italians feel like third-class Catholics. My sister Angie and I upped and walked out one day. You might have saved a couple of Neapolitans if you'd been around."

"It's not too late, Jenny."

They heard the wild howling again. The priest looked at Joe. "If you feel I shouldn't intervene . . . maybe you should."

Joe scowled. "Jen, we better keep a girl on duty all night. Tell them to wake us if any of these p-people go sour. I'll see what Kakai Chok is up to."

There was a stone-and-cement building on the distant side of the buffalo pond. Joe had been told it was an unfinished enclosure for a generator.

Joe walked in.

The Ilaga prisoner was chained to a sawhorse. The center of his spine rested on the cross piece. His legs dangled over one part, his trunk lolled backward. He was shirtless. There were red welts on his chest.

Larrizabal was standing over him with a studded leather belt in his hand. Santiago and two other constables stood in the shadows and watched impassively. Zavala reached out and put the tip of his cigar to the Ilaga's bare soles. The howls were fainter now.

"Tough bastard," Larrizabal said. "Na, tell him once more we'll chop his head off an inch at a time if he doesn't tell us where his friends are."

Na spoke to the prisoner.

"He swears he doesn't know, Kakai Chok," Na said. "He says he's telling the truth."

Zavala placed the burning tip against the man's sole. A vile odor of scorched flesh soiled the air.

"For Chrissake, Chuck, enough," Joe said.

"Sure, Joe. Danny, give him the frog."

Na Bong seemed unmoved. The constables rested on their guns in the shadows. They were from Luzon. They did not understand these savages.

Larrizabal unscrewed the cap on the bottle around the man's neck and fished out a half-dead frog.

330

The prisoner began to wail. Larrizabal cracked him across the chest with his belt.

Santiago put his gun aside and came toward the sawhorse. He grabbed the man's hands and held them underneath the cross piece. Another soldier forced open the prisoner's mouth.

"Blue-plate special," Chuck said, and laughed. "Shove it in. Make sure he swallows it." He looked at Joe. "Once he eats his fucking charm, he's finished."

Larrizabal jammed the frog into the man's mouth. The Ilaga tried to vomit, hurled his head from side to side.

Finally Danny shoved the frog into the man's throat, the way a veterinarian forces a dog to swallow a large pill. It went down in one spasmodic gulp.

Dr. Zavala got up, slapping his thigh. He was wearing his pearl-handled revolvers.

They stood back and watched. Santiago untied the man's arms and let him fall from the sawhorse. He collapsed on the dirt floor, babbling to Na Bong.

"He says no more, boss," Na Bong translated. "Ilo-Ilos got a cave up beyond Suraga. Can't see it from the air or the forest. Three holes in the mountain. They wait there for Perpetua. When he says the land is free, they come out."

"What I figured," Zavala said. He looked at Joe. "Was I right or was I right?"

"Boss is always right," Larrizabal said. "What do we do with this guy now?"

"Dump him in front of Perpetua's real-estate office."

"No," Joe said. He stood in front of Zavala. "I said n-no."

"Joe," said Zavala, "you run a hell of a hospital. I love you and Jen. But these people, all they know is kill or get killed. Now he's eaten his frog, he's willing to croak. Right, Na?"

The chief nodded sorrowfully.

"You kill him, Chuck, and I w-walk out tomorrow. Run your own h-hospital."

"Cool it, buddy boy," Zavala said. "You say no, it's no." He nodded at Santiago. "Put the bastard back in his cage. We'll give him to the cops. Make sure they get his confession. Have Ramon take it down with a thumbprint."

Father Kelly poked his scholarly face into the stone hut. "May I?"

"Sorry, no last rites, Padre," Chuck said. "He's yours when he croaks. They're Catholics, these guys. Not the best, but that's what they are."

"Get Tifak," Zavala ordered Mai. "Tell him we're looking for the caves at dawn. I want twenty men. If the fuckers won't fight we'll burn 'em out."

"I'm going also," Joe said.

"Sure, buddy," Chuck said. "Army medic. Run the field hospital."

I'll do more, Joe thought. *I'll try and keep you and your friends from turning it into a massacre.*

To Kevin's astonishment, his mother balked at the operation. Felder had talked to her. Leave it to Sam, Kevin thought. The Island's top heart man and a leading cardiovascular surgeon recommended it, but Doc Felder disagreed.

"It's nothing to worry about, Mother," Kevin told her.

She sighed and gave in. When had she ever been able to oppose Kevin? Had they told Joseph? she asked. Had Bridie reached him? Kevin explained that there was no telephone to Batati, only a shortwave radio. Bridie would arrange for the UBC newsroom to send a message to the Manila correspondent. In turn he would phone Dr. Zavala's office, who would get the information to Joe.

"I hope you told him not to come rushing home on my account," Meg said. "I don't want to upset him. With all he has to do, and the little boy they adopted."

Normally Kevin did not show up for the first few hours when one of his patients was undergoing open-heart surgery. He knew the Luff team was efficient, expert. But the following morning he was at Upper County at seven. His mother had been prepped and was dozing off when he kissed her forehead. She looked serene, resigned.

In surgical greens, Kevin stood in the OR and watched Potsy go to work.

He had seen the procedure hundreds of times, but it was a strange sensation seeing his mother's chest exposed, the flesh slit open, the tissues pulled apart, the breastbone separated by the electric saw. Clamps and scissors pulled back the blood-rimmed flesh. Kevin saw

332

her heart beating under the pericardium.

Soon the pump was being readied for Potsy to place her on bypass. A cannula was placed into her right arm so venous blood could drain into the cardiac tank. A second cannula was inserted into her left leg, to return the blood to an artery, once surgery around the exsanguinated heart began.

Kevin shivered. It was too easy watching strangers, even friends, undergo this. But to see one's mother, the source of one's life, reduced to a square of bloody tissue, muscle and bone was different. For the first time in his life Kevin felt faint in an operating room.

Dr. Blum and Dr. Armas, the assistant surgeons on Potsy's team, worked methodically. Bits of flesh and bone sizzled as blood vessels were cauterized. The breastbone was stretched with a retractor. *Christ, what the human body can endure,* Kevin thought. He wondered why he was so rarely affected by suffering, pain. Maybe his aloofness, his lack of passion, were failings. *Maybe I am really the son of a bitch my sister-in-law says I am.*

Potsy swept into the room with a flourish. The preliminaries were over. It was time for him to take charge. Miss Peralta, the circulating nurse, helped him into sterile gown, mask, gloves.

He examined the stitching around the tubing leading into Meg's arms, legs, throat. "Keep 'em small, boys. Incidentally, who left a clamp on Mrs. Cohen's aorta last week? Just joking."

There was silence. Dr. Armas and Dr. Blum knew enough not to engage the chief surgeon in conversation. Most of the talk was like a third baseman's fast chatter. *Run it past him, Charley baby; can't hit what he can't see. . . .*

"Draw off two units of blood and keep it in the cardiotomy tank," Potsy said. "Replace with bank blood as soon as possible. Understood?"

"It's been done, Walter," Dr. Nakamura, the anesthesiologist, said. "Look at the tank."

"No wonder you guys creamed us at Pearl Harbor."

A few minor crises preceded Potsy's cutting into the pericardium. A kink developed in the arterial line. Miss Peralta flew from her side of the table and with deft hands found the faulty section of tube and straightened it.

"That's my girl, Imelda," Potsy joked. "Kev, you ever see moves

333

like that? Does she know your brother is working with her people?"

Shy to the point of muteness, Nurse Peralta did not respond.

"She knows," Kevin said. For once Potsy's egotistical gabbiness did not amuse him. Nor did it reduce the tension in the room. All of the members of the team, Kevin sensed, realized this was Dr. Derry's mother on the table. Blum and Armas, he was certain, had heard about Felder's objections to the surgery.

Meg was on bypass. Her uncovered heart stopped beating and deflated as blood left it, to be circulated and reoxygenated by the heart-lung machine. Clamps were placed on the aorta. Potsy made an incision and opened the aortic valve.

"Take a look, Kevin," he said. "Was I right or was I right?"

Meg's aortic valve was heavy with calcified growths. Small white chunks impeded the operation of the valve. It was a malformation of the nodular type. The orifice leading from valve to aorta through which the blood had to flow was severely narrowed.

"We were both right," Kevin said. *And so was Sam Felder sixteen years ago,* he thought.

"We can guess later why they grew so fast the last few years," Potsy said. "But it's there."

Potsy cut the diseased valve. He dropped the chunks of tissue into a curved pan. "Save that for the path lab," he said. "Never know what we'll learn. Okay, prosthetic valve."

From a sterile envelope Miss O'Farrell extracted the plastic ball-like unit that would be sewn into Meg's aorta to do the work of the defective valve.

Potsy, Armas and Blum began drawing green sutures around the edge of the prosthetic device, pulling on the filaments.

Kevin walked around the room, checked his mother's blood pressure and her breathing rate with Nakamura. She seemed to be doing well.

"Get a load of that stitching," Potsy bragged. "I could win needlepoint contests. Kevin, you watching? I always like a cardiologist to see what us surgeons can do when we're challenged."

With a flourish, Potsy placed the artificial valve in position and began attaching it with tiny stitches to the aorta.

"Look at that left ventricle, everybody," Potsy said. "Hypertrophied because it had to work too hard. Forward blood flow was impaired because of calcium around the orifice. Coronary arteries had to work too hard. Result, angina. Correct, Dr. Derry?"

"Almost as good a diagnosis as a cardiologist would make," Kevin said. He thought of his mother's delicate complexion—paler as she aged. What they called the "Dresden-china look."

"Good old valve," Potsy said. "Never lets a man down."

Dr. Nakamura, at his gauges and monitors, was frowning. "Drop in blood pressure. Just went from seventy-five to fifty."

Kevin walked to the monitoring machines and watched the needle descend.

"Read it again, Nak," Potsy said.

"It's at forty-five."

Kevin breathed deeply. What was happening? He wondered if air in the arterial line might have formed an embolus. Unlikely. His mother had been subjected to it only briefly. "She's warming up," said Potsy. "Getting her back on her own power soon, boys. Stand by."

He glaned at the technician's half-hidden black face. "Ready, man?"

"Ready."

"Partial bypass. On."

"On, Doctor."

The valve was fully secured to the heart and the aorta. They watched the malformed orange heart return to life. The blood was returning to Meg's circulatory system.

"Bleeding," Dr. Blum said.

"Where?" asked Potsy. "Sponge, nurse. Oh, I see it. Nothing."

Kevin peered over his cousin's shoulder. The heart was bleeding. "What is it?" he asked.

"Nothing major. Sometimes the stitching . . ."

He studied the heart a moment. "Tell you what. Let's fibrillate her and go back on bypass so I can look it over. Hand me the paddles."

Nurse O'Farrell gave Potsy the two plastic handles with the aluminum discs at the end. He raised them. "Ready?"

"Ready," Dr. Nakamura said.

"On."

"On."

The heart settled into a slower, irregular, noncoordinated beat, a step necessary before putting the patient on total bypass.

To Kevin's horror his mother's heart appeared awash in blood. It was leaking badly. Even while no longer pumping it was losing blood.

"There's a puncture somewhere," Potsy said. His voice shook a little. "Somebody let a scalpel slip. Right in the heart muscle."

Neither Armas nor Blum spoke. Potsy had done all the cutting around the heart.

"How long has she been on bypass?" Kevin asked.

Nakamura checked his watch. "Hour and forty minutes."

"Lots of time," Dr. Walter Luff, Jr., said. "Lots of time."

Kevin felt his knees go watery. *Christ, what a mess.* The operation had gone so well. Now something had fouled up. No wonder her blood pressure was dipping. There was a minuscule cut somewhere in the heart.

"Pledgets," Potsy said. "Fast, dammit."

O'Farrell handed him gauze patches. Armas intercepted them, gave them to Potsy. "Everybody keep their hands out of my way. There's got to be a cut somewhere."

He was working damned near blind, Kevin saw. So much blood was oozing that as much as the nurses sponged and wiped, the heart remained obscured.

Potsy anchored cotton patches. And still the blood oozed. The heart muscle was tricky, thick-walled. It could hide the minutest tear.

"Wipe my forehead, will you, Imelda?" Potsy asked. "All I need is to contaminate the cardiac cavity. It's bleeding again. Another pledget, Harold. Dammit, don't hold it that way."

It took thirty-five minutes for the bleeding to stop.

Kevin checked his watch. Over three hours on bypass. It was not a good sign, not with someone his mother's age. Potsy's patching had stopped the oozing of blood, but no one was certain where the cut was located, what had caused the loss of blood after the valve had been inserted.

"We've got it now," Potsy said. "Tolliver, you with me?"

"Yes, Doctor," the heart-lung technician said.

"Start taking Mrs. Derry off bypass. Give her back two-fifty cc. at a time, nice and slow. Ready?"

"Ready."

"Go."

"Going." The technician began closing the venous line and loosening the clamp on the arterial line.

Potsy nodded. "Just great. We'll give her a big dose of Inderal and we'll be out of the woods. Kev?"

"She looks better." But her blood pressure had not noticeably improved, Kevin saw.

"Goddammit to hell," Potsy muttered. "Bleeding again."

No sooner was blood returned to Meg's heart than the bleeding started. The upper surface of the heart was a red splotch.

"Put her on bypass," Potsy said. "We're going to redo the suture line. From the back this time. Where the hell is that incision?"

Kevin breathed deeply. If his mother remained on bypass too long she might suffer brain or kidney damage. The excessive handling of the heart could induce any number of complications. And the leaking would not stop. Each time blood was returned to Meg's heart, the bleeding started again.

"Aunt Meg was never a bleeder," Potsy said to Kevin. "Was she?"

"No. And I have to assume she got a full dosage of coagulants."

"Just the right amount for her age and weight," Nakamura said. "And I'm adding a little."

Silence settled over the OR. Once the muscle began to tear, shredding could proceed quickly.

"The heart came back terrifically after the first run on the pump," Potsy said. "What went wrong?"

"We're over three and a half hours on the pump, Dr. Luff," Nakamura said.

Potsy snapped at him. "If I want to know, I'll ask you."

Kevin remained silent. For all his knowledge, all the open-heart surgery he had seen, he had nothing to suggest. Potsy rarely failed. His cousin resutured the stitching around the prosthetic valve. A neat, quick job. He looked at Kevin. "That should do it. She's getting perfusion. Heart looks better."

Once more Meg was taken off the pump. Another 250 cc. units of her blood were returned. There seemed to be less bleeding this time. Only a red trickle appeared across the face of the heart.

Potsy growled, "Dammit, we've made it. Kevin, she's going to be all right."

Kevin wondered. Perhaps coagulation was setting in and the invisible wound was healing. Perhaps.

337

The heart beat faintly, barely acknowledging life.

"I'll take the defibrillators," Potsy said. "This time it's for real. Ready?"

"Ready," Nakamura said.

"Hit it."

The anesthesiologist threw the switch. Potsy applied the metal wands to the surface of the heart and its base.

There was no response. The heart continued its irregular fluttering.

"Once more, Nak."

Nakamura threw the switch again. Again Potsy applied the paddles. If anything the heartbeat was more erratic.

The third time Potsy tried to shock the heart into a beat, nothing registered on the EKG on the wall monitor.

She's dead, Kevin thought.

No one spoke. *Dr. Derry's mother. Dr. Luff's aunt.* The team watched, solemn-eyed, apologetic.

"Give me a syringe loaded with adrenalin," Potsy said.

He jammed it into the dying heart. *Blood of my blood,* he thought. *My mother's sister.* . . . He massaged the heart with his hands and kneaded the muscles until his fingers were crimson.

He looked at Kevin. "Sorry, Kevin. A crazy one. I don't know what went wrong. Any life signs, Nak?"

"Sorry, Dr. Luff. Nothing."

"Brain waves?"

Nakamura shook his head.

Nurse O'Farrell cleared her throat. "We're all sorry, Dr. Derry. Your mother was a wonderful person. She never complained once, when she had to take all those tests."

Blum came around from the table and stood in front of Kevin. Armas, more reserved, tidied up the corpse. Blum was crying. *Strange,* Kevin thought. *He barely knew my mother. He's thirty-five, ready to storm the surgical world, and he seems to care.*

"Dr. Derry, what Miss O'Farrell says . . . I'm sorry. . . . I don't know how it happened. . . ."

Potsy frowned at him and yanked the mask down. "Okay, Harold. You and Armas take over."

The family had been waiting in Lawton Curtis' second-floor suite of rooms. Curtis had canceled meetings and calls. Bridie was there with Aunt Katherine and Uncle Walter. Cynthia had remained at the Cape. Kevin had assured her it was a routine operation. Serious, but one that was bound to make his mother's life easier. Anyway, Kevin did not have the strength to deal with her. Better to let her stay in Orleans and learn of the good results when it was all over.

When Kevin and Potsy came upstairs they were surprised to find Manship present. He was holding Bridie's hand.

"I'm sorry," Kevin said. "Bridie, come to me, please."

She got up. "Oh, Kevin . . ."

"Mother died ten minutes ago."

The tears flooded Bridie's face. She grabbed her brother's shoulders and rested her head on the white coat.

Katherine wept discreetly. Walter touched her shoulder. Not demonstrative people. For God's sake, Harold Blum, who barely knew Meg, had shown more emotion, Kevin thought.

"Sorry, dammit," Potsy said. He began to cry. "It was a crazy thing. The valve went in beautifully, the prosthesis was perfect, but the heart gave way . . . no indication it would happen . . . her signs were good . . . God, I'm sorry. I do these every week, and I've never lost one. . . ."

"Potsy's right," Kevin said. He stroked his sister's hair. "He did his best. So did the people on his team. The heart gave way."

Neither mentioned Potsy's suspicion that he had made a minute tear in the heart muscle. Medically they were right. The valve was severely calcified. Meg could have expected increasingly painful attacks of angina, weakness, shortness of breath.

"Kevin, Kevin," Bridie cried. "She never hurt anyone in her life. She was so good, so kind. And all of us, we ignored her. . . ."

Manship came forward and touched Bridie's arm. "No you didn't, Bridget. She adored all of you. And no mother I know got as much joy from her children as Meg did. You made her happy. That's what counts."

Bridie sobbed. "We hardly ever visited her. . . . We were all so busy with our big careers. When did we last spend a Christmas together?"

"Bridie, Meg understood," said Katherine. "She appreciated your success."

Potsy sank into Curtis' chair. The administrator was standing in the doorway, offering condolences.

"I've never felt so lousy in my life about anything," Potsy said.

"Kevin, this was a one in a thousand, wasn't it?"

"Right." He was dry-eyed. He had loved and pitied his mother. But there was a block of ice inside him. He had been a stranger to tears and sorrow all his life. There was always too much to get done. Had he cried at Jack's funeral twelve years ago? He could not remember. But he could recall Bridie and Joe's tears as they watched John Kennedy's funeral, and he had stood by dry-eyed.

"Someone's got to call Joe," Kevin said. "Bridie, you didn't get through to him the other day, did you?"

They had agreed to wait until after surgery, she reminded him. She'd call the network. Should Joe come home?

"I think so," Kevin said. "If there's a problem, I'll get the airplane tickets."

Manship was looking at him curiously. In almost a whisper he asked, "And Cynthia? The children?"

"I'll call right away."

Bridie, dabbing at her eyes, looked from E.E.'s face to Kevin's. How alike they had become, she thought.

Potsy's beeper went off. A patient waiting for a bypass was prepped and waiting for him. Would Dr. Luff rather Dr. Blum handled the case?

"No," Potsy said. "It's my job. Aunt Meg would forgive me. Okay, Kevin?"

"Sure, Potsy. It won't bring Mom back if we stand around wringing our hands."

Potsy left. He looked beaten, sagging.

"Poor Walter," Katherine cried. "He wanted so much to help Meg. . . ."

"Why don't all of you come to my place," Manship said. "We still have to consider funeral arrangements, notifying people. . . ."

Kevin agreed. Bridie said she had to leave. She had stopped weeping, but was still holding his arm. He felt her hand—as strong as his own. She left to freshen up, meet Kevin later.

At the end of the corridor, Kevin saw Sam Felder seated glumly on a bench. There was a young woman sitting alongside him.

Doc got up and came toward Kevin. "Sorry, kid. Believe me, this isn't going to be an 'I told you so.' You and Luff may have been right. Blum tells me it was a crazy thing. Bleeding wouldn't stop. Kevin, your mother was a real lady, one of the last. Always reminded me of Mrs. Felder. I never heard her raise her voice."

Felder touched something in Kevin that no one in his family had been able to do. He saw again the sagging Derry house, the dingy pharmacy. His father and Doc swapping stories.

"Thanks, Sam. You were always good to her. And to all of us. Best damned GP on the Island. Maybe we should have listened to you."

"Nah, nah. You guys are experts. The way Blum described it, it was no one's fault. What a shame, the way good people have to go sometimes."

The young woman on the bench got up and came toward Kevin. "I'm sorry also, Kevin."

Kevin almost failed to recognize the oval face, the extraordinary dark eyes.

"My daughter, Kevin," said Sam.

"For goodness' sake," Kevin said. "I haven't seen you since . . . since you and Bridie graduated."

"That's right. A restaurant on Broadway. I'm sorry about your mother. Tell Joe and Bridie I asked about them."

Sam Felder bragged a little. Annette Felder was in New York to read a paper on genetic studies of cancer. She had driven him to the hospital to find out how his patient had been doing. They had heard the sad news, didn't want to bother the family.

"Pop, please," Nan said. "Kevin's got other things on his mind."

Almost involuntarily, Kevin looked at her ring finger. No wedding band. Hadn't he heard she was married? She caught his inquisitive glance and said to her father, "I don't think a cardiologist is much interested in cancer-bearing mice."

"Kevin, if I can help," Felder said. "I'm not that busy. Let me know when the funeral is, huh? That's all I seem to do lately. Help bury people."

Kevin said he would. He turned, then smiled at Nan with the Derry charm. "Where can I reach you? I'm in charge of a monthly lecture series here for house staff. We try to keep it as varied as possible. I think they'd like to hear a report on your work."

"It's the Boston Institute for Genetic Studies. But this is wrong. We shouldn't be talking medicine."

"That's what keeps me going." Kevin stared at her intense eyes. A woman who spent long hours in the lab, peered into microscopes. "If

341

we didn't have the work, we'd lose our minds. I'm glad I met you again, Nan."

"Terrific girl," Dr. Felder said, unashamed to brag. "Won the Emmett Prize last year. What do you think keeps an *alte kocker* like me alive?"

"Pop, cut it *out.*"

"Yeah I talk too much. Kevin, I'm sorry about your mother, I really am."

Kevin thanked Doc again for his kindnesses and left. When he got home he scrawled on a pad N. FELDER, BOSTON.

7

UBC had trouble finding Joe. In Batati the raid on the Ilagas was underway. Father Kelly was standing on the dirt track, waving his hands. The first of three Jeeps halted in front of him. Five armed men rode in the back. Zavala drove.

"Chuck," Father Kelly said. "A last appeal. Don't go ahead with this. I have no sympathy for the Ilagas. But this is wrong."

"Give us a blessing, Father," Zavala mocked.

"Not for what you are about to do, Chuck."

"Then forgive us."

"If you'll turn around and go back, and refer the affair to the authorities, I would find it in my heart to forgive you. So you'll kill some of those people. More will come down."

"Not if we make an example of them."

Father Kelly walked down the small convoy, terrified by the automatic weapons, the somber faces.

"Joe, use your influence," he said. "Chuck respects you. You may be the only one he does. I know there's justice on his side, but he can't run a private army. Let him defend the Batati, but don't escalate the fighting."

It was the same argument Jenny had given Joe, crying and shouting that morning, trying to convince him to stay behind, to let Zavala, that runt in battle dress, run his own war.

"It's no use, Father Tom," Joe said. "He's g-got his mind made up. I don't think we'll find anyone. Those caves'll be empty."

Zavala stood up. With a wave of his Armalite, he signaled the

343

convoy to proceed. The Jeeps grumbled over the pitted track. Joe looked into the back of his vehicle. Na Bong winked at him.

"Tell that kid next to you to p-point his rifle barrel up," Joe said morosely. "One bounce of this Jeep and he'll blow my head off."

Na Bong bawled the boy out. A barefoot, rail-skinny kid. He was a tracker, not more than seventeen. He laughed, pointed the bolt-action Springfield to the sky.

They left the Jeeps three miles beyond the huts that had burned the previous night. Zavala spent ten minutes poking in the ruins. The houses had been reduced to heaps of ashes. Joe saw scorched tin plates, bits of broken china, a clay doll.

Ferdie, the radio operator, met them at the edge of the settlement. He could not explain why the Ilagas had not left the mutilated dead. Maybe they had taken hostages.

"Fuckers," Zavala said. "You too, Ferdie, you dumb asshole."

"Lay off," Joe said. "What c-could he do?"

Cursing, Zavala climbed out of the Jeep. He was Patton in Normandy, Monty at El Alamein. Beyond the undulant green terraces, they saw the beginning of the rainforest. Somewhere, to the east and north, the Ilaga prisoner had said, there were caves.

"Tifak," Zavala called. "Which way?"

The barefoot hunter ran to Chuck's side. A Springfield rifle was on one shoulder; a bolo dangled at his hip.

The party followed Tifak up a narrow trail. It was overgrown with vines. Their progress was impeded by undergrowth so thick as to be impenetrable. Above them tropical birds screamed; they heard the chatter of monkeys. Joe had never seen terrain like this. The trees were so lofty and thick that only occasional shafts of light slanted through. As the ascent grew steeper, his breathing became labored. Danny Larrizabal, in camouflage suit and jungle boots, walked with him.

"Sure you don't want a gun, Doc?" he asked.

"No. I'm your m-medic."

"You can have my forty-five," Larrizabal said. "I'm gonna use the BAR on those fuckers."

Joe had not noticed it in the Jeeps. Now he saw that Larrizabal was not only carrying two .45s; a Batati boy was bearing a Browning automatic rifle.

"Know what that is, Doc?"

"Sure. Even medics had to learn to use them."

"Blow a guy into small turds with one."

Tifak paused at a ledge in the side of the mountain. There was less cover now. The green vegetation screened off the valley where they had left the Jeeps.

Tifak got on his knees and sniffed the ground. He ran his graceful fingers over the earth around the ledge. All at once there was a crashing noise in the bush. Tifak grinned. Wild pig, number-one meat.

Chuck was wheezing from the climb.

"Maybe we'll go home," Joe whispered to Larrizabal. "Y-your boss looks beat."

They sipped from canteens, waited. Tifak pointed east, into the slanting rays of the sun. The escarpment, sparsely covered with twisting vines and shrubs, wound its way upward.

Joe scowled at Larrizabal. "Not much cover," he said. "If they're up there, we're w-wide open."

"We'll have to go up in two columns," said Zavala. "One file stay close to the mountain, the other at the edge. First shot, take cover. Tifak says he remembers the caves. He slept there once."

They continued their slow ascent. Joe noticed that the Batati boys, undernourished and barefoot, seemed the least tired. Tifak was singing. A hell of a way to sneak up on someone.

They heard shots as the first four men emerged above the treeline.

"Up there!" Zavala shouted. "Take cover! Goddammit, take cover!"

The party hugged the sides of the escarpment. Despite Zavala's training, the men bunched together. The Batati looked terrified, jabbering, pointing. They were not gunfighters, Joe knew. Their weapons were bolos and spears.

Santiago went crashing off into the brush with another soldier. Joe could see what he was doing. He would circle the hiding place, come up from another side.

There was another burst from above. Joe saw the slugs stitching the ground. They were using rapid-fire weapons.

Another constable, accompanied by a Batati boy, broke from the wall, zigzagged close to the ground and vanished into a patch of shrubbery. A professional, he lay prone and ripped off a few shots. Zavala led three men after him, shouting. "Everyone else stay back."

There were more shots from the caves. Then answering fire from Zavala's men.

"Shit," Zavala said. "They're inside. Have to burn the bastards out." He cupped his hands. "Danny!"

Larrizabal and a Batati boy carrying two cans of gasoline crawled up the cliffside to the boss. Joe decided to follow. Above him, on the ledge, he heard Santiago chattering. They'd seen one man, a sentry, who had fired the shots. They thought they'd wounded him. He had dropped off the top of the cave, Santiago shouted.

One of the Batati with Zavala had been hit. Joe helped the boy into the woods, poured iodine on the wound in his leg, and bound it. There did not seem to be any arterial bleeding, just a jagged hole.

Now there were heavier volleys of fire from the cave. Everyone hugged the ground. Bullets spit and crackled over them, snapping branches, whipping the leaves.

"Son of a bitch," Chuck said. Their position was precarious. Zavala shouted at them to spread out.

From above they could hear Santiago firing back.

"One grenade in there, and a can of gasoline," Zavala was moaning, "and it would all be over."

Larrizabal fingered the grenades on his jacket. "I'll go, boss. Just gimme two Batati with a can of gas apiece. We'll smoke them out."

Joe snaked along the ground. Memories of the infiltration course at Sam Houston. A guy who looked into a rattlesnake's face, jumped up, and was cut in half by machine-gun bullets.

"Look, Chuck," Joe gasped, "talk to them first." He was getting old. Forty and playing stupid games. Like starting at nose guard with two bad knees, wanting to cry with the pain.

"They're killers. I don't talk to them."

"Take 'em alive, Chuck. You have enough c-clout in Manila to put them on trial. Get them to testify against Perpetua."

Na Bong's honest face was nodding. "Kakai Dokka right, boss. Give them a chance to surrender."

Larrizabal had not heard the discussions. With brainless daring he burst from the undergrowth and, with his Batatis following, raced toward the cave. He tossed a grenade. It fell short, detonated, raised a fountain of dirt, rocks, metal splinters.

Bullets whizzed through the air, and they heard Danny cursing and shouting. The Batati boys dragged him back. He had caught two slugs in his right thigh. He was bleeding, crippled.

Joe helped pull him away. Larrizabal's coppery face had turned white. He kept grabbing at his injured leg and cursing. "Fuckers. Dirty fuckers."

Joe gave him morphine and cut away his green and yellow camouflage suit. One wound bled too rapidly to suit Joe. He undid his musette bag, found rubber tubing, tied a tourniquet around Larrizabal's thigh.

"He all right?" Zavala shouted.

"Yeah, he's okay," Joe said. "Let's g-get the hell out of here."

"Not me, buddy boy." He was on his feet, shouting to Santiago and the other soldier to get closer to the cave and lob grenades into it.

Na Bong put his hand on Zavala's arm. "Boss, maybe Kakai Dokka is right. Maybe we can talk them out."

"Talk, shit. I want them carried out in pieces."

"Maybe not so easy, boss. I talk. They know me. They know I am datu of Batati."

Zavala wiped his forehead. "They got a price on your head. You can't even go into Labat without a bodyguard."

Joe inched his way toward them. "Then you go, Chuck. They'll think twice before they shoot you."

"No," Na said. "I go."

The datu took off his white shirt and tied it to a branch.

Zavala cursed. He hated any situation he could not dominate. "Go on, Na," he said sullenly. "You guys up there, cover him. If they shoot Na, charge them."

Na Bong walked from the patch of forest, waving the white flag. He shouted in Ilo-Ilo, stopped halfway along the ledge, facing the cave opening. It was obscured with the dust and smoke of Larrizabal's grenade.

A voice responded. Na shouted back. They spoke for a few minutes. No shots were fired. Joe breathed easier. Hell, two men wounded. Both would live. They could pack up and go home.

Na walked back to Zavala.

"Well?" Zavala asked.

"They say they have four of our people in there alive. Three men and a woman. If we don't go away, they'll chop them up a little bit at a time. And throw out a piece at a time. We have to go away and let them go to Labat and meet Perpetua. They say the Batati attacked them last night."

"Go back and tell 'em we don't believe them," Zavala said.

Na was standing fifty feet from the cave shouting at the entrance. They got a glimpse of a head with a long black ponytail. Sunlight glinted on the bottle around his neck. Another frog-worshipper, Joe thought.

Suddenly they heard a scream. The wails intensified, then faded to an undulating moan.

A human foot came flying from the cave opening. It was brown, dusty, bloody. Around the shredded ankle and protruding bone were the brass rings of the Batati.

Na called out again. He was pleading with the Ilagas.

"Na, get back here," Zavala barked. "We should charge them. I'm ready." He looked at Joe.

"You'll kill the hostages."

"Okay, so they die. They're not afraid. Are they, Na?"

"No, boss."

"You stay with the wounded, Joe. We need a doctor. They need a God. That's me."

Another bloody object came flying out of the cave. Joe shuddered. No screaming this time. A dismembered hand lay in the earth.

Crawling close to Tifak and Na, Joe asked Na, "What's the c-cave like inside? Tifak says he slept there."

"Deep, Kakai Dokka. Go all the way back."

"Open anywhere else? Another way in?"

Tifak shook his head. Then he made a curious gesture, patting his mouth, chattering, miming something's rising from his head.

"Maybe hole in the roof," Na said. "For smoke. Hunters use cave."

Joe asked Zavala for his binoculars. He focused on the crown of the cave. Was it his imagination, or was there a wisp of smoke rising from it?

"What you have in mind, buddy boy?" Zavala asked.

"Give me two grenades," Joe said.

Zavala shook his head. "Unh-unh. You're high-priced help. Anyone can pull a grenade pin. Besides, I thought you were against blowing them out."

Zavala will never understand me, thought Joe. Throwing a punch at Johnson, the medic who hated the Batatis. Standing up to the noncoms who ran Curtis' drug racket. Sticking up for hardheads like

348

Felder. Sometimes there was no other way.

"If I drop two eggs on them," Joe said, "the Ilagas may run so fast they won't have time to think about killing anyone. You g-guys charge as soon as the grenades go off. You have flashlights?"

Zavala nodded.

"Go in with all the light you can manage; try to grab them."

Chuck gave Joe the grenades and embraced him. He split his men into two groups. Three of the Batati climbed to the high point to join Santiago. Na and the others would charge from below.

Joe borrowed a .45 from Larrizabal, who, faint from loss of blood, insisted on setting up the BAR. He couldn't walk, but he could shoot.

Joe put a grenade in each pocket of his bush jacket, jammed the .45 into his belt, and made a wide circle through the forest around the cave. He descended for fifty yards, then climbed the stream-soaked side of the rock. His arms ached. The old burn scars were paining him.

The Ilagas had trusted their frogs too much. If there were a hole in the cave roof, they should have posted a man there. Joe saw the smoke now. He scrambled across the top of the cave. Below him he saw Santiago wave his rifle, then let loose three rounds.

Scarcely breathing, Joe pulled the pin on the grenade. The hole in the rock was about a foot wide. He dropped the grenade in as if tossing a lead sinker over the side of a boat. He followed it with the second.

He was halfway down the rock face when the grenades exploded. A geyser of dirt and ashes spewed from the hole. He could hear screams, the *dut-dut-dut* of the automatic weapons.

Na was shouting for surrender, screaming at the Ilagas to come out, not to hurt the hostages. The gunfire was continuous now—loud, shattering. Larrizabal was firing the BAR. Joe hoped that the morphine-doped hoodlum had the sense not to kill his own men.

Joe ran down the escarpment, leaped ten feet to the forest floor, raced across the terrain to the clearing.

It was over.

Four Ilaga men, holding their hands over their heads, had emerged. Their eyes were smudges of fear.

"Tell them to squat," Zavala yelled at Na. "Tell them to squat or I'll blow their fucking heads off."

Na barked the order. The four men did as told. One, a boy of no more than eighteen, began to crap. Feces oozed from his soiled pants as soon as he assumed the squatting position.

Santiago came out of the cave carrying the mutilated corpse of the Batati farmer.

Joe turned and vomited. Dry heaves. Bile and gastric juice.

"Attaboy, Joey," Zavala shouted. "Scared the shit out of them. The other hostages are okay."

One of the prisoners made a break for the jungle.

Waving his hands, he ran past Larrizabal's BAR. The bursts from the weapon cut through his midsection. He ran a few steps with his entrails flying behind him like a blue hawser. Then he tumbled to the ground and died with his guts in an untidy pile.

Joe staggered over to Chuck, who was having trouble disentangling himself from the grateful hostages.

"Good job, buddy boy. Didn't you know medics aren't supposed to carry weapons?"

Joe mopped his face. Christ, what a day. He'd never get anyone to believe it.

"We're going to n-need stretchers," Joe said. "One for Danny, one for the kid with the shoulder wound."

The three hostages—an old man, a younger man and a scrawny woman—were wrapping the remains of the mutilated Batati in giant leaves.

"What about the guy Danny blasted?" Joe asked. "Why don't you let the other th-three prisoners carry him? Give them something to think about."

"Carry him?" Zavala said, and laughed. "When we're through with these fuckers, they'll be crawling back to Labat." He turned to Na Bong. "Gimme your bolo."

Na unsheathed the long razor-sharp knife.

The prisoners began to finger their frogs.

Zavala swaggered toward the man with the loose bowels and pointed the tip of the bolo at his nose. "You first, shitass."

Na shouted at the man to stand up. He got to his feet, hands clutching the frog around his neck.

Joe dropped his musette bags and walked between Zavala and the captive. He put his hand on the blade. "No reprisals, no slicing n-noses or ears. They're prisoners and they'll go on trial."

"I pay your salary, Joe."

"Yeah. But I'm not one of your expensive hookers, or a goon carrying a g-gun for you. I can leave tomorrow."

Zavala giggled and dropped the bolo. "Oh, Joey, what an ace. Okay, you win. We take them back whole. You're right. We'll let them do the carrying."

Na picked up his bolo and resheathed it. His dark eyes looked thankfully at Dr. Derry. There was a time to stop killing.

Jenny, obscured by the rain, was waiting for them in a hooded green slicker and boots.

She flung herself at Joe, hugged him, inspected him for wounds. A mob of screaming Batati surrounded them. The women made birdlike cooing noises. The men laughed and fired old guns into the air.

Zavala, shoving away mouths that tried to kiss him, hands that tried to touch him, drove to the hospital. Larrizabal was asleep, full of morphine.

"I'm okay," Joe said. He kissed Jenny several times.

"You're not hurt? You're okay?" Jenny wept. "Joey, all that blood all over you."

"It's over. I th-think I convinced Zavala he's got to put those guys on trial." He put his arm around her and hugged her as they waded through a lake of mud.

"We'll scrub, get into greens, and work on Larrizabal. He's got two slugs in his leg. The Batati aren't badly hurt. Maybe I should have been a trauma surgeon. Think it's too l-late?"

She kept weeping.

"What's wrong. Jen? I'm here. I'm in one piece."

"Joey, I can't . . . Joey, this came on the wireless from Manila after you left. . . . I've been trying to get a message to the states. Joey . . . your mother . . ."

She handed him a rain-soaked sheet of yellow paper.

The rain clouded his eyes and made the ink run in gray rivulets.

DEAREST JOEY TERRIBLE NEWS BE BRAVE MOTHER DIED OF COMPLICATIONS AFTER HEART SURGERY TODAY PLEASE CONTACT US ALL OUR LOVE BRIDIE AND KEVIN

He swallowed, took off his hat, let the rain beat down on his bare head.

"Oh God. Why didn't Kevin tell me she was s-sick? It's not true . . . it's . . ."

She held him. Her man, her boy, her angry doctor. Always in Kevin's shadow. The famous Bridget Derry's brother. And never the best-loved of the three, neither by Jack or Meg.

"Christ, she wasn't seventy," Joey muttered. "She was okay when we l-left. Why heart surgery?"

Bereft of that power of control in which Kevin prided himself, Joe wept on Jenny's shoulder.

"Joey, Joey, we'll call later. There's nothing you can do now."

Na Bong was standing a few feet away. His ankles were deep in the mud of the village street. Something bad had happened to Kakai Dokka. A man he loved. Na had seen the heart in this plain man, seen it sixteen years ago when he had fought the sergeant and saved Gantu's life.

"Kakai Dokka," the datu said. "I help in hospital?"

Joe looked up. He was ashamed of his bawling. "Sure, Na. Stay with us, huh?"

They saw the generator-fed lights go on in the hospital, heard its confident hum. Father Kelly was mopping rainwater from the doorway.

Work to do. Knowledge to be used. Jenny at his side. He would cry later. They would have to tell Nicky about Grandma Meg.

Hands locked, they sloshed through the mud. Jenny stayed close to him. Yes, she said, he should go home for the funeral. She would stay with Nicky and Peter.

With a surge of sorrow, Joe heard his mother's voice.

Joey, is that you tracking mud into the house? Another fistfight? Why can't you be like Kevin? Oh, look at your bloody nose, and the sweater ripped. Do you realize your father didn't earn the price of that sweater today?

Joe pushed the thoughts from his mind. But as he walked into the hospital, he knew his time in Manila was drawing to a close. His home was America. At the end of the next year he would return for good.

PART SIX
1970

1

"What's 'hematemesis'?" Eliot Sparling asked in a whisper.

"Vomiting blood," the medical student replied.

The reporter had sneaked into the auditorium of Upper County Hospital and taken a seat in the rear row next to a bearded intern.

"And 'melena'?"

"Black, tarry stool."

Sparling hunched low. *Melena hematemesis.* Sounded like a Greek folk singer. He had entered the hospital furtively, sneaking past the uniformed guards. He had a late-afternoon appointment with Kevin, but he had arrived early to sit in on "grand rounds."

Grand rounds. It had a marvelous ring. He imagined it would have been a kind of processional, with banners, as Derry, Luff and the other medical lords paraded their way from ward to ward.

But it was nothing more than a lecture. Dr. Derry was discussing a baffling case. Woman, age sixty-one, dying in the hospital after thirty-two days of intense suffering following a valve replacement and a cardiopulmonary bypass. It was one of the few cases that Potsy had lost, and it was not established that the surgery had anything to do with the patient's death. Sparling could see Luff's cherubic face, his air of studied concern.

Kevin was discussing the patient's final symptoms. The bloody black stool and the vomiting of blood occurred on the last day of the woman's life. The events leading up to it could have filled a medical textbook.

Sparling sat fascinated, now and then asking his neighbor—an

355

intern named Donald Weisbrod—to explain things.

"How often does Dr. Derry hold grand rounds?" Eliot whispered.

"Maybe once a month. Star time. He and Luff, the capitalistic cousins. Know what Luff earned last year?"

"Beats me."

"Million and a half dollars. Paid no taxes. Tax shelters, dodges, corporations, deals."

"And Dr. Derry?"

"Empire builder. He's got all the money he needs. He just wants the power. Medical establishment's front man."

The auditorium was lavish, with blue cushioned chairs, royal blue drapes, mosaic friezes.

Kevin cleared his throat. "Whoever's mumbling in the rear seats, could you please hold it down? Go outside if you want to talk."

What Eliot was gathering from Kevin's discussion was that whereas it was not a full-blown medical fuck-up, it surely was a case where physicians were stumbling around in the dark.

"The patient had been discharged after four weeks, showing temporary aphasia, hemiplegia and jaundice. . . ."

"Loss of memory, paralysis on one side," Dr. Weisbrod whispered, anticipating Eliot. "You know what jaundice is. These conditions cleared up and she was sent home."

"Two weeks later," Kevin continued, "she's readmitted. Anorexia, nausea, vomiting, light stools, dark urine, jaundice. A dehydrated and desperately ill woman."

There were two other physicians sitting on the stage with Dr. Kevin Derry. Sparling recognized one—Dr. Abraham Gold, a big wheel at Beth Moses. The other was a white-haired chap. Dr. Howard, Weisbrod muttered. Old-type society fella, emeritus this, emeritus that.

"How about it, Dr. Gold?" Kevin asked pleasantly. "She was your patient."

It sounded to Sparling like "Your witness."

"I agree with Dr. Derry," Dr. Gold said, "that this is a baffler. Obviously consumption coagulopathy is indicated. But what else? Mitral valvular disease, but that, we trust, should have been corrected by surgery. . . ."

A resident raised his hand. "What about the jaundice?"

"I might attribute it to the halothane anesthesia. It was halothane that was used, wasn't it, Dr. Luff?"

Potsy nodded.

"We know halothane can cause hepatic change, yes."

Gold went on. "There was certainly chronic consumption coagulopathy, associated with mitral valvular disease and acute bacterial endocarditis. The most baffling symptom is the bleeding. She developed the clotting problem only after surgery."

Dr. Luff, speaking in measured tones, disagreed politely with some of Dr. Gold's findings. "I wonder if Dr. Gold has perhaps fallen into a situation, as I often have, of trying to combine a number of unrelated findings. We may be wrong in trying to come to a unifying diagnosis. . . . I am not sure we can find a major underlying disease."

Sparling was sorting things out. An anesthetic that brought on jaundice? An artificial valve that kept the blood from clotting properly and caused hemorrhaging? He wanted to pump Weisbrod, but to his surprise, the intern was standing in the aisle.

"Let's keep in mind," Kevin was saying, "that both the open-heart surgery and mitral-valve disease offered an opportunity for virulent organisms to be seeded into the heart valve."

"Not in my OR, Dr. Derry," Potsy called from his front-row seat. "We are sterile, Doctor, sterile."

Jesus Christ, Sparling wondered, *they can screw you up as much as they cure you.* He had to hand it to Kevin Derry, the way he layed it all out in the open.

Suddenly Dr. Weisbrod walked down the aisle.

"Attention, all members of house staff," Weisbrod shouted. "There will be a meeting of the Progressive Medical Association at three P.M. today in conference room B! Issues to be discussed—lower cost of hospital care, an increase in minority students, community participation in hospital management. Please join us!"

With that, Weisbrod began handing out mimeographed sheets. Eliot grabbed one. As he read, he was astonished by the attendings' silence. Derry, Gold and Luff seemed paralyzed.

"Down with the money machine!" Weisbrod shouted as he returned to his seat. "Power to the people! Serve the communities, the poor, the blacks, not the rich who use this place as a rest home!"

357

Abe Gold got up. "Dr. Weisbrod, this is inappropriate," he said. "These are grand rounds. You want to call a meeting, do it in a civilized way. We are discussing medical matters here. This auditorium is not your soapbox."

"I speak for the people," Weisbrod shouted. "You don't. Everyone, read our twelve non-negotiable demands! Attend today's important meeting! Details on the paper!"

"Who is that man?" Kevin asked Gold.

"Weisbrod. New intern. He was at Mid-Island last year. Took an elective in community medicine. Joe warned me about him. A brilliant kid, but he thinks he's Che Guevara."

Kevin called out, "Dr. Weisbrod, you can stay and participate in medical discussions if you want to. But you may not make this a political forum. Either leave or shut up."

"I'm leaving," Weisbrod shouted. "Dr. Derry, you're the one who'd better think about getting out. There won't be any place for medical empires."

The intern left. Kevin quickly brought grand rounds to a close. The cause of the woman's death was never fully determined.

As the doctors dispersed, Sparling noticed that most of them left Weisbrod's papers on their seats. Then he went off to Kevin's office. Dr. Derry greeted him with a reserved smile.

"What's Bridie up to?" Kevin asked the reporter.

"Haven't heard from her for a while," Eliot said. "She's settling down in Paris. I'll talk to her on the phone one of these days when she's ready to broadcast. Any messages?"

Kevin, clouded in cigarette smoke, laughed. "She doesn't need my advice. She goes her own way."

Sparling watched his tongue. Bridget Derry had not precisely gone her own way to Paris. The network brass had sent her there— not exactly as a punishment, but to end her affair with Ling, which had become potentially damaging for everyone's comfort. Either she goes, the network president said to Christopher Ling, or you go. Dolores Ling had had her way. And so Bridie, too valuable a property to be cast off, was made a foreign correspondent. Ling had broken her heart, she told Eliot. She had truly loved him. Maybe Paris would help her forget.

Eliot had no idea how much Dr. Derry knew. He was not the kind of man with whom you discussed his kid sister's affairs. So he just mentioned how quickly she had mastered a crash course of Berlitz French, and then changed the subject.

"Quite a show, grand rounds," Sparling said.

"You mean that kid Weisbrod with his grandstand play?"

"Actually, no. I've heard something about the radical movement among medical students. He didn't impress me."

"He doesn't mean a damn. In five years he'll want a big practice, a winter home in the Barbados and a ski lodge in Vermont. We'll see how much he cares about blacks then."

Dr. Derry placed a fresh pack of cigarettes on his desk, ripped the cellophane off, and lit up. *Hell of a habit for a heart man,* the reporter thought. Yet Derry looked lean and fit. A bit more gray in the red hair was the only sign of aging.

"I was fascinated by the medical discussion," Sparling said. "I couldn't exactly follow all of it, but the case must have been a doozy."

"Yes, a pity. The surgery had nothing to do with the lousy outcome. She was a sick woman. The valve disease and the endocarditis were more severe than we realized."

"I hope I'm not being rude," Sparling said cautiously, "but it sounded as if every medical procedure made her worse. The anesthetic. The surgery. The catheters."

Kevin did not disagree. "All possibilities. We'll never know. You'd be surprised how little we know in some cases."

He dragged deeply, stared at the photograph of his wife on a corner of his desk. "I know I promised you some time this afternoon, but I'm late." He was due back at Bay Medical Group. As the group expanded, problems multiplied. Kevin had brought in a new internist with a subspecialty in cardiology, to take some of his work load, a man named Donald Eck, medically superb but abrasive. Dr. Eck and Dr. Graubart were locked in a battle over scheduling, days off, office use.

Eliot took the hint.

"I have no idea what kind of TV report we will end up doing. My boss is interested in the medical empire you're building."

"I don't like the word. But if you mean are we expanding the Danforth medical complex, it's true. This is one of the fastest-growing areas in the country. As population increases, we have an obligation to increase and improve medical services. You should talk to Lawton Curtis, the executive director of the hospital."

"He sent me to you."

"I don't get into things like capital budgets or appropriations. At least if I can avoid them. That's for the trustees."

Eliot pointed out the window to a new wing. "There was some fuss over that," he said. "The Mary Laura Manship maternity wing. People said it was a waste of money."

Kevin smiled and turned in his swivel chair. "I don't agree. So it's a little lavish. Mr. Manship wanted to honor his late wife's memory. The bequest stipulated an OB wing."

"Mr. Manship's your father-in-law?"

"Come on, Eliot, you knew that years ago."

"Sure, sure. Some of the reform political crowd say the money should have gone to Mid-Island to keep the ceiling from caving in."

"Not true. We try to upgrade Mid-Island. It's only loosely connected with Danforth, anyway. Have you been there lately?"

Eliot nodded.

"And?"

"I'm not sure what to think. Your brother Joe and his wife used to put in a fourteen-hour day—"

"So do I."

"—looking after drunks, addicts, pregnant teenagers, psychos, all the garbage and leavings in the area. Maybe I'm prejudiced because I've always admired Joe and Jenny. But it seems to me Mid-Island needs thirty more people like them. Maybe those long-haired kids are on to something when they holler about medical care for the poor."

"Sheer bullshit," Kevin said.

"Why?"

"There isn't a person in this region who can't get medical care, no matter what his color or economic condition. What Medicaid and Medicare don't cover, the state and county will. Half of those people are too lazy and stupid to know it's available."

"Then why is Mid-Island called Hell City?"

"There are lots of reasons. But those radicals don't have the answers."

Sparling got up. "One thing I wanted to ask. What's a proprietary hospital?"

"In business for profit."

360

"But Upper County and Mid-Island are both voluntary, right? Supported by third-party payments, bequests, public funds?"

"More or less. Beth Moses is a voluntary hospital par excellence. Federation of Jewish Charities. Terrific operation."

Sparling stroked his nose. "About these proprietary hospitals . . . know of any locally?"

"Nursing homes."

"Sort of combining nursing care and medical care? I hear there's several being built by an outfit called Concordia Medical Supply. Know them?"

What the hell is he driving at? Kevin wondered. "We buy supplies from Concordia, but we also buy from BD, and lots of others."

"Does it bother you that profit-oriented hospitals and nursing homes are catching on? They tell me Uncle Sam will pick up the tab under Medicare. Outfits like Concordia will write their own ticket. They'll put these places up in high-income areas, turn away nonpaying patients, cut out clinics and emergency services. Not only that, outfits like Concordia plan to sell *stock* to local M.D.'s and make it worth their while to send them patients. . . ."

"I haven't given them much thought. Voluntary and public hospitals will always call the tune. Someday when I have more time I'll explain tertiary care to you, and why it costs so much and why only places like Upper County can do it."

How the hell did Sparling learn so much? And when was he going to go for the jugular and start asking about Concordia's son and heir? Lawton Curtis was executive director of Upper County. E.E. Manship was on Concordia's board of directors. All too close for comfort or publicity. Sparling was fishing, and for the moment Kevin refused to bite. What Sparling perhaps did not know was that Concordia was going *nationwide* with its proprietary-hospital program. Anywhere there was money, older people willing to pay, Medicare and third-party sources to be tapped, Concordia had its scouts out.

"Are these places needed?" Eliot asked. "I mean, when the cities are rotting slums, when medical care in Harlem or Cleveland or Detroit is so lousy?"

"It's not my area, Eliot," Kevin said. "I'm a heart man. Maybe you should do a report on our research programs. We pioneered a long-term study of smoking and heart disease." He smiled ruefully.

The old Derry charm. Kevin shuffled through medical literature on the windowsill, found two abstracts and gave them to Sparling.

"Thanks. I'll enjoy reading them. I didn't mean to get snotty. But the producer wants a report on the so-called medical empires. I picked Danforth because I knew you."

Kevin walked the reporter to the door. "You want to get a peek at some outstanding research funded by this so-called empire, go to the genetic lab and talk to Dr. Felder."

"Who's he?"

"She."

Sparling made a note on his pad. "Full name?"

"Dr. Annette Felder. She's running an experiment with generations of mice. Potential Nobel Laureate. But for God's sake don't say that to her."

"Local girl?"

"Churchport."

"Oh, yeah. Bridie told me about her. Only she called her *Nan.* Charley Felder's kid sister. Their old man was a doctor."

"Right."

"Good old Charley. Power behind the gang fighting for community control at Mid-Island. Right from his storefront law office. So his sister is a research hotshot."

Sparling left. As soon as he was gone, Kevin dialed Nan's office to warn her.

He heard her low, warm voice, and he experienced that inevitable desire to see her and touch her. "Kevin, I don't want any reporters around here. I'm too busy."

"How busy?"

She lowered her voice. "Too busy to see you later."

"Oh, no. I'll be there."

They tried to speak in code. They had to be careful. Kevin was never sure of the hospital's telephone operators or his own secretary. He rarely ventured down to what the residents called Mouse Valley, although their affair had been going on for over a year.

After several wrong turns Sparling found an area of the basement marked GENETIC RESEARCH UNIT. It was a low-ceilinged suite of toxic green rooms.

An animal odor assailed him as he walked through the open door. He could see shelves filled with numbered cages of squeaking, nattering, twitching mice.

Beyond the animal dormitories were rooms filled with slate-topped tables, test tubes in racks, centrifuges. A lot of the work was apparently computerized. There were TV-type screens on which numbers flashed and changed.

Sparling poked his long face into one of the rooms. A stout gray-haired woman in a white smock was injecting something into a squirming gray mouse. She returned the animal to its cage and made a notation on an index card attached to the side.

"'Wee, sleekit, cowrin, tim'rous beastie,'" Sparling said.

"I beg your pardon?"

"Robert Burns. Poem called 'To a Mouse.'"

She stared at him through distorting bifocals. *Old battle of science and the humanities*, Sparling thought. *Guess what side I'm on and guess who'll win.* He let his eyes wander around the bleak efficient room. "Are you Dr. Felder, by any chance?" he asked.

"I'm Dr. Roush. Who are you?" She had a throaty baritone.

"My name is Eliot Sparling. From UBC."

"Dr. Felder doesn't talk to news people."

"Dr. Derry suggested I see her."

The change in Dr. Roush was instantaneous. "I'll see if she's free."

Sparling studied a set of Petri dishes distrustfully.

"Can I help you?"

Sparling turned. "Dr. Felder?"

"Yes."

He introduced himself and told her Dr. Derry had approved his visit.

"Dr. Derry may be the president of the medical board, but he has nothing to do with this department." Her voice was low and soft, but her manner was faintly antagonistic.

"I, ah, I'm sorry, Doctor. Maybe some other time. . . ."

"I'll give you five minutes and some literature. I'm opposed to publicizing our work."

He followed her into an inner office. A technician was sitting at one of the TV monitors, punching up responses.

"Sunichi, will you excuse us a moment."

The assistant nodded and left.

Sparling, his eyes now seeing beyond the shapeless smock, the severe hairstyle, realized that Annette Felder was a truly beautiful woman. She was olive-dark, smooth-skinned, her face a perfect oval.

The forehead was high and serene. Her eyes were wide, the same mahogany shade as her hair.

Sparling said, "I know your brother Charley and your old friend Bridie Derry. Used to date her, as a matter of fact."

Dr. Felder crossed her legs. Good ones, Sparling noticed, though she hid them in the smock, minimized them with flat-heeled shoes. Yes, she seemed to recall his name. Not from Bridget, whom she hadn't seen in years—wasn't that a rocketing career!—but from her brother.

"Charley's helped me a lot covering local politics. The sewer scandals. Police rackets. I understand he's giving legal advice to the groups pressing for community control at Mid-Island."

"Maybe he has a better story for you," she said. The hint was clear: get out.

Sparling was not offended. "How long have you been here?" he asked.

"A year and a half. I don't want to give you a *curriculum vitae*. I haven't time to explain my work. It would take a week. And it might take you a year to understand what I'm doing. That's why I detest half-baked journalistic reports."

"Sorry. But I'm genuinely interested. You were always into genetic work?"

She shook her head. She was not an M.D., she said. She had a Ph.D. in biology and her field was genetics, the study of heredity and variation. "We try to understand the mechanisms causing resemblances and variations between parents and progeny," she explained patiently. In her case, she and her associates were trying to find out whether cancer was transmitted through the genes.

"Some of it is in that published material," she said. "I suggest you read it. You may find it dreadfully dull. Even if you are interested, I reserve the right to say no."

Tough cookie, Eliot saw. Another Bridie. Yet he seemed to recall Bridie's saying once what a gentle girl Nan was. Maybe she'd been burned. A man? A colleague?

"How did you come to Upper County?"

There was a pause. "I'd published a piece in the *Proceedings of the National Institute for Genetics*. Some people here were after a federal grant and needed a demonstration project. That's how things get done these days. They offered me more money and a bigger staff than I had in Boston."

"I guess Dr. Derry was delighted to have you."

"Why do you mention him?"

"Well, he's president of the medical board. Swings a big bat. Feather in his cap to land a top scientist like you. . . ."

"He was no more involved than other board members."

A bit too contentious, the reporter sensed. Some tender nerve touched. He changed the subject. "I just remembered. Your father was an M.D. Bridie told me. He delivered the Derry children."

"My father died over a year ago."

Nan Felder got up. The interview was over. "Would you believe, Mr. Sparling, that not too long ago my father was barred from this hospital for sticking up for a patient's rights? Now I'm back here running their genetics-studies program."

"Justice," said Sparling. "Spies tell me you may land a Nobel Prize one of these days. You've won a few of the big ones already."

The intense brown eyes looked suspicious. "Who told you that?"

"Newsman's instinct."

"Dr. Derry, probably. Usually the people he tells this to are warned not to repeat it to me."

"Sorry. I can see why you don't want it talked about. We can't give it a *kine-ahora*."

At the mention of the Yiddish word she smiled. A lovely Jewish girl, hiding her beauty and emotions behind a brilliant mind. Sparling shook hands and left, his admiration for her heightened.

The rules were explicit. Nan made them and enforced them. She and Kevin were never to be seen leaving work together. They were to meet as little as possible in the hospital, and when they did, to stick closely to professional matters.

They arrived separately at the one-room apartment in an expensive highrise in West Cohammet, which had been purchased by Kevin. He gave her the funds for the maintenance payments, which were minimal. They could not use her own apartment because of her fourteen-year-old daughter, Carol. The child was self-sufficient, reconciled to a hardworking divorced mother. Understandably Nan did not want her to know about Kevin.

"It must give you a sense of accomplishment," Nan said once when they had finished making love, "to make a whore out of a Ph.D."

"It's an honor to make love to you," Kevin said.

He maneuvered upward in the double bed. They kissed, and she sighed. "And I love you, Kevin. But I hate this arrangement."

"But you keep coming back. We need each other."

"I'm not sure I need you that much. If you really love me, divorce that horsewoman and marry me. It's been done before, you know."

"I can't. I can't hurt her any more than I have."

"Liar. You don't want to lose the family connection. What would Dad say? E.E. might not let you run the Danforth show if you dumped his crazy daughter."

"Don't be cruel, Nan."

"I'm being realistic."

Her anger aroused him again. He could always divert her with a caress. They were supreme sexual partners—adoring and uninhibited.

Her first husband, Kevin had learned, had been an icicle. Dr. George Beauchamps was ten years older than Nan. Neurotic, prone to migraine and ulcers, a professor at Nan's graduate school. He had divorced a nagging wife and married Nan. The work, they felt, would keep them together. Once they were married, bed had been a failure.

"Why?" Kevin had asked. "What happened to the guy? You're a beautiful woman. The best sex I've ever had is with you."

"Jealousy. Poor George. He trained the brightest girl in his class, taught her how to grow carcinomas in mice. Then she goes off and wins the Denkerman Prize and an NIH fellowship. All his male vanity went up in smoke. So he had his revenge. He'd deny me his penis, which, I might add, was not that big a deal."

Kevin put his arm around her. She was warm and soft, a woman meant to be treated gently, in many ways like his long-dead mother.

He tried to remember when they had started sleeping together. It was odd how death and sex, the last functioning of the body and its ultimate ecstasy, so often went together. Kevin remembered years ago making passionate love to Jenny Connetta to exorcise a patient's death.

It was Doc Felder's death that had started his affair with Nan. The old man, warned not to climb stairs, had left his home in Churchport on a July night and puffed up four flights to look after an eighty-year-old patient.

On the third landing, the angina attack doubled him over. He staggered up another flight and had the patient call a cop to drive him home. He died in the old frame house a day later of a massive myocardial infarction.

Kevin had been at the Cape with Cynthia and the children. It was the July Fourth weekend. Charley had called him. Had he any suggestions? Young Dr. Eck, a good heart man, had looked Doc over, but he didn't offer much hope. Doc died on July 5. Kevin, motivated by memories of Felder's affection for his parents, left Orleans early to attend the funeral.

He could remember sitting in the gloomy funeral parlor with a handful of older physicians and distant relatives as a rabbi extolled Dr. Felder for his devotion to his community and his calling.

Outside the funeral parlor, as the cars gathered for the ride to the cemetery, Kevin had approached Charley and Nan.

"I'm sorry, Nan. Really."

She thanked him. Clear-eyed, unfaltering, her dignity shamed him. She knew that years ago he had made a deal with DeBeers and Rhodes to blackball Sam Felder.

"It was kind of you to come, Kevin. Daddy always liked the Derry kids."

After the funeral Kevin could not blot Nan's face from his mind. A week later he resumed the inquiries he had begun two years ago, at which time she had told him she would not leave Boston. Her daughter liked her private school. The Boston Institute was generous.

Kevin was a hard man to resist. The new offer was a generous one. She could select her field of study, hire her own people. In the spring of 1968, a time when campuses were erupting, Nan Felder came to Upper County and recommenced breeding generations of mice.

Three months later she was having an affair with Kevin, three nights a week, at the one-bedroom apartment. Her daughter probably suspected nothing. Nor did Cynthia. Nor did anyone at the hospitals. They were discreet, careful.

Only Potsy Luff, his antennae bristling for scandal, remarked to Kevin one day after a utilization-committee meeting, "Not a bad piece, the little Jewish professor. Take off the rags and I bet she's stacked."

"I never noticed."

"Never?"

Potsy knew Kevin rarely slept with Cynthia. Who could blame him? She'd become an undernourished pain in the ass, in and out of depression, maintained on drugs. Sometimes, high on uppers, she seemed to be coming off the wall, full of fake energy.

Joined to Nan in the darkness of an April evening, Kevin experienced a sense of rightness that he could not define. His lovemaking with Cynthia, even before they were married, had always been tinged with hostility, conquest. *Sticking it to her.* And his other affairs had been no more than mechanical acts.

"I love you, Nan. I adore you. How can we do better than this?"

"Marry me. I'm an old-fashioned Jewish girl."

"Tomorrow. We'll have a huge wedding in the Huntington Manor. Two rabbis, a cantor, and all the relatives. The Damelio brothers can provide the music."

"You joke. I cry when you leave."

"Don't, Nan. I can't hurt you." He embraced her, kissed her forehead, her dark eyes, her nose. "Jewish women have a curve in them. Who said that?"

"Thomas Wolfe. I read that when I was in Barnard with your sister. He was also an anti-Semite. He didn't know what he was talking about."

"But I know. You're warm, responsive, good. And dammit, you do something; you mean something; you function in the real world."

"Love me, love my career."

"I do. One of these days I'll spend some time in the lab, and you can explain to me the significance of a color gene."

"The lab is off limits, sweetheart."

"My Nan. All business."

"Except here." She kissed his ear, circled it with her tongue.

Kevin sat up in bed. It was seven-thirty. Time to go. Mrs. Cottrell had informed Cynthia that there was a late meeting of the Beth Moses building committee, and that Dr. Gold wanted Kevin there. Cynthia never bothered checking on him. He knew why. She preferred to believe the deceits.

Nan stroked his bony back. As lean as when he was a boy. Bridie's big brother, playing in the tennis finals in ragged sneakers. And she, seven years younger, knock-kneed, with braces on her teeth, hanging behind Bridie, her friend and protector.

"I get the blues after you go, Kevin," she said. "But I've given up

368

complaining. I wish something would happen so we could be man and wife."

"I do too, Nan."

"You won't leave her."

"I can't. I owe her something. Her father treats me like a son. He'd go into orbit if I left her. She's miserable, but she has a right to live."

Nan began to dress. She telephoned her daughter, Carol. Late work at the lab, she explained. Carol had made her own dinner, was watching TV and doing her trig homework. She was a brilliant child, almost too smart.

"Good girl, Carol," Nan said. "Mother's a rat coming home so late."

"A mouse, Mom."

Kevin left first. That was one of the rules. Dressed, he kissed her at the door. "I'm jealous of your relationship with that girl. You're both great people." He left unsaid his own thought: *I was never much of a father to mine. Thank God,* Kevin thought, *for all the money, all the servants.*

"She needs a father, Kev. Interested?"

"Don't lay any more guilt on me. I'll work something out. I don't know what. Just keep loving me. God, I love you."

They kissed once more. "Oh, I need you," she sighed.

"I need you even more. You see, Nan, I've always been the cold, calculating fellow. It's not true."

She touched his cheek and waved him out the door.

Opening his front door, Kevin was surprised to find Clayton, Serena's husband, waiting to take his coat.

"Guests?" Kevin asked.

"Yes, Doctor. Two couples. Mr. Doberhauser and his wife, and some folks whose name I can't recall."

Goddammit to hell, Kevin thought. *She did not tell me. I know she didn't. It wasn't on my calendar. A dinner party in the middle of the week?*

"He's here!" Cynthia cried. "Kevin! You forgot all about dinner!"

"Did I?"

She was wearing a scarlet lounge suit—gold chain, gold earrings, hair snipped short, more makeup than usual. The anorexia had been stemmed. Lithium had done wonders for her. But the depression that had been the underlying cause had been replaced by a perpetual high. She manifested a crackling electric quality that grated on his nerves, forced him into noncommittal silences.

Her friends at the hunt club, at Hobe Sound, in Orleans, said it was miraculous how energetic Cynthia was. Kevin saw it differently. One set of aberrancies had been replaced by another. He was thankful they were rich enough to send Johnny to Choate and Karen to Emma Willard. Subjecting the children to her eternal chatter would have been ordeals for them.

"I must apologize," Kevin said. "Late meeting. Hello, Evan, Letty."

Evan Doberhauser, Manship's adviser on art, real estate and tax shelters took Kevin's hand. Kevin disliked him. A furtive, smarmy man. Letty, his wife, made a career of being at the right galleries, opening nights, parties. She wore contact lenses, false eyelashes, and for all Kevin knew had had a face lift and nose job.

"And this is Craig Rouse, the head of Cedar Grove Books, and Lucy Rouse. My husband, Kevin."

Rouse was a pudgy man with a mass of black hair and a black beard. He appeared to be wearing more hound's teeth than were in evidence at the American Kennel Club show.

Kevin helped himself to a scotch and tried to be pleasant. This evening cannot last forever, he told himself.

"Sorry if there was a misunderstanding," Evan Doberhauser said. "Really, if you're exhausted, Kevin, we'll call it a night. Right, Letty?"

"Absolutely. I mean, I really. . . ."

"No, it's all right. Just a slip-up somewhere. My secretary's fault." He sat down in one of the leathery chairs that Cynthia had ordered from San Miguel de Allende.

"Yes, yes," Cynthia said. She was almost shouting. "It's nothing at all. We're both so busy, Kevin with his practice, and his teaching, and the hospitals, and me with my writing. . . . Look at my desk over there . . . all my notes, my research, my day's work. . . ."

Writing?

Kevin had suggested it himself. Courses at C.W. Post or SUNY. Cynthia had grown savagely jealous of Bridie and her zooming career. Every time she saw her sister-in-law on the nightly news, she made a barbed comment. "Screwed a vice-president and became a correspondent. . . ."

It developed that Doberhauser had introduced Rouse to Cynthia's father. Craig Rouse "packaged" books. *How?* Kevin wanted to ask. *In cardboard boxes? Wooden crates?* Anyway, Craig felt that Cynthia's writings might make a book. And there'd be tax benefits, shelters, write-offs.

"And just from a letter from me!" Cynthia shouted. "I outlined my ideas and Craig saw the book right away!"

Kevin sipped his drink. He saw the scheme at once. Get Manship to finance the project, hire a ghostwriter. Hell, if it would help Cynthia, boost her ego, it might do some good. But what would he do about Nan? Would a healthy Cynthia make his involvement with Nan any easier?

He looked at his wife's willowy form, gold bangles glinting, scarlet folds billowing, and felt a rush of sorrow for her. Something wrong in the chemistry, in the blood, in the nervous system.

She was shuffling papers at the desk, muttering what a mess it was. She wanted to read the first twelve pages of her book aloud for the Rouses and Doberhausers.

"Maybe Mr. Rouse should read it by himself," Kevin said. "He can use my study."

Rouse fluffed his beard. "I'd love to hear Mrs. Derry do it. She's wonderfully emotive."

"I call it *A Woman's Odyssey*," Cynthia said. She walked to the center of the floor. Adjusting her butterfly goggles, she held the papers high, like an actress auditioning with an unfamiliar script.

"Maybe we should eat first," Kevin said.

"You'll hate dinner, darling," Cynthia said. "Rock Cornish hen and wild rice. What you refer to as 'North Shore kosher.'"

"Not bad, not bad," Doberhauser chuckled.

Kevin remained silent. Christ, he was sorry for her. To subject herself to these fakes, to let them use her. But had he been different?

Cynthia began to read.

"'One would think to look at me, to hear my history, that I would be the happiest woman in the world. I was born to great wealth. People tell me I am a beautiful woman. I was graduated from a select women's college, made my debut in New York City and eventually married the man I loved. I am an accomplished horsewoman, a breeder of prizewinning dogs and not without talent as a writer.

"'I have two beautiful adoring, well-adjusted children, who have given me nothing but joy. My parents treated me wonderfully. My brother is a distinguished artist whose works are in major collections.

"'One may ask, then, why for so many years was I unhappy? Why was I a woman unfulfilled, unable to respond to my loving husband, my kind parents, my beloved children? I am not sure that this book will answer the questions that it raises. But suffice it to say that I am now cured of my inability to relate to my family and friends, and for the first time in my life feel secure.'"

Her voice was rising, and Kevin felt he could not abide another word.

"'This, then, is a woman's story of the conquest of her fears and failings, how a compassionate husband and dear friends helped her through her crisis and . . .'"

She was all but screaming.

Kevin was filled with a draining pity for her. Some chemical imbalance of the nervous system was at fault.

"Fascinating stuff," Rouse rumbled. "People appreciate candor. It sells. Personal revelations. And these are marvelously honest. Your name should be on the book, and there should be no bones made about it. It's *your* story—Cynthia Manship Derry."

Cynthia was running her hand rhythmically up and down her gold chains. "Perseveration," Bridie called it. Repetitive acts, over and over. The way Rosemary Luff used to rock against a wall.

"'Yes,'" Cynthia continued, "'I have had affairs. In my illness I sought comfort from other men. But I did not realize what I was doing, who I was hurting. I was hurting myself more than anyone, punishing myself.'"

Kevin walked toward her. He put one arm around her waist and took the pages from her.

"I'm sure it gets better, darling," he said. "I agree with Mr. Rice. It's extremely interesting. But I'd much rather he read it in his office. Isn't that so, Mr. Rice?"

"Rouse," Cynthia whispered.

"Ah, yes," Rouse said. "There's something to be said for that. I'm intrigued with what I've heard. Cynthia, perhaps I could take the pages home. And the outline for the balance of the book."

"No. I want to read it now." She glared at Kevin. "There's a great deal about you. Give me my manuscript."

He kept the papers behind his back and did not release his grip on her arm.

"We can hear it after dinner," Doberhauser said. "Frankly, I'm hungry also."

"Give me those papers," Cynthia wailed. "They're mine. You've taken everything from me; at least give me my book."

"I will, dear. But let's dispense with the public reading."

"Why?" she screamed. "Why? Afraid of what I'll say about you?"

"No more, Cynthia. Maybe our guests should leave. We're both tired." He smiled at Doberhauser. "I think the evening's over, Evan. Sorry."

"Yes, yes. Maybe the emotional strain for Cynthia was a bit too much. No problem, Kevin."

He and his wife rose. The Rouses took the cue.

"Why? Why must you always have your way?" Cynthia was shrieking.

Kevin began to lead her toward the stairs. She did not resist.

"We understand, Cynthia. It isn't easy," Letty Doberhauser said. "You're a brave girl to do what you did. I'm sure Kevin understands."

Clayton opened the door. A cold rush of April air blew through the house. Serena appeared in the alcove leading from kitchen to dining room and said to her husband, "Looks like you and me got six rock Cornish hens to eat."

In the bedroom Cynthia became violent. She began hurling her vermeil toilet articles at him—brush, comb, powder box, a mirror that shattered against the wall, scattering glass shards on the blue velvet carpeting.

"You son of a bitch," she screamed. "You rotten, cold, superior son of a bitch! You won't let me do anything. You won't let me be a person. You won't let me write, have a career, try anything."

"You've tried a great many things, Cynthia. I have no objection to your writing. I encouraged it. But you were reading nonsense. I don't care to have our lives exposed to fakers like Doberhauser and Rouse."

"Bastard. Cold, mean bastard."

He began to retrieve glass bits, cutting his hand, sucking blood from his right thumb.

"Get out of my room," she screamed. "Who are you screwing now? Who keeps you at those phony meetings? I've known for over a year that you lie to me, that your secretaries cover up for you! Where do you do it? Who's your latest?"

"You're disturbed, Cynthia. I'll get you something."

"You can get out of my life! You selfish, self-centered shit! Why in God's name does my father keep backing you? Does he know what a wreck you've made of me?"

"I suspect he doesn't, because it isn't true."

She fell on the bed with a rustle of raw silk. She seemed stretched on a rack of luxury, sobbing, pounding her fists.

"Cynthia, I wasn't the one who ran off to strange beds."

"No, you weren't. But god damn you, you never forgave me, never forgot; you damned near shoved me into them. What is wrong with me? Why can't . . . can't . . . can't . . ."

Choking, her voice ceased making intelligible sounds.

Kevin sat beside her and held her. He began to stroke her back with firm, gentle movements. The massage seemed to comfort her. But soon she was gagging, stumbling to the bathroom, bringing up bile. Spittle depended from her agonized mouth. Her eyes teared.

He got her back to the bed, unloosened the chains and belts, removed her earrings and necklace.

"Take it easy, Cynthia."

"Kevin," she said breathily. "Don't go away."

"I'm not. I want to get you something to calm you down. I'm not angry with you. I don't want you to be angry with me. Let's forget what happened tonight. I apologize."

"But don't leave me."

"Just to get something to help you sleep."

She stirred, wiped her eyes. The blue makeup left smudges. He agonized for her. He wished he could love her. But when passion died, it was hard to revive.

"My stomach won't take anything. I'm sick of those drugs they force on me. I want to be healthy on my own."

"You will, sweetheart."

In his bathroom he found a disposable syringe, ripped open the sealed envelope, filled the plastic cylinder with Thorazine. He had done it many times to halt crying jags that could be controlled in no other way.

He came back, carrying a wad of absorbent cotton drenched with alcohol, and the syringe.

"Dr. Feel-Good," she muttered. "Always ready to calm the kooky wife. When does the straitjacket arrive?"

"Cut it out, Cynthia. You'll get a good night's rest."

"And tomorrow?"

"We'll talk. You should keep writing. But keep those phonies out of it."

With a gentleness suggesting a sexual preliminary, he pulled down the scarlet harem pants, peeled down the flesh-colored bikini panties and turned her on her side.

"You're so subtle," she said.

"You said that years ago to me. Somewhere in Churchport. You didn't mind my directness then."

"I didn't. I never did." She started with pain as he jabbed the needle into her buttocks.

He sat at the side of the bed, holding her hand until she relaxed. Once she asked him to kiss her. He did, gently, then watched her eyes close, her figure go limp under the comfort of the drug.

Later he undressed her and helped her into her nightgown. Her flesh was smooth and firm.

Kevin turned the lights out and sat in the easy chair alongside the bed. He looked in the dark at the rise of her body and was engulfed in sorrow. All wrong. The whole damn thing had gone wrong. His mind scurried about for a solution—cure her, divorce her, find her another mate, marry Nan. All impossible.

Once, he got up to go to the study, and she stirred and called to him in a child's voice, "Don't leave me. I'm afraid."

He came back. "Of course not, Cynthia."

"Sit on the side of the bed. And hold my hand."

He did. And knew it could not help.

2

Early one Sunday morning, Joe Derry was awakened by the telephone. Jenny, exhausted, sat up in bed rubbing her eyes. It was two-thirty. They had been back in the states for over a year, slipping back into their niches at Mid-Island. Joe was now assistant chief of medicine. He was much happier than when he had been struggling with a marginal practice.

"Dr. Derry? Dr. Mikulski. You've got to get out here. I'm calling everyone. It's awful." Mikulski was a second-year resident, a goodnatured and bright Polish boy. Joe had never heard him so agitated.

"What's up, Albert?" Joe yawned.

"Fire in Whitmanville. Lots of kids burned. God, more than a dozen. Three DOAs. I've never seen anything so awful."

"Get everyone you can," Joe said. "Call Upper County and see if they can raise Gottlieb. He's the best dermatologist around. And all the surgeons you can find. Who's got a burn unit?"

"I don't know."

"Christ, find out."

Jenny was climbing into white slacks and buttoning her tunic. Joe dressed quickly and asked her what to do about the children. Nicky, only eleven, was too young to be left alone with Peter.

"When in doubt," Jenny said, combing her hair, yanking angrily at her curls, "call a Damelio."

Since their return from the Philippines they had lived a few minutes from Mid-Island in a split-level house, as alike as a hundred

376

and three of its sisters, in North Shinnaway. She phoned Tony Damelio, whose wife, Rose, answered. Could Tony drive their oldest daughter, Yolande, over right away to stay with the boys? No problem. Yolande had just gone to sleep after a double feature at a drive-in.

"Burns," Joe said, as they sped down the turnpike. "I don't think we got a guy on staff knows how to handle them—not as bad as these sound anyway."

"Prevent hypovolemic shock," Jenny yawned. "Hydrotherapy. Got to clip away the dead tissue. Feel like a surgeon tonight, Joey?"

"How in hell do you remember so much?"

"I'm older than you. Oh, look at the ambulances and the police cars."

Mid-Island, with its sooty stained twin towers, hardly seemed up to the challenge. The entrance was jammed with three ambulances, a half-dozen police cars. Lights flashed red and orange.

Joe snaked his Ford around one ambulance, rammed it into a parking space. As they got out they saw three EMTs pulling a stretcher from an ambulance. A small figure, with only the black blistered face exposed, lay on it.

"What's up?" Joe asked.

"Fire in a frame house in Whitmanville. Foster home or something. Filled with colored kids."

The stretcher bearers raced up the rear steps. Sirens wailed in the distance. A policeman made a path for Joe through a mob of weeping relatives and reporters.

"How many?" Joe asked him.

"Four dead so far. They pulled nine or ten out alive, but from what I seen of them, Doc. *Whew.* I never want to look at a mess like this again, ever."

"What happened?"

"Party downstairs. Something blew up. House went like an orange crate. Most of the grown-ups got out, and they dragged some kids with them. Upstairs—forget it."

Joe and Jenny ran down the hallway. Another stretcher was wheeled in. Joe recognized Matt Cross, his old friend from the ambulance.

"Bad?" he asked Cross.

"Bad, Doc. Real bad."

The burned face of a girl, blinded, insensate, peeked from the blankets. Her hair was singed to spiked nubbins and her eyelids were swollen shut.

Dr. Mikulski came running out to meet Joe as they waited for an elevator. "Oh, boy, I'm glad you're here, Joe. I couldn't raise Gottlieb, but I located a dermatologist. Saturday night. Everyone's out."

"How are you doing?" Joe asked.

"Not too good. We're short two men. I got two Indians, a Pak, a Panamanian and a Greek."

Joe rubbed his nose. "Pull out all the lactated Ringer's solution you can find. If the pharmacy is closed, I'll break someone's neck. Tetanus toxoid, penicillin, erythromycin."

"And household bleach," Jenny said sharply.

They walked down the hall to the wards where Mikulski had assigned the burn victims. "Bleach?"

"Sodium hypochlorite. One quart to fifteen gallons of water. It's a bactericidal remedy for burns. If the supply room is short, have someone smash open a supermarket and clean out the shelves."

"Trauma surgeons?" Jenny asked. "Any surgeons?"

"They're on their way. The chief surgical resident is out sick. I got a few others up."

"Deakins?" Joe asked.

"He's coming."

Dr. Ellsworth Deakins was Joe's superior—chief of medicine at Mid-Island. He was black. A cool type, wary of the white man's world.

There were nine children alive, all suffering extensive third-degree burns. The dead had been sent to the morgue. Joe heard a cop saying that there were still several bodies in the ruined house.

Joe and Jenny entered the ward where the children had been placed. It was an eerie silence, no weeping, no screaming. Joe knew why. In third-degree burns there was often an absence of pain. Moreover, the youngsters—they varied in age from four to twelve—were in shock, their superficial nerve endings destroyed. The agony would come later.

Wet compresses were being applied to the limbs, trunks and faces of the children. It was crazy how the coloration of the third-degree-burn lesions varied—from a deathly marble white to a mahogany caused by thrombosed veins to charred black wounds. Flesh flaked and peeled from scorched torsos and limbs.

"Holy Jesus," Joe whispered. "We need s-surgeons fast. Mikulski, get every surgical nurse on duty, the whole trauma staff."

"First things first, Joe," Jenny said. "These kids need fluids. They're in hypovolemic shock. Or they will be before long. No surgeon in the world will be worth a damn if they die of shock."

"Blood pressure and pulses have to be monitored," Joe said. "Urine output. They all have f-fluid loss. Check urine output *and* concentration. There's always loss of serum protein. I remember that's what they told me when my b-back got burned. U-use isotonic fluids and albumin."

Already nurses were wheeling in metal poles, plastic jugs of lactated Ringer's solution. A nurse went to work putting an intravenous lead into a boy's arm.

Jenny grabbed the next jug and went to the bedside of a girl of about eleven. Her face and chest were severely burned. A large edematous lump was forming around her left breast.

Joe went to work at the bed of a third child, a boy of about fourteen. They had no names, no ID tags as yet. Unidentified black kids. Eternal victims.

Dr. Deakins, in starched white coat, entered the room. He nodded at Jenny and the other nurses. It was evident they did not have enough people trained in burn therapy to handle the crisis.

"How goes it, Joe?" Dr. Deakins asked.

"Just cranking up, Deak," Joe said. He found a vein, jabbed the needle in, let the fluid flow into the boy's arm.

Joe watched Deakins' masklike face. He was advising the nurses to put Foley catheters in the bladders for better urine monitoring. They were also to check for any drop in blood pressure or changes in respiration.

Dr. Mikulski, who had left to track down Clorox, had found a new handbook on burn therapy issued by a pharmaceutical house.

"If they're already in shock, hypotensive and not producing urine," the resident said, scanning the pages, "we can assume a loss of twenty-five to forty percent of circulating volume. It says they should get one to two grams per kilogram of body weight each day, and twenty cc. of fluid per kilogram of body weight."

Each child would have to be weighed and the extent of body burns determined. Then a formula for each would be appended to each chart.

"If hypotension persists, the fluids can be doubled, up to forty cc. per kilogram," Mikulski read.

"Some of these kids have burns over fifty percent of their bodies, Joe," Jenny called from the corner of a room. She was inserting an IV into a five-year-old girl's arm.

"She'll need more," Joe said. "Is she sh-shocky?"

"She looks it," Jenny shouted. "For heaven's sake, get house staff in and keep them taking blood pressures and pulses hourly. We don't want to overload them with fluids if some of them don't need it."

In a half hour all nine children—there were three in the adjacent ward—were being infused. Joe and Mikulski drew up a chart showing the amounts of lactated Ringer's with albumin, depending on the child's weight and the severity of the burns.

Jenny remained in the ward with the six children, running from bed to bed, changing dressings, chivying the house staff, trying to make herself understood to the Pakistani. More nurses had arrived, including Potsy's old conquest, Miss Bezerska. She was a dependable worker.

"Jen," Joe said, "we ought to be able to start gastrointestinal alimentation once the IVs are functioning."

"You're going to feed these kids? Their mouths are so scorched they can't move their lips."

"We'll force them to drink. They probably have gastric dilatation. We'll put in nasogastric tubes to decompress the GI system. Then you can start an ounce of milk every hour. If they don't v-vomit, double the amount. The more f-fluids we can get into the stomach the less we have to use IVs."

Joe, Deakins and the house staff began to check each child's respiratory system.

They asked them to speak. Three children manifested hoarse, indistinct voices. Their tongues were soot-coated. Nasal mucosa and hairs were singed.

Revived by intravenous fluids, the children now wept and called for help. One screamed hoarsely. Joe and Jenny raised one girl whose nose and mouth were badly burned. Dr. Deakins listened to her breathing. He looked perplexed.

"Bronchospasm," Deakins said. "Upper airway injury. They'll need inhalation therapy."

Dr. Fels, an ear-nose-and-throat man, arrived and began checking the children's ears. "They don't feel pain in these third-degree burns," he explained. "Look out they don't bend the ear as they rest on the pillow. It can cause cartilage fracture. I'd suggest splinting the worst with a wad of cotton and a circular bandage. It's not my field, but start examining eyes if you haven't. You want to be on the safe side, open their eyes with retractors, because the lids look edematous. Once they shut, you run a greater danger of infection."

"T-too much to think of," Joe said. He cursed the old hospital, its inefficiency, its lack of personnel and equipment.

The children howled as their swollen lids were peeled back.

"Mama, Mama," a boy wailed. "Mama, it hurt, it hurt."

Miss Bezerska found tubes of penicillin ointment. They began to work on the eyes. Wide, staring, terrified, the children's eyes— eyelashes singed, lids and conjunctiva engorged—stared at Joe like challenges. Like the wounded Batati farmers.

Deakins watched. Deceptive fellow, Joe Derry. With the stammer, the smashed nose, the blunt manner, you'd never guess he knew his stuff so well.

"L-listen," Joe shouted from a bedside. "Keep an eye open for numb digits, cyanosis of nail beds. It means compromised venous drainage. Look for edemas under the injury."

Deakins took him aside. "What happens if it develops?"

"Surgeons' job. Where the hell are they? Not even a surgical resident? You have to relieve vascular compression with an escharotomy. I've s-seen it done. A general surgeon c-can handle it."

"We forgotten anything?"

"Tetanus prophylaxis, wound cultures. We've g-got to put a hold on every bathtub on the floor. They'll need Clorox baths to control bacteria. What we really need are agitators, compressed air."

"In this dump?" asked Dr. Deakins. He didn't relish his job or the hospital. He had been told he was assigned there to ease relationships with the black community. Polite words for a front man. He guessed they hadn't found a white physician who would accept the post. And the top job had never been offered to Dr. Joe Derry. He was considered too short-tempered, a lax administrator.

"The baths are the best way to effect d-debridement," Joe said.

He squeezed penicillin ointment into the frightened eyes of a small boy.

"Won't hurt, son," Joe said. "Make your eyes f-feel better."

"Debridement?" Deakins asked. "Don't the surgeons cut away the dead stuff?"

"Sure. But it can be damned t-traumatic for the kids, even with minimal pain. I remember when they snipped crap off my back for a week. Drove me nuts. The b-baths are better. J-Jen, these kids may need four or five weeks of bathing to get the skin in shape."

An hour later, Jenny, Joe, Deakins and the house staff had got emergency procedures underway. The children seemed more aware of what was happening. Many were crying.

Foster children, Joe recalled the EMT saying. They'd get the best attention Mid-Island could give, with all its failings. Maybe once they were stronger it would be wiser to move them to a hospital with a burn unit. Kevin could pull strings.

Jenny looked haggard, worn, her hair undone, her white uniform marked with charred flesh.

"Oh, Joe, Dr. Deakins. We're losing one of them. A ten-year-old girl in the second ward. She's gone into shock. Nothing seems to help."

The physicians ran to the ward.

The dying girl lay very still. Her eyes were wide, held back by retractors, greasy with ointment. Her limbs were swathed in wet gauze. Nurse Bezerska kept changing the gauze, soaking it in a basin of Clorox-laced water.

"Not responding?" Joe asked.

Joe felt her pulse. They stood around the bed and watched her die.

"More than sixty percent of her body surface was burned," Deakins said gloomily. "Anyone know her name?"

No one answered. Unknown. Identification would take place later. The foster parents would have to be brought in to identify her.

"Can we resuscitate?" Joe asked.

"Too late," Deakins said. "She's finished."

The brown head shuddered violently. There was a long expiration of air and the body went rigid. Jenny drew the curtains around the bed.

Of the nine children admitted seven survived. A total of seven had died—two in Mid-Island, five at the fire.

Among the surviving children, one who would need massive skin grafting was the fourteen-year-old, whose name was Jerome Hudson. Yes, the boy murmured through swollen lips, he was the brother of Eric Hudson, the boy who had died after open-heart surgery some years ago.

Joe made a point to wait for his parents. He was puzzled that Jerome was in a foster home. The Hudsons had seemed reliable people. The woman was employed on an estate, he recalled. Mr. Hudson had been a handyman.

Mrs. Hudson, crying softly, came alone. She thanked Dr. Derry. She remembered him from the time Eric died. Things had gone bad for them after that, the woman said. Her husband had started to drink, lost his job, run away. She did not know where he was. It had been too much for him—the loss of his son, unemployment.

"Jerome, he's bright, Doctor," she said. "Got a B-plus average in Whitmanville High School. He isn't tough or mean. I got to live at the estate, and he needs a home. That's why he was in that house."

Joe looked at the boy's peeling face. He was recovering. Fluids, ointments, baths. But he would need skin grafts on a third of his body.

"He'll be okay, Mrs. Hudson," Joe said. "J-Jerome's gonna finish high school, and we'll get him to college also. Right, Jerome?"

The black head nodded, managed a smile. *I owe them something,* Joe thought. He prayed that the sickle-cell trait was absent in Eric's brother.

Bridie Derry read about the fire in the Paris *Herald Tribune.* The Whitmanville dateline caught her eye at once.

East Whitmanville, New York, April 20 (AP)—Five children were burned to death and nine others seriously injured when fire roared through a two-story frame home in this eastern Long Island community. The children were all members of a foster home run by Mr. and Mrs. Cyril Russell.

Fire department spokesmen said a blaze of unknown origin started on the ground floor, where the foster parents and friends were having a party.

Of course they'd been taken to Mid-Island. It was less than ten minutes away. Joe and Jenny had probably been in the thick of it.

Bridie knew Jenny had offers from Upper County, Christ the King, and a new proprietary complex. She had turned them all down. She and Joe worked as a team. If nobody but Mid-Island Hospital wanted Joe Derry, they got Jenny. And she was deemed a prize.

Bridie looked out at the Champs-Elysées from the Paris bureau of United Broadcasting. A number-two job, to be sure, under the renowned foreign correspondent Farley DeGroot. Bridie had made it clear to the UBC brass six months ago when she was given the assignment—no fashion shows, no art shows, no back-of-the-book fluff. She was a seasoned reporter. And since DeGroot loved Paris and disliked traveling, Bridie was to be a "roving correspondent," dispatched to Africa, Asia, and Eastern Europe on major stories.

Outside her office she could hear the secretaries—one French and one English—chattering. She liked both girls and they did not seem jealous of her. As ever Bridie was frank and outspoken. Her French was excellent, whereas DeGroot, after ten years as bureau chief, could barely manage *bonjour*. Moreover he was lazy, inept and scheming. No cameraman, soundman, secretary or fellow reporter was safe from DeGroot's spies. The bureau chief knew what they were doing every second, played one against the other—a formidable task, given his ignorance of French.

"*Voilà,*" Bridie could hear Solange saying to the English girl, Dovina, "*tous les journaux sont prêts pour le boss.*" (Because Farley was illiterate in French, Solange had to scan the Paris newspapers and make English extracts for him.)

Bridie came out and helped herself to coffee from the pot the technicians kept bubbling in the equipment room. She liked them. She knew the difference between an Auricon and an Arriflex camera. The coffee was hot and strong, and helped brace her for another day with DeGroot. She detested him, despised his spying, his evasiveness.

The Telex machine from New York chattered. Bridie walked to it. Some vice-president was coming over in a few days. Could Mr. DeGroot make sure he was booked at the Plaza-Athenée, and would they make certain that he got a special suite on the tenth floor? And could they arrange opera tickets for him? And a chauffeured limousine to meet him at Orly?

Christ, Bridie thought, that is all these high-salaried idiots think of. Hotels. Restaurants. Limousines. Half the teleprinter messages to and from Paris had to do with hotels, evenings at Laperouse or the Tour d'Argent. DeGroot shrewdly understood this. Of all the bureau chiefs, he was the most solicitous of executive comfort. Champagne in the room. Flowers for the wives. Hookers for those without wives. He had made a life's work of ass-kissing, honed it into an art, and even that most cynical of men, Christopher Ling, succumbed.

On the wall above the clattering AP, UP and Reuters machines DeGroot displayed signed photos of his superiors, including one of Christopher Ling, executive vice-president for news, sports and public affairs. He looked handsomer than ever, the hair white and thick at the temples.

Public affairs, and a few private ones, Bridie thought, as she ripped off copy. He'd dropped her like a hot coal after Dolores Ling threatened to sue for divorce, nail him with photographs (she claimed) and a private eye's tapes of him and Bridie moaning in the Sutton Place pad.

"But I love you," Bridie had bawled. "I thought you loved me."

"I love you too, angel. But it's finished. Over."

She had cried for a week. Dolores Ling triumphed. Ling moved upward in the network. Bridie missed the hedonistic languor of the apartment, the champagne, the lavish rooms. Most of all, she missed him.

She conceded she had loved him, more than anyone she had ever known. Poor Sparling learned of the break and tried to console her, but she was too unhappy to tolerate his mournful blatherings. Two months later, embittered, toughened, emotionally empty, Bridie was on her way to Paris. No man would ever take her for a joy ride again. No more con games, no more handsome liars.

In the outer office, where Solange and Dovina worked, Bridie picked up a copy of *Elle* and thought again of Ling. She flipped pages. Fancy lace underwear was coming back—sleek lounging robes, nightgowns, chemises. Ling had always been aroused by her underclothing. A fetishist deep in his simple Kansas heart.

Screw him, she thought. Yet he was the direct reason she was now in Paris, a full-fledged foreign correspondent. She was taking Spanish and Italian lessons, had leased an elegant apartment on the Avenue Charles Floquet overlooking a sea of chestnut trees. It had a view of the Eiffel Tower and the Ecole Militaire. She had had a few interesting affairs.

Bridie sometimes had to stop and wonder what she had done to be so lucky, to have had such a marvelous life thrust upon her. When she thought of all the people in the world consigned to dull mean work, she battled a rising sense of guilt. Worse, she often thought of the children she had deserted at the Brambier Institute. "You're one of my best people, Bridget," Helen McGrory had told her. McGrory had suggested the Institute would pay for her doctorate. There were no limits to how high she could go. But she had lost the desire to serve. She was selfish. A bit like Kevin.

She ripped more pages from *Elle*—a Givenchy robe, a Dior dress. Why not? She would take all they gave her, pad expense accounts, live in the best hotels, run up bills at the best restaurants. The captains at Le Grand Vefour and the Tour d'Argent already knew her: the beautiful *poil de carotte* journalist.

In a sense it was her revenge on Ling. Not that anyone cared in New York about Bridget Derry's frantic spending. In fact they encouraged it. It proved she was high class. Besides, she delivered. Interviews, exclusives, big stories. The news department was Ling's, and she enjoyed using it the way he had used her. Along with a truncated love affair, he had taught her to be tough, cynical and greedy.

Unlike Ling, DeGroot was insecure. Instead of using Bridie's talents he felt threatened by them. She'd tangled with him after three days on the job. They were each giving radio reports from the broadcast booth, and when the mike was open, she corrected his pronunciation of a French politician's name.

DeGroot had clapped a white-knuckled hand over the microphone and, in a shivering voice, had said, "Don't you ever, *ever* dare correct me—on or off the air."

The flare of anger in his cornflower-blue eyes had upset her. Then she saw him for what he was: a four-star fake, a coward.

After she had done her report (on the fad for canned wine), she knocked on his office door. The dutiful Solange was seated at DeGroot's right hand, taking calls, translating bits from French papers. The bureau chief saw the fire in Bridie's eyes. He dismissed his secretary.

"Before you start," DeGroot had said, "get this straight. I run this bureau. You work for me. You aren't the New York princess any more."

I am past crying over men, Bridie thought. "Well, Farley honey," she said, *"you* better get something straight. I don't need Chris Ling or anyone else to make a career for me. I tried to save your ass when you mispronounced Vaubanard's name this morning. Next time I'll let you mangle the language. No wonder the New York staff calls you Captain Queeg. Now, go work on your irregular verbs, and if I ever suspect you of monitoring my calls or opening my mail, I'll sue you. Understood?"

"We—we'll see who has influence in New York," DeGroot said. The richness had fled his voice. He was shaken. Why had they sent him this tigress?

"I was warned about you, Farley," Bridie said. "And it's all true. You try to fuck me up, I'll have your job in six months. You'll be covering fires in Minneapolis."

Solange had eavesdropped at the door and heard every word. Her mother was a concierge. She knew the tricks. By early afternoon the entire bureau knew the story. Bridget Derry was a heroine to the cameramen, sound engineers, the secretaries, even the office messenger, a one-legged veteran named André.

387

3

The ringing phone made Nan start. No one knew the number except Kevin and Carol. An outside laboratory, she had told her daughter, where she sometimes had work done.

"Mom? Carol."

Sated with sex, Kevin's head resting wearily on her small breasts, she tried to sound crisp. "Yes?"

"Dr. Luff called about five minutes ago. He wondered if you knew where Dr. Derry was. Said something about a meeting with med students the two of you might be at."

"I . . . I don't know where Dr. Derry is. Did Dr. Luff say anything else?"

"No."

Nan returned the phone to the cradle. She relayed the conversation to Kevin. He sat up in bed and lit a cigarette. "What the hell has gotten into Potsy?"

"He doesn't know about us, does he?"

"No. But he's a suspicious bastard. What could he want?"

"Call him."

"No way. He'll know we were together."

Nan got up. "Think of an excuse and call him."

Kevin looked at his watch. It was eight-thirty. He had stayed later than usual.

He began to dress. Potsy probably had run into a bad case. He was turning out cardiovascular bypasses the way the oldtime surgeons used to run appendectomies in and out of the operating room. A terrific heart man. But too ready, some said, to shove people into the OR.

Nan came out in a blue velvet robe Kevin had bought for her. She had no interest in clothing. The elegant robe had replaced a tattered viyella plaid she'd worn since graduate school.

They kissed, desperate for each other. He had never felt this sense of loss on leaving a woman. He could remember his teenage partings from Cynthia. There had always been a sense of relief, of a battle ended.

Not so with Nan. A *helluva thing,* Kevin thought as he left the apartment: *I am in love at age forty-six.*

Two police cars were parked in the circular driveway of his house. The garage door was open. Cynthia's Mercedes 280 was not in it.

Robbery? A possibility. The golden retrievers were not aggressive watchdogs. But Serena had been at home. Cynthia had been making preparations for the annual two months in Orleans. There had been a rash of burglaries in East Cohammet.

He drove into the garage, relieved that the children were away at school. They'd be home in a week or so, excited about the summer. Johnny was going out West for a rough-and-ready horseback tour through Wyoming, and Karen, complaining a little about the "squares" she was forced to bunk with, would spend another summer at the sailing camp on the Cape.

Kevin entered the house via the garage door that led to the kitchen. He heard men's voices—subdued, somber. And Jenny's— low, broken by a cry.

In the living room, facing him like a jury, he saw Potsy, Joe and Jenny. And two men in business suits, with the beefy look of policemen. Two uniformed cops were standing at the door. One was on the telephone.

"What's happened?" Kevin asked. "Was the house broken into?"

Jenny, in her nurse's uniform, got up and dabbed at her eyes. Potsy and Joe looked at each other. Potsy started forward. Joe stopped him. He walked toward his brother and said, "Easy, Kev. Cynthia's d-dead."

Jenny ran to him and put her arms around him. She smelled of disinfectant. "Oh, Kevin. Poor Cynthia. I guess none of us were ever decent enough to her."

"Dead," Kevin repeated. "How? Where?" Guiltless all his life, he at once sensed some failing, some flagrant act of abandonment. But it was too late; much too late.

"Sorry, Kev, sorry as hell," said Potsy. "Jen's right. We never tried. I mean, the rest of us, the family. I guess we figured the money was enough. . . ."

Jenny said, "Shut up, Potsy."

Joe kept holding his brother's arms. "Kev, it's not a nice story."

"Tell me."

"She took her life. Pills. Sometime late this afternoon. We couldn't find you. . . ."

Kevin disengaged Joe's hands. He nodded. *Be calm. Don't show your feelings now.*

"Anyone tell the children?" Kevin asked.

"We were waiting for you, Kevin," Jenny said. "We called Mr. Manship. He's in Tucson. He's flying in on the company plane."

Kevin rubbed his cheek. Gone. His goddess in the striped bathing suit. And the rottenness in both of them. Her weakness. His selfishness. A rich woman's keeper. Paid off by a wealthy father-in-law. No emotion in those people, those old Churchport Beach summer lords. With their sunburned faces and good backhands and horses. They had ruled the earth for so long they took it for granted. Everything went their way. No disasters could hurt them, so they needed only scraps of emotion. And he had become like them; he should have been better, like Meg and Jack and Joe.

"Dr. Derry," one of the detectives said. "Can I talk to you?"

"Yes, of course," Kevin said. Jenny squeezed his hand.

It must have been in the blood, in the central nervous system. He felt a need for Bridie, tough, bright, competent, telling him about new discoveries in mental illness. Chemical. Biological. It made it easier to accept the fact that at forty-five his wife was dead. Who could be guilty when she was, in damned near fundamentalist fashion, preordained at birth to fail in life and look for death? The empty bed, the separate bedrooms, the mutual silences, he tried to tell himself, had not killed her. Destruction was seeded in her nerves, muscles, bones, blood and connective tissues.

"Can we go somewhere alone?" the detective asked. His name was

Malloy. The other man in plainclothes was named Herron, a scholarly-looking young man. Malloy had a heavy sorrowing face.

"My study," Kevin said.

"I'll go along," Joe said.

Malloy looked at Kevin. "Okay, Dr. Derry? It's a little rough."

Kevin nodded.

Joe grabbed his hand. "J-just me. The t-two of us."

Jenny asked, "Shall I call the children, Kev?"

"No, I'll do it, Jenny."

He glanced at her. She seemed lost in the vast living room with its modern paintings and Danish rugs, the custom-made furniture. None of the possessions had ever interested him. He wondered how much they had interested Cynthia. She hired people to buy for her, accepted their judgments. All her life, he realized, she had been incapable of making critical decisions. All problems had been resolved for her, schools decided upon, vacations paid for. She had never once confronted a truly difficult choice. And he had never encouraged her or sustained her.

Seated in his study, he had a vision of Rathman Lal's body under Dr. Rhodes' window. *We die so easily,* Kevin thought. Perhaps that explained his fourteen-hour day, the board meetings, the lectures, the lucrative group, the empire itself. Stay alive, keep working, occupy each minute. Perhaps his limitless energy, his endless involvement in his profession, had rendered her bereft of self-confidence.

Kevin sat behind his desk and stared a moment at Cynthia, in riding helmet and habit, smiling toothily atop her bay hunter.

"Sorry I have to be the one to break it, Dr. Derry," Malloy said.

Herron, the young detective, entered and stood by the door.

"Tell me," Kevin said. "I should be used to death by now."

Joe moved his head from side to side. He wiped his eyes.

"Mrs. Derry was found dead in the Cove Gardens Motel at five-forty-five this afternoon," the detective said. "There was an empty bottle of pills at the bedside. They were prescribed by you about a month ago."

"Yes. I recall."

"We tried to revive her with oxygen and pumped her stomach. It was too late. She was DOA. Evidently she tried to phone someone while she was conscious. Maybe she changed her mind after she swallowed them. Anyway, the motel manager came to the room and found her."

Kevin looked at Joe. "A motel? Why?"

Joe lowered his eyes.

"Dr. Derry, I hate being the guy has to tell you this," Malloy went on. "I know you and your brother. I remember your father's drugstore."

"Go on, Sergeant Malloy."

"There was a man stayed there with her. They registered at about three this afternoon as Mr. and Mrs. John Walker of Dallas, Texas. The motel didn't ask any questions. Even though she and the man came in different cars—hers the Mercedes, and his a rented Olds from New York."

"Who was it? Have you found him?"

Malloy nodded. "A man named Haslam."

"From North Carolina."

"He's being questioned in New York now. Near as we can figure, they registered, and well, you know what happens in motel rooms. I'm sorry, Dr. Derry, real sorry."

"Kev, you want a shot of booze?" Joe asked.

"I'm okay, Joe."

"Your wife was nude when we found her. The coroner gave her a preliminary examination. You realize there'll have to be an autopsy."

"I understand."

"There were traces of semen in the vagina and the anus. She hadn't been beaten. Haslam admitted they had relations. He left her at four o'clock, maybe four-fifteen. Some time later she took the pills. That's about it."

Cigarette smoke formed a protective haze around Kevin. He remained immobile in his leather chair. "I don't understand. If she knocked the phone off the hook, someone should have come to the room sooner. . . ."

"In her death throes maybe. The lady who manages the place knocked on the door a few times, heard nothing, figured she was asleep."

Joe sounded angry. "Your guys didn't get there any too fast. Might have saved her."

"I don't think so," Malloy said. "She emptied the bottle. Some reporter read the police ticker. He has most of the story. Not about Haslam; we're trying to keep that part out of it. Just the suicide, nothing about what went on before. Mr. Manship got in touch with the chief of police and a couple other people and we've had the motel owners change the registration."

Fixing and manipulating to the end, his father-in-law. No scandal would attach to the death of Cynthia Manship Haslam Derry. A suicide. The reports would say she had had severe mental problems, had been committed for psychiatric care on several occasions. Who knew why she took her life? No one. It was in the cellular intricacies of the mysterious body. Between Manship's power and Haslam's there would be nothing made public about the screwing that had preceded Cynthia's last assertion of will.

"Nobody's b-business anyway," Joe said. "Christ, Kevin, why? W-why did she do it?"

"Maybe we should have seen it coming. Cynthia was an ill woman. She'd been under care for a long time. It doesn't matter in terms of your report. Will you have to say anything about Haslam?"

Sgt. Malloy's eyes sought the beamed ceiling. "Between us, no. The chief got the word from the county commissioner. Someone from the governor's office called. Don't either of you ever say I told you." He looked at Dr. Derry. "Did you know Mr. Haslam?"

"Met him once. Mrs. Derry's first husband. Is he being held?"

"There's nothing to hold him for. He admits he met her there. He admits they had sex. He left while she was alive. The motel manager saw him go. Haslam's wife and another couple—they're staying at the Regency—they backed him up as to what time he got back to New York."

"Their name is Crist?"

Malloy looked at his copy book. "Mr. and Mrs. Edward Crist of Morganton, North Carolina. They were having drinks in Mr. Haslam's suite when they got the news."

Joe tried to say something. Kevin's controlled approach to the terrifying death of his wife was bothering him. There had to be sorrow and anguish and guilt roiling Kevin's guts. Yet he manifested nothing.

"We'll need an identification of the body from you, Dr. Derry," Malloy said.

"Where is she?"

"County morgue."

"Let's do it now."

Malloy and Herron walked out. Joe came to the desk. "That

bastard Haslam. That son of a bitch. Kevin, we ought to beat the shit out of him. He must have done something to her."

"No, Joe. She did it to herself."

In the living room, Kevin started to follow the detectives. Jenny stopped them.

"Kevin, the children. I can get a day off and run up and pick them both up. Someone from the family should be with them."

For the first time since he had learned of his wife's death, Kevin gave way to tears. A damp underlining of his eyes, an involuntary act, as if Jenny's goodness was shaming him into crying.

"I'll call now, Jen. It might make a radio newscast. I wouldn't want them to hear that way."

Kevin went to the phone. When had he last talked to Johnny? To Karen? He and Cynthia had sent them off as if shedding unwanted property. He loved the children, kept assuring himself that given the demands on his time, he tried to do things with them, guide them. A lie. They had been trapped, in riches enough for a thousand children, between an unbalanced mother and in invisible father.

As he dialed the number for Choate, rehearsing in his mind how he would tell Johnny the news, he had the shameful thought that if Nan had been the mother of his children, he would have been a better father.

In death Cynthia looked astonishingly healthy—tanned and firm. The white left by her bathing-suit halter startled Joe.

Out of her misery, Kevin thought. He was not that lacking in self-knowledge to realize that he was relieved that she had died. Manship, of course, would never know his feelings. So long as Cynthia had lived, he was bound to stay with her or lose her father's support. Now he could retain E.E.'s patronage and be free to pursue Nan.

Joe must have divined some of his thoughts, but all he said was, "Helluva thing. So awful you can't think about it. To go that way. With all she had."

"Maybe it was less than everyone thought," Kevin said.

"Positive ID?" asked Sgt. Malloy.

"Yes. She's my wife."

Joe drove Kevin back to his home. They listened to the news on

394

the car radio. Nothing about Cynthia. Manship had taken care of everything.

"Kev, why'd she do it?"

"She quit. A long time ago."

"On what?"

"Everything. Me. The children. Nothing interested her. She played around, Joe. That crowd in North Carolina, some people up here."

"I guess it wasn't as much fun as it's supposed to be."

"What is? Except working?" Kevin asked. Finally he cried. For Cynthia, for his children. Karen seemed all right, but he was certain Johnny'd been into drugs.

"Want Jen and me at the house when they come home?"

"No, I'll manage."

He and Joe rode the rest of the way in silence.

The following afternoon he sat with Johnny and Karen in the living room and lied about Cynthia. Gently, he tried to restore some communication with his children. Karen, an exquisite, fine-boned twelve-year-old, seemed to have inherited the Derry strength. She was the most popular girl in her class. The headmistress had told him. Bright, generous, concerned. She worked as a volunteer in a Troy ghetto.

Johnny, almost fifteen, did less well. He had Kevin's hair and eyes but apparently some of his mother's instability. Although powerfully built, he did not like contact sports, and sneered at "jocks." The alternative, being a "grub," elicited from him even more contempt. At Choate he had gone out for ninth-grade football, quit after a week. He wouldn't, as he told Kevin, "take any bullshit from the coach."

What bothered Kevin most was that his son did not seem involved in *anything*. He'd had endless hours of tennis lessons and he was fast and strong, but he would not play to win. "Let's just hit, Dad," he would say. None of his studies interested him. "It's bullshit anyway," Johnny muttered, as Kevin looked disconsolately at the C's and D's. "Grampa will get me into any college I want, right?"

Now learning that their mother had died, both children sat in paralyzed silence until Karen began to bawl, her mouth twisting downward. She ran to her father and rested her head on his shoulder.

"M-mother, Mother," she sobbed. "Daddy, we'll never see her again. And we weren't very nice to her. None of us."

"That's not so, baby."

Johnny slumped on the leather sofa. He seemed to have turned to rubber. He held his long hands—Cynthia's hands—over his mouth and nose and whistled softly.

"Is it true she killed herself, Dad?" he asked. His voice was flat.

The story had been in the morning papers and on the radio. Nothing about Wells Haslam. Mrs. Derry had presumably taken her life with an overdose of sleeping tablets . . . wife of the well-known Long Island physician, head of the medical board at Upper County Hospital, and professor at Danforth Medical College . . . Mrs. Derry had been under treatment for some years for depression. . . .

"We aren't sure, John," Kevin said.

"Radio said so."

"They said it was presumed. She may have made an error— wanted to go to sleep—and taken too many."

The boy's eyes, which had been studying the ceiling, abruptly riveted themselves on Kevin. "What was she doing in that motel, huh?"

"Your mother was a disturbed woman, John. You knew about the time when she refused to eat and had to go away. It was a manifestation of a deeper mental illness. We aren't sure what."

"Heck, you're a doctor. You should have figured it out."

"Dope," Karen said. "What a thing to say." She nestled against Kevin, wiping her eyes, resting her flaxen head on his chest. "Daddy's a cardiologist. There are other doctors for people's minds. None of them were able to help. Mother was nervous all the time."

"And nobody knew why?" Johnny asked insolently. "None of those guys could figure it out?"

"Maybe they could," Kevin said, "but that doesn't mean they could find a cure. Mental illness is a complex matter, John."

"So Mom was nuts. I figured that."

"Shut up!" Karen shouted. "Daddy, make him shut up."

"Mother is dead, children," Kevin said. "Using crude language won't help her, or us." He kissed his daughter's head. Hair like fine silk, skin like satin. He prayed she would not suffer from Cynthia's self-destructive propensities.

"We never saw much of her anyway," Johnny said cruelly.

"Be tolerant, son. I told you that Mother had problems. They got worse as she got older. Who knew why?"

John's eyes found the wall over Kevin's head. "I know. That idiot half brother we've got, locked up somewhere. So what? There's lots of mental retards around. Women don't go crazy when they have them."

"That was part of it," Kevin said. He tried to find the right words. "Your mother was a sensitive woman, John. But not too strong. I don't mean physically. She had a lot of money and a good education and a fine family—but no hold on life. We can learn something from tragedies, even ones that hurt us. Don't just *exist*—help people, get into the world. I guess I sound like the chaplain at Sunday services. But I mean it. Look at Aunt Bridie. She was always involved, always active, always learning."

Karen smiled. "The kids in my class want Aunt Bridie to come up to school and talk to them. They think I'm super because I'm Bridget Derry's niece."

"Terrific idea, Karen. Aunt Bridie said she'd be home for the year-end news roundup in December. I'm sure she'll find time to talk to your class."

The girl dug fists into her eyes and revived. It was as if the life force in Bridie was making up for Cynthia's degraded life.

"John, we should grieve for Mother and respect her," Kevin said. He felt stodgy, but did not know what else to say.

The boy lowered his head. "Mother was okay. I mean, considering none of us knew her too well."

"Be generous, son. Think of all she gave you. . . ."

And he stopped, flustered, because apart from the gifts of wealth, the expensive vacations, the private schools, she had given the children damned little.

"Daddy's right, John," Karen said. "We have to take a lesson from what happened to Mother. There are a lot of things to do in the world. Right, Daddy?"

"Right, Karen."

"You're so busy all the time. There's this doctor at school. And he knew right away who you were. He said you were the best heart man in the state. That when you lectured, other cardiologists came and listened."

"It's all bullshit," Johnny said.

"What is?" Kevin asked.

"All of it. All this." His arm made a sweep, taking in the room, the house, the grounds. "What good did it do Mom? She killed herself. Because it was bullshit."

"Does that include my work?" Kevin asked.

"A lot of it. I mean, all that really matters is to be yourself, to do your thing."

"You'll learn differently when you're older. I hate to hear you talk like that, John."

"It's bullshit. What they teach us in school, what's happening outside. I mean, like Vietnam and all."

"If you don't like what's happening in Vietnam, do something about it."

"Why don't *you?*" the boy asked with a sneer.

"I'm busy sending you to Choate. I work fourteen hours a day. I'll leave the future to you, John. Get into politics, if you want."

"That's bullshit also."

"Only in this family," Jenny said. She was looking out the bay window at Nicky and Peter, who were waiting for the camp bus. "One kid who's Italian-Irish, one who's a Filipino, and they go to the Jewish Center Day Camp."

It was an oppressively hot day in August, a month after Cynthia's death. The flat housing development with its scrawny trees was bathed in steamy haze at eight in the morning.

Joe, yanking on a frazzled tie, gathered up the papers he had been working on the night before—a plan to test young Negroes in the Mid-Island area for sickle-cell anemia. He smiled as he looked at his children.

Nicky, star of the camp's twelve-and-under baseball team, had an arm around Peter and was warding off Irwin Needleman. Irwin was Nicky's best friend, and the reason Nicky had insisted on going to the Jewish camp instead of The Friends' School camp. But he had recently taken to taunting Peter. "Chinky," Irwin and his friends called him. Nicky, to be sure, was not blameless. He had led the first insults against Peter. Now he was beginning to resent them.

Jenny tied the belt around her starched white shirt, took a last sip of coffee, and walked out to the car with Joe.

They could hear Nicky's husky authoritative voice. "You don't call him knucklehead, hear? Only *I* call him knucklehead."

Jenny and Joe watched. *Ah, progress.* At last Nicky was defending his brother. Among the tiniest kids in camp, Peter was proving one of the best runners and swimmers in his group. Mr. Feldman, camp director, praised the boy continually. "Adapted marvelously, Joe," Feldman said. "We've got five black kids on scholarship—good kids, mind you—but they've got problems Peter will never have."

Jenny wondered. That dreadful childhood experience—buried head down in the earth. Yet he seemed a happy child. His work in kindergarten had been good; his psychological testing showed no danger signs.

Joe and Jenny waved goodbye and backed the Ford down the driveway. Mid-Island Hospital appeared asleep, simmering in August torpor. Joe and Jenny were planning a winter vacation trip to the Philippines. Dr. Carlos Zavala would pick up the tab for everything—plane fares, hotels, tours. He wanted them to visit Batati Village again. He'd got a young Filipino physician to take over the clinic, but Zavala wasn't satisfied with him. Since Kakai Dokka and Kakai Jen had left, medical care had deteriorated.

Joe carried his briefcase with his sickle-cell-testing plan to the executive director's office. The vast room had been refurbished, but it still looked dreary. The new director, a Ph.D. in hospital administration, was from Puerto Rico. His name was Angel Rios and he was very American, educated in Iowa. Joe liked him and worried about him. He had been told—by Kevin perhaps?—that if he got Mid-Island back in running order, better things would be in the offing for him, perhaps running one of Concordia's private nursing homes.

An attempt had been made to enlist more black doctors at Mid-Island. The nursing staff, aides and technicians were almost fifty percent black now. But oddly, house staff—interns and residents—were almost to a man foreigners. Smart white American kids avoided Mid-Island, and young black M.D.'s were in short supply. As a result Asians and Latin Americans dominated the house staff.

Two months had passed since the fire that had taken seven lives. The surviving children had been left with considerable scarring. As Joe and Dr. Deakins sat down, Rios asked for a report on their status. Joe had the facts at hand. The last patient, Jerome Hudson, suffering hypertrophic scarring and burn-wound contracture of the neck—his face was yanked downward thirty degrees by the thick scar tissues around chin and throat—had been sent to a burn unit in upstate New York. Others had undergone a variety of skin grafts. Two had had autografts, tissues taken from other parts of the patient's body, and two were being treated with so-called xenografts. These consisted of temporary grafts of pigskin.

"Pigskin?" asked Rios. A nonmedical man, he tried to stay out of the doctors' way. He worried about personnel, budget, the imminent physical collapse of the west wing. Moreover, some patients and local residents seemed intent on tearing down Mid-Island before it fell of its own weight. Plumbing and electrical supplies were stolen regularly. Purses were snatched, nurses mugged on their way home. Graffiti festooned the walls. Winos and addicts lounged in the hallways. No amount of security seemed to work. The guards were old and feeble.

"It's in common use," Joe said. "Split-thickness pigskin. You sh-should have seen that girl they fixed up. It functions as a biological dressing. Cells regenerate under it."

"Good thing there were no Moslems among those kids," Deakins said.

Rios smiled, then turned his attention to Joe's papers. "What's this sickle-cell deal going to cost us, Joe?"

"Very little, Angel."

Joe presented his case. He explained he had got interested in sickle-cell anemia some years ago, after Eric Hudson's death. It was a strange disease, Joe explained, found almost entirely among blacks. It occurred in one out of every five hundred Negro births and was more prevalent among black people than such disorders as cystic fibrosis, leukemia and PKU. Yet no one recognized it as a serious health problem.

"Sounds like a dead end," Rios said.

"Prevention is the answer," Joe said. "Mass screening. Advising people who have a possibility of transmitting the g-gene from having children. Th-that's the only hope until someone comes up with a cure."

Dr. Deakins stifled a smile. Fat chance. He liked Joe Derry, but the man, despite his tough face and stubbornness, was an innocent.

"So you are saying we determine which people carry the sickle-cell gene, then let them decide whether they want to risk having kids?" asked Rios.

"Yes. We start a screening program for every b-black couple in the area. Only one Negro in twelve carries the sickle-cell trait. The chance that both parents will carry it is about one in one hundred and forty-four. Extrapolate that, and it means that only about p-point-seven percent of Negro families run the risk of having kids with sickle-cell anemia. If we can get their cooperation, we can cut down on the d-disease."

Rios asked how he proposed to do it.

Publicity, Joe said. Get the Board of Education, the county health departments to cooperate. Make the screening free. Anticipating Rios' next question, Joe added quietly, "And it w-won't cost much. We can even ask for a grant from Danforth. I'll talk to m-my brother."

Smiling, Deakins thought of Dr. Kevin Derry throwing Mid-Island a bone. A little money to run blood tests on blacks.

"You talk about this to our community friends?" Rios asked.

"I asked Charley Felder about it."

"Ah, the lawyer. Guy gives me fits."

Dr. Rios knew Charles Felder from a dozen battles over Mid-Island and its role in maintaining community health standards. Charley was counsel for a consortium of minority activists.

"Charley sees no objection," Joe said.

Deakins blew softly through his tented hands. "Has he gone to his clients? They may think it's a plot. A subtle form of genocide."

"Why sh-should they?" asked Joe.

"They always do," Deakins said.

In one of those maddening coincidences which to Joe seemed to characterize the practice of medicine, two deaths associated with sickle-cell anemia occurred late that afternoon.

The heat, the humid Island air, seeped through the air-conditioning. Units broke down. The emergency ward was filled with people with heat prostration. Rills of sweat ran down Joe's wash-and-wear shirt. House staff vanished, cut rounds.

At about half past four, the ambulance roared into the emergency-room parking lot, bearing a thirty-two-year-old black man named Treat. He was a migrant farm worker who had been picking tomatoes. At the end of a long exhausting day, he had lost consciousness.

401

Dr. Mikulski assumed it was heat prostration. But after regaining consciousness, Treat continued to complain of shortness of breath and faintness.

Mikulski called Joe. "Crazy one, Dr. Derry. Pulse is one-thirty and blood pressure is one-thirty over sixty. Boy, he looks sick. More gray than black. He wasn't boozing, or smoking, had his regular lunch. Pepsi and a cheese sandwich."

"Run blood tests, Albert."

An hour and a half later, long after Jenny had driven home to look after the boys, Mikulski phoned. The patient, his blood pressure dropping sharply, was suffering from sickle-cell anemia.

"Son of a bitch," Joe said. "All bets are off."

"Why?" asked the resident.

They stood at the bedside in the ward. A stray cockroach made its erratic way up the wall, darted into a crack. Treat was lapsing into coma.

"I've heard of this, but I've never seen it," Joe said angrily. "Sudden death from s-sickle-cell trait. He's gone into crisis."

Joe ordered oxygen administered from a bedside tank. Christ, every hospital in the area had a central oxygen supply. All you had to do was plug a jack into the wall. Mid-Island's oxygen installation had never been completed.

Treat began hemorrhaging from the nose. Additional blood tests showed that his clotting time was below normal. Joe paced the ward, but could think of no further treatment.

Treat died five hours later. He had no family; the medical examiner would have to be asked for permission for the autopsy.

After midnight, a second black migrant was brought in with similar symptoms. He too was suffering hypotension verging on shock. He had no urinary output and his white-cell count was high. Again Joe looked at the lab tests on his blood. *Another sickle-cell case.* Once more he and Mikulski tried to revive the patient with fluids. Like Treat, he began to hemorrhage from the nose. Toward morning he died.

Joe caught three hours of sleep on the couch in the head of medicine's office, apologizing the next morning when Dr. Deakins arrived for work.

"It's all right, Joe. What's up?"

Joe told him about the two deaths.

"New one on me. I thought sickle cell was a progressive disease. Patients don't keel over and die."

"They d-did this time. The cases are important for the screening program we want to set up. People don't know it can cause sudden d-death. My own guess is that these guys suffered hypoxia, acidosis and dehydration. Couldn't even produce urine. Exertion and loss of fluids hastened the reaction and lowered blood pressure and caused hemorrhaging."

"Nothing we could have done?"

"I g-guess not. That's why we should publicize the cases. Tell the people that if they have kids with sickle-cell trait, they're p-playing with fire. I tell you s-something else, Deak, any time we find sudden death in a black, whatever his p-previous state of health, sickle-cell anemia should be considered as a differential diagnosis."

Deakins disagreed with Joe's approach.

"Joseph, if we publicize these cases it will just be put down as one more example of a Mid-Island foul-up. You let out that two blacks died here after a day's work in the fields and the radicals will blame us. We didn't create migrants, or sickle-cell trait, or three hundred years of dumping on my people. But we'll catch it. You and Mikulski gave these patients every possible attention, did you not?"

"Yeah, yeah."

"Then keep it quiet. Why don't you go home and get some sleep?"

Joe left, bothered. There was heat on the administrative and medical staff at the hospital. Deakins was constantly attending crucial meetings. Subject: what to do with Mid-Island? There were no answers.

Before going home Joe found Mikulski. If any other black farmworkers were brought in with what appeared to be heat prostration, he wanted a full blood workup.

4

The following morning, when Joe and Jenny arrived at Mid-Island, there were a half-dozen police cars stationed around the hospital. A picket line was parading in front of the main entrance.

Joe recognized some of the kids from the radical Student Health Organization.

Joe and Jenny stopped to read the signs. They could not disagree with the sentiments

BETTER HELP FOR THE POOR
FULL-TIME ATTENDING DOCTORS IN THE CLINICS
WHY NO COMMUNITY PREVENTIVE MEDICINE PROGRAM?
FREE DAY CARE CENTER FOR HOSPITAL WORKERS' CHILDREN
STOP LEAD POISONING

But one sign made Joe draw in his breath. It read WHO MURDERED THE MIGRANTS? Damn, Deakins was right.

Dr. Mikulski, flushed and perspiring, was talking to Charley Felder and two black men in black T-shirts. They were standing at the main entrance to Mid-Island, in front of the glass doors.

Joe and Jenny made their way past the police and the pickets and walked up the steps.

"Charley, what's happening?" Joe asked.

"Hi, Joe. Hi, Jenny." Charley sounded apologetic. He served as legal adviser to community groups. At different times he had bailed out Black Panthers, defended Hispanic activists, drawn up petitions for radical students. He had got fat and sloppy, and although he was only in his forties, he looked older. Joe never saw him without remembering Doc Felder's angry face.

"What's h-happening?" Joe asked.

"I don't like that crack about murdering migrant workers," Jenny said. She was ready for a fight. With Charley or anyone.

"They go a little overboard, Jen." Charley mopped his forehead. "I was against the whole deal. They wouldn't listen, and it's their game plan. Oh, Dr. Derry, Mrs. Derry. Brother Shabazz and Brother Ishmael."

The blacks nodded. They were secretive behind dark sunglasses and heavy beards.

"You on staff here?" Shabazz asked.

"I'm associate d-director of medicine. My w-wife is assistant chief nurse."

"Good," Shabazz said. "You workin' for us now."

Charley cleared his throat. "Shabazz, I know these people. They do a hell of a job. The hospital stinks, but it isn't their fault."

"Well, if you're in charge," Jenny said, "I want a raise."

Shabazz and Ishmael were not offended. They laughed. "Oh, we raisin' salaries of the kitchen help, maintenance people, the brothers and sisters who clean toilets, before we git around to you, you know."

Mikulski said, "They've taken over inside, Joe. Everywhere. I mean, no rough stuff, no violence. It happened during the night, about four A.M. They say it's the people's hospital."

Joe rubbed his nose. "Deakins here?"

"They're holding him and Rios. Giving them a lecture on the rights of the people. They got a guy in house staff lounge lecturing the interns and residents on something called a commune. Scared the pants off the Indians and Paks and Mexicans. They got some Puerto Rican guy in a beret and an army shirt hollering at them on the needs of the Hispanic community."

"Who's with Deakins and Rios?"

"Kid named Alan Weisbrod and a couple of others. You know Weisbrod? He's a resident at Upper County."

"Yeah. Is he the head of this operation?"

Shabazz grinned. "He no head. We got no head. We a brotherhood of the people, and we gonna run this hospital for the

405

people. You perfectly free to go about your business, do your work, take care of the sick people, you know. But we runnin' the hospital. We watchin' every move you make. We gonna git to the trustees next, you know."

"That's who you sh-should go to first," Joe said. "I have no argument with you guys. This hospital should be better. It needs more funds. More house staff. More nurses."

Below, riot police in helmets and boots lounged against the parked cars, taunting the pickets. Joe heard one tease a white college girl about her preference for dark meat.

"Ground rules, Joe," Charley said. "I got Shabazz and Ishmael, and the Hispanics, and Dr. Weisbrod—"

"Who does he represent?" Jenny asked.

"Progressive Medical Association," the lawyer said.

Joe nodded. He knew about them. The smartest kids, the ones who claimed they weren't interested in big-money practices. Joe sympathized with them. They were right on a lot of issues. But they did not seem to have staying power. The radical activists of a few years ago were now in prosperous groups, coining dough.

Charley went on. "Absolutely no violence of any kind. Nobody is armed. Nobody. I searched them myself. No looting, no addicts lifting stuff from the pharmacy. No interference with medical duties."

"Then what's this all about?" asked Jenny. "You guys going to teach me how to run an IV line? You walking into surgery and scrubbing?"

"No, we ain't," Shabazz said. He seemed on the verge of an insulting remark, but he had heard about Joe Derry. He sensed that he was not a man to push too far.

"Then what's the big deal?" she asked.

Ishmael lifted his chin. "We announcin' plans to run a hospital to serve the people. We liberatin' it for the people."

"Good luck," Jenny said.

"Joe, listen," Charley said nervously. "The guys mean well. I mean, let's face it, the joint doesn't do the job. This is to wake up the people at Danforth. Kevin and his crowd."

"Power to the people!" chanted the parading pickets. *"Who killed the migrants? Who killed the migrants?"*

"Yeah, yeah," Joe said. "No argument. But tell them to shut up about the migrants. Mikulski and I and a lot of other people worked our asses off to save those m-men. You want to protest, protest. But lay off that crap."

"I'll try," Charley said. "How about it, Shabazz?"

The black's face remained unresponsive.

Jenny ran down the steps to the girl carrying the sign that read WHO MURDERED THE MIGRANTS? In a move worthy of a Damelio, Jenny ripped the placard from the student's hand, cracked the stick over her knee and tore the cardboard in half.

The black pickets kept marching. Radcliffe girls in coveralls were not their idea of allies. *Let whitey fight whitey.* Joe ran down the steps.

"Fascist," the girl said to Jenny.

"Fascist, your Boston ass. Nobody murdered those men. They died of hypoxia and shock. Everything possible was done for them." Her voice rose—loud, angry. "And my husband stayed up all night trying to save them."

"Fascist," the girl repeated. And she chanted, *"Who killed the migrants? Who killed the migrants?"*

Charley and Joe pulled Jenny away as she lunged at the girl. Shabazz and Ishmael watched, grinning.

"Come on, Jen," Joe said. "Nothing'll help here. Let's go in and s-see what's doing."

"Nobody calls you a murderer and gets away with it."

Charley accompanied them into the hospital. "I'm sorry as hell, Joe. They're using the migrant business to point up Mid-Island inadequacies. I tried to stop them."

"Yeah, you're a big help," Jenny said.

"Easy, Jen," Joe said. "Charley knows the t-truth. If he keeps them in line, this thing may d-do some good."

Mid-Island's lobby was unrecognizable. Behind the admissions desk, Nurse Bezerska was seated, asking questions of an elderly white woman in a wheelchair. Behind the admitting nurse, two youths in berets were nailing up a hand-lettered banner: THIS HOSPITAL WILL SERVE THE PEOPLE AND THE PEOPLE WILL RUN IT

"How you doin'?" Joe asked Miss Bezerska.

"I don't like it, but so far they haven't bothered me. Name, please?"

The old lady fidgeted. "What are all these coloreds doing around here? What do they want?"

"Justice, lady," said the black boy.

"Some justice," Bezerska said to Joe and Jenny. "They got all

the side doors barred. Only the front and back are open. They got their guys checking people in and out."

Felder looked upset. He had not wanted the confrontation. He was working behind the scenes to get the hospital covered by state funding with a grant for community medicine.

Two bridge tables had been set up in front of the elevators. Behind them two medical students wearing badges reading PMA—Progressive Medical Association—handed out literature.

"Join us, Dr. Derry," one said. "Join us, please." He was a dark boy named Messer. Joe remembered him from medical rotation. One of those who'd pulled a low lottery number and ended up, grumbling and sullen, at Mid-Island.

"Join what?" Joe asked.

"The Medical Commune. We're going to take over Mid-Island Hospital in the people's name."

Joe and Jenny glanced at the mimeographed sheet. It listed twelve non-negotiable demands. One included full amnesty for participants in the Medical Commune.

"H-how can you ask for amnesty wh-when you haven't done anything yet?" Joe asked.

"Rios and the Uncle Toms and the white establishment are getting ready to call the cops in later today. They'll bust heads." Dr. Messer seemed to relish the thought.

Joe shrugged. "Kid, I've been a combat medic, and I did three years in a Philippine village where they lived on rice and bananas, and had endemic amebiasis. Don't lecture me on community medicine."

Jenny was reading the demands. *Day care center for hospital workers. Screening tests for TB, anemia, dietary deficiencies. New one-on-one drug program. Community medical centers. More minority medical students under Affirmative Action. Increased clinic facilities, no more four-hour waits.*

She stopped and glared at Messer and his associate. "Okay, you've made your point. But what's this crap about an investigation into the Whitmanville fire scandal and the migrant deaths?"

Messer smirked. "Everyone knows the burn treatment given those kids was substandard. That's why four of them died and—"

Jenny swept the stack of papers off the table. "You idiots. They were in shock when they were admitted. The doctors and nurses worked twenty-four hours straight to save the others, and they

408

succeeded. And the migrants had sickle-cell anemia. People die of it. Don't you tell lies about us. Understand?"

"We wanted to make dramatic impact," Messer said. "We felt that—"

Jenny was too angry to listen. Joe guided her toward the elevator. He wanted to see Dr. Deakins and find out what was happening in Rios' office. At the elevator another young man in a beret was on duty, a light-skinned black who saluted Joe and doffed his hat to Jenny.

"Hold it," Charley said. "Let's take a look at the auditorium before you go up."

A dozen black children lolled around the huge hall. On the stage was another hand-lettered sign: MEDICAL COMMUNE DAY CARE CENTER. A young black woman in a yellow dashiki and a green bandana was trying to get the children to eat their breakfast. They did not seem interested. A white girl in a medical smock, wearing the PMA badge, was setting up tables on the stage, placing coloring books and crayons on each.

"It's a good idea," Joe said. "But where do we hold grand rounds?"

"Wanna Pepsi," a black boy wailed. Others took up the chant.

They left the nursery and took the elevator to Dr. Rios' office. Outside the elevator Shabazz and Ishmael were waiting.

"Everyone is free to come and go, do his or her job," Shabazz said, as Joe, Jenny and Felder came out of the elevator. "Our marshals will see to it that no doctor, no nurse, no technicians be interfered with. All we aks is that they be for the people."

"Can your marshals raise the money for a new intensive-care unit? For a central oxygen supply?" Jenny asked.

"This a beginnin'," Shabazz said.

"I don't get it," Joe said. "Th-there's the Progressive Medical Association, and the Commune, and the Students' Association. Who's running the sh-show?"

Shabazz smiled. "*We* runnin' it. We lettin' the students and any doctors or nurses want join us. But we in charge."

Dr. Mikulski, trailed by a black teenager in beret and T-shirt, came down the hall. The boy was waving papers in his hand. "Tell this kid to stay out of the wards and leave the nurses alone. They got enough to do without reading the collected wisdom of Mao,

409

Mohammed and Che Guevara. I got four floors full of sick people and they shouldn't be bugged with mimeographed propaganda."

The boy in the beret looked menacing, determined to assert his mastery over Mikulski. Shabazz cautioned him. "Do as this doctor say. We runnin' the hospital, but they got to be allowed to do their work. Understand, Omar?"

Jenny and Joe approached Rios' office. One of the guards was a yellow-skinned teenager in a beret. He wore the Puerto Rican liberation flag on his jacket. The other was a fat medical student in a soiled white coat who had the anxious expression of a despairing missionary.

"It's okay," Charley said. "Dr. Derry is the associate chief of medicine. Nurse Derry is his wife."

"We don't need their permission to go into Mr. Rios' office," Jenny said. "Stand aside, children."

Charley knocked at the door. Rios' terrified secretary, Miss Trapani, opened it.

Rios and Dr. Deakins sat facing Dr. Alan Weisbrod, "brigade leader" of the Progressive Medical Association.

Miss Trapani whispered to Jenny that twenty nurses had refused to come in, having heard on the radio of the "People's Takeover." Kitchen and maintenance help, many of them black and Hispanic, had awarded themselves a day off.

Shabazz leaned against the door and watched.

"We have seized the hospital to serve the people," Dr. Weisbrod said shrilly. "You have to understand that, Dr. Rios. And you too, Dr. Deakins."

"Who appointed you?" Rios spluttered. "Who gave you the right?"

"The people!" Weisbrod cried. "You will give in to our nonnegotiable demands."

"Goddammit, I've heard enough," Rios cried. "You have been here two hours insulting Dr. Deakins and myself and I have had enough. It's time we threw you out."

"Why not leave peacefully?" Deakins asked placatingly. He looked at Shabazz. "How about it, brother? You've made your points. Set up a committee and we'll negotiate."

"Not yet," Shabazz said.

"Then you'll go when the cops drag you out!" Rios yelled. "This

410

is a hospital, not a guerrilla camp!" He reached for the phone. "I am calling the police. I don't care who gets hurt. You will not interrupt services in my hospital, understood?"

Deakins tried to salvage the situation. "Dr. Weisbrod, call it off. We are trying. You know about Dr. Derry's sickle-cell screening program. That's a start."

Weisbrod sneered. "Throwing us a bone?"

Joe walked over to the young man. Instinctively, Weisbrod jerked his head back, as if fearful Joe would belt him. Joe merely put a hand on the resident's shoulder.

"Look, kid," Joe said, "lay off that. You have legitimate complaints. This place isn't all it sh-should be. Nobody knows it b-better than Dr. Rios and Dr. Deakins and me. There are a lot of reasons for it. Yeah, I'm st-starting sickle-cell screening. And we should test for TB. But don't f-fight us. Work with us."

"That's what we're asking!" Weisbrod shouted.

"Then lay off th-that stuff about murdering migrant workers. Or the Whitmanville fire. We worked hard to s-save those kids. You want to help us, put pressure on the state, the county, and on the D-Danforth medical complex."

"Yes!" Weisbrod crowed. "Your brother! The medical emperor! Do they cut you in?"

"Belt him, Joey," Jenny said.

Joe was tired. He no longer wanted to hit or be hit.

"Stop!" Rios cried. "I am giving these people fifteen minutes to leave and then I am ordering the police to clear the place."

From the window, Joe could see additional squad cars pulling up in front of the entrance.

"Ten minutes," Rios said. "I mean it. If there's blood in this hospital, it won't be my doing!"

Joe said, "Shabazz, you know me. You know the Hudsons, the Lakes, the Robinsons. Ask black people around here if I ever did them a bad turn. I'm no hero and I'm no liberal, but there's never been a black or a Puerto Rican who didn't get the best treatment we could provide."

Shabazz did not respond.

"Five minutes," Rios said. "You got five minutes, Weisbrod; then you'll be carried out."

"Angel," Joe said. "H-he wants a bust. Guys getting beat. Front-

411

page photos." He turned to Shabazz. "Shabazz, you know better. You know the bust won't solve anything. I know a little about you g-guys. You'll deal."

"Don't!" Weisbrod yelled. "No deals! The demands are non-negotiable!"

"Everything's negotiable," Jenny said. "You jerky kid, keep the hospital running. Then talk. Listen to my husband."

"Two minutes," Rios said. He sounded shaken.

Ishmael opened the door. "All the press are here. We got the story out." He looked contemptuously at Weisbrod. "We made our point, sonny. The one the people care about. We just make sure Dr. Rios forget his calls to the police. Understood?"

On the morning that the Commune occupied Mid-Island, Kevin was meeting with Manship, Miles Curtis, and Manship's attorney, Evan Doberhauser. The subject under discussion was Concordia's expanding chain of nursing homes. Manship had invested Kevin's and Potsy's money as well as his own in them. Supported by Medicare and Medicaid, the nursing homes were a source of enormous profits.

The connection to Danforth disturbed Kevin. He looked at Curtis' bloated face and remembered how he had started his company on profits from black-market drugs. And damned near sent Joe to prison.

"Let's put it this way, E.E.," Curtis was saying. "The nursing home is proving to be the *perfect* vehicle for federal funds. Every old person is a potential customer. We're rarely audited. No one seems to care in Washington."

"Care about what?" asked Kevin in a hostile voice. He was thinking of Joe's struggle to raise money to screen black kids for sickle-cell disease.

"How we dispense funds," Curtis said. He was careful with Dr. Derry. He remembered the encounter with Kevin and Joe in Germany.

"You mean the people who run Medicare don't check on how their funds are spent?" Kevin asked.

"It's too complex a job," Curtis said. "Concordia has a superb reputation. When they see names like Manship and Derry on the board, they know they're dealing with a quality operation. The audits are perfunctory."

"And our profits quadrupled last year," Kevin said, letting his eyes scan the financial statement, "although we've only doubled our number of patients."

Manship said, "Costs have risen, Kevin."

Doberhauser was quick to agree. "We give a dollar's worth of care for every dollar the government gives us. They're delighted to have us do the job for them."

"Crazy, isn't it?" Kevin said. "Medicare was supposed to be the end of private medicine and look what it's done for us. We don't suffer from government interference. Uncle Sam pays the bills. . . ."

"You sound bitter, Kevin," Manship said.

"Dad, I'm not so sure it's proper for me, with my position at Danforth, to be tied so directly to Curtis's operation."

"You have no objection to your quarterly dividend," Curtis said sharply. "You've never returned one."

Manship let a breathy sound escape him. "Kevin's got too much on his mind. The group, the medical school, my daughter's tragic death. Kevin, you aren't going to ask to have your name removed from the board of directors of Concordia, are you?"

"I'm considering it."

"Look at it this way," Curtis said. "We're like the aerospace industry ten years ago. We may soon be the most heavily subsidized private business in the country. And with an absolute minimum of regulation."

"That's what makes me suspicious," Kevin said. Then he shrugged. Who was he to complain? For years he had played along, approved contracts, given the Curtises a free rein.

"I resent that," Miles Curtis said. "E.E., I respect Kevin and admire his medical achievements, but he has no right to make such insinuations."

Manship silenced him with a gesture. "All right, Miles. Kevin is overworked. I think that instead of arguing we should be gratified that the nursing-home program has taken off so marvelously. Don't you agree, Kevin?"

His son-in-law remained silent.

Back at Upper County, instead of going to his office, Kevin went to Nan's laboratory in the basement.

Sunichi Matsuma, her assistant, and Dr. Etta Roush were

injecting cancerous cells into mouse embryos. Kevin walked past them and closed Nan's door.

"Stop," she said. "Off limits. You're not to come to the lab."

"The hell I'm not. I'm president of the medical board, Dr. Felder. You work for me."

She shoved him away, wanting at the same time to hug him.

"Besides, we're getting married, Nan."

She looked up. Really?"

"Yes. I've waited long enough. I love you."

"Oh, Kevin. Are we sure? Are we right? I mean, apart from bed?"

"We're right, Nan. I don't only love you. I admire you. You're one of the few people in the world I truly admire. You and Joe."

She looked at him with warmth and compassion, but avoided his embrace.

"No, Kevin. Let me catch my breath. What would I do in that twenty-room mansion with Cynthia in every room? What would I do with the stables?"

"Fill 'em with mice." He kissed her forehead.

"Enough," she said. "You know, I'm getting somewhere. After seven years. Dr. Roush and I think we're breeding normal mice again."

Kevin left, full of tenderness and desire. He would sell the apartment. They would marry. Then he would sell the estate in East Cohammet with its memories of Cynthia. Maybe it was time even for him to abandon the group and give up practice. He was a rich man.

As he entered his office, changing from his cord jacket to a white coat, the phone rang. His secretary hurried in, looking flustered.

"It must be your brother, Doctor. He's been after you all morning."

Kevin heard Joe's husky voice. "Kev?"

"Yeah, kid. Just got here. I have rounds in ten minutes."

"No you don't. We need you at Mid-Island." Joe filled him in on the radical takeover. He sounded worried.

"Where are you, Joe?" Kevin asked.

"In Rios' office. Me, Deakins and Rios. We're hostages. Couple of the occupying f-forces got sore when Angel wanted to call the cops to clear the place."

"Oh, Christ, none of that," Kevin moaned. He took off his white coat and gestured to his secretary to help him into his jacket. "Where does it stand now?"

Joe explained. He had persuaded Rios not to order the cops to arrest the pickets.

"What do they want?" Kevin asked.

"Lots of things," Joe said. "And they aren't wrong. This dump doesn't serve the community. It hasn't for years. Not since you and everyone else at Danforth d-decided to let it die."

Kevin thought of Manship and Doberhauser and Curtis. Their America. Not the blacks parading outside Mid-Island.

He heard arguing voices at the other end of the line. "Lay off, Weisbrod," he heard Joe say. "If I'm a hostage, I have rights. Besides, I may have to b-belt you if you grab at the phone again. Kev, you there? Dr. Weisbrod wants to talk to you."

"Dr. Derry?" Weisbrod shouted.

Kevin's voice was low and cold. "You hurt Dr. Rios or Ellsworth Deakins or my brother and I'll burn your ass. What do you want?"

"Don't be so high and mighty, Derry. We have a file on you. Up to your neck in Concordia Medical stock."

"Weisbrod, what do you want?"

"We want answers to our demands. Someone from the medical school to sit down and talk to us. Rios is a front man. Everyone knows Danforth doles out the money."

"Calm down," Kevin said. "I'm on my way. You can have a fourth hostage."

5

Kevin had never seen so many police massed in one place. As he walked up the hospital steps he noticed his old Churchport friend, Al Kilduff. Al was now a sergeant with the county police.

"Crack a few heads; that'll stop it," Al said nervously to Kevin. "They got Joe prisoner up there."

Kevin nodded and continued pushing through the crowds. The chanting followed him into the lobby.

"More pay, more pay!"

"Screen TB! Screen TB!"

"More clinics! More doctors!"

Reasonable demands, Kevin thought. *But how answer them?* He did know that some of the federal grants enriching the Curtises of the medical world could be diverted to the inner cities.

He smiled at the PMA doctors at the information desk, noted the marshals in berets and armbands. Nurse Bezerska greeted him. She was admitting a drunken black youth, propped up by two friends.

"Hi, Dr. Derry," she said. "The lunatics took over the asylum."

"Hang in, Miss Bezerska."

Reporters and cameramen lounged at the distant end of the lobby around a hand-lettered sign: MINISTER OF INFORMATION. Kevin could see Bridie's friend Eliot Sparling chatting with a black man in a beret.

A Puerto Rican in a worn field jacket escorted Kevin to Rios' office. Miss Trapani was crying. "Oh, Dr. Derry, thank God. If

416

anyone can straighten this out, you can."

"I'll try."

The first thing Kevin saw was Jenny talking angrily to Shabazz. "I'm not a hostage, right? So I can get back to the wards and do my job?"

"Please do," Shabazz said.

"Hey," said Jenny, as she left, "the other Dr. Derry is here. He can work miracles. Bye."

Charley Felder got up and shook Kevin's hand. Rios was seething, sputtering. They'd sent him a mimeo'd sheet attacking him: OUT WITH THE FASCIST RIOS, FRONT MAN FOR THE EMPIRE. ANGEL RIOS, ALLEGED FRIEND OF MINORITIES, IS A TÍO TOMAS.

"Mexican standoff, Kev," Joe said. He looked weary. Younger than Kevin, he was aging faster.

"What can I do?" Kevin asked Charley.

"Ask me, Dr. Derry," Dr. Weisbrod said shrilly. "Mr. Felder isn't running this occupation. We have taken over Mid-Island Hospital in the name of the people."

Kevin sat down and crossed his legs. "I'm listening."

"You better. This is the start of a new day at Mid-Island, and you and everyone at Danforth better realize it. You dropped this place because it was a money loser. Who needs sick blacks and Puerto Ricans? This area has the highest rates of VD, infant mortality, lead poisoning, rat bites. The clinics can't handle the people who need help. But where does the Danforth dollar go? Into cat scanners and research projects and bypass surgery. A third of the people around here have to shlep out to Queens for medical help."

Miss Trapani poked her head in. "I'm sorry, Mr. Rios, but the house staff just walked out. All of them. Dr. Hassan and Dr. Wong led the parade."

"Whose s-side are they on?" Joe asked.

"Dr. Hassan says he refuses to work with some hoodlum watching over his shoulder. The residents want the building cleared and the pickets removed before they come back."

Kevin drew on his cigarette. Dr. Weisbrod appeared flustered. "Happy, Weisbrod?" Kevin asked. "You want to improve services, right? You have a point. But you've just succeeded in scaring the hell out of the interns and residents. Tell me how we run a hospital without them."

Shabazz said, "The brothers do it."

"You look smarter than that," Kevin said. "Are you going to screen teenagers for sickle-cell disease?"

"He got a point there," Ishmael said.

"No! No backing down until our demands are met!" Dr. Weisbrod shoved the sheet at Kevin.

Joe got up. "I'm needed in the wards. How about it, Weisbrod? We can't do any good s-sitting on our asses here."

Deakins also got up. He appealed to Shabazz and Ishmael.

"No!" Weisbrod cried. "They are hostages!"

"Calm down, will you, Weisbrod?" Kevin said. He crushed his cigarette. "Joe, Deak, hold it a minute. This thing can be resolved. There isn't a point you raise that hasn't merit. Sure, we've neglected Mid-Island. Let me say in defense of Danforth that it wasn't all our fault. Professors of medicine and specialists don't like the sound of community control. Five years ago, when this ruckus started, you scared them off. But you're right. This place needs an overhaul. I'll give you my word that if you create a negotiating committee, including yourself, Charley Felder, and that gentleman over there"—Kevin indicated Shabazz—"I'll invite you to the board room at Danforth to meet with our people. Within limitations of budget and personnel, we'll try to take action on your demands."

"They're non-negotiable," Weisbrod snapped.

"You can always occupy Mid-Island again," Kevin said smoothly. "You can make it a weekly event, like grand rounds. Or a mortality review."

"Very funny, Dr. Derry," the resident said. He went to a corner of the office and whispered with Felder and Shabazz.

"S-some good can come out of this, Kev," Joe said. "I mean, you g-guys up there needed a prod. Maybe this is it."

"They're right, and you're right, Joey," Kevin said.

The phone rang. It was Nurse Bezerska. Two attendings had got into a shouting argument with the pickets, and a fight had broken out. Dr. DeMario, an endocrinologist, had been knocked to the steps. Bloody nose. As a result, the nurses were now walking out en masse. Miss Bezerska herself would lead the parade.

Joe looked out the window. He could see DeMario shaking a fist at the pickets, patting his nose. The police had moved closer.

Weisbrod walked back to Kevin. "No deal, Derry. We know you're Manship's boy. We want you to sign this agreement. In the

418

name of the board of trustees of this hospital and the Danforth Medical College, you will agree to all demands."

"Nonsense. I can't speak for forty other people."

"If you back us it will swing the others. How'd you like the Commune to publicize what we know about the nursing homes?"

"For Chrissake, Weisbrod, s-stick to one subject," Joe said. "You guys got an offer; take it."

Kevin stretched and walked to the window. It was getting ugly. The picket line was longer. Hospital workers in large numbers had joined. He turned and spoke to Shabazz. "Excuse me, I forgot your name."

"Shabazz, son of Syed, descendant of the Prophet."

Kevin smiled. "A lot fancier genealogy than mine. My brother and I are clamdigging Irish. Mr. Shabazz, I've made a decision."

"I'm listenin'," Shabazz said.

"Dr. Weisbrod will not be moved," Kevin said. "Nor will the medical students. They don't understand that in this country the right things get done for the wrong reasons. You are a religious man, I take it, one who takes his faith seriously. I'm no student of the Koran, but I'll bet it counsels brotherhood and understanding. I want to settle these problems with dignity."

Joe watched Kevin closely. Older brother at his best. He was dividing the enemy camp. Black against white. Proletariat against elitists, the clever bastard.

"Speak, man," Shabazz said.

"Get your people out of the building and off the picket line. I promise you you'll get a better hospital. Knock down the barricades; remove the signs; pull off your pickets."

Joe got up. "K-Kevin, let 'em keep the kids in the day nursery. No one uses the au-auditorium anyway. The kids can't hurt anyone."

"Why not?" Kevin agreed.

Shabazz whispered with his lieutenants. He turned. "You got you a deal, Dr. Derry. But we wants forcible ejection. Escorted by the pigs."

"Why?" Kevin asked.

"Show the world as how Allah give us courage to stand our ground."

Kevin nodded. "You want us to ask the cops to escort you? Of

419

course, you'll be arrested. But if you don't resist it shouldn't be too bad."

Felder was quick to agree. "Shabazz, you'll be out on bail in an hour."

"He's a liar!" Dr. Weisbrod shouted. "Derry's a liar!"

Shabazz and his troops left. They were spreading the gospel to their marshals. The blacks and the Hispanics agreed to the plan. In the lobby, reporters and cameramen dashed about, getting ready for the bust.

Kevin picked up a phone and called Sergeant Kilduff. "They'll go quietly, Al," Kevin said. "No rough stuff, no insults."

A woman medical student supporting Weisbrod collapsed on a chair and began to sob. "Oh, God, I always wondered how I'd react in a crisis, and now I see I've failed. Alan, what's wrong with us?"

"It's that clever bastard Derry!" Weisbrod shouted. "He conned them."

Joe shoved him into his chair. "Shut up. I've had more than enough from you today."

"Oh, Alan," Radcliffe moaned. "Where did we go wrong?"

Joe looked at Weisbrod and smiled for the first time that morning. "H-Harvard," he said.

The evacuation did not go as smoothly as Kevin had hoped. Shabazz and his friends maintained order, but the hospital workers were another matter. Egged on by the students, they refused to go, fell to the pavement, grabbed at trees and fences. The cops became rougher. Kevin and Joe could see Eliot Sparling, dodging police clubs, at the edge of the surging mob.

Two state policemen entered Rios' office. They went immediately for Dr. Weisbrod and the female medical student. They even knew her name—Katherine Tench.

"Let's go, folks," one of the policemen said.

"No," Weisbrod said. "I'm staying."

"Come on, Doc, we don't want to hurt you."

"Go on, Alan; go on, Katherine," Charley Felder said. "Sergeant, will they be taken to the county courthouse?"

"That's right, Mr. Felder."

From the window, the Derry brothers, Rios and Deakins watched the police escort Weisbrod and the girl to the waiting van. As he got in, Weisbrod raised a clenched fist to the window.

Goddammit, he's right, Joe thought. *He's a pain in the ass,*

420

but he's right. And he has more guts than I have, more insight into what's wrong. Joe raced to the door.

"Where are you going?" Kevin called.

"With them."

Minutes later Kevin saw Joe walk up to Al Kilduff. Then Al took off his helmet. Joe, his homely face full of mischief, shoved the sergeant.

Kevin opened the window. "What the hell are you doing, Joe? You gone crazy?"

Kilduff looked up. "Kevin! Your crazy brother wants to be arrested. He wants to go with those animals."

Kevin laughed. You couldn't change Joe. He knew where the fault rested, and he knew that as obnoxious as Weisbrod was, he was *right.*

"Dr. Derry," Rios shouted. "Don't do anything foolish!"

Sgt. Kilduff looked up. "Kevin, tell him I refuse to arrest him."

"For Chrissake, Al, g-get it over with." Joe shoved the sergeant again. "Assaulting an officer. Resisting arrest. L-let me in." He pushed past Al and climbed into the Black Maria. He squeezed onto a bench, between a weeping Puerto Rican girl with a bleeding ear and old Matt Cross.

"Yeah. I figured you be with us." Cross shook his hand.

"Oh dear," Rios quivered. "Someone tell Mrs. Derry, please. Mr. Felder, do something. Get him out."

Charley went to the door. "Don't worry. They'll be out in a few hours."

"I wish Joe and Jenny were with us," Bridie said. "Get all of the Derrys together for a change."

She and her escort, a lean, graying man with a tanned face and infinite charm, were dining at the Tour d'Argent, playing host to the newlyweds, Kevin and Nan.

"Old Joe," Kevin laughed. "A night in the slammer. Judge Hanratty almost fainted when he saw Joe in court. Hanratty was a cornerback on that famous losing football team. He worshipped Joe because Joe *stuck,* and Hanratty was afraid to. Nan's brother bailed them out, and Joe's now the community rep for Mid-Island at Danforth."

"Any progress?" asked Bridie.

Her escort, whose name was Hayward Tillotson, and whose family bred horses on Maryland's Eastern Shore, listened with a winning smile. He was a traveling representative for a variety of middle-sized American corporations and maintained a lavish Paris penthouse. Nan and Kevin found him genial and elegant. He seemed to worship Bridie.

"The going is slow," Kevin said. "It's not just medical care they need. It's a whole damned new society. Doctors can't do it all."

Outside, Notre-Dame loomed over the moon-brilliant Seine. Nan was silent, enchanted. Her honeymoon with Kevin seemed like a dream. London had been marvelous. Paris even better. Bridie and the obliging Tillotson took them everywhere. Nan decided she liked the Brancusi studio in the Modern Art Museum best.

Tillotson agreed. He knew a great deal about modern art, and had known Cynthia's brother some years ago. Buzzy and Celeste had moved to Crete, where he could perfect his style.

Bridie was regaling them with a story about her office. DeGroot feared flying. He was usually dining with "Couve" or "Giscard" when a major story broke, so Bridget Derry was the one usually found in tailored khakis interviewing a black president, an Arab king, a mercenary. The camera crews loved her. She had been the first correspondent to tell DeGroot to shove it.

Kevin realized how much his sister had changed. She was no longer the compassionate, giving girl who had worked with retarded kids. Not even the compliant woman whom Christopher Ling had made his mistress. Kevin could see it in the way she handled Tillotson.

Later, after Kevin and Nan made leisurely love in their suite in the Elysée-Parc, Nan decided that Bridie would marry Tillotson. Kevin doubted it.

"Perhaps you're right. Perhaps she'll only use him," Nan said. "He's the perfect partner for her. No competition, but lots of class."

Kevin chuckled. He recalled Abe Gold's rule on M.D.'s for the group: *no geniuses, just noncomplainers.* Tillotson seemed to fit the category.

The day before they left Paris for Nice, Nan read a paper at the Institut Pasteur about the generations of cancer-bearing mice she had bred. When she finished, she made a point of sharing credit with Dr. Etta Roush. This irritated Kevin. Why did she mention her assistant? It was *her* work. She'd planned the study and carried it

422

out. But he decided not to say anything. Not for the moment anyway.

Their last night in Paris, Kevin and Nan sat up late with Bridie after Tillotson had left. He was off to Hungary early the next day—selling lipstick, or pantyhose, or some item which the citizens of the communist paradises craved.

"Do you love him?" Nan asked.

"No. But he's sweet, terrific at parties, knows all about opera and wine."

"Will you marry him?" Kevin asked. Tillotson had been with them every night—attentive, intelligent, intrigued with the Derrys and their medical careers.

"I think so."

Kevin and Nan said nothing. Both were vaguely shocked. Bridie appeared to be choosing a husband the way she would buy a dress.

The next day Kevin and Nan flew to Nice. They rented a Peugeot 404. Nan stocked up on art books and they toured Provence. They walked, holding hands, through the Maeght Foundation museum, went to the Pont du Gard, the Roman amphitheatre in Orange, the colosseum in Nîmes, Cézanne's studio.

Kevin had left an itinerary with Bridie at UBC. There were a few cases hanging fire. That night, back in their hotel, the phone rang. Kevin picked it up and heard Joe's husky voice.

"Hate like hell to call you on your honeymoon." Joe paused. "Johnny's in trouble."

"How bad?" "Johnny's in trouble."

"He's going to be expelled from Choate."

"Why?"

"Dealing in drugs. He stole a batch of your prescriptions and a pad of Graubart's. Took them to school and started a business. He had the kids buying everything from dilaudid to bennies. One of the pharmacists got suspicious and phoned Bay Medical Group. Graubart is screaming about your rotten kid." *And he is right,* Kevin thought. "Anyway, it didn't take the cops long to figure out where the prescriptions with the name D-Derry came from. They questioned Johnny and he confessed, naming every kid he'd ever sold stuff to."

"What else?"

423

"The k-kids he'd squealed on beat the shit out of him. They stripped him, whipped his ass red, punched him silly."

"Is he all right?"

"Bruises and contusions. I drove up to g-get him this morning and I admitted him to Mid-Island. Nothing made the papers."

"Has he been using drugs himself?"

"I'm afraid so, Kev. Mainlining. Track mark on his arm. He's got a hematoma on his thigh where they b-beat him and his left eye is closed. But it's his ego that's really hurting. He talks to Jenny, but that's about all. He says he's sorry."

"Sorry he stole prescriptions and went into business?"

"No. Sorry he got caught."

Kevin paused. "Does Manship know?"

"N-not the details."

"Call him, Joe. Have him talk to the headmaster."

"It won't help, Kevin. The cops up there are going to make an example of Johnny. They were waiting to catch one of th-those smartass preppies and hold him up as an example. Maybe Cynthia's death hit him harder than anyone knows. The kid keeps to himself too much. We're going to t-try to take him to the Jets g-game on Sunday. I think you better get on the next plane. Nan will understand."

Nan did. She tried to console him after Joe hung up, but she barely knew his children. The crisis frightened her.

"I feel I'm to blame," she said, as she took his hand. "I'm the intruder. What do your children make of me? After the goddess they knew as a mother."

"Believe me, she was no goddess," said Kevin, lighting a cigarette. "Maybe we didn't talk to the kids enough. We held back . . . kept our distance. Johnny's always worried me."

"It wasn't your fault, Kevin," Nan said. She rested her head on his chest.

"I don't know where to start," Kevin said. "I hope the boy isn't deeply hooked. I've been through addiction wards. When they start that early, it's hell getting them straight."

"We'll try, Kev; we'll try."

They flew back to Paris, telephoned Bridie from the airport. She was shocked by the news. Out of her experience as a psychiatric nurse, she tried to be encouraging, and told Kevin to call Dr.

McGrory. Kevin agreed. He tried to sound optimistic, but when they had boarded the Air France 747 and locked their seatbelts, he said, "It's wrong, but I'm furious with Johnny. I know I'm supposed to be loving and understanding. But what got into him? You and Bridie, Joe and me, we never had what he had. And we managed."

"Maybe he had too much, Kevin," Nan said softly.

The four engines roared, whirred, and the plane circled the city and headed west. *Never, never again,* Kevin thought, *will I be as happy as I was these past ten days.*

PART SEVEN
1974

"Slow down," Jenny said. "I always like to see how the local medical mill is doing."

Joe braked the VW. It was a cloudy March morning, cold winds whipping in from Long Island Sound. But under the chill, Jenny sensed the hint of spring, the reassuring renewal of life.

We've made it one more year, Joe thought. Mid-Island was improving imperceptibly. But it was not the success that they had hoped for. Proof lay in the "medical mill" to which Jenny referred. To their right, occupying a storefront, was the Central Medical Group. Beneath the sign was a list of services:

OBSTETRICS

GYNECOLOGY

MINOR SURGERY

GASTRIC AND LIVER AILMENTS

BLOOD DISEASES

ALLERGIES

X-RAY

"Lined up at eight in the morning," Joe said.

Shivering, huddling in pile-lined jackets and mufflers, a dozen blacks stood outside waiting. Through the cracked window, Joe glimpsed the chief, Dr. Behari Ghosh.

Central Medical Group was a notorious racket. The doctors shoved people in and out, overcharged, gave useless diagnostic treatments, endless prescriptions (to be filled at their own pharmacy), and had chalked up close to six hundred thousand dollars over the past year. Not bad for a slum practice. Medicare and Medicaid paid the bills, never questioning the need for or quality of the medical services.

"It's a reflection on us," Joe said. "If w-we did a better job, they wouldn't go there."

"We'd do a better job if we ever got the money from Danforth."

Joe wheeled the VW under the arcade connecting the towers of Mid-Island, parked in the space marked DIRECTOR OF MEDICINE. He had had the job for almost a year. Some months after the occupation of the hospital Dr. Deakins had quit. He had no interest in further confrontations with his brethren. He now held a safe teaching position in Pennsylvania.

"Kevin's trying," Joe said, as he helped Jenny out of the car. She struggled a little, smoothing her heavy plaid coat. "Why do Eye-talian girls get big in the behind and nowhere else?" she said.

"No complaints, Jen."

"Forty-seven and on the job. How come you didn't mind my being two years older than you?"

"How can I? You were the only g-girl ever gave me the time of day."

They crossed the parking area, waved at Matt Cross, huddled in his blue parka, next to his ambulance. Cross must be sixty now, Joe thought; he's been here even longer than we have.

In his office Joe checked the overnight report. Dr. Weisbrod had admitted a woman with cardiac arrest. She'd been rushed to the CCU and was improving. *Weisbrod.* Joe had to laugh. The firebrand of four years ago who'd organized the Progressive Medical Association and the Medical Commune was now coining eighty thousand dollars a year in private practice. As his income rose, his radicalism shriveled.

Nothing really tangible had resulted from the historic occupation of 1970. Mid-Island had expanded its psychiatric services and reopened the narcotics center. A few floors had been refurbished, an extra dialysis unit added. But the hospital remained grossly understaffed and poorly equipped. The success of the local medical mill proved that they were hardly the model of a community health center. Joe was even surprised that Weisbrod had deigned to send a heart case to Mid-Island.

Cunningly, Nixon had pointed the accusatory finger at angry blacks, welfare mothers, long-haired kids and addicts, every time a union member asked for a raise. The strategy was superb. It would work for a long time, Joe thought.

Shabazz and Ishmael, who had once impressed Joe with their sincerity, had made the mistake of circulating a crudely anti-Semitic leaflet in the hospital. Joe had gone into a rage. So had Gold, Gottlieb, and the Jewish medical establishment. Who could blame them? They'd been in the vanguard of the reform movement. Now they discovered they were "Zionist Fascists," bigots, black-haters. "You dumb bastard," Joe raged at Shabazz. "Who do you think has been taking your s-side all these years?"

The blacks withdrew. Hopes for an effective coalition vaporized. And now, two years later, Joe was doing the best he could. He put on his white coat and went off to morning report. The new chief resident was a Dr. Naw from Bermuda, who had done his training at Oxford.

Naw was an excellent chief. His accent alone terrified the house staff.

"One rather odd one," Dr. Naw said as Joe sat down. "A bleeder." '

"Hemophiliac?"

"Yes. Dr. Soong, it was yours, wasn't it?"

Soong and one of the junior medical clerks, Alvin Rhodes, Jr., Dusty's younger boy, had examined the "bleeder." He was a twelve-year-old male, unable to walk. Pepe Colon had fallen down a flight of stairs after his drunken father had decided that the kid needed a lesson.

Pepe could not get up after he hit the bottom step. A hemophiliac, his blood vessels ruptured and his knee joints had filled with blood. The condition, a serious one that could lead to permanent crippling, was known as hemarthrosis.

"Both knees?" Joe asked.

"Yes, sir," Soong said. "They're immobilized. Very purple. No breaks in the skin, but there is internal bleeding."

Joe rubbed his eyes. "Has he ever had plasma therapy?"

Dr. Naw shook his head. "The mother couldn't recall. The old man had beaten her pretty badly too."

"Okay," Joe said. "I'd l-like to see him. Start him on plasma.

431

"We'll have to d-determine how much mobility is left. I think it's ten-U thromboplastin component for every kilo of body weight."

It was a rare case, and Joseph Derry, M.D., was developing a reputation as a hematologist. Four years ago he had launched the screenings for sickle-cell trait among blacks. The hospital had coded and card-indexed carriers of the defective gene. And yet, Joe had to concede, it hadn't helped a great deal. Black couples bearing the deformed cells had children anyway—in or out of wedlock.

Kevin was right. The problems went deeper than medication or diagnosis. But in the course of his work in sickle-cell anemia, Joe had become fascinated with blood diseases and metabolic changes and had taken a few PG courses at night.

"How about splinting the boy's knees?" asked Dr. Naw.

"Wrong," Joe said. "Y-you do that, you w-weaken the muscle structure. Get him ambulant as soon as possible. Let's try cortico-steroids in addition to the plasma."

"Sir?" Naw asked.

"One mg. of prednisone per pound per day in two divided doses for three days," said Joe. "I think you'll see dramatic results."

The residents looked awed. A new one. Sometimes Dr. Derry, in his stuttering way, was capable of surprises.

"Any extra blood tests?" Dr. Naw asked.

"N-not at the moment. This isn't Upper County. No defensive medicine practiced here."

They laughed. The meeting dispersed. But Joe had not meant to be funny. He knew that Bay Medical Group, under Kevin's guidance, was one of the major offenders in ordering unnecessary tests. Blessed with middle- and upper-class patients, the doctors submitted people to interminable diagnostic procedures, had them admitted to Upper County, Beth Moses or Christ the King at the slightest sign of complications.

"You're like the g-goddamn medical mill," Joe once told Kevin.

"Not quite, Joe. We give first-rate medical care. Okay, costs are up, so we charge more."

"And the g-government picks up the tab. And people who aren't covered go broke if they have l-long-term illnesses."

"That's why we make the workup as thorough as possible."

"H-horseshit, Kevin. It's to protect yourself from malpractice suits. Not to mention the vacation houses and cabin cruisers and ski lodges. G-Graubart ever buy that condominium in Palm Beach?"

432

"Not just the apartment. The whole building, fifty units with a beach view. Terrific investment."

"It figures," said Joe bluntly. "Though why you play ball with them I'll never know. You certainly don't need the money."

Joe and Jenny ate lunch late in the steamy cafeteria. Dr. Weisbrod joined them. He looked considerably different from the way he had four years ago. The beard was gone; the hair was of normal length, the suit from Paul Stuart. Weisbrod had married well. Some doctors, it seemed to Joe, had a homing instinct where rich girls were concerned.

Abe Gold ambled over with his tray. "I get to sit next to Jenny," Gold said. "Makes my day." He opened his medical bag, pulled out a tiny transistor radio and pressed it to his ear.

"Watergate?" Joe asked.

"I'm loving every minute of it," Abe said. "I always said Nixon was basically a criminal."

Weisbrod leaned across the table to catch some of the reports from the radio. "What's happening, Abe?"

Gold turned up the volume. A federal grand jury had indicted seven of Nixon's top aides on charges of conspiracy, including Haldeman, Ehrlichman, and Mitchell.

The political discussion was interrupted by Dr. Naw, who came to tell Joe that the boy with hemophilia was doing fine. The steroids had made a dramatic difference.

"Good man, Naw," said Joe. He winked at Jenny. "I sh-should have been a hematologist. We can discharge him if his parents will bring him in for medication. I'd rather have him ambulant and at home."

"That'll be a problem," said Jenny. "The social worker says his father is in jail and his mother is here with two broken ribs. He's a cute kid."

Joe knew what was coming. He and Jenny had done it dozens of times in the past. Their house was an unofficial shelter. Nicky and Peter never knew when some stray would show up to occupy the extra bedroom for a few days.

"How long is the treatment?" Jenny asked.

"Five days," said Joe.

"Not even a week. We can keep him with no trouble."

Gold switched off the radio. He and Weisbrod were staring at

Jenny with wonder. Their wives would never countenance such a thing. There were foster homes, charities, orphanages, for such as Pepe Colon.

"Okay, okay," Joe grumbled. "S-so long as he isn't a steady tenant."

That night Nicky and Peter studied the undersized boy. He was as dark as Peter, with the same straight black hair.

"He stayin'?" Nicky asked.

"No," Jenny said. "Eat your meatballs, and if you're good and don't insult him, you can watch the first half of the Knicks game."

"We got one of *them* already. We don't need *two*," Nicky said. He was fifteen, a natural athlete who played ice hockey, football, baseball. His room was a mound of pads, steel cups, leather gloves and helmets.

"What does *that* mean, Nick?" Jenny asked. *"Them?"*

"Yeah," Peter said. He was a happy boy, full of zest for living. He did not fear his big older brother a bit. "He means *me*. I ain't no PR. I'm a Namerican."

"I am too," Pepe Colon said.

"Got it, pal?" Jenny asked Nicky. "Lay off that *them* stuff. There's no *them* in this house. It's all *us*. Pepe, you can watch the first half of the Knicks game also."

"I didn't mean nothin'," Nicky said. "You go to school, kid?"

"Sure. But I don' like it," Pepe said. "The kids pick on me 'cause I can't run."

"Pick up a rock," Nicky said. "And throw it at them."

"Whatcha gonna be when you grow up?" Peter asked.

Pepe hesitated. Then he looked at Joe. "A doctor. Like him."

"Hah," Nicky hooted. "You? You can't even speak English."

"One more crack like that and it's no Knicks game," Jenny said.

Later that night, when they were getting ready for bed, Joe said, "Why shouldn't that little squirt make it as an M.D.? We fill the hospitals with Asians and Europeans. But I don't see any more blacks or Puerto Ricans."

"They don't qualify," said Jenny. "Not enough of them."

"Then the system's no good. Got to talk to Tolland, the new community guy, about it. Maybe an intensive high-school science p-program would help. I'll talk to Kevin about trying to recruit more of these kids for Danforth."

"Oh, he's a big help," said Jenny. "But a losing cause never stopped you yet."

"Well," sighed Joe, turning off the light, "I think these days Kevin's got a lot of problems of his own."

A week later Kevin was asking E.E. Manship why the Danforth trustees had vetoed an affiliation with a new Concordia nursing home.

"They're wary of any proprietary operation."

"Anything fishy with Concordia?" Kevin asked bluntly. Curtis' empire was sweeping the East and the Midwest. The corporation's stock had zoomed.

"Not at all," Manship said. "It's simply that nursing homes are proving to be even more profitable than anyone imagined. They might prove an embarrassment."

Kevin sighed. He'd worry about it later. It didn't affect him. He was spending more of his time teaching and less in practice.

"I'll look at the trustees' report tonight, E.E.," Kevin said. "I noticed an expanded allocation for research. That'll make Nan happy. Maybe we can buy that computerized setup she's been talking about."

Manship pursed his lips in agreement. No problem. But it hurt him slightly that Kevin's second wife was so hardworking, so creative. So unlike his own children. Manship admired Jews.

"I don't see that most of this report should concern me," Kevin yawned. "Whatever the trustees and the administration want, I'll go along with." He stretched, wearily. He did not exercise any more. But he remained youthful and trim at forty-nine.

"It *does* concern you," Manship said. "There is unanimous feeling among the trustees that you be the new president and dean."

"Me?" said Kevin, realizing that Manship's unannounced visit to his office had a purpose.

"You're considering giving up practice. You are a wealthy man, Kevin. The group will survive without you."

"I didn't want to go into administration. I was thinking of research."

"You can do whatever you want. Research, teach. But the top job should be yours at Danforth."

"Why?"

"People listen to you. You are a top-flight medical man. You should be in a position where the teaching hospitals are under your control."

Kevin rested his head in his hands and stared at the framed photograph of his children. None of Nan. She refused to be on display. The sulkiness showed on John's handsome face. It was a picture taken at his graduation from his fourth prep school, an obscure institution specializing in problem children. None of Manship's contacts could get John Derry into Yale.

"I'll have to talk it over with Nan," Kevin said.

"I can't see her disagreeing. It will be a boost for her also. I had in mind a special department of genetic research to speed up her study."

"Can't hurry the mice, Dad. Or the cancer cells."

"I understand. I had in mind a special chair for Dr. Felder. A distinguished-service professorship funded by the Manship Foundation. My spies tell me her work is important."

"True enough. I'm grateful for your interest. It would be understandable if you resented her."

"I never have. I wish she'd be less formal with me."

"She's a shy woman."

E.E. got up and patted Kevin's shoulder. "President and dean. You would retain your professorship. You could organize cardiac research. Power is pleasant and invigorating, Kevin. Those who reject it usually regret having done so."

He left Kevin staring at Johnny's picture.

It was a relief, thought Kevin, a refreshing conclusion to the long day, to visit Nan's laboratory, even though Dr. Etta Roush, eyes hostile behind bifocals, barely greeted him. Kevin's appealing smiles and interest in Nan's work made no impression on plain Dr. Roush.

Nan was reviewing printouts from a computer. Her dark-brown bun was frazzled and her horn-rimmed glasses perched precariously on her nose. With a delicious lift in his heart, he realized once more how beautiful his wife was, a beauty that went far beyond her pretty face.

As he sat down opposite her, Dr. Roush, shapeless and distrustful, appeared in the doorway. She held a cage of twitching mice. "What shall I do with lot two-forty-five?"

Nan raised her eyeglasses. "Have they gotten the intraperitoneal transfers?"

"The usual. Cells from the original tumor."

"And you made sure the cells were treated in the usual way? We don't want any more false leads."

"No mistake, Annette."

"I guess we can let them stew. Continue the transplants for two weeks and let's see what develops."

Roush nodded and left. He could hear her calling good night to Nan. But not a word to Kevin.

"She resents me," he said. "She has for four years."

Nan tapped the pencil against her teeth. "You aren't her notion of a man of science. You earn too much money and you're too involved in hospital politics."

"Is that Dr. Roush or Dr. Felder speaking?"

"It's Dr. Felder's interpretation of Dr. Roush's feelings."

"Maybe she has a crush on you. It happens."

"Nonsense. Stay out of psychiatry. Stick to murmurs."

Nan got up, changed from her Loafers to a pair of low-heeled pumps. "I respect her scientific talents, which are considerable, and she respects mine. If it makes you feel any better, she had no use for Beauchamps either."

On the drive to their new home, Kevin told her about Manship's proposal—an appointment as both president and dean of Danforth Medical College.

Nan whistled. "And what did you tell him?"

"I said we'd think about it."

"I'm flattered you included me. But I can't advise you, Kevin."

"It's a challenge. I'll be fifty in a year. If I'm going to make a change this would be the time."

"If it's what you want, darling."

Kevin smiled at her. "It will mean good news for you. Manship suggested we put your final report under the aegis of Danforth. You'd get a lab twice the size, and all that computerized stuff."

Nan reached for his hand. She did not fully trust Manship or the men around him. Too many had become wealthy and powerful through nothing more than correct breeding, good connections, proper marriages, the right schools. She thought of her father, trudging up flights of drafty stairs to visit an impoverished fisherman.

They drove to the house. It was old and eccentric, with turrets and wide porches and vistas of Long Island Sound. Nan had refused to live in the Tudor mansion with its echoes of Cynthia.

Carol greeted them with a wave. She was eating a TV dinner, watching the evening news and writing a term paper for high school at the same time. Kevin had offered to send her to Emma Willard along with her stepsister, Karen, who was two years older, but Nan and Carol both objected. She'd liked public high school, and was a straight-A student.

Now she called to them. "Hey, Kevin. Your sister's coming on."

He and Nan stopped and watched as the anchorman threw Bridie her cue. She was standing on the balcony of the UBC offices on the Champs-Elysées and reporting on the French reaction to Watergate. What she said was nothing of importance, but she made it sound relevant, worthy of attention.

"Nice work if you can get it," Kevin said. "Sixty grand a year for a minute's worth of nothing."

"She earns her money," Carol said. "After all, she got shot at in the Middle East."

They ate a light supper in the kitchen. Kevin enjoyed the liberation from the big house and servants. He didn't need the estate. The children were rarely at home. Nan and he liked sitting on an upper balcony and looking at the lights winking around the cove.

"You remember my father's cornfield?" Nan said suddenly.

On a patch of earth behind his home, Doc Felder had grown dahlias, peonies, roses, corn.

"Once when Charley and I were kids, Daddy found an Indian arrowhead while he was hoeing. I'll never forget how thrilled we were. I think I decided that day I'd be an archaeologist."

"Good thing you didn't. What a loss to genetics."

At two-fifteen that morning the phone awakened them. Kevin picked it up and heard an unfamiliar voice.

"Dr. Kevin Derry?"

"Yes."

"This is Sergeant Yablock, New York State Police."

Kevin turned on the bed lamp and sat up.

"Dr. Derry, are you the father of John Derry, a freshman at Syracuse University?"

"Yes, yes." He reached for his cigarettes, managed to light one with one hand.

"Your son smashed up a VW Combi two hours ago on U.S. eighty-four outside of Binghamton. We're holding him at the state-police barracks."

"For God's sake. Is he all right?"

"Bruises and cuts. He ran onto the divider of the six-lane section outside Binghamton and hit two cars."

"Anyone in the other cars injured?"

"Two women. They're in Central Hospital."

Kevin's mind made connections. He held the insurance on John's Combi. If the women's insurance carriers learned he was the owner, they would try to hit him with a big suit. Something for Manship's lawyers.

"I guess I'd better get up there," Kevin said. He paused. "Or send my attorney. What can we do about posting bail?"

"Not till morning, Doctor. I think you'd better come up yourself. Your son's car was loaded with narcotics. He seems to have been running a big business on a half-dozen campuses around here."

"Could the stuff have been planted on him?"

"Not the load he had, Doctor. You want to frame somebody, you don't give him fifty thousand dollars' worth of dope. Dr. Derry, your boy is in trouble. He won't be arraigned until tomorrow, after we clean him up and get him to stand straight."

"Stand straight?"

"The medical examiner says he was using his own merchandise."

Kevin jotted down the address of the police barracks and hung up.

His back to Nan, he said, "That lousy kid. He should have been killed in the crash. Save us all a lot of trouble. Goddamn him."

"Kevin, you mustn't say that. And you can't abandon him. I'm not that smart that I can diagnose what's wrong with John. But he's your son. He has no mother. I can't fill the role."

"I didn't marry you for that purpose." He groaned and walked into the bathroom.

"Kevin, you have got to go to Binghamton yourself."

"Can't. I've got two people in open-heart surgery." He began to cough violently.

"Are you all right?" Nan got out of bed and came to the bathroom door. It was locked.

"Don't come in, Nan. I'm okay. We'll call Manship's lawyer in the morning. Send him up by plane."

Nan went back to bed. She did not understand these people. She never would. They frightened her. It was their absolute power, their talent for suppressing emotion. But Kevin had not always been this way. She hoped he would open his emotions in time to save his son.

In the preternaturally bright bathroom, Kevin exhaled a cloud of smoke, put out the butt in an onyx ashtray. Christ, it was almost morning. In three hours he would be showering, ready for another arduous day.

He tried to tell himself it was Cynthia's fault that John was forever in trouble. Heedless, inattentive, she had left the children to maids and private schools. But the truth was he had not been much better, with his interminable work, his absence from the home. Suddenly he was filled with longing for Johnny as a small, blond, laughing child. The innocence and freshness, the clear skin and golden hair. Gone. He wanted to cry, but no tears came.

As he started to open the door, pain flared in his chest like an electric charge, radiating down his left arm to the fourth and fifth fingers.

Kevin gasped and staggered. He heard Mozart filtering through the locked door. *Thank God.* Nan would not hear him. He sank to the toilet seat, lowered his head. In a minute or two the pain eased.

"Goddamn angina attack," he whispered. *Classical Heberden type of pain. . . .* He'd have to get an EKG. But for the moment he didn't want anyone to know.

The next morning he called one of Manship's lawyers and asked him to charter a plane and arrange for John's release. E.E. was informed. He showed no emotion, but said if there were any problems, Kevin should call at once. Cynthia and Kevin's son could not be abandoned, old Manship said. These matters were susceptible to solutions.

2

It proved to be a grim day.

Kevin glanced at the *Times* in the OR lockerroom and read that Max Landeck had died of cancer. Member of the Shinnaway Medical Group. He left a wife and three children. "Dr. Landeck was born in Stuttgart, Germany. . . .

One of the residents saw Kevin studying the obituary. "Too bad about Dr. Landeck, isn't it?" He was a soft-spoken young man with a toothy grin. A Churchport boy.

"Know him?" Kevin asked.

"I had him for tutorials at Christ the King. Terrific hepatologist."

"We were medical students twenty-four years ago," said Kevin. "I never forgot that blue number on his arm."

"Number?" asked the boy. An era had passed him by.

"Concentration-camp number. He told me once he counted every day of his life precious after that."

"Gosh, Dr. Landeck never mentioned that," the resident said. "Why'd they put him in prison?"

Kevin looked at him with numb wonder. Amazing how little any of them knew about anything but medicine.

"He was a Jew," Kevin said, and went back to his paper.

There was nothing in print about John's arrest. Kevin guessed that such incidents were not infrequent in upstate New York. All you needed was a beard or a decorated van to be stopped by state troopers.

Potsy entered the lockerroom like a gust of wind. He had little time to waste either on Landeck's death or Johnny's arrest. He was busy complaining about one of Kevin's partners, Donald Eck, the cardiologist.

"He tried to screw me out of an operation. Fifty-five-year-old man, badly occluded arteries. A natural for bypass."

"But the left main coronary artery was healthy, Potsy."

Dr. Luff grimaced. "You sound like Eck. Why in hell did you take him into the group? Kevin, he's *anti*surgeon. All that medical-maintenance crap. He wants to put me out of business."

And quite a business, Kevin thought. A million-plus a year in bypasses. Potsy paid an accountant more than Joe Derry earned.

He gave his cousin a placating answer. Eck was a good doctor. Late in the day Kevin went to him and described his own angina attack. Eck nodded, set Kevin up on the table for an EKG. It was normal. Probably just a temporary spasm. Yes, he should carry nitroglycerin with him. There was no cause for immediate concern. But he should stop smoking. "Kevin, you're the only cardiologist I know who smokes. The surgeons, sure. They don't know any better."

Kevin smiled. He liked Eck, who had some of Joe's blunt honesty. "You've got a thing about surgeons."

"Some. That patient Luff cut this morning? He could have been cured medically. And for a lot less than eleven thousand dollars."

"I understand you raised some objections at the medical-surgical conference. I'm not disturbed. We need different opinions."

Dr. Eck ran a hand through thinning blond hair. "I understand you're ticketed to be the next president of Danforth. Excuse me, Kevin, but word gets around. The Italians who pick up the garbage were talking about it."

"They always know first. The Damelio brothers. Buddies of mine."

"True or not?"

"A possibility, Donald."

"The school needs you, Kevin. You hear the rumors?"

"Which ones?"

Eck got up. Kevin was his superior and it took a lot of guts to confront him. But the younger doctor—*dammit, he was like Joe!*—didn't hesitate. "Someone on the Danforth admissions board is on the take. I heard some parents have made twenty-thousand-dollar bequests to get their kids into Danforth."

"Impossible."

"I hate to say this, Kevin. But you'd better keep an eye on our esteemed executive director."

"Curtis? I don't believe it."

Eck's long face confronted Kevin like his own conscience. "A Mr. Kahn and a Mr. Lobello have told me that Curtis asked for the money. Said if they paid, he'd get the kids in."

"Did they give him the money?"

"No. Lobello was my patient. He'd checked notes with Kahn. Kevin, if two men are complaining, maybe it's happened before. When you get the top job, you'd better look into it."

Kevin shuddered. Curtis again. The crooked son of a crooked father.

He was glad when Eck changed the subject. Would Kevin back him in a study of chronic stable angina? A project in which they could compare angina sufferers treated with bypass surgery, with a similar group treated medically?

"Hell, yes, Donald," said Kevin. "I may even be one of your first guinea pigs."

Kevin picked up Nan at six and they drove home to face Johnny. He had been released on bail. The stereo was booming with the noises of a new rock group.

John Derry, in jeans and torn sweatshirt, lay on the long sofa, his booted feet on a pillow, two cans of beer by his side. The boy's head was bandaged but he seemed in reasonable health.

Kevin crossed the room and turned off the stereo. Frate, Manship's lawyer, looked relieved to be rid of his client.

Kevin walked over to his son. "You might stand up when Nan walks into the room."

"I'm hurtin', Dad."

"Try it. It isn't hard." He hooked an arm under John's shoulder and yanked him to his feet.

"Ouch," John said. "Do you want to break my arm?"

"I would if it would help." He looked at his son. All ego, everything turned inward. "Try greeting me and your stepmother in civilized fashion."

"Okay, okay. Leggo. Hi, Dad. Hello, Nan. Mr. Frate says I may

443

not have to stand trial. Can I sit down? My back is killing me."

Kevin turned away.

"Yes, Johnny, sit down," Nan said. She crossed the living room and sat beside him.

"I'm okay," John said. "And it's not as bad as you think."

Kevin turned back and started to speak, but Nan shook her head at him. No point in starting an argument.

"Have you eaten?" she asked.

Johnny grunted. Yes or no?

"Mr. Frate, would you care to join us?" Nan asked.

"Thank you, Mrs. Derry. I mean, Dr. Felder, but my wife expects me. It's been a long day."

"We're grateful to you."

Kevin walked into the front hall with the lawyer. "What happened?" he asked.

"Mr. Manship arranged bail. I thought it rather steep—thirty thousand. The boy is restricted to within five miles of his house. He's remanded to your custody."

"What about a trial?"

The attorney lowered his voice. "There won't be one. The two women weren't badly injured and they don't seem very bright. I doubt they'll sue. The insurance company will make good on medical bills and the car."

"And the drug charge?"

The lawyer flashed his teeth. "The judge was impressed with John's background—Manship, Dr. Derry, Dr. Felder. He gave John a lecture on dishonoring such fine people, and said that he was taking the nature of the family into consideration."

"I don't want my son to go to prison," said Kevin. "Although I have a feeling it might not hurt him. But I'm curious. How does one get away with an obvious crime?"

"There's always a defense. Other boys may have used the van and left the stuff in it." Frate shrugged. "There are possibilities." He looked sly, secretive.

Kevin returned and lit a cigarette. "We'll give you a work-up at the group tomorrow, John."

"You want an aspirin?" Nan asked the boy. "Maybe something

stronger? Sorry, Kevin."

"Don't be sorry," said her husband. "Aspirin probably acts on him like an M and M." He got up. "Come on, John, I'll give you a look. Those bandages need changing."

In the study John took off his flannel shirt. Kevin listened to his chest, probed the bruises. There was a dark-blue hematoma below the last rib on the right side of his back. As he put on the clean dressings, he kept remembering John as a four-year-old. Skin bronzed, the hair like pale gold, digging in sand at Churchport Beach. How did it end so soon?

"Watcha thinkin' about, Dad?" Johnny asked. His voice was full of fear.

"Nothing important, John.;"

"You're pissed off at me, huh?"

"Pissed off is putting it mildly."

John winced as his father pulled adhesive tapes taut. "Dad, look at it this way. I'm no good. I never was. Why bother with me? Gramps is going to settle a big chunk on Karen and me. I heard him say so. Why not let me split and do my thing?"

"And what is your thing?"

The boy got off the edge of the desk, ran his fingers through dirty hair. Kevin saw again in his mind's eye the perfectly formed child's head, the tender neck, the browned arms. Building a sandcastle. Crying when a jellyfish stung him. He wanted to weep.

"I'm looking for it."

"A little discipline might help you find it. Some interest in your studies."

"Thought I'd try driving a cab in New York. Or maybe go out West. Work the ski resorts."

"No college? No career? Your grades were good in elementary school."

"I'm dumb. I'm dumb. I couldn't pass freshman chemistry. That little grub upstairs—Carol—she's twenty times smarter."

"Don't refer to Nan's daughter that way. There are worse things than being good at your studies. John, look at yourself. You don't want to do anything. What's wrong? What are you trying to prove?"

His voice was faint. "I'm not sure."

"Can I help? Can Nan help?"

"Nah. I'm like Mother. She was stupid also. I heard you say it once. You're smart. Nan's smart. I'm dumb."

"I never said any such thing." But did he? Christ, the agonies of the old marriage, the interminable recriminations.

"Mom never got the handle on anything; I know that. Booze, getting skinny all the time. Killing herself. I'm like her, not you or Karen."

"I'm not convinced of that. Your life is your own. You can be a lot of things. Syracuse has a good business school. Gramps will see to it you get an interesting job."

"Gramps, shit. Anyway, what he does is bullshit. Everything's bullshit when you look at it close enough."

"My work included?"

Johnny closed his eyes and leaned back. "Oh, you have to know lots of things. You're smart; I admit it. That's why I can't be around you. Reminds me of how stupid I am."

Kevin had a desire to embrace the boy. To bring back a sun-browned child in a green playsuit.

"You're better off checking me out, Dad. I'll work on a ranch. Maybe tend bar in Denver. Lotsa guys do that."

Kevin was silent. After a while he said awkwardly, "Well let's get our dinner."

Nan and Carol were waiting for them. Carol, who had come downstairs in her robe, kept staring at John.

"Watcha lookin' at?" John asked.

"You."

"Watcha see? The real live dope pusher? Guy who wrecked a Combi loaded with smack?"

"John, please," Nan said.

"Oh, Mom, I know all that stuff," Carol said. "And that's not what I'm looking at anyway. I'm trying to figure out if you're a brachycephalic or a dolichocephalic type."

Johnny moaned and pushed his plate away. "Jesus, my head is ringing. I'm going to bed."

"Ask Nan if you can be excused," Kevin said sharply.

Nan looked ruefully at her husband, as if to say, *He's troubled enough; don't make him aware of his manners.*

"Sorry, Nan. Can I be excused?"

"Of course, John. Leave your laundry in the hall. The maid will do it tomorrow. And there's lots of goodies for breakfast. Your father, Carol and I are all out of the house by seven-thirty."

Johnny Derry bobbed his head, as if sorry he were not part of the busy family. "That's all she wrote," he said, as he clomped upstairs.

"Oh, Kevin, he has to be helped," Nan said when he left.

"You figure something out."

"Carol, go to your room. We want to talk."

She pushed her glasses up her nose. She jiggled her bite plate and got up. "Poor guy. I wish I could help him."

When she had gone they discussed a number of possibilities, but came to no conclusions. Perhaps Dr. McGrory might help. It was worth a try. Anything was.

"You're in agony, aren't you?" Nan asked. "I can't bear for you to hurt like this."

"Don't suffer for me or for him. I can manage. And he isn't worth it."

"Kevin, that isn't so. You don't believe it."

She shut her eyes. Thank God for work, for the rewards of the mind. Pity would not help her stepson. But what could?

In March 1974 Bridie had been reassigned to the United States. She came home with a husband—she had married Tillotson—and a new job. She was now a network star.

After an apprenticeship in Washington, she and Tillotson bought a beachfront home in Easthampton and a co-op on Park Avenue.

"She's changed," Jenny said, after an uncomfortable dinner at Bridie's apartment. "Talks about herself all the time. I guess it goes with the territory."

"Pretty good t-territory," Joe said.

It had been a painful evening. Joe and Jenny were shabby intruders. Kevin and Nan had been there too, but both seemed too exhausted to smooth things over. Kevin had just been elected president and dean of Danforth Medical College.

Manship had assured Kevin that whatever he lost from his group income would be more than made up by his Concordia stock, which was soaring. Kevin seemed to have more on his mind than money. Yet even he noted the change in Bridie. She never called. She showed little interest in the family. Johnny and Karen were strangers to her, as were Nicky and Peter. "Christ," Kevin said as he and Joe went to pick up the car. "It's another world. All she talks about are contracts, salaries and sponsors."

"Almost like a medical-board m-meeting," Joe said.

Several months later Eliot Sparling caught up with Bridie. He had ambled into her office when she was mercilessly reaming out a film editor over the phone. He'd screwed up a sequence she'd worked hard to put together, an exposé of housing in the South Bronx.

Sparling could scarcely believe that the harsh voice belonged to his old friend Bridie. She had always been shrewd and demanding, but she had softened her approach to others with humor and tolerance. Now she seemed so devoured by ambition that she had jettisoned simple courtesies.

"Eliot, old buddy," Bridie said. "What have they got you doing?"

"Suburban beat. Long Island, Queens. I make the network once a month. I didn't come to gossip about myself. I wanted you to get this bulletin from me since indirectly it involves your family."

A scandal was about to blow the roof off the Danforth medical empire, he said. Kevin wasn't involved, as far as Eliot know. But her brother had apparently walked into a snake pit. Then he listed several stories that were bound to hit the papers.

"First," Sparling said, "several parents with kids applying to Danforth Medical College say they were asked to make donations. I have three affidavits. One man claims he was asked to lay out thirty grand. Another twenty-five."

"I don't believe it. Kevin would never allow that."

"He wasn't dean at the time. If you ask me, Manship insisted he take over because he knows Kevin is the only one who might pull them through. Kevin is respected. Everyone's favorite."

Sparling went on. He'd been digging on the story for months. He had a report that the college's administration had skimmed over *seven hundred thousand dollars* from federal grants for hospital costs—new living quarters, unauthorized salary increases. It was money earmarked for medical care. Somehow it had gone for "overhead," a violation of government guidelines.

"And there's that crazy tie-in with Concordia," Sparling said. "It's not directly connected to Danforth or any of the hospitals, but Kevin and your cousin Dr. Luff own Concordia stock. Concordia always seems to get the fattest contracts. I tell you, Bridie, it's going to explode. I wouldn't want to be your brother when it does."

Bridie asked Sparling to show her his notes.

"Why? What are you planning to do?"

"I'm not sure," said Bridie. "But when I decide, I'll want to have all the facts straight."

"Bridie, I don't mind you warning Kevin. That's why I told you. But you can't interfere with the investigation."

She was silent for a minute. Then she said, "I'm not all that sure I'm going to be on Kevin's side."

He was about to question her when the phone rang. She took the call—from her agent—and dismissed Sparling with a wave of her manicured hand. Then she studied her appointment book—4 P.M., leg waxing at Helena Rubinstein.

3

On an evening in late June, Joe and Jenny were summoned to the hospital to take care of Jenny's cousin Carmine. The fat man appeared to have had a massive coronary.

A clutch of Damelios in garbage-stained work clothes—except for Tony, unaccountably suave in black silk suit and white turtleneck—were swarming outside the dying man's room.

Jenny got the story in bits and pieces. Carmine—Johnny Farrell—was making the run from JFK to their "office" in East Shinnaway. He was loaded, after a "pickup."

Her eyes on fire, Jenny interrupted Tony. "Garbage, Tony? Or loot?"

He ducked his head. With Carmine dying, he was next in line to take over the trash empire. He respected and feared Jenny.

"Ah, you know, Jen, a little business on the side."

She knew. They were into a lot more than trash, her esteemed cousins. They were ferrying stolen goods in vast quantities from the airports to secret storerooms. Hi-fis, bicycles, typewriters. . . . "Name brands," Tony boasted. "We don't ask where it comes from; we just move it and take our cut."

Usually (a chastened Tony went on) he or Vince or Louie rode shotgun with Carmine, who was almost sixty. Tonight he had been alone. As he turned off the parkway, and headed down a deserted street for their "warehouse," he was rammed by one of Ravetta's trucks. Ravetta personally never went in for strong-arm anymore. He ran his business out of a florist shop in the best section of Cohammet, dispensing orders from telephones in the rear office. The three goons who slammed into the garbage truck laden with Sonys and Panasonics were greasers off the boat, ship jumpers.

They started dumping the load into the street, smashing cartons with sledgehammers. Raging, Carmine got out of the cab waving a .38. One of the goons belted him in the gut with the sledge; the other let him have it across the knees. The cops found him gasping like a dying hippo.

Joe came out of the ER. He'd taken an EKG and was shaking his head. "Tony, he c-can't last another two or three hours." He held the roll of paper in his hand—jagged peaks and valleys.

"Isn't there anything you can do, Doc?" Tony pleaded. "Maybe your brother could come and look at him." He was crying.

"Kevin's in Albany."

"Johnny loved him. No offense, Joe, you're aces with us also. But he always said Doc Kevin Derry was the greatest guy inna world. Ever since he took care of him right here in this hospital twenny-fi' years ago."

An orderly and a nurse wheeled Johnny out. An oxygen mask covered his bloated face. End of the road for the trash collector, Carmine Damelio, the legendary Johnny Farrell.

One of the younger brothers went to call Serafina, Carmine's wife.

"What about his s-son?" Joe asked. "That skinny kid, the one who was on d-drugs?"

"Yeah, Kenny," Tony said.

"He should be here."

Vince snickered. "Some chance, Doc. Kenny's doin' ten to twenty for dealing. They framed him."

Jenny and Joe followed the stretcher into the elevator. An hour, maybe two, and the overworked heart would die, the blood refusing to be pushed any further.

Three days after Johnny's death, a black Cadillac rolled past Ravetta's Florist Shop. Two men got out and hurled Molotov cocktails through the window. A week's supply of geraniums, roses, dahlias and carnations was roasted. The next morning Mr. Ravetta told the police he hadn't the faintest idea who would perpetrate such a brutal act, but if he ever got his hands on the dirty animals who did this to his flowers, "they'd get fucking worster than they give me, and that's a fucking promise."

451

That summer Kevin took over as president of Danforth. He was not aware of the force of the scandal about to break. He seemed to enjoy the easier hours. For a while he would drop by Nan's office at five-thirty—early for him—and pretend to be surprised that she was not ready to leave. She had not seen him so carefree since their honeymoon.

Nan had almost finished her project.

"Naturally you'll present the paper at Danforth," Kevin teased. "Get us into *Time*. I'll call Sparling and he'll put you on TV."

"No, Kevin. I did the work at Upper County, and I'll present the paper there."

"Then you'll resign."

"What?"

"I've put through a grant for you. You'll hold the Winston Manship Chair of Genetics. Full professorship. No teaching, just the perks, all the research facilities you need. Double the space you have now. Twice as many people."

Nan pushed the horn-rimmed glasses up her nose. "Kevin, don't. As much as I love and respect you, it's wrong for me to advance because of my husband's influence. I made it on my own before we were married. I want to keep it that way."

"You didn't object to my help when you got the appointment."

"We weren't married then. Who is Winston Manship anyway?"

Kevin laughed. "E.E.'s father. An old railroad pirate."

"Well, that convinces me. Kevin, I think we should keep our professional lives apart. You run Danforth; I'll stick to my mice."

At times he found it hard to believe that he could love her so, surrender to her sexual attractions so hungrily and with such adolescent fervor. Sometimes he caught a glimpse of her in the corridors at the hospital, and he felt his heart flutter—the way he did when Cynthia was eighteen, nineteen. . . .

"You're the one person in the world I can't work my Irish charm on," Kevin said. "Why?" They were both sitting up in bed, reading. WNCN filled the room with *Siegfried's Rhine Journey*.

"You did well enough. I guess it's my memories. Ask Charley about those Irish kids coming out of St. John Chrysostom's and shouting at me and Charley, 'Go back to Germany.'"

"Why hold that against me?"

"I don't. But it's in my subconscious, Kevin. And we're going to keep our careers apart anyway."

He kissed her neck. "Is this Dr. Felder's ego trip? Don't want me to cash in on the glory? Nan, don't be stubborn. I'll see you get all the credit. Our PR people will make it your show."

"I'll decide that."

He laughed, lit a cigarette as she went to the bathroom. Nan complained of his smoking. Some kind of punishment, she called it. Destroying himself with a temporary pleasure. "Don't come to me when you have an angina attack again," she had said once.

He looked at the draft of her report, which lay on a night table. To his astonishment he saw that the byline read ANNETTE FELDER, PH.D. AND ETTA F. ROUSH, PH.D.

What was she doing surrendering half the credit? For the first time he resented the absence of his own name. Dammit, she was Annette Felder Derry. On the last page, he noted that both Sunichi Matsuma and her ex-husband, Beauchamps, were cited for their help in the experiments.

When she came back to bed, he expressed his annoyance.

"You weren't supposed to see it. I'm sorry I brought the papers home."

"Etta Roush has no right to share the credit. Put her down in the afterword."

"No."

"This was your project. Roush hasn't been more than a technician. You owe her no more than a mention."

"You're wrong, Kevin. I'm not greedy. I'm not one to hurt people who help me."

"Am I?"

"I don't know that you've knowingly hurt anyone. But you can be careless of their feelings. Etta Roush contributed important work to the study. She worked out the computer printouts, helped design the machines, supervised the transplants."

"Technicians are a dime a dozen."

"She was more than that. She's a brilliant, kind woman, without a friend in the world."

"Don't let your compassion stand in the way of your career, Nan. Listen to me. You're the real scientist. You did the early work. You don't catch me or Potsy tossing bouquets to underlings. Potsy makes sure his assistants are well hidden, he —"

"Don't say another word about Potsy," Nan said. She shuddered. "He epitomizes everything mean and greedy in medicine." She sat on the edge of the bed and collected her papers. "Kevin, the few nasty things in you—and they're very few—are reflections of Walter Luff. The subject is closed. Dr. Roush is sharing the byline."

He knew better than to argue with her. She frustrated him with her intellect, her immovable integrity. Why should he have expected less of Sam Felder's daughter?

He was about to turn off the light when Johnny, never considerate of the time difference, called from Denver, where he was entering the university. Kevin heard the apologetic tone. John needed money. The Combi had broken down. The mechanics were ripoff artists. They were giving him a hard time on the guarantee, claimed he had ruined the motor by not using the right oil, or some shit. He sounded full of self-pity. What about college? Would he give it his best shot now? Kevin asked. Was he going to try to get the handle on something? Oh, sure, Johnny said. He met this terrific girl, this great kid who had a ski lodge and a Porsche. . . .

Kevin suppressed a groan. A world in terms of ski lodges and Porsches was not what he had in mind. He told John he'd have to await the next check from his trust. The boy grumbled and hung up.

An hour later, the pains germinated in Kevin's chest, bending him double. He put a nitroglycerine tablet under his tongue and lay back. Frightened for the first time in his life, he told Nan nothing.

"Ten bucks to cure a s-strep throat when that kid was six years old," Joe said moodily, "c-could have spared him a t-twelve-thousand-dollar operation today."

"Joe, come off it." Potsy patted his tanned abdomen.

The three couples—Nan and Kevin, Joe and Jenny, Potsy and Rosemary—were seated around the Luffs' forty-four-foot Wagner pool.

Nan was silent, wary. She told Kevin that in some peculiar way, she feared the Luffs, feared them as much as she liked Joe and Jenny. They had a kind of power, a sureness of foot, that she found disturbing. Kevin laughed. Potsy and Rosemary *adored* her. They were in awe of her achievements.

"I'm interested, Joe," Nan said. "You say if the man had had a strep throat taken care of years ago he wouldn't have needed open heart surgery?"

Shadows extended across the lawn. Some of the younger children were batting a shuttlecock. Potsy's oldest son, Walter Luff III, just graduated from Holy Cross, swam furious splashing laps. His fiancée, a silent blonde girl from Texas, daughter of one of his grandfather's business associates, watched him while reading *Time*. Nan had talked to them and rather liked them.

Joe described the case. Potsy had done a mitral-valve replacement on a twenty-eight-year-old TV repairman named Mulhearn. He had no third-party insurance, and was ineligible for Medicare or Medicaid. Self-employed, it had meant canceling plans for his children's education, selling his house, taking staggering loans.

"I ch-checked Mulhearn's history," Joe said. "As a kid he had a series of sore throats. Never treated. And three bouts of rheumatic fever. Come on, Potsy, you know that can c-cause mitral-valve stenosis. But when Jimmy Mulhearn was a sick kid, his aunt couldn't afford a f-five-dollar medical fee to have his throat treated. So twenty-three years later he has heart disease and needs twelve grand for surgery, and now he's broke."

"Don't look at me," Potsy said. "Not my fault they didn't take him to a clinic when he was a kid."

"Th-that's not the point. I'm arguing for primary medicine, dammit."

Kevin looked at Joe sympathetically. The old burn scars made a pale splash on his tanned back. Incredibly, the ancient helmet scab had left a white mark on the bridge of his smashed nose.

"I'm not against primary medicine," Potsy said. "You, Kevin?"

"No. We need more GPs and family physicians."

"But all of the effort, all the federal grants, go for r-research and hospital expansion. Every kid in med school wants to specialize. So, there's no one to treat a s-strep throat. Why not treat the source of the illness, rather than spend a f-fortune to cure the eventual damage?"

"You're picking on Walter," Rosemary said. "You always do."

"No he isn't, Rosie," Potsy said. "That's Joe. Dr. Underdog. Anyone who wants to can get medical care, no matter how poor. Admit it Joseph."

Before Joe could answer, Jenny, feeling fat and flabby in a too-

455

tight black suit, responded. "Like fun, Potsy. Have you been to Mid-Island lately? Or South Shinnaway? A four-hour wait in the clinic? And when the patients finally get to the pharmacy, they've run out of what they need. We're all so busy with cat scanners and research—"

"And open-heart surgery?" Kevin asked. He winked at Potsy.

"Yes," Jenny said. "Too damn much of it. I agree with Dr. Eck. Wait till he publishes his study. Sure, it's the fast, expensive way— shove 'em in, cut, bypass, wow."

"Now take it easy, Jen," Potsy said.

"Walter earns every dollar he gets, doesn't he, Kevin?" Rosemary asked.

"Of course. It's a rare skill. Highly specialized form of surgery. Jenny and Joe know that."

"Worth over a billion b-bucks a year?" Joe asked. "When there aren't enough M.D.'s in the South Bronx, in Harlem, in rural areas? W-when the clinics in the inner cities are madhouses?"

"You have a point, Joe," Kevin said. "But it's a free country. You can't force students into primary medicine. No one wants to practice in Harlem or Bed Stuy. No one wants to be a family doctor, make calls, deliver kids for one-third what an OB man gets paid. You're dreaming."

"M-maybe not. Why don't you have a p-program at Danforth for that k-kind of training?"

Kevin sighed. Joe had been after him for the past few months, arguing for more courses in community medicine, training in nutrition, sanitation, decentralized medical care.

"I think it's a good idea," Nan said. "Even though I'm one of the beneficiaries of those research grants."

Kevin shook his head. "The students don't want to study community medicine. HEW's lost interest. The trustees hate it. You know what happened when the radicals occupied Mid-Island— nothing. Those so-called community groups pull no weight. They're too busy battling each other."

"That's unfair, Kevin," Jenny said. "You've got the power. Use it. *Get* students into the communities. *Make* them work in the ghettos."

"They don't want to, Jenny."

"Hell, all the blacks want are loose shoes, a warm place to crap, and free you know what," Potsy said.

Nan's face darkened. She covered her eyes. Jenny made a hissing noise.

"Or someone to mug," Rosemary said. "Look what they did in Boston when they integrated the schools."

Kevin saw the fury in Jenny's eyes. "I can't find enough qualified blacks for our freshman classes," he said. "And we look for them. Those kids don't have the MCATs to make it."

"I wouldn't want one treating me," Rosemary said. "I'm not prejudiced, but who wants a doctor who doesn't know what he's doing?"

"Rosie," Joe said, "y-you'd be surprised how many of us don't know what we're doing. I c-could tell you about foul-ups in hospitals committed by some pretty-high-priced s-specialists."

"But at least they're smart, they're trained properly," said Rosemary.

Jenny was ready to explode. And how did Meg Derry die? On Walter Luff's operating table, her heart bleeding from a slip of the scalpel? But she said nothing.

Joe and Kevin continued to argue, but without anger. Kevin wasn't against it. He couldn't interest anyone in it—from the trustees who lavished millions on Danforth, the heart of the empire, down to the black and Hispanic students. Potsy, bored by the argument, left to broil steaks on the hibachi.

Joe was reminding Kevin about the kids they'd lost after the Whitmanville fire. Jerome Hudson, now eighteen, recipient of eleven skin grafts, had come to Joe after graduating high school. He had a B average, had done well in science and wanted to study medicine. He was entering Whitman State College and needed a nighttime job. Joe had found him kitchen work. It was the Jerome Hudsons, Joe felt, who should be encouraged to attend medical school, and then sent to the inner cities.

After dinner they watched the evening news. The anchorman introduced Bridget Derry, who would present a special report on a "medical scandal."

"What the hell is this?" asked Potsy.

The camera revealed Bridie standing in front of Concordia Medical

457

Corporation's plant in Pennsylvania. It was a bright, breezy day. Her abundant auburn hair was tightly bound with a ribbon. She looked ravishing, almost too beautiful to be a crusading journalist.

"Concordia?" Kevin asked. "What's she up to?"

"M-maybe send that b-bastard Curtis to jail," Joe said. "Go get him, Bridie."

There was a shot of Miles Curtis, tall and flabby, warding off cameras and microphones. Bridie identified him as the chairman of the board. He would not be interviewed.

"This multi-million-dollar corporation," Bridie said after Curtis entered the building, "specializes in hospital and medical supplies, and, since 1972, nursing homes. Concordia owns and operates eighteen nursing homes. Their stock has gone from seven in 1972 to a current listing of twenty-six and one half. Concordia is rated one of the country's fastest-growing conglomerates and is now branching into cosmetics, health foods, and vending machines. . . ."

"Get it out, Bridie," Jenny said. "Drop the other shoe."

"One month ago federal marshals served a subpoena on Colonel Curtis, ordering him to produce Concordia's books for the years 1972 and 1973. As yet the corporation has refused to comply, challenging the legality of the subpoena. UBC has learned that Concordia will also be charged with cheating Medicaid of four million dollars in fraudulent billings.

"Government prosecutors have indicated that the legal battle will be a long and difficult one, that Concordia has important political connections, and that its lawyers will battle the attorney-general's charges down to the wire."

"Miles Curtis," Joe said. "F-finally caught the c-crook." He started to explain the old connection, when Kevin shushed him and pointed to the screen. Bridie had not finished.

"Concordia's tentacles reach deep into the medical establishment. . . ."

There was an exterior shot of Upper County Hospital, followed by one of Lawton Curtis seated at his desk.

"This is Upper County, part of the Danforth College medical empire. The executive director of this hospital, Lawton Curtis, is Colonel Curtis's son. Channel Six reporters have established that Concordia Medical is Upper County's main supplier of drugs and equipment. It gets many of its contracts without competitive bidding. Lawton Curtis refused to be interviewed but through a spokesman denied the charges and hinted at a libel suit."

Kevin felt his stomach turn over. He reached out for Nan's hand, but it was cold and unresponsive. What the hell was Bridie trying to do? Destroy him?

"But there is more to the Concordia story than this. I have in my hand a list of the corporate officers." She waved a copy of the company's financial report, a handsome brochure, full of color photographs, intricate charts, earnings statements.

"Concordia's board of directors includes some of Danforth College's most distinguished physicians. And Mr. Everett E. Manship, Danforth's principal benefactor, is listed as board chairman emeritus of Concordia.

"These interlocking relationships should concern not only the attorney-general but the public that relies on Upper County for care. This is not the first time the Danforth empire has come under fire. Some years ago the community questioned Danforth's treatment of Mid-Island Hospital, which serves the poorer section of Long Island."

"Let's hear it for Mid-Island!" Jenny cried.

Kevin moved to turn the set off.

"K-keep it on, Kev," said Joe.

"I think we've heard enough."

"All lousy rumors," said Potsy. "Bridie should have more sense. Some loyalty to the family. They haven't proven a thing against Curtis."

Kevin's mind raced ahead. What had got into Bridie? Didn't she realize she was attacking *him?* Oh, no harm would come to him, he was sure. The Curtises, father and son, might get into trouble, but Dr. Kevin Derry had removed his name from the Concordia board of directors some weeks ago. It might be a good idea for Potsy and the others on Concordia's board to do the same. Manship, of course, was untouchable. He could not be held responsible for any shady deals by Curtis.

Later that evening, Kevin again emphasized to Nan the importance of transferring her work to Danforth. He wanted her to call herself Dr. Annette Derry.

"I won't be used, Kevin," she said.

"That's a cruel thing to say to me."

459

"You're frightened by what Bridie said tonight. You and Manship and those awful Curtis people. It's not such a big step from black marketing to five-hundred percent markups on drugs, is it? Or cheating Medicare. You let yourself get involved. It would be just dandy to counteract the bad publicity with a hot new discovery in genetics, wouldn't it?"

"I'm not afraid of Bridie's report. We're clean. Danforth is one of the best schools in the East. We don't owe apologies to anyone. If Curtis broke the law, he'll pay for what he did. It's not my business."

"That's right. You have no worries, do you Kevin? You never do."

"Not when I'm unfairly attacked. I pulled my name off Concordia's board. I don't know a bloody thing about their nursing homes."

"You have stock in them."

"Manship's people manage my portfolio. I never know what they buy or sell."

But, she thought, *you care about buying and selling people. Perhaps,* Nan mused, as she lay awake in the dark, *you think you bought me. And now you want a return on the investment.*

4

"Tolland, for Chrissake," Joe shouted, "you want a decent ambulance service, tell your soul brothers to stop r-ripping off the vehicles."

Joe Derry was one of the few white physicians who could talk to Wilson Tolland, head of the Community Care Office, in that manner. Tolland was black, Afro-headed, cool. He had a master's degree in social work. He, Charley Felder, a Puerto Rican woman named Alicia Martinez, Dr. Donald Eck, and a few others sat in Mid-Island's conference room for the monthly review of local health care.

The complaints had grown drearily alike. Long waits in the clinics. Drug shortages. No one to make calls. No preventive medicine. No programs in nutrition or sanitation.

Tolland growled. He knew damned well why the ambulances were breaking down. Local punks stole spare parts. One of the black mechanics was probably in on the thefts. Anything salable around Mid-Island was robbed.

"Police the ER," Joe said. "Tell the guys who are ruining the service you'll have them jugged. Jesus, is th-that our main worry?"

The old hospital was sliding downhill again. Short on attendings. Short on house staff. And, oddly, full of unused beds. Even the poor avoided the place, preferring to stay at home or patronize the medical mill.

"Okay, Tolland," Joe said brusquely, "y-you've made your point about the ambulances. Dr. Eck and I have a more important idea

461

that we want to discuss. W-we want more minority doctors and we want them to practice around Mid-Island."

"Fat chance," Wilson Tolland said.

Joe ignored him. Charley had told him many times that he and Jenny were among the few people at Mid-Island that the community trusted; Tolland's surliness was pro forma.

"It w-won't solve the problem tomorrow," Joe said. "But it will help. Here's what Donald Eck and I have been t-talking about."

They had approached Whitman State College, a good school that offered the B.A., B.S. and master's degrees in teaching, business and a few other fields, to work with them on a special medical preparatory center."

"What does it mean?" asked Tolland warily.

"To start with, a special premedical program for qualified blacks and other minorities," Joe said. "Kids whose board scores were too low to get into other colleges, but kids with promise and ambition. Like Jerome Hudson. He was in his freshman year at Whitman. A perfect candidate."

"What could Whitman do for Jerome Hudson?" Tolland asked.

"Make a physician out of him," Joe said. "Not only that, but a physician who would agree to practice primary care in poor areas. The students would be given an intensive six-year program—four years of pre-med and two years of medical school. Teachers could be rotated from Danforth, Stony Brook and Downstate to augment Whitman's faculty in specialized disciplines such as microbiology and pathology. There'd be no easy courses, no passing of students who didn't qualify."

"What happens after the six years?" asked Charley Felder.

"We get them into a qualified medical school for their last two years. They have to pass boards, keep up with the w-work. Dr. Eck and I can tell you that pre-med is tougher than med school, and the l-last two years of med school are the easiest—clinical work and electives."

"Sounds fine," Tolland said. "But they gonna fight you."

"Who?" Joe asked.

"Danforth. Your brother."

"Don't be so sure, Tolland. Kevin knows he'll be under pressure to provide care for the slums. Dr. Eck, read the proposal."

Eck, in his dry Midwestern voice, began to read. They would seek

462

out minority students unable to afford premedical education, put them through an intensive course in the sciences, eventually place those who qualified in accredited medical schools. Contractually, the students would have to agree to practice in underserviced communities.

Charley looked cynical. The plan sounded fine, but . . . "The white middle class won't like it. Faculty at Whitman might object to diverting funds in this manner. The medical schools will say your kids aren't well trained."

"W-we'll show 'em they're wrong," Joe said. "Dr. Eck and I think a k-kid with four hundred SATs who's motivated and basically bright can do it. Hell, ninety percent of the high schools don't offer more than two m-math courses. We'll make up for that. If necessary, give the kid an extra year before he starts the college program."

"Just what I mean," Charley said. "Remediation on top of remediation. Who'll want to use an M.D. who's gone that route?"

Joe rubbed his nose. "People who've never had decent care. To hell with the big hospitals and research c-centers. Let's get M.D.'s where they're needed. So our M.D. isn't the world's greatest genius on renal failure. He'll know how to treat a strep throat."

"It sounds fine," Miss Martinez said. "But how can we cut down clinic waiting time right now? We can't wait eight years."

"You're right, Alicia," Joe said. "We'll have to do both. I intend to get these kids, even while they're at Whitman, working s-summers at Mid-Island, and at community health centers. Part of their curriculum. I want to get the doctors back to the people."

When the meeting broke up, Charley Felder stayed behind with the two physicians.

"This might work," the lawyer said. He had contacts at Whitman. There was a state assemblyman who would run interference for them. Owed Charley a few. They'd need funding, an HEW grant. Charley knew where to go. Joe's proposal for "family physicians" might sound good.

"Tell 'em there's too much duplication in pre-med and med-school courses," Joe said. "Dr. Eck and I can combine it, save them money. A million and a half bucks a year on open-heart surgery? And w-we can't run a decent ambulatory-care center for twenty thousand p-people?"

They were about to go when the door burst open and Alvin Rhodes, Jr., poked his head into the conference room. "Dr. Derry? Can I see you? Urgent."

"Don't tell me the pharmacy ran out of Valium again." Joe got up and stretched. Meetings wore him down.

"Can we talk outside, sir?" young Rhodes asked.

In the night-dimmed hallway the boy looked grave.

"What's up, kid?" asked Joe.

"Your wife, sir. She was in an accident."

"Accident? How bad?"

"Ambulance is bringing her in. Near as I could find out, she's okay."

"Car?"

"No sir. Gunshot wounds." Rhodes swallowed, brushed back his hair. "Riley was on the radio a few minutes ago. She isn't conscious but her life signs are good."

"What the hell happened?"

"I'm not sure, Dr. Derry. Near as Riley could figure out, your wife was being driven home by one of those garbagemen. Her cousins. Her car wouldn't start, and she didn't want to bother you."

Joe flew down the hallway to the emergency room.

"Those goddamn idiots, the Damelios," he gasped. "Kill the bastards. N-not funny anymore. Jenny. Jesus Christ, Jenny . . ."

He was watery-kneed, dizzy. Jenny was everything good in life. She walked into a ward and people felt better. They faced pain, outrageous insults to their bodies, the prospect of death with more courage at the sight of Jenny's smile.

The Emergency Room had not changed much in twenty years, except for a central oxygen supply and an overhead trolley for IVs. A resident was bandaging the bloodied head of a drunk who kept cursing, trying to get up.

"Get him out," Joe shouted. "He doesn't need the table. Move."

Miss Bezerska came running in. "We raised Riley again. One bullet wound in the side, another in the arm."

"You call a surgeon?"

Bezerska nodded. "Dr. Gertz is getting dressed. He'll be here in a minute. He heard it was Jenny . . ." Her voice broke. She dabbed at her nose and began to cry.

Joe paced the floor, pounding one fist into another. The old rage,

464

which he had suppressed for many years, welled up.

Dr. Bernard Gertz came in. "Anything new?" he asked Joe.

"Bernie. Someone says Jenny has two gunshot wounds. Arm and side. They think they've stopped the bleeding."

"Take it easy, Joseph. If the bleeding's stopped, it's a good bet the vascular system wasn't affected."

They heard the shriek of the Klaxon, saw the flashing red lights. The ambulance, preceded by a police car, zoomed into the parking lot.

Joe ran outside. Dr. Gertz ordered his residents to get the table ready.

Cross and Riley opened the rear door and with assistance from Joe and Rhodes eased the stretcher out. Jenny's upper body was swathed in bandages. She managed a weak smile. Joe took her hand.

"Jen, Jen, how are you?" he asked.

She could not speak. But she smiled and would not let go of his hand. *A goddamn wonder, my wife. She has never complained in her life.*

"She's full of Demerol," Riley said. "She was in a lotta pain when we got her. There was a guy dead."

Joe kissed her forehead, brushed the graying hair back. He could see bloodstains on her bandages, but he saw no rhythmic pumping of blood.

Sgt. Al Kilduff climbed out of the patrol car and followed them inside.

"What happened, Al?" Joe asked.

"Shootup. Her cousins were the pigeons. Tony Damelio was driving. A kid brother was in back."

In the ER, Dr. Gertz, scrubbed and gowned, was supervising the nurses and technicians as they eased Jenny from the stretcher to the table.

"Tony's dead," Kilduff said. "Right through the eyes. Blood all over his three-hundred-dollar suit. The kid in back wasn't touched. Hid on the floor. Jenny picked up the shots intended for him. They were caught in a blind switch as they came off the Parkway. Two cars rammed them and drove them onto the shoulder. Then a third pulled alongside and someone started shooting."

Joe nodded. "Anyone catch them?"

"Not yet. You know how those Damelios are. They won't talk to the cops. The kid says he'll settle it himself. Tony didn't last very long as *numero uno*. What was Jenny doing riding with them?"

"Her car broke down. I was at a meeting and she didn't want to bother me. Hang around, Al. I may need somebody to lean on."

Gertz worked swiftly. He cut away Jenny's blood-soaked blouse and snipped off the bandages.

Joe wept at the sight of her defenseless bleeding flesh. Miss Bezerska touched his arm. "Dr. Derry . . . you don't have to stay."

"It's okay. Let me give you a hand, Bernie." He scrubbed quickly.

"Metzenbaum scissors," Dr. Gertz said. "I hate doing this in the ER, but she looks pretty good. Check her blood pressure and put in a central-venous monitor."

They saw the holes. There was a red oozing gouge in Jenny's left forearm and another in the left side of her chest.

"Heavy coat she was wearing," Joe said. "It m-must have helped." He cursed the Damelios and their contemptible life, their petty criminalities. They worshipped him and adored Jenny. But why, *why* did they have to do favors for her? Irrationally he was furious with her for racing home to see that their sons got "a hot meal." Risking her life for a plate of lasagna.

"The one in the arm doesn't bother me," Dr. Gertz said to Joe. "I doubt the bone's injured."

Jenny was trying to talk.

"Q-quiet, kid," Joe said. "Dr. Gertz is fixing you up."

Gertz sprayed antiseptic on the arm wound, then probed the wound in her side. "Breathe easy, Joe. I think we got lucky."

"What do you see?"

"It looks to me like the bleeding is venous." The bandages removed, blood oozed slowly. "Jenny, you have any pain? Shake your head yes or no."

Jenny gave a small shrug.

"You're her husband," Gertz said. "What did that mean?"

"A little bit of pain. She'd never admit it. She's got an Italian martyr complex."

Jenny smiled.

"Increase the Demerol," Dr. Gertz said, studying the wound. "She may not even need surgery. After we take X-rays I'll know more. Nature's got its own way of preventing hemorrhaging, Joe. I don't think the systemic arteries were hit. If they were, the blood would be gushing."

Joe kissed her forehead as they wheeled her out.

"I don't even think she'll need a thoracotomy," said Gertz. "We'll get the OR ready, in case. But I think she'll make it with nonsurgical care."

He took Rhodes aside. "Stay with Mrs. Derry, Alvin."

"Yes, sir."

In the corridor Gertz lit a giant cigar. "She'll be okay, Joe. I've seen these before. If they miss the vital organs, even at close range, they get better. Jenny's healthy. Anyone who can scoot around wards the way she does has to be."

Joe started to thank him but found his voice choked with tears. He turned away. Gertz continued down the hall. *Not many wives like Jenny,* he thought. *No wonder Joe was so upset.*

The X-rays confirmed the good news. Jenny would have to spend some time in the hospital but the wounds were clean. No further surgery was needed.

Joe went up to visit her. A nasogastric tube had been inserted in her nose, and there were two IV leads in her arms. She was heavily sedated, but she smiled and whispered, "The boys."

"What about them?"

"Didn't get dinner."

"They'll survive."

He stroked her forehead. "Dinner," he scoffed. "She's got two bullet holes in her and she's worried those two *scugnizzi* didn't get their minestrone."

"Call Nicky, Joe," she whispered. "Call my folks."

"Nicky, yes. Your folks, no. They can wait'll tomorrow. I don't w-want any hysterics at ten o'clock at night."

But he did call Fort Lauderdale. And weathered Carmela's screaming, Nick's hoarse shouts for vengeance. He had his police .38 and he would come up and use it on Ravetta or whoever shot his daughter. Too bad about Tony, but those dumb Damelios were asking for it. They weren't as tough as they thought, trying to be wise-guys. Well, they'd learn there was nothing like a legitimate business. He'd as soon shoot a few of his nephews as the bastards who shot Jenny.

467

Jenny's sister, Angie, came to visit. She cried briefly, and sat with Joe in his office. Angie had aged—but she was pretty. Many of the younger doctors still sighed after her.

"Next time a Damelio offers me a ride," Angie said, "I'll spit at him. Poor Jen."

"Don't blame them. They're p-part of the times, Angie."

"Whatcha gonna do, Joe?" she asked.

"What do you mean?"

"I mean, the guys who killed Tony. They almost killed my sister."

"The cops are handling it. Paulie says he knows who they were but he won't tell anyone."

"I know what I'd do. I'd go looking for them. So would my father."

"Keep him in Florida. I need him like I need malaria."

Joe yawned. The endless nonsense. You kill me, I'll kill you.

Angie volunteered to spend the night with Nicky and Peter and get them off to school. Joe was grateful, and grateful also to be left alone. Jenny's family could be as big a pain in the neck as his own.

In less than a week Jenny was home. But the splintered bone in her left arm was proving more of a problem than the wound in her side. True to Dr. Gertz' prediction, the pulmonary artery healed itself and the lung was sound. But the fractured radius needed a metal peg, splinting, and an awkward raised cast.

Nick and Carmela flew up from Fort Lauderdale to look after her, annoying her with their fluttery if well-meant attentions.

The immobilization bothered her. She took it as a personal affront and harassed Dr. Gertz until he assured her she would have the cast off by Christmas.

Joe did not attend Tony Damelio's funeral. He had had his fill of these hoods. He had tried to question Paulie but drew no response. "No way, Doc. This is our business."

One day Jerome Hudson stopped Joe outside the kitchen.

"Dr. Derry," he said, "you was talkin' to the garbageman about your wife?"

"That's right."

"Woodson says he knows who did it."

"Who?"

Jerome led Joe into the kitchen. Woodson was a black giant. He was slicing cucumbers.

Joe recognized him. "Hey, you're the guy my wife told to stop selling policy in the corridors."

"That's me. I got nothin' against Miz Derry. Sorry she got hit. She just say, 'You wanna sell numbers or take bets, keep it in the kitchen.'"

Jerome Hudson said innocently, "Woodson knows everything."

And what he doesn't, he'll learn, Joe thought.

"Them guineas on the garbage, they afraid, but I ain't," he said. "We run *both* mobs outta here. Black folks deserve black service. I handle the bets here."

"What else is new?"

"Ravetta send his hoods to shoot up that car. He knowed your missus was in it."

Rage exploded in Joe's head, but he said calmly, "What do you have in mind, Woodson?"

"We go visit his flower store."

"Is he armed?"

"I guess so. But he never figure a doctor would belt him one. He a real yellowbelly. I'll wait to make sure the others don't make trouble. Me and Hudson."

Joe rode in the cab of the ambulance with Woodson. Jerome Hudson sat in the back.

"You know, Doc," Woodson said, "you and the missus are okay. Tolland tell us what you tryin' to do."

They parked the ambulance a few feet from Ravetta's florist shop. Calla lilies, roses and dahlias bloomed in the window. A blue neon sign was set in a bower of mums and carnations.

RAVETTA'S FINE FLOWERS

WE DELIVER

"I f-feel like a goddamn fool," Joe said. "I don't want to kill anyone."

"Me neither," Woodson said. "But you used to be pretty tough, I hear. Just hit him once't or twice't. Unless you want me to?"

"No. It was *my* wife almost got killed. All you got to k-kick about are your runners."

Woodson cocked his head and peered through the window. Inside they could see a stout dark-haired man with hooded eyes arranging white roses in a refrigerated glass case.

Joe felt his anger mount, the old irrational urge for justice. Make the bastards know they could not hurt people forever.

Woodson winked. "I'm goin' around the back way. Sometimes one of his friends is there unloadin'. You know how to punch, Doc?"

I am a goddamn idiot, Joe thought. *I should know better.* He remembered how Jenny had looked in the ER.

"Good luck, Doc.," Woodson whispered. "Just remember he's yellow."

Joe walked into the florist shop. Potted plants covered half the floor. From the ceilings macramé hangings held terra-cotta and copper planters rich with wandering Jew, philodendron, ivy.

Behind a counter, Ravetta was wrapping pink roses in green paper. He certainly did not look menacing. He was of medium size and stout, with sloping shoulders under his starched gray coat.

"You Ravetta?"

"That's me. Can I help you?" His voice was husky.

"I'm Dr. Joseph Derry from Mid-Island Hospital."

"Pleasure." The voice was almost inaudible. "Interest you in hothouse roses? I make up a nice assortment—pink, white, red. Fifteen dollars a dozen. Throw in the baby's breath."

"I d-don't want any flowers."

"How can I help?"

"Y-your goons shot my wife ten days ago. Don't look so dumb. Mrs. Derry, the n-nurse at Mid-Island. She was r-riding with Tony Damelio. They killed him and put two bullets in her."

Ravetta smiled. The lips retreated; the yellow teeth emerged. "I don't know what you're talking about, Doc. I'm a florist. What would I be doin' shootin' people? I read about that bastard Damelio. He deserved what he got, but don' look at me. I'm sorry your wife was inna car. You ride around with shit you get treated like shit."

Joe lunged across the counter. He grabbed Ravetta's collar, lifted him off his feet and dragged him around to the side. "You b-bastard, admit it. You don't care who you kill. It w-was your hoods shot my wife."

"Hands off, Doc. You'll get yourself in bad trouble."

Holding Ravetta with his right hand, Joe lowered his left fist and rammed it into Ravetta's gut.

Ravetta grunted. Air whooshed from his mouth. Then he

470

wriggled out of Joe's grasp and reached under the counter. Joe saw a small automatic in the florist's hand.

"Augie!" Ravetta screamed. "Augie, *vieni qui!*"

Without thinking, Joe cracked Ravetta's hand, sent the gun flying. Then he straightened him up, and with a right fist to the florist's throat sent him smashing into the panes of the display case.

Simultaneously Augie ran into the shop from the rear. He carried a pair of elongated shears. As Ravetta exploded through the glass, Augie pointed them at Joe's face. Before he could move, Woodson burst through the rear door and belted Augie across the kidneys with a tire iron. The man crumpled. Woodson kicked him in the side until he lay still.

Joe wanted to vomit with shame. Lying amidst the brightly colored flowers, Ravetta looked like an ugly piece of garden statuary.

Woodson raised the iron over Ravetta's head. "Once more, Doc?"

"Lay off, Woodson. He's had enough." Joe knelt next to him.

"Cocksucker," Ravetta murmured. "I get your whole fuckin' family."

"No you won't, Ravetta," Joe said. "Y-you do what you want to those g-garbage collectors, but don't you ever hurt m-my wife or my kids or anyone from my hospital. You w-want to fight over garbage or numbers, fight with your own kind. But you start on my family or my staff, I'll kill you. With my own hands, you hear?"

"Aw, lay off," Ravetta moaned. He plucked pink carnations from his chest. "Lemme up. I ain't makin' no trouble for you or the wife. I'm sorry she got hit. It wasn't for her."

Joe nodded at Woodson. They left.

Outside Jerome Hudson had the motor running. They climbed in. Woodson smiled at Joe. "You hit him like you know how to hit."

Joe did not respond. Shame and revulsion overwhelmed him. Some director of medicine. He made Woodson and Jerome swear never to tell anyone. As they returned to the hospital he felt an unexpected surge of satisfaction. *From a life of frustrations,* he thought, *a small victory.*

5

When the September session began, and a new batch of students was being rotated through the hospitals, Joe and Charley Felder visited the president of Whitman State College. Andrew Schwartzbaum, Ph.D., was a cousin of Dr. Abe Gold's wife. That would help.

Joe, in his halting way, explained his idea. He and Dr. Donald Eck had spent weeks preparing the proposal.

"Six years here for the students. Bachelor's degree and t-two years of medical school. You give an M.S. and an M.A. in sciences already. Then we g-get them into a regular medical school for the last two years."

"Why not just pressure the medical schools to take more poor kids?" Schwartzbaum asked.

"W-we want to get the dead hand of the admissions office out of the process. We want minority kids who'll practice in their own neighborhoods."

"We're not equipped to teach things like pharmacology and pathology."

"Dr. Eck and I have covered that. You'll have v-visiting professors from other schools."

Schwartzbaum frowned. "What makes you think those teachers will come to a state college?"

"For money, they'll teach kindergarten."

Schwartzbaum chuckled, "Getting cynical, Dr. Derry?"

"Truthful."

"This will need federal funding."

472

Charley said, "I think we can get it. Seed money from a foundation. An HEW grant. It's worth a try. I agree with Joe. We can't let medical practice be run by the big hospitals. No one's against research and machinery. But not at the expense of the community. The poor get sicker and the sick get poorer, and it won't stop until we develop physicians who'll go into their homes and preach preventive medicine."

Schwartzbaum liked the idea. He'd talk to Dr. Gold and feel him out. Next to Kevin, Abe was one of the most influential medical men in the area.

"Have you spoken to your brother?" Schwartzbaum asked Joe.

"Casually. Kevin's up to his neck with his own p-problems. Wants Danforth's reputation to outweigh any scandal."

Charley smiled. "That doesn't do much for black kids with sickle-cell trait, or their VD rate, or the increasing number of abused children."

Schwartzbaum cocked his head. "Abused children? Is that a medical problem also?"

"U-under our scheme," Joe said. "Medicine doesn't operate in a v-vacuum. Parents sock their kids for lots of reasons. Let's stop the causes. Hell, there was th-this M.D. ran a rural health center in Mississippi some years ago. Know the first thing he did? He started writing prescriptions for *food*. That's right. On his prescription pad—whole-wheat bread, meat, milk, vegetables. Medicine or social work, Dr. Schwartzbaum?"

"You've got a point. Let me talk to my faculty."

Bridie visited her brothers in October for the first time in months. They knew her now more as a face on the TV tube. She shared major assignments with a man named Sensenbaugh. Hostility between them was evident. It made for spicy items in the newspapers, but she was clearly emerging as the winner. In fact it was rumored he was on the way out. And as they sat down to lunch they learned that he was not the only man departing from her life.

Hayward Tillotson had not come along. Jenny, her arm in a sling, asked why.

"We're getting a divorce," Bridie said.

Nan's eyes opened. "Bridie, you were married so short a time. . . .

473

"Nan, not that middle-class bit. Not from you."

"From me, then," Jenny said. "What happened, Bridie?"

Kevin and Joe did not seem distressed. They had become inured to Bridie's outrageous behavior, her overwhelming ambition. She seemed to do any damned thing she wanted.

"He was a spook," Bridie said.

Kevin pushed his food away. "A spy?"

"CIA up to his eyebrows. Handsome Hayward Tillotson. All that Maryland horseshit and wine tasting. He was using me as his cover. Can you top that?"

"N-not by much," Joe said.

"All those years in Paris he was escorting me to parties? He was milking me for information, using UBC as a conduit, running errands for the CIA. I got the tip on him from another journalist."

"But . . . but . . . didn't you love each other?" asked Jenny.

"No. I liked him. I think."

Kevin wondered. Was there someone else? And then he decided that it did not matter. She was all ego and drive. He saw her photograph on magazine covers and did not recognize her. Certainly not the lively open kid he remembered from Churchport and nursing school.

What the hell, Kevin thought. *They accuse me of being without emotions.* But looking at Nan, he knew he was not. He adored her more every day. And his children. He yearned to reach them, find out what was troubling John, now drifting around the West in his van. Or Karen, pretty and bright, but wary of him.

"So we scrub Tillotson," Jenny said. "Any replacement?"

"Nope. I'm too busy."

And I know how, Jenny thought. It didn't bother her that Bridie was now a famous personality, but rather the ease with which she assumed the role. Her old cynicism, her quickness to attack fraud and greed—a trait Joe still possessed—had vanished. She seemed to enjoy the useless, self-promoting, vain and rich. It disgusted Jenny. One could be a good journalist, she imagined, without spending all one's time with fakes.

Later, Joe drew Kevin aside and asked if he had given any thought to Joe's idea for a medical preparatory center at Whitman State? Kevin's support would be important to the program's success. If

Danforth would agree to rotate a few teaching professors. . . . If Danforth would open its lab and hospital facilities. . . . If Danforth would take a few qualified students for their last two years. . . .

"I'm looking it over, Joe," Kevin said. "It's got plusses and minuses."

"Such as?"

"I agree we need more family doctors. And I agree they should practice where they're needed, not on East Seventy-ninth Street."

"But?"

"I'm worried about the kind of student you'll turn out."

Joe pursed his lips. "Won't know till we try, w-will we, Kev?"

"But the effort, the expense. It may not be worth it. Why not stick with the traditional medical-school pattern?"

"Because it only turns out those guys who want to practice on East Seventy-ninth Street. I wish I could convince you, Kev."

"I've got an open mind."

How open? wondered Joe.

In November, corrected proofs of Nan's report on her eight-year experiment arrived from the printer. Nan rushed to open them, but when she pulled them out she was stunned.

The byline read

ANNETTE FELDER DERRY, PH.D.
UPPER COUNTY HOSPITAL GENETIC RESEARCH UNIT

She read no further. Etta Roush came in with a question about a breakdown in one of the computers. Nan responded vaguely. She put her hand over the pages.

"Corrected proofs?" Dr. Roush asked. "Hot from the printer?"

"More or less, Etta."

"Great. Love to see it. Although I know the darn thing by heart already. Publication set for February?"

"Yes. We may make a presentation at the convention in Dallas. You'll go with me, of course."

Etta left. Nan dialed Kevin's office. He was in conference with the senior faculty. Nan tried to control her anger.

She thumbed the pages, trying to keep her hands from shaking. She saw on the last page that Dr. Etta Roush was listed in the footnote with Sunichi Matsuma, Georges Beauchamps and two other aides. Kevin's secret editing. She walked into the frigid December air and drove to Danforth Medical College.

Kevin came in from his meeting shortly after she arrived. Two secretaries hovered over her. "Coffee, Dr. Felder? Something to read? We're sorry you didn't call; we're sure Dr. Derry would have ended the meeting earlier. . . "

Kevin kissed her cheek, touched her arm. As always, she seemed to him somewhat frail and defenseless.

She pulled the sheets from the envelope and placed them on his desk. "I suggest you hold all calls," Nan said. "I know that fund raising and the admissions problems are headaches. But please look at the byline."

"I see it."

"You changed it without consulting me."

"I thought I'd present you with a *fait accompli* and you'd agree."

"It will be precisely the way I wanted it. Etta Roush will share the credit. Kevin, we made an agreement a long time ago. I am Mrs. Derry in my private life. I am Annette Felder in my professional life. Don't start any Freudian analysis about my father fixation and how I'm trying to honor his memory by using his name."

Kevin stared at her with aggrieved eyes. "I did this because I love you, Nan."

"I wonder."

"Do you doubt my love?"

"I never have. But I won't be sucked into the Derry empire and I won't betray Etta Roush."

"Dammit, it's not a question of betrayal. We've been through this before. You did the work. You originated it."

"Kevin, I think you've reached the stage where you feel you can do anything you want as long as it advances Danforth. You don't seem in the least disturbed by the Concordia mess, for example. Sparling was on the air again hinting that you and Luff are involved."

"None of it is true. Besides, Curtis is blaming it on his accountants. Manship's lawyer says—"

"Goddamn Manship and goddamn Curtis. Kevin, you're getting to be like them. Blaming it on accountants? Four million dollars' worth of cheating? Kevin, I'm sick of the lies and evasions."

"Listen to my side of it, Nan." He got up and touched the nape of her neck where the bun of her hair rested on the soft skin. "Please, Nan . . ."

She was crying. "Kevin, you're always the winner. You always make your mind up things will be thus and so, and that's how they end up. Not this time."

"Listen to me, darling. I'm after the biggest haul we've ever got for genetic research. A million and a half dollars from the NIH, and matching funds from the foundations. This paper of yours will clinch it. It means a new lab, a blank check for your work. Roush's name doesn't mean a thing. The connection with me is the important one. Don't ruin our chances by diluting the byline. Let 'em know you're *my* wife, that you did this thing on your own. You're one of the leading geneticists in the world. Nan, when that Nobel Prize comes through, you should be Mrs. Kevin Derry."

"Stop it Kevin!"

"You can put Danforth on the map. Get us anything we want for research. And no one's going to interfere with your work or dare to steal you from me."

"From you?" she asked. "What makes you think you own me, Kevin? Or that you can use me?"

"I'm not using you. I love you. I respect you more than anyone in the world. Do you call it using to get you the best genetic research unit in the East?"

"I'm happy in my basement. My mice make no demands. And neither does Etta Roush. She isn't pretty or aggressive and she has no bigtime medical husband to make deals in her name."

"Be reasonable. Let the paper stand as corrected. Please."

Nan got up. "I only believe half of what you're saying, Kevin. If the work is as important as you think, you'll get the grant with Etta's name on it. The Derry imprimatur need not be on this paper. I'm changing it back to the way it was."

He saw he could not bend her, charm her into agreeing as he had done all his life with so many people. "A stroke of the pen. But I won't fight with you. I have too much admiration for you."

She got up, wiped her eyes and walked to the door.

"A stroke of the pen," Nan said. "So easy to change back. But not so easy to restore our relationship. I'm sorry."

"Nonsense, Nan. You're overdramatizing. Married people are entitled to professional differences."

"This goes a bit deeper. It tells me things about you I'd rather not know."

She did not say goodbye. She dabbed at her eyes again and left, walking past the solemn-faced secretaries.

For ten minutes Kevin sat morosely in his chair, taking no calls. Then his secretary asked that he speak to Lawton Curtis.

"Kevin, the bastards have done it," the executive director said on the phone. "They've indicted Dad. They claim he cheated Medicaid out of a bundle. Our lawyers say it can't stick. Dad's free on bail and he's confident. I was thinking, maybe the top faculty people could draw up a petition supporting Dad? You know, vouch for his character, the way he's assisted in medical research. Kevin? Kevin, are you with me?"

Kevin coughed and lit a cigarette. "Lawton," he said. "I hope they send your fucking father to jail forever." He hung up, spun in his chair, and looked out the window. Nan was turning out of the driveway.

A week before Christmas, Joe sat in his brother's office. It had been a month since Joe had sent him the proposal for the medical preparatory center at Whitman. He had not heard from him.

"Well?" Joe asked.

"It won't fly, kid."

"Why?"

"Lots of reasons. First off, the smart minority kids will get into regular medical schools. Hell, the Ivy League schools have scouts out for blacks and Puerto Ricans with talent and good board scores."

"Not good enough, Kevin. I want the kids whose SATs are lower, who want to work in the slums, who can make it with re—"

"Remediation. Not my notion of an M.D."

"Who is? Potsy Luff? Making a million a year?"

"You know me better. Besides, there won't be any money for your Whitman scheme. Hospital costs are going up fifteen percent a year. That's where the money goes. Forget about Potsy. He's an exception. Most doctors aren't earning much more than they did ten years ago. It's the equipment, malpractice insurance, operating costs that are skyrocketing. I fight it every day. No one's going to cough up for a pie-in-the-sky deal like yours."

"Meaning Manship."

"The old man likes you, Joe. But his foundation read this and said

478

no." He indicated the plastic-bound presentation Joe and Eck had written.

"We'll get the d-dough."

"Charley'll wheedle some out of the state, the feds. But in the long haul, what'll you get? A dozen badly trained doctors. You won't even have a guarantee once they get their M.D.'s that they'll practice in South Jamaica."

"We should give it a try, Kev."

Kevin looked at the photograph of Nan on his desk. Joe had heard they'd had a fight over her paper and that she was threatening to move out. He and Jenny had wanted to say something, but had been afraid.

"You may not get a chance to," Kevin said. "Our medical board and our trustees don't like the idea."

"What? What the hell b-business is it of theirs?"

"They think Danforth is setting an extremely high standard out here. We're in the big leagues now. Sinai, P and S, Cornell. Why dilute our medical service with the sort of half-assed school you have in mind?"

Joe felt color staining his cheeks. Why couldn't he control himself the way Kevin did? "You're the president of this place. You tell hospitals what to do. What did you say to the trustees and the medical board?"

Kevin leaned forward. One brother, lean, handsome, fox-faced. The other with his battered nose and seamed face. "I gave you a hearing. I tried to be impartial. I couldn't look as if I was favoring my own brother."

"But you didn't go to bat for me, did you? Or for Eck. Or for Charley. You didn't say, yes, we'll give the Whitman project a leg up, help them get funded?"

"It never got that far. There was such complete disapproval that I couldn't pursue it."

"Thanks, buddy. Jenny's been right about you a long time. Haul up the ladder, I'm aboard."

"It's not finished, Joe. We can talk about the project next year."

"But I'm finished with you."

Joe walked to the door. He had assured Charley Felder, Dr. Schwartzbaum, Wilson Tolland, that Kevin would be in their

479

corner. Joe thought of the old joke: keep your eye on the referee, someone's beating the crap out of me.

"Look," said Kevin. "All I see is third-rate doctors. Don't think the working-class whites won't be on your back. They'll take you to court. You'll end up with Italian and Greek and Polish kids instead of those blacks you want."

Joe turned at the door. "Go to hell, Kevin. You can be a solid-gold prick. I've never figured out why. Maybe b-because you always had your way."

Kevin sat silently for a moment. He wanted to cry out to Joe, appeal to him. *Stop tilting at windmills, bucking the system.* But he did not move. He buzzed his secretary to call his wife at Upper County. For the fourth time that day he was told she was unable to come to the phone.

"I have to level with you, Joe," Abe Gold said. "Kevin wasn't even neutral. He hated your idea. Don Eck and I were the only ones who supported you."

Joe and Abe were in Charley Felder's storefront office in downtown Shinnaway. Outside black kids played noisily in the snow, slamming garbage lids, battling with broomsticks. "Kevin said even though he was your brother, he had to oppose the medical prep idea."

"How about you, Abe?"

"Joe, if you get it off the ground, Don Eck and I will be glad to teach and serve on the board. Kevin won't like it, but he can't stop us."

Joe looked at Felder's drooping face. "So?"

"We'll get it going, Joey. The seed money doesn't amount to that much, but I think it's available."

"That bastard brother of mine. I don't know what the h-hell is eating him. He and Nan aren't getting along. Maybe that's it. Why should he foul us up?"

"Let's go public, Joe," Charlie said. "You know about the Concordia scandal. Curtis was indicted. His son was suspended from Upper County. That's all part of Danforth's image."

"What does that m-mean for us?"

"Get your sister on our side. One more example of the way Danforth tries to manipulate and dominate medical care at the expense of the community."

"Bridie?" Joe smiled. "Not a bad idea. She's always been Kevin's fan. But I think all that interests her now is a good s-story."

The following week Joe had lunch with Bridie and Eliot Sparling. As Joe began to explain his concept she looked bored. But Sparling, who was assigned to her as a writer and associate producer, did not. "You think this thing can work?" he asked as they were served *moules marinière*.

"W-won't know till we try. Everyone except Charley Felder and a f-few doctors is against it. Even that kid Weisbrod who led the commune in sixty-eight doesn't give a d-damn. Too busy coining money."

Bridie looked affectionately at Joe's blunt plain face. Too much honesty in him. Too much trust. He was different from Kevin, and, she realized now, different from her. Joe retained the goodness, the simplicity, the innocence, that she herself had had twenty years ago. It was his failing. And his virtue.

"I can't believe Kevin is against it," Bridie said.

"He w-went easy with me. But he shot it down behind my back. Maybe Charley can dig up the money and work on the state college, but unless the hospitals and medical schools cooperate, it w-won't get off the g-ground."

I love them both, Bridie thought. *And they are both good men, but Joe has a sense of outrage and decency that won't be stilled.* She thought of his ramshackle house in the suburbs—the house of a doggedly middle-class man with a hard-working wife. And then she thought of the fakes and self-promoters she dealt with every day. Maybe it was time she did something worthwhile.

"What do you think, Eliot?" she said.

"I'm with Joe. I think we should do a whole program. I mean a one-hour takeout on the state of medical care in the country. That way we won't have to focus on Danforth. There are a lot worse guys than Kevin Derry."

"I d-don't want to hang him," Joe said. "Maybe this isn't such a hot idea."

Bridie's mind was racing ahead. An hour on medical care today. Who gets cured. Who doesn't. It had to get a good rating. Everyone was interested in medical care.

"We'll do it," she said. "Eliot, write up the proposal, sign my name to it, but let me read it before it goes to Chris."

Sparling made notes in a copybook. Joe could see he hungered for Bridie. But she was too rich for Sparling's blood. Maybe anyone's.

Joe lapsed into silence. He was afraid that in the end he and Bridie would appear to be lined up against their brother.

"M-maybe this program's a lousy idea," he said. "Maybe you should do it on New York City."

"No," Bridie said. "On my own turf."

"Or as someone once said," Sparling added, "on native grounds."

Bridie kissed Joe, snapped a few orders to Sparling, and left before the coffee arrived.

"You look tired, Joe," Sparling said. "But then, Bridie tends to wear people down."

Medical Empires, a UBC Special Report by Bridget Derry, drew a tremendous audience. It seemed, Eliot Sparling said, after the ratings came in, that every American citizen was pissed off at medical costs.

"It hit a nerve," Sparling said as he and Bridie looked at the Nielson ratings. "Jesus, the fourth-highest rating for the week, right in back of *All in the Family.*"

"The talent helped," Bridie said. "Don't you know I have a loyal following?"

Then she dismissed him. She was off to the Middle East. She barely looked up when he returned to her office with the news that the state legislature was setting up an ad hoc committee on medical practices.

"Look, Eliot," she said. "Once I do a story it's *done* for all time. Be a good guy and take the Albany calls for me, huh?"

Eliot went back to his office to pick up the phone. It was Dr. Joe Derry. He and Charley Felder wanted a list of Eliot's contacts for the program. Did Eliot mind lending them his notes?

"I never could say no to a Derry." Sparling said.

Kevin had refused to appear on the program, saying he could not be interviewed by his own sister. "You want to put the knife in us and I can't stop you. But I won't help you find the place in my neck." It was a legitimate excuse, but it was a mistake. His assistant had been evasive and upset.

A professor of medicine, a chief attending in OB and a prizewinning radiologist defended the Danforth complex. But their laudatory words were intercut with scenes of plaster flaking from the walls of Mid-Island, black mothers and kids packing the waiting rooms at the clinic, and zonked-out teenagers in the detox center.

"I knew it would be a setup," Kevin said to his staff. "But to hell with them. Maybe they have a point. But where is the money coming from? I'd like to give nutritious meals and free medical care to every black kid in the county. Somebody fund us and we'll supply the services."

Donald Eck started to reply, thought better of it, said nothing. The TV program had touched on the misuse of National Institute of Health funds intended for medical care—money illegally redirected toward salary raises and capital improvements. What Sparling and Bridget Derry had not learned was that the extent of the misuse of funds was far greater at other hospitals in the area. Eck held his peace. In his plodding midwestern way, he was working with Joe, with Dr. Schwartzbaum, and with Charley Felder, to shake up the establishment.

"You want to say something, Dr. Eck?" Kevin asked. He looked peaked, bloodless. His associates worried about him.

"Nothing, Kevin."

"You weren't exactly silent on that program. Don't misunderstand me, Don. But you didn't have to wax so eloquent about primary care. We all believe in it."

A few doctors laughed. Eck's reticence had become a Danforth joke.

"You wouldn't have wanted me to dissemble, Kevin," Eck said. "We need the machinery and the plant and tertiary-care programs. But we also—"

"I know, I know," Kevin said irritably. "The kid with the strep throat. Christ, I wish my brother would find him, cure him, and get off our back." He looked at the ceiling. "Any new business?"

"Malpractice review," Abe Gold said. "New rates are due out this week. They'll be outrageous. Want me to tackle it?"

"Do that, will you, Abe? And look into that insurance pool. It may be our only hope."

Eck allowed himself a faint smile. Very much in control, Kevin Derry. Eck knew the exposure had hurt him. Coming as it did on top of the Concordia scandal and the suspension of Lawton Curtis.

"The one-on-one narcotics program is a bust," a staff psychiatrist said. "I want a full-scale reevaluation, Dr. Derry."

"You'll have it. Maybe we should reevaluate a lot of special programs."

No one quite knew what he meant. Eck told Gold later, as they gossiped over coffee, that Derry's marital problems were eating at him, affecting his health.

Jenny got the news first. Charley Felder had called Mid-Island asking for Joe. Joe, as he was so often these days, was reaming out a resident. Another foul-up, another bungled workup. The foreign house staff meant well, but Christ, the language problem! Now that "Ghettoese" was accepted by the schools, it was even harder for them to communicate with blacks. Nor did some young intern from Delhi appreciate being called "motherfucker" at three in the morning.

It was almost a month since Bridie's program. The state committee had gone into action. Felder had fed them reports, statistics and Joe's proposal for the medical preparatory program at Whitman.

"Jen, baby, great news!" Charley shouted. "We won. The whole thing."

"You're kidding." She eased herself out of the swivel chair at the nurse's island. "Joe's school?"

"The regents went for it. Unanimous vote. Of course, our guys on the committee helped. Who could argue against lower medical costs through preventive care? My friendly assemblymen and senators assure me the funds will be voted within two weeks."

Jenny, flushed with joy, told Charley to call Joe.

Joe picked up a phone in the house-staff lounge, dismissing a perspiring intern with a warning to always, *always* take blood-pressure readings before and *after* administering digitalis.

"The m-medical schools will want in, Charley," he said. "All except D-Danforth. It's a shame. Kevin could get off the hook with a nod of his head."

"He's your brother."

"Th-that's the problem."

Joe kept his distance from Kevin for a week or so. He didn't want to appear to be gloating. The Whitman State College plan was no skin off Kevin's nose. He had objected to it on professional grounds, and maybe, Joe confessed one afternoon at a meeting with Schwartzbaum, Kevin had some justice on his side. But they'd never know until they tried it.

Local politicians were already trying to get mileage out of the medical preparatory program. Joe warned Charley to lie back. "We have to handle this like those smart asses at Harvard," Joe said. "M-make believe we are not favoring minorities even when we *are,* so we can't get sued for establishing quotas."

Schwartzbaum raised the issue of teaching hospitals. It would look odd, he said, if Joe's own base of operations, Mid-Island, an inner-city hospital, was not included.

"Try Kevin," Felder laughed. "He owns all those guys."

One evening Joe called on his older brother in the Victorian frame house on the North Shore.

They sat in the high-ceilinged study with its view of the sound. The house seemed eerily quiet.

"Nan around?" Joe asked.

"Meeting. They invited her to speak at P and S. I don't know where she gets the energy." Kevin covered his face. "Hell, I can't lie to you. She's left me."

"*Left* you?"

"Too long a story, Joe. It might not be permanent. If I told you what set it off, you'd laugh."

"I w-wouldn't, Kev." And he thought, *Something about the research. Kevin trying to grab credit for the Danforth monster.* Or was it more personal? They had seemed so in love, so close. But he was not by nature a nosy man, and he realized how far apart he and Kevin had drifted. He felt ashamed to be bothering his brother in a moment of private crisis. Kevin looked appalling. Pallor making the spray of freckles look more like liver spots. His hand shook as he lit a cigarette.

"I hear you got your vocational school for oppressed minorities," Kevin said, after a long silence. "Good luck."

"Doesn't sound like you, Kev."

"Why not? You know my reputation. The Empire Builder. That's what people want to believe."

"That isn't like you either. I can't remember you ever feeling sorry for yourself, or worrying what p-people said about you." Joe

485

thought, *It's Nan that's bugging him, and I don't blame him.*

"I'm sorry about Nan, Kevin. R-really."

"Oh, it'll work out. Maybe it's for the best."

"Yeah. Kevin . . ."

"What can I do for you, kid? You want Danforth to tie in with the Whitman program? Not a chance. Not us, not Sinai, not P and S, not Cornell. Maybe not even Bellevue. The state schools will handle your charity cases. Maybe we'll join after we look over the first crop."

Manship's snobbishness had rubbed off on him, Joe realized sadly. Abe Gold had explained it once to Joe as the Gatsby syndrome. Joe had never realized how deeply it had got into Kevin's blood.

"No, we don't n-need you," Joe said. "We'll manage with the s-state schools, and a few others. It's Mid-Island I w-want to talk about. Eck and I want it accredited and fully staffed for teaching. It should be s-saved. I know the ph-pharmacy gets ripped off and there are four-hour waits in the clinics, but if the primary-medicine program is going to work, why not improve Mid-Island?"

"Why come to me?"

Joe sensed the old anger at Kevin's casual power. He had come to Kevin because Kevin got what he wanted, controlled the money and knew how to convince the directors.

"Goddammit, Kev, you know why. All y-you have to do is say, 'Let's upgrade Mid-Island—'"

"No go. We're running a tight ship. Tertiary-care costs are flying out of sight. Malpractice insurance may damn near break us. Sorry, Joe. The last thing we want is to start shoveling dollars into Mid-Island. It might be better if we scrapped it."

Joe got up and pounded his fist on Kevin's desk. "Go screw yourself. I sh-should be feeling sorry for you, but I'll be damned if I will. Nan m-must have had good reason to walk out on you. You've forgotten you were once a druggist's son who married rich. M-maybe I'll get Mid-Island to disaffiliate altogether, get Charley to p-plug us into the state. I'm through asking you favors. It's not that you're a real shit, Kevin. You just sort of f-fall into the pattern."

Kevin drained the brandy. "Ah, the hell with it, Joe. Sometimes I think maybe the two of us should have gone into the Public Health Service the way you did when you were a kid. The daring Derry brothers . . ."

486

"Go to h-hell." Joe walked out of the study.

"Hey, Joe. Come back. I'll bring up the Mid-Island deal. Maybe the medical board will like the idea. Win them brownie points."

Joe had already left. A wave of shame engulfed Kevin, and, for the first time in more years than he could recall, guilt. When? When Cynthia killed herself?

The pain began a few seconds later, angina so severe he gasped with each convulsive assault on his chest. He tried nitroglycerine, got little relief, popped Demerol, found it nauseated him.

In the morning, weak and unsteady, he canceled his meetings and went to see Potsy for a workup.

"Bypass, old buddy," Dr. Luff said. He squinted at the X-rays taken in the cath lab at Upper County. Kevin had asked that the work be done at night, holding the technicians over. The less people who knew the better.

"Left main coronary and the diagonal," Potsy said briskly. "A piece of cake, Kevin. The sooner the better. You'll never miss that vein from your leg."

They sat in Kevin's office, studying the shadowy pictures.

Potsy knocked a carton of cigarettes off his cousin's desk. "No more, friend."

What the hell, Kevin thought. My son won't speak to me, my wife has left me, and my brother thinks I'm a heel.

He'd have to start patching his life together again. Maybe after Potsy was finished patching his abused heart.

PART EIGHT
1978

Kevin rested on a hospital bed at Upper County, recovering from his second open-heart operation. Over the last six months the anginal pain had recurred. Potsy's airy promises had been vindicated for somewhat less than four years. Then the pain had resumed, and tests showed that the vein grafts were occluding, narrowing, limiting the flow of blood. Donald Eck scoffed; Kevin would have been better off on a diet, medication. Now a second round of surgery was needed.

Kevin wondered how long his luck would hold out. Eck, now working with Joe at the medical preparatory center, had come up with depressing statistics. Surgical patients did not have that long a survival rate. Yes, pain lessened, energy returned. Superficially the postoperative patient functioned very well. But the pathological process, the blocking of vessels, was not changed. Certainly in Kevin's case, the prognosis did not seem cheering.

He was roused from his gloomy thoughts by the phone.

The hoarse voice baffled Kevin for a few seconds. Finally it identified itself as his son, now twenty-three, living . . . where?

"Jesus loves you, Dad."

"I'm glad, John. I need all the help I can get."

"But he does, Dad. Jesus loves us all, especially you. You're a sinner, but He forgives you. I was a sinner and He forgave me."

Kevin, under the watchful eye of a CCU nurse—they all seemed to be small perky women, reminding him of Jenny Connetta thirty years ago—tried to look calm.

"Where are you, John?"

"This really cool place outside of Portland. Sort of a commune."

"Oregon or Maine?"

"It's Oregon. Dad, I've never been happier. I'm with Jesus. So is Sue Jeanie, my companion in Jesus. We live the way He did. And He loves us."

And what, John Derry, have you done with your brain? Kevin asked himself. His son was living on Manship's remittances. Since the old man's death of lung cancer ten months before, Karen and Johnny had both become independently wealthy. The money was in trust, but the allowances were generous.

"I've become someone else, Dad," John said. "We kind of live in the woods, farm, but mostly experience Jesus. I'm much better than I was."

"You think you might give college a try, John? You're not that old."

"I don't need it, Dad. The checks come on the dot. I donate them to the commune. Dad, if you live with Jesus, you'll get better and you'll live a fuller life. I was thinking, Dad, maybe your medical school could give a course in Divine Blessedness."

Kevin declined. At least he was relieved to realize his son was off drugs and busy at something not totally useless.

He handed the receiver to the nurse who put it back in its cradle.

"Your boy?" she asked.

"Yes. Good kid. I'd sort of lost track of him."

"It was sweet of him to call. I tell you, some of these kids. Their parents sick, and no calls, no letters."

Kevin didn't answer. He had the feeling he would never be able to talk to John again, at least make real contact with him. The boy would drift, seek new gods, all to no purpose.

Kevin looked at the tree of get-well cards and letters the nurses had rigged on an IV pole in the middle of his room. There was Karen's letter from Mount Holyoke. Others from old friends from Churchport. Matt Cross and Ed Riley and Jerome Hudson. And notes from his staff and Manship's colleagues, who carried on the old man's interest in the college and the hospitals.

Joe and Jenny came by in the afternoon. Joe looked at the charts and told Kevin he appeared to be great. Back to the suite of offices at Danforth in a few weeks. Privately, Potsy told Joe that Kevin had signs of emphysema. All those butts over the years.

492

"What's new at med prep?" Kevin asked them.

"Taking fifty kids this year."

"Great."

"I keep track of them. Only three or four are h-having trouble. Not bad, considering everyone's predictions."

"Tell the truth, Joey," Jenny said. "You flunked out two thirds of the first class. And more than half the second."

"So what? If we can turn out twenty doctors a year, I'll be happy. Can't wait till they start practicing in the old neighborhoods."

"I know," Kevin said. "And start looking at strep throats." But he was not sarcastic. He wanted the experiment to succeed despite its problems. Whitman State was about to be sued in a class action by white students who claimed the college practiced reverse discrimination. They contended they were as qualified as Joe's minorities. Who could say who was right? "The back wheels will never catch up with the front wheels," Charley Felder said, "if we don't give the blacks a chance." He was preparing Whitman's defense.

"Know what the answer is?" Kevin asked. "They should all get a crack at medical school."

Joe scowled. "Yeah. But if they don't go where they're needed after they get the M.D., we're b-back where we started."

"I've heard *this* before," Jenny said. "Joe's obsessed with it, Kevin."

"Not a bad obsession. Let me know if you need help."

He'd come around, Joe understood. Four years ago Bridie had blown the whistle on inadequate medical care in the slums and rural communities, while a billion and a half dollars were funneled into bypass surgery. And not one doctor within fifty miles of some towns!

Whitman had got its premedical experiment. Joe had joined the board as a consultant in premedical education. Moreover, he was constantly recruiting teachers, doctors and financial supporters.

When Joe and Jenny left, Kevin sensed his isolation, his appalling loneliness. So much promise had come to nothing. His kids were virtual strangers. And Nan. She had left him four years ago. They met professionally from time to time. She had not remarried, had no boyfriend, seemed utterly involved in a new study of hormonal involvements in cancer. Her first project had made front-page news.

He shuddered, remembering the night she had left, after an

493

uncomfortable period of sleeping in separate rooms, both of them unable to gather up the frayed remnants of what had been a warm marriage.

I don't want a thing, Kevin. No money, not the house, nothing. I'll take my clothes, my books, my papers, and my office furniture. I don't even want one of those damned Mercedes. They always embarrassed me. . . .

She had left. Her daughter, Carol, damned near as brilliant as her mother, was a premedical student at Stanford. Gawky, not as pretty as Nan. Kevin missed her, missed her as much as he regretted the loss of John. He was like Manship, he supposed, treasuring someone else's child.

I love you, Kevin, but I can't stay with you, Nan had said. *I won't be part of your empire. I can't forgive the way you tried denying Etta Roush the credit she deserved. Or the way you fought Joe on Whitman State. Kevin, you don't even realize how you're acting, how you want to control everything. . . .*

He found himself at a loss for a response. His ease with words, the old charm, deserted him. "But . . . we were good with each other . . . the times I held you and loved you."

"I know, Kevin. That's what makes this so hard. Oh, God, don't make me say it."

He protested and kissed her. But Nan had stood firm. Remembering their affair, the honeymoon in Europe, Kevin drifted off to sleep.

"Wake up, sleeping beauty."

Kevin opened his eyes and saw Potsy standing at his side, taking his pulse.

"Healthier than a two-miler. Get you on your feet tomorrow, buddy. Pull all the tubes and wires out."

He sat down and tried to distract Kevin with hospital gossip. He chattered on about who was sleeping with whom, which doctor had got sued, which had found a terrific new tax shelter. Finally he got around to what he had come to say.

"Got to hand it to Miles Curtis."

"Hand it to him?" asked Kevin.

"Yeah. Found him guilty two years ago, and he's still walking around. They say he'll never do an hour in jail."

"Breaks my heart," Kevin said. "Two-year jail sentence for Medicaid fraud, a year for bribing a public official. And he hasn't done a day's time."

Kevin shut his eyes. Oh, the bastards, cheats and liars he'd played ball with. They had terminated Lawton Curtis from the hospital with minimum publicity. Young Curtis threatened to sue. He was being punished for his father's sins. Sparling had dug up some interesting billings, canceled checks, correspondence. Lawton had inherited his father's fine hand. He was skimming profits, taking kickbacks from Concordia.

The damning information had been enough to force him to resign. Kevin had not been touched. He'd long divested himself of Concordia, knew nothing about the nursing-home scandal. But in the fallout Danforth had been smeared. The events had moved state legislators to support Joe's plan. After Potsy left, Kevin regretted again opposing Joe. He tossed restlessly on his pillow, falling finally into drug-induced sleep.

He woke with a start four hours later.

In one of those ill-formed visions which the convalescent experience, he was certain he saw a familiar woman in a white smock walk past his room.

He sat up in bed, his mind shaking off the drugs, trying to catch a glimpse of the woman.

"Nan?" Kevin called. "Nan?"

The nurse heard his voice. "Dr. Derry? Do you want anything?"

"Woman who just walked by. Who is she?"

"A paraprofessional. Goodness, it's three in the morning. I'll have to give you another round of knockout drops if you don't sleep."

Long Island in October, Joe recalled his father saying years ago, had it all over New England. Brighter skies, better air, foliage to match Vermont and New Hampshire. This day, he knew what Jack meant.

There could not have been more than five hundred people in the wooden stands. Joe and Jenny were among them. Jenny found herself hating the game, angry that Nicky, at one hundred seventy pounds, with a knee twisted from injuries suffered his freshman year, insisted on playing.

Whitman State was taking its usual shellacking. Joe watched the teams, banging heads and bodies, hitting the turf, and thought of his own inglorious career. *I cannot understand how a human being cannot know how to block.* Well, he had known how; it hadn't kept them from losing. Nicky, a second-string linebacker against a team of two-hundred-twenty-pound linemen, also knew.

"Is this necessary?" Jenny asked.

"It's a n-nice way to spend a sunny Saturday afternoon."

It was early in the first quarter. Whitman was down thirteen to nothing. The opponents from upstate kicked off. As the Whitman back caught the kickoff and ran for the sidelines, Nicky tore into a defensive lineman and leveled him. The ball carrier made it to midfield. The play was called back. Someone on Whitman had clipped.

"J-Jesus," Joe moaned. "They can't do anything right."

Nicky returned to the bench. Too small. Too injury-prone to play first string. Joe looked at his son's dark face, smudged with shoeblack, the curling dark hair—Jenny's hair.

Down on the sidelines, Peter, undersized and skinny, stood admiringly in back of the bench, shouting encouragement. *Our Filipino son,* Joe thought. *He'll make it; he's gutsy.*

Jerome Hudson was sent in to play tight end.

Joe could see the rebuilt face. Jerome was in his third year of the medical preparatory program. He was getting by with tutoring and special classes. *Christ,* Joe wondered, *will it ever be easier?* They lost half of every freshman class. Kids who couldn't take the workload. But it was a start. Young Hudson had become a symbol to him. If Jerome could make it, others could.

The boy caught a sideline pass with one hand, held on, picked up five more yards as he reversed field.

"If he c-can pass qualitative analysis the way he runs the buttonhook, he'll make it to m-med school."

"Oh, Joey," Jenny sighed. "My beloved optimist."

Whitman fumbled and lost the ball. The upstate team was driving for another score.

"Do we have to stay to the bitter end?" Jenny asked. She was stouter, still beautiful. Her eyes had the same luminous glow they had when Joe first saw her.

"Kevin s-said he'd show up."

"Surprise. He usually spends Saturdays with his Dict-a-belt."

"Lay off, Jen. For a guy with emphysema and a patched heart he does okay."

"But he won't talk to his own son."

"N-not Kevin's fault. He's tried."

Nicky was sent back in, made two crisp tackles, racing sideways, stringing out blockers, slamming into the runner. The second time he got up slowly.

"I hate this game," Jenny said. "He doesn't have to prove to me he's tough. He's got cops, firemen, prizefighters and hoodlums in his blood. Nicky can go out for tennis."

There was love in her voice, and she thought, *How lucky we have been with our children*. She felt a profound pity for Kevin.

Before the half ended Kevin arrived.

Joe saw him walking toward the wooden seats with a woman in a checked coat. Kevin wore a rakish trenchcoat. For him, this was informality.

"Who's the girl with Kevin?" Joe asked. "I d-don't believe it. Take a look, Jen."

"It's Nan."

"Unbelievable. All the way from California?"

Kevin had told him he'd been trying to reach her. She had called him after his second operation. Joe thought she would never come back.

Perhaps this was just a visit. She traveled a great deal, lecturing, giving conferences. Her paper had made her famous.

Joe and Jenny left their seats and waved at Kevin and Nan as they climbed the stairs.

My brother moves slowly, Joe thought. Years of smoking and overwork, of hidden tension, masked anxieties, had exacted a toll. He was fifty-four and he looked sixty.

Nan Felder looked marvelous, Jenny thought. Her dark skin was clear. A cautious smile lit her oval face.

They embraced and kissed, and for a moment they had little to say.

"Nicky play yet?" Kevin asked.

"Special teams," Joe said. "He stuck a few guys. I think he got his bell rung on the last tackle. That's him. Middle linebacker. Number fifty-one."

"Your old number."

"And the t-two of us on losing teams."

They talked (avoiding the subject of Nan's presence) about

497

medical-school problems, about Potsy's acrimonious debate with Dr. Eck over the proper treatment of coronary-artery disease.

"Where d-do you stand?" Joe asked.

"Neutral. Let 'em fight it out. We'll learn more about the problem." Danforth was backing a new research program. Kevin laughed. "I'll fund it and I'll be a statistic in it. Been to the well twice with my defective arteries."

Nicky tackled the opponent's star back, shoving him out of bounds savagely as the runner tried to turn an end.

"Way to st-stick!" Joe called. He looked at Kevin's pale eyes. They were rimmed with a fretwork of lines. Ever since the first operation. No, earlier. After Nan left him, after Joe had defied him on the inner-city program.

"Nicky going into medicine?" Kevin asked. Sunlight dazzled the field. The trees ringing the stadium sparkled green and gold, orange, red and purple.

"He's not in the six-two p-program," Joe said. "W-wants to keep his distance from me. But he'll end up in medicine, Kev. The kid's smart, but he doesn't work hard enough. If his boards had been better he might h-have made it to the Ivy League."

"Or if he weighed two-twenty and was all-state."

Jenny was talking to Nan. She had come east to read a paper at Sloan-Kettering, called Kevin for old time's sake. Elated, he had asked her to dinner. No, she had no close male friends, lived alone in Palo Alto. She admitted to Jenny—one of the few people to whom she would make the admission—that she was lonely. Her daughter was on scholarship at Stanford.

"So?" Jenny asked. "You and Kevin? Another shot at it?" She shaded her eyes. "Thank God Nicky's on the bench again. I can't bear this."

"You're not subtle, Jenny."

"I never have been. A big-mouth Neapolitan. We're all on the surface."

"I love you for it." She touched Jenny's gloved hand. "We're thinking about it. I love him. I always did. But . . ."

"I know. Nobody's ever really disliked Kevin, one of his problems. And, what the heck. He's *different*. I don't mean just that he's stopped smoking or doesn't drive as hard. The edges aren't as sharp. Know what I mean?"

"I know."

Jenny kissed Nan's cheek. "God, I wish you were back in the family. Bridie would be happy, too. Gee, we hardly ever see her. Kevin and Joe tried all summer to get her out here—no go. Too busy. She goes to discothèque openings and runs with that gossip-column crowd."

"I guess it's part of her job."

"Yeah, I guess. Anyway, Nan, when you and Kevin decide to do it, we want to be the first to know."

"Don't rush us, Jenny."

Kevin, circumspect as ever, said little to Joe. Nan "happened to be in town" and had called him. It was a casual date. In their fifties, people did not talk freely about intimate relationships, Kevin felt.

As the half ended, Nicky rammed his head into the fullback's shoulder pads, took a blindside block, fell unconscious to the turf.

Jenny moaned and ran from the seat. Joe ran after her. By the time they reached the field Nicky was being helped to his feet by the trainer.

"You okay, Nick?" Joe asked.

"Yeah, yeah. Hey, Dad, willya beat it?"

"Nicky!" Jenny shouted. "Are you all right? You recognize me?"

"Sure. You're Linda Ronstadt. Ma, willya beat it? I'm okay."

The trainer yanked Nicky's helmet off. "He's okay, Dr. D."

"I don't want him to play again!" Jenny shouted.

Nicky shook his head a few times and walked toward the lockerroom.

"Got his bell rung," the trainer said. "Nick never quits. We'll get those guys in the second half."

Not with the score twenty-five to nothing, Joe thought. But there was no harm in being optimistic. *Winners never quit and quitters never win,* Nicky used to say when he played Little League ball and was seven runs behind.

Kevin watched Nick, helmet in hand, walk out of sight. Number fifty-one. Joe's old number. Losers? Hardly. Kevin had never admired his kid brother more. He took Nan's hand. He was determined to have her back. Maybe he could yet infuse his life with some of the warmth and closeness and compassion that Joe and Jenny had always found so effortlessly. It was worth a try.

He saw Joe's rugged thick-shouldered body, leading a sniffling Jenny up the stairs. Autumn sunlight gleamed on the vivid green turf. In the red brick buildings in the distance, Joe's students

499

labored with "qual" and "quant." Some would fall by the wayside; a few might fulfill Joe's dream and become doctors who were willing to care for the poor.

The years formed a jumbled mosaic in Kevin's mind. The bay at Churchport. He and Joe with their father trolling for snappers. Clamming. Tennis tournaments. Doc Felder, Jack Derry, Meg. . . .

He would have to see more of Joe. Perhaps give him a hand with the medical preparatory program. They were not meant to be opponents. He looked at Nan. "Do me a favor, Nan? How about a lecture for Joe's kids at Whitman?"

"Anything for Joe."

"And for me?"

Nan was silent. But she took his hand and smiled.

Kevin decided the four of them would have dinner at his house that night. They'd phone Bridie. She'd not be able to come, they were certain, but they would all talk to her.

Nan edged closer to Kevin. She looked at the aging face. Yet a hint of the boyishness remained. *He has always had his way,* she thought. *And will have it now with me. . . .*

Whitman's rinky-dink band was marching down the field. *There will always be a band and Saturday football,* Kevin thought.

Jenny laughed. "Sounds like the Damelio brothers' orchestra. Nice day, huh, Joey? I hope Nicky isn't hurt. Poor kid."

"He's a Derry," said Joe. "They were born to take punishment and bounce back."

"The bouncing gets a little harder when you turn fifty," Kevin said.

He changed seats with Jenny, sat alongside Joe—as if to draw strength and courage from him. *Brother physician,* Kevin thought. *Indomitable, outraged, forever honest. Maybe it is time,* he mused, *to learn from him.*